MECHA CORPS

"Patton brings the transformer games to life to create superweapons using the brains of cadets to manage them. He provides plenty of action . . . and enough planetary destruction to satisfy most game players."
—SFRevu

"Brett Patton has written a thrill-a-minute military science fiction starring a fascinating hero."
—*Midwest Book Review*

"Part *Starship Troopers* . . . part *Transformers*. I love it. Well-written mecha action."
—Sporadic Reviews

"Filled with twists and secrets. Fans will enjoy . . . combat with the *Mecha Corps*."
—Alternative Worlds

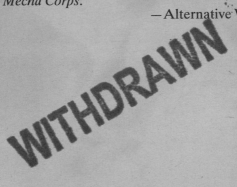

Novels of the Armor Wars

Mecha Corps
Mecha Rogue

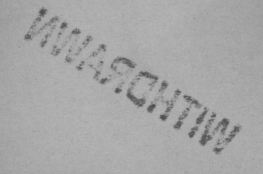

MECHA
ROGUE

A NOVEL OF THE ARMOR WARS

BRETT PATTON

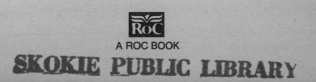

A ROC BOOK

ROC
Published by New American Library, a division of
Penguin Group (USA) Inc., 375 Hudson Street,
New York, New York 10014, USA
Penguin Group (Canada), 90 Eglinton Avenue East, Suite 700, Toronto,
Ontario M4P 2Y3, Canada (a division of Pearson Penguin Canada Inc.)
Penguin Books Ltd., 80 Strand, London WC2R 0RL, England
Penguin Ireland, 25 St. Stephen's Green, Dublin 2,
Ireland (a division of Penguin Books Ltd.)
Penguin Group (Australia), 250 Camberwell Road, Camberwell, Victoria 3124,
Australia (a division of Pearson Australia Group Pty. Ltd.)
Penguin Books India Pvt. Ltd., 11 Community Centre, Panchsheel Park,
New Delhi - 110 017, India
Penguin Group (NZ), 67 Apollo Drive, Rosedale, Auckland 0632,
New Zealand (a division of Pearson New Zealand Ltd.)
Penguin Books (South Africa) (Pty.) Ltd., 24 Sturdee Avenue,
Rosebank, Johannesburg 2196, South Africa

Penguin Books Ltd., Registered Offices:
80 Strand, London WC2R 0RL, England

First published by Roc, an imprint of New American Library,
a division of Penguin Group (USA) Inc.

First Printing, December 2012
10   9   8   7   6   5   4   3   2   1

To Rina, for making it through.

ACKNOWLEDGMENTS

Thank you to the following individuals. Without their support, this book would never have been written:

Pete Harris, who was my mentor throughout.

Jessica Wade, for her input and insight.

Lisa, and her unending patience and understanding.

PART ONE

EVIL

"Mankind are governed more by their feelings than by reason."

—Samuel Adams
American Statesman
Founding Father of the United States

"The Universal Union is humankind's grand hope for a rational, long-term expansion into the last great frontier."

—Patrica M. Powell
First Union Prime
Founding Member of the Universal Union

ORIENTATION/MISSION BRIEF
OPERATION PUSHBACK

Excerpted from Keller Corsair Occupation Documents

Version 0.95.1, 06.04.2322

CORSAIR FACTION INTELLIGENCE

UNIDENTIFIED: the Corsair Confederacy faction currently holding Keller has been tagged an Aggressive Corsair Cell (ACC). The faction's LEADERSHIP, GOALS, and ARMAMENT are undefined. The faction has not stated its goals.

ENVIRONMENT REVIEW

KELLER is a Class 3 Universal Union colony world.

Keller's strategic importance is in easily accessible deposits of rare Earth metals, as well as extensive lithium and beryllium resources. In addition, its location near the margin of the Universal Union and Corsair Confederacy space make it an important potential buffer between the Core and Emerging worlds of the Universal Union.

OFFWORLD: Keller is protected by Union Army automated emplacements. It is believed these were compromised in the Corsair occupation.

ONWORLD: Keller's environment is arid in its equatorial areas, with daytime temperatures that exceed fifty degrees Celsius. A thin oxygen-argon atmosphere is breathable by most persons in good physical condition.

CURRENT SITUATION

On 06.02.2322, Union Army Automated Emplacements recorded the arrival of an UNREGIS-TERED DISPLACEMENT DRIVE ship. Approximately 140 minutes after arrival of the Displacement Drive ship, ORBITAL EMPLACEMENTS were taken offline. Associated VIDEO shows Corsair freighters landing at Placerville Mine, Keller's largest population center (c.80K). Communications have ceased from Keller's FTLcomm. No demands have been made to date.

OBJECTIVES

Determine Corsair stronghold or strongholds, effective armament, and presence or absence of the Corsair Displacement Drive carrier ship.

Destroy Displacement Drive ship, assuming its presence.

Remove Corsairs from Keller and assumed additional landing points.

If possible, capture Corsair leadership for interrogation.

KEY TEAM

UNIVERSAL UNION COLONEL John Ivers, UUS Helios Strategic Command

MECHA CORPS MAJOR Guiliano Soto, Mecha Corps Lead

MECHA CORPS CAPTAIN Matt Lowell, Mecha Corps Tactical Specialist

MECHA CORPS CAPTAIN Michelle Kind, Mecha Corps Tactical Specialist

MECHA CORPS AUXILIARY SERGEANT Peal Khoury, Mecha Corps Technical Specialist

1

KELLER

The Corsair Confederacy faction currently holding Keller has been tagged an Aggressive Corsair Cell (ACC).

Matt Lowell read the words on the mission brief one more time, shaking his head in disbelief. The Corsairs were an interstellar confederacy of terrorists and pirates that had long been a thorn in the side of the Universal Union, but attacking one of the Union's colony worlds went beyond aggression. And trying to hold Keller against the might of the Union's Mecha Corps was suicidal.

What were they thinking? Were the Corsairs just throwing their lives away, now that their leader Rayder was dead?

And there were no demands, no identity, no threats. It made no sense.

His giant Demon Mecha mimicked his shaking head perfectly.

"Question, Captain Lowell?" Major Guiliano Soto's voice boomed in Matt's ears as his comms icon flared to life.

Matt jumped. Deep in thought, he'd forgotten for a moment he was suspended in magnetorheological gel within a giant biomechanical Mecha, seeing the outside world only through his viewmask.

Matt turned to look at Major Soto. Like Matt, Soto wore a Demon-class Mecha. Thirty meters tall and dull red, the Demon lived up to its namesake. Huge trifurcated legs bulging with biometallic muscle supported an angular, mirror-smooth torso. Hundreds of carbon-ringed, orange-glowing apertures along its side hinted at the fusion power hidden within. Serrated ridges ran down the Demon's arms and flowed over its shoulders. Its head was tiny, little more than an upturned slit for the sensor array and two spiked protrusions, like horns, at its very top. The latest in Union-funded biomechanical technology, the Demon packed scaled weaponry versatile enough to take out a single sniper in a crowded Union city, or to destroy an entire asteroid-derived Displacement Drive ship.

And Soto's Mecha wasn't the only one in the UUS *Helios*'s Mecha Dock. Beyond Major Soto, floating tags in Matt's viewmask identified Captain Michelle Kind in her own Demon, as well as Sergeant Peal Khoury at the front of a platoon of Hellions, a much smaller biomechanical Mecha.

Three Demons and a full platoon. Another clue the Union had no idea what to expect, and they weren't taking any chances.

"No questions, Major," Matt said, keeping his voice even.

But doubt burned in his mind. Could the Corsairs possibly hope to hold Keller? They should never have made it past the automated heavy-matter guns. Did that mean they had some new weapon?

Or was the Union withholding information? They

protected their secrets well. Matt had been told point-blank: *"You shall not state or imply you were part of the team that killed Rayder."* Even though Rayder's death was the crowning achievement of Matt's life. Revenge, at long last, for Rayder killing his crippled father, after the monster had what he wanted.

Even if the Mecha Corps worked for the Union, and did whatever they asked, Matt had to admit that his last year's worth of missions were on the up and up. He'd been able to help—really help—Union citizens at the edge of the frontier. He'd personally destroyed a Corsair Displacement Drive ship that was preying on the refugees in the Independent Displacement Alliance.

"The Union has a good reason for everything they do," Captain Michelle Kind had told him.

Matt stole a glance at Michelle's Demon. They'd orbited each other like worlds gravitationally locked on the opposite sides of a sun.

Michelle's Demon turned to regard Matt. In its visor's fun-house-mirror reflection, his Demon looked grotesque and deformed. What was she thinking? he wondered.

"Damn," Matt said under his breath.

"Damn what?" Major Soto asked.

Matt silently cursed the sensitive throatmike. But he had to roll with it. "Damn, let's get to it," he said, nodding at the giant steel air lock at the front of the Mecha Dock. "I thought this ship was fast. Sir."

"It is fast, Cadet," Colonel John Ivers broke in from the bridge, his comms icon flaring brightly in Matt's POV.

"Captain," Matt said.

Colonel Ivers chuckled. "Right. Captain. You've moved up fast in the Corps. Thirty seconds between Displacements is amazing good. Forty light-years a minute, at maximum Displacement. You should've lived when the barges took an hour to charge."

"Yes, sir," Matt said.

But Colonel Ivers's comms icon was still on. It flickered a moment, as if he was thinking about clicking off. He continued. "This isn't just about pace. This is about precision. We're inserting direct into low orbit, below the range of the Union Army automated emplacements."

"How low, sir?" Major Soto asked.

"Eighty kilometers, Major."

"That's not orbit, sir!" Sergeant Peal Khoury told them. "We'll have significant atmospheric heating! Even with the *Helios*'s armor, we may take damage—"

Colonel Ivers cut him off. "We won't be there long enough."

Silence fell over the comms. For a long time, all Matt heard was the hiss of his respirator and the fast thud of his heartbeat. Too fast. Inside his biomechanical Demon, Matt was deep in Mesh high. It was the best feeling in the world, but it colored everything he thought. Everything he felt. It was why he was going from excitement to doubt in an instant.

"Why, Colonel?" Matt asked.

"Why what, Captain?" Colonel Ivers emphasized the "Captain."

"Why are we going in so heavy, sir?"

More silence from Captain Ivers's side, but again, his comms icon stayed on. Matt could almost imagine him on the big hemispherical bridge, floating in zero g, his brow furrowed as he thought of what to tell them.

Finally Ivers continued. "This is the biggest Corsair action since Rayder's attacks on Geos. The Union wants a decisive victory here, Captain."

Matt shook his head. The plan still didn't make sense. A decisive victory here at Keller wouldn't require three Demons and a full platoon.

Soto saw Matt's Demon mimic his head shake and

laughed. "And we don't know what's down there waiting for us."

Another pause. Finally, in a gravelly voice, Ivers grated, "Expect surprises."

Ivers's comms icon snapped off, as if to close the matter. When he came back, he was all business.

"Mecha Corps, ready!" Ivers barked. "Beginning countdown to final Displacement. Twenty-seven seconds, mark."

Matt glanced at the brief one more time, then pushed it aside. He'd sort it out when they arrived.

"This was Ash's world," Michelle said.

"Cease unnecessary comms, Captain," Major Soto said. But his tone was understanding.

Ash Moore. She'd been part of Matt's and Michelle's Mecha Training Camp group under Major Soto. She'd walked away from her husband and her kids for her one chance at the Mecha Corps, knowing only a few ever completed their training. And more than a handful died.

Ash had never gotten a chance to complete her training.

"Twenty seconds," Colonel Ivers said.

Matt's emotions surged in the rush of Mesh, as his Perfect Record, his photographic memory, brought back every instant of Ash's death. She'd died in Mecha Merge, sharing her deepest feelings with everyone who'd been joined with her. Matt. Michelle. Soto. They'd had to watch while each moment of her life was abraded away, like brilliant sparks coming off a grinding wheel.

"Let's do this for Ash," Matt said.

"Yes," Michelle replied.

"Agreed," Soto added.

"Ten seconds," Ivers said, over the comms. "Mecha, prepare to deploy."

In the *Helios*'s Mecha Dock, sleek forms of destruction tensed against their steel scaffolding and the raw rock of the asteroid. Three red Demons and twenty Hellions stood bow-taut, ready to leap.

"Five seconds," Ivers said.

Matt remembered Ash's children, staring happily into the pale yellow sky of Keller.

"Four."

He remembered her husband, filthy from the lithium mines, grinning as if he hadn't a care in the world.

"Three."

He remembered her words about Michelle. *"She's a skittish one."* Oh how right she'd been.

"Two."

And he remembered that thing, that dusty-static thing, that clawed at him when he was this deep in Mesh. It had been there when Ash died, as if feeding on her pain.

"One."

Matt closed his eyes, cursing his memory. His Perfect Record. His father's gift. Such a burden. He could never forget anything he experienced. Ever.

"Displace."

The UUS *Helios* rocked and shuddered as the air-lock doors slammed open. Superheated orange plasma and dust billowed into the Mecha Dock, peppering the Demons and Hellions with shards of rock and droplets of molten steel. Through the hellish haze, the arid wastes of Keller's equator were seemingly close enough to touch. The UUS *Helios* was deep in Keller's atmosphere, and it was taking a beating.

"Deploy!" Colonel Ivers said.

Matt released his grip on the scaffold and dove into the fire.

Matt fell free into the thin atmosphere of Keller. Faintly, he felt the chill of space and the rush of wind on the biometallic skin of his Demon.

In that weightless moment, everything was perfect. Deep in the rush of Mesh, there was no place he'd rather be. He was born to be a Demonrider, meant to fall from low orbit onto desert worlds held by anti-Union terrorists. Matt closed his eyes, imagining the coming inferno. He was the ultimate force that would bring the universe back into balance.

Matt turned to look back at the UUS *Helios*. Ten billion metric tons of armor-plated asteroid, streaking through Keller's hazy sky like a comet. Its forward section glowed an angry yellow-orange from atmospheric friction, and red veins of hot metal wrapped halfway around its girth.

Directly above Matt, Major Soto's and Captain Kind's Demons fell from the conflagration. Their Mechas quickly transformed into delta-winged aerodynamic shapes, biometal flowing like mercury. Engines lit on the Mechas' backs, driving them toward the hot planet surface.

Behind Soto and Kind, polished black Hellions darted out of the UUS *Helios*'s Mecha Dock. Their bulky flight packs were clumsy, almost antique. Matt remembered his overwhelming awe when he first saw a Hellion. It now seemed so long ago.

With an earsplitting clap, the UUS *Helios* disappeared. Superheated air condensed into swirling white clouds where the giant ship had just been. The UUS *Helios* had Displaced to safety.

"All eyes front!" Major Soto snapped. But his voice wasn't angry. It quavered with excitement. Soto was in his element too.

"Yes, sir!" Matt said, turning his gaze back to the planet. Below him, yellow and salmon-colored wastes stretched into the gray haze of atmosphere. Brown-black mountain ranges punctuated the desolate landscape, their razor-sharp peaks slicing the sky. There wasn't a single green growing thing in the entire vista, no blue lakes, no vast cloud-shrouded oceans. Keller seemed to be a near-dead world. All the value must be underground, in the mines.

Ash had raised her kids here. Matt remembered their grinning faces in her images from home.

On the horizon, tags popped into view in Matt's viewmask:

OBJECTIVE: PLACERVILLE (SUBSURFACE, POP: 80,000)
RELATED OBJECTIVE: PLACERVILLE SPACEPORT (SURFACE)
PRESERVE WITHIN REASONABLE COST: PLACERVILLE FARMS (SURFACE)

More tags floated, farther away, showing the location of Keller's other primary mines. Clusters of Hellions rocketed toward each of the tags. One was tagged SERGEANT PEAL KHOURY.

Good luck, Peal, Matt thought. That kid and his brother had been through a lot. His brother would never be a Mecha pilot, but Peal had stuck with it, and he was one of the best Hellion pilots they had.

"No Corsair Displacement ship in orbit," Colonel Ivers barked over the comms. "Automated emplacements intact but noncommmunicative and noncombative. Redirecting all Hellions to the surface. Looks like the fight's on the ground, Corps."

"Good news, sir," Major Soto said.

Ivers broke comms without commenting. Matt frowned. Were the Corsairs so cocky they thought they could hold a Union world with only ground troops?

Placerville swelled as they fell toward the dry surface

of Keller. Sand fountained in the wake of their delta-winged Mecha. Cracked, heat-crazed ground flew by at a blur.

"Slow up!" Major Soto commanded as the tags for Placerville Farms exploded in size. Matt braked his Mecha, forward thrusters momentarily blinding him. They were passing over square kilometers of milky plastic-covered crops, vaguely green beneath their shroud. Mechanical harvesters did their mindless work, as if nothing was amiss.

Keller Spaceport came into view beyond a low rise, its vast expanses of sand and rock blasted into shiny green glass by ten thousand passing cargo shuttles. At one edge of the field, a low tower built of aluminum scaffolding glinted in the scorching daylight.

And directly under the tower were two Corsair freighters, wearing the familiar thousand-daggers insignia of the terrorists. They'd been converted from Taikong stock, hastily refitted with amplified cutting lasers.

But cutting lasers were really low-grade weapons. Not something a leading Corsair faction would use.

On the field, figures tagged as KELLER CITIZEN were working with figures tagged CORSAIRS, unloading battered yellow storage crates from the ship. Not one figure held a gun.

A deep shard of anger ripped through Matt. Union and Corsairs, working together? How could that be?

"Fire Sidewinders," Soto said. But even his voice sounded hollow, uncertain.

Fire, Matt thought. Sidewinder missiles exploded from Matt's chest apertures, tracing brilliant white lines toward the Corsair ships. The spaceport staff looked up and ran for cover as the Corsairs' amplified cutting lasers finally began jerking toward the incoming Mecha.

Too late. The first of the Sidewinders hit the ships. Actinic light burned Matt's retinas as the big freighters rocked. Corsair crew bailed out of the ships as they crumpled inward and collapsed.

That was way too easy, Matt thought. The Corsairs were as weak as they looked. Sending Demons against them was like using a nuke to kill a spider.

Michelle's Demon gestured frantically at the mine entrance, a hangar-style door set into the side of gray-brown cliffs. The name PLACERVILLE was laser-cut into the cliff face to the right of the door.

The door was slowly closing.

"Shit," Soto cursed, diving toward the mine entrance. Matt and Michelle followed, zooming in sideways as the door slammed shut.

Matt, Michelle, and Soto landed just inside the door, Demon Mecha transforming seamlessly back into their basic humanoid form.

They stood in a vast, warehouselike space. Union shuttles and ancient Shark-class fighters stood to one side of the cavern, while stacked crates of refined metals and supplies towered on the other. Sunlight streamed down on them from dusty skylights cut through the stone ceiling.

Ahead, Placerville's living areas stretched on either side of a boulevard for more than a kilometer. Functional aluminum-and-glass apartments sat shoulder to shoulder with buildings constructed of native stone. Skinny trees grew in a row down the middle of the boulevard, each carefully placed to get the maximum amount of light from the skylights.

Matt turned on his Demon's Sensory Amplification. The city was quiet, seemingly deserted.

"Enable Fireflies, antipersonnel mode only," Major Soto told them.

"Major, what was that out there?" Matt asked. "Uh, sir."

Soto didn't answer for a long time. After a while, he said, "We can discuss that later, Captain."

"Were the citizens helping the Corsairs?" Why would anyone help a Corsair?

"Proceed forward," Ivers's voice boomed, cutting Matt off. "Escalate weapons to Sidewinders or Fusion Handshake if necessary. Do not, repeat, do not, use Zap Gun. It may destabilize the mine."

Matt, Michelle, and Soto proceeded cautiously through the city toward a dark opening tagged MINE EN-TRANCE. Heat signatures showed citizens watching them through windows as they passed, but nobody challenged them.

The three rode a massive platform down into the mine. Rough-hewn rock walls, pockmarked by inset lights and ribbed with scaffolding, passed swiftly by as they descended. The outside temperature reading dropped, then leveled off and began to rise.

"Out here on the frontier, Corsairs aren't as black-and-white as you'd expect," Soto grumbled in grudging response to Matt's earlier question. "But that doesn't change anything. This isn't any different than Rayder and Geos. We're here to knock them down hard."

Matt didn't respond, feeling his anger rise at the mention of Rayder and Geos. Five million dead. The biggest Corsair assault ever on the Union.

They continued to descend in silence. One thousand meters, two thousand, five thousand. The faint sounds of metal on rock came through the Mecha's enhanced senses. It seemed that even with the attack, the work in the mine went on.

When they reached the bottom, dust billowed ahead of them, coming from a new, jagged shaft that descended at a sharp angle even deeper into the planet. Matt's viewmask tagged the rest of the mine as UNOCCUPIED. Only the newly hewn shaft reverberated with the desperate grinding of steel through bedrock.

Was it the Corsairs who were digging? Matt wondered. If so, digging for what?

"Forward," Soto said, descending into the shaft. Only a single climbing scaffold had been hastily welded in place; they were working fast and desperately.

Matt and Michelle followed. The clank of machinery swelled to a cacophonous symphony, hidden in the all-encompassing dust.

As they reached the bottom, shapes resolved. Giant mining machines, fronted by immense rasps, ground the shaft ever deeper, while men in battered PowerSuits cleared away the mounting piles of rubble.

Matt's viewmask tagged the workers as both KELLER CITIZEN and INFERRED CORSAIR. But they worked together seamlessly, again without guards or guns. There was no doubt now. The people in Placerville were actually helping these Corsairs.

Matt clenched his fists, fighting down the urge to fire every single one of his Fireflies and wipe them all out.

Finally the men in PowerSuits noticed them. One by one, heads rose, their dirty faces peering up at the hulking Demons above them. In his Demon's augmented senses, Matt saw frustration, anger, and fear—not even a tiny bit of relief.

"But we're Mecha Corps," Matt whispered. "We're here to help you."

"Captain—" Major Soto began. But before he could get any further, something struck him and took him down to the ground with a reverberating boom. Soto yelled in pain.

Crouched on top of Major Soto's Demon was a Mecha unlike any Matt had ever seen. Smaller than a Hellion and dull silver, with overlapping metallic scales covering a thin, whiplike body and long, multijointed arms and legs. Next to a Demon, it was a frail thing. How had it toppled the major? The giant red Demon spasmed and shook, but Soto wasn't trying to get up.

Michelle launched a small burst of Fireflies. They knocked the silver Mecha off its perch, and Soto started to get back on his feet.

The silver Mecha came back at them, blurring fast. Michelle moved forward to grapple with it.

"Don't let it touch you!" Soto hissed.

Too late. The silver Mecha impacted with Michelle, and she went down, groaning in pain. Like Soto, she made no move to get up.

"Michelle!" Matt cried.

"Get back!" she hissed. "Pain—it's got—pain!"

Matt ignored her. All he wanted to do was rip that spindly scaled Mecha apart. He ran at it, grabbed the thing with his Mecha arms, and prepared a Fusion Handshake to take it out for good.

Matt's world exploded in a burst of agony. Every muscle in his Mecha spasmed as pain arced through Matt like an electric shock. He collapsed against Michelle's Mecha hard, his visor banging on her chest plate.

Matt thrashed and tried to move, but he had almost no control over his Demon. The silver Mecha was doing something to his Mecha's systems! Boring deeper into its code, screaming feedback through every nerve of his interface suit. It had to be some kind of neural interrupter, bent on total domination of his Mecha. The feel of the Demon's own mind, the familiar prickle of dust and static, ramped upward as the multifaceted eyes of the silver Mecha peered down at him.

"Situation report!" Ivers barked.

"Down, sir," Soto grated.

"I see that! Why?"

Soto's Demon gave a mighty push, but it wasn't able to get to its feet. The small Mecha held the giant Demon down effortlessly. Soto was in the grip of the same pain as Michelle and Matt.

Matt tried to aim his Fireflies at the silver Mecha, but his Demon didn't respond to his request. There was nothing in the system but reverberating pain. It was his entire world.

Can't . . . use weapons . . . either. Michelle's thoughts came to him through contact with her Demon, amplified by the Mecha's neural interface.

Merge, he thought. *Two minds are better than one.*

The two Demons flowed together like drops of molten metal. Matt was dimly aware of the pilot's chamber re-forming to accommodate the two of them. He reached out and touched Michelle, feeling the smooth surface of her interface suit. The beating pain of the silver Mecha fell away, just a little.

The configuration diagram in Matt's viewmask showed the two Demons had become a completely new form, something almost wasplike. Matt grinned. He and Michelle did make a great team.

Matt didn't hesitate. He threw the Demon's body against the raw rock walls, knocking the silver Mecha off its perch. The stuttering pain left Matt/Michelle. They grabbed the silver Mecha before it could react, pinning it with sharp pincers.

Fusion Handshake, Matt/Michelle ordered. Blue power rammed down his arm, and the silver Mecha exploded in a hundred shards.

Matt/Michelle went for the remaining silver Mecha on top of Soto. It turned and leapt at them, but Matt/Michelle loosed a volley of Fireflies, driving it back into

Soto's own Fusion Handshake. The boom of actinic power shook dust from the rough tunnels, and rocks pattered down on the Mecha.

Sudden silence fell over the mine. Matt/Michelle and Soto turned to face the diggers, who'd powered down the mining machines. Keller citizens and Corsairs alike stepped away from their machines, raising their hands in the universal sign of surrender.

"What?" Matt asked. They were just giving up now? That wasn't how Corsairs acted.

Helping Corsairs wasn't how the Union acted. Who could side with them?

"Placerville Mine secure, sir," Soto told Ivers.

"I see. Round them up, pull the mining gear out, and collapse the shaft they created."

"Collapse the shaft? Sir?"

"Are you questioning my orders, Major?"

"No, sir." But Soto's Demon stood tense, uneasy.

When they were back up top, Soto's Demon clapped Matt on the back. "Good thinking," he told Matt. "That Merge saved our asses."

"It was all of us," Matt said, beaming with pride. "Sir."

But through his happiness, doubts ate at Matt. Why had Union citizens been helping Corsairs? What were they digging for? Why had they gone in so hot, when this job was so easy? Was the Union trying to hide something?

And just how much more powerful were the Corsairs, now that they had their own Mecha?

2

CAPITOL

Matt didn't have time to stew on his questions. Less than twenty hours after their arrival at Keller, the UUS *Helios* Displaced for Eridani, the first planet in the Union and capital of the largest interstellar governmental organization of humankind. The official line was that the Mecha pilots were being shuttled to another stop on their scheduled R&R rotation.

But it felt undeserved. Yes, they'd destroyed the Corsair Mecha and the transports, and yes, Peal and his Hellion platoon had confirmed no Corsair presence in the other major mine cities. But that was it. They'd wasted far too much firepower on a tiny little job. Sure, it was a surprise that the Corsairs had Mecha, but they were weak and pathetic, except for the "corrosive system meme"—Peal's words—that disrupted the Demon's systems.

Why was the Union acting as if they had to pay them hush money?

"The heroes' reward," Major Guiliano Soto said, sardonically, as he lounged with Matt and Michelle in a first-class cabin on the Eridani Space Elevator Transport. The curved room was a slice of a toroid-shaped passenger cabin riding a meter-wide ribbon of carbon nanotubes from orbit down to Eridani. Floor-to-ceiling windows showed the gentle curve of Eridani's surface, wrapped in a thick blue atmosphere and striped with bright white clouds. Eridani's oceans covered almost eighty percent of the planet, and their deep teal depths reflected sheets of brilliant sunlight.

As they fell toward the planet in the elevator, there was no vibration, no sensation of motion. Only a high, thin whistle of atmosphere confirmed what the room's status screen showed: they were descending toward Eridani at almost five hundred kilometers an hour. The eight-hundred-kilometer drop would take less than ninety minutes.

"Such luxury. They're showing off for us," Matt said.

"Why shouldn't they? And why shouldn't we enjoy it?" Michelle asked, leaning over to look out the curved window at the ground. "We are the saviors of the Union, after all."

"That pathetic fight on Keller?" Soto said.

"Not that."

Soto frowned and nodded. He knew exactly what she was talking about. They'd killed Rayder together.

Matt sighed. HuMax. Genetically engineered superpersons who had almost destroyed the Union over a century ago. They were supposed to have been all wiped out in the Human/HuMax wars of almost a century past. But Rayder had somehow survived. And much of his crew was HuMax. It was entirely possible there were even more of them out there, hiding past the edge of the Union.

Michelle grabbed Matt's sleeve and pointed down at Eridani's surface. "You can see Newhome now. Come look!"

Matt shook his head. He was wiped out. His head beat

like a drum, and his stomach still churned from Mesh hangover, the unavoidable effect of using a biomechanical Mecha. They were all suffering from it. Demons were the worst for Mesh hangover. It was amazing they weren't flat on their backs in bed.

At the same time, a constant chant repeated in his mind: *Get back into that Mecha. Mesh, and you'll feel fine. Mesh is the best thing in all the worlds!*

"We're above the Union capital, and you don't even want to look?" Michelle looked at him incredulously. Even though she also had the well-used look of a Mecha pilot coming down from Mesh, her eyes sparkled.

"A planet's a planet," Matt mumbled.

Michelle frowned and crossed her arms, turning away from him. "No, it's not. If each planet wasn't special in its own way, we wouldn't fight in Mecha to protect them. If a planet was a planet, we wouldn't have created Mecha at all! We would've just kept lobbing atomic weapons at each other until they were all dust!"

Righteously angry like that, she was even more beautiful than usual. The curve of her cheek was backlit by the teal-tinged reflected Eridani sunlight, and her face was lit like a halo. Her utilitarian blue Mecha Corps uniform didn't hide her generous curves. Matt remembered the first day he saw her, the lone Union Army recruit at Mecha Training Camp. Beautiful and deadly. If she hadn't known what she was doing, he might not have made it through the first mock battle.

And . . . she was right. Planets truly suited for human life were incredibly rare. Uninhabitable rocks or borderline wastelands like Keller were the norm. Eridani was special, one of four worlds in the entire Union that were truly Earthlike.

You should be making nice, not pissing her off, Matt thought. Michelle was amazing, the kind of woman you could spend your whole life with. And she was a Mecha pilot. How could it get any better?

But when Matt tried to imagine a future with her, his vision blurred. Things wouldn't resolve. There always seemed to be something between them. First Cadet Kyle Peterov. Then Rayder.

No excuses now, he told himself.

"I'm sorry," Matt told her. "It's just that—"

"It's just that you're an asshole," Michelle said, with real heat. She didn't turn around.

Matt felt a red-hot stab of anger, and he clenched his fists. He had to grit his teeth to keep from biting off a sharp comment. More Mesh hangover. It tweaked your emotions. Had to keep that in mind.

Soto went to the window to look down with Michelle. He held a small snifter of some golden liquid he'd gotten from the bar. Matt's gorge rose. How could he drink now?

But Soto was always like that. Soto didn't waver. Soto was tough, gristly, made of muscle and determination. Even in his forties, he was a pinnacle of fitness. Washboard abs showed even under his Mecha Corps uniform. Bulging biceps strained the limit of the fabric. Matt could see Michelle easily going for someone like him, even though he was twice their age.

Would that happen? On Eridani? They were supposed to be going to some Mecha Corps retreat overlooking Newhome Basin. And if not Soto, what about the other Corps who were undoubtedly there?

Always something in the way.

Matt sighed and looked down at the swelling city. It was late in the afternoon, and shadows stretched long from Newhome's concentric rings of brilliant chrome-glass and white-stone buildings. The Capitol Plaza was a hilly green park at the very center of Newhome, ringed by wide canals and dotted with neoclassical buildings housing the Universal Union Congress, its High Court, the Union's most important monuments, and the Prime Residence. It looked far too perfect and regular to be real.

Sudden vertigo made Matt sway, but he forced himself to stay there and look down.

"You're right," he told Michelle.

Michelle said nothing. Her expression, visible in the reflection from the window, remained set and hard. After a time, though, her lips twitched into a smile.

"Yes," she said. "I am."

The trio watched the rest of the way in silence as the space elevator hurtled down toward Newhome.

A whisper-quiet electric shuttle took the Corps to a resort that sprawled atop a hill overlooking Newhome. In the gathering twilight, the city was a vision in porcelain white and green glass, towers soaring gracefully as they approached spires soaring nearly a kilometer high. At one edge of the city, Atlantis, Eridani's largest ocean, fed canals that snaked through the outermost concentric rings of Newhome, glowing a pale teal from artificial light. Small personal watercraft and larger yachts peppered the canals, lit with pinpricks of brilliant white light. Low, purple-tinted clouds stood in banks off the edge of the shoreline, as if politely waiting for nightfall to move in. Above the clouds, the first stars had begun to speckle the sky, and two of Eridani's five moons were visible as tiny crescents.

"It's beautiful," Michelle said.

The resort itself was a collection of low, post-and-beam buildings of raw native wood and glass. A single stone slab outside read MECHA CORPS I: SHANGRI-LA.

"Not subtle, are they?" Soto asked, nodding at the sign.

It's not a heroes' reward, Matt told himself. *It's a bribe. Forget your questions, here in the lap of luxury. Do your job, and you can live like this for a time.* They technically had an entire week off. Matt had no idea what he would do.

Inside, graceful, sculpted furniture and abstract art were the order of the day. The lobby looked out over carefully pruned grounds of Eridani's native, spiky, purple-tinged foliage, with a lighted turquoise pool the size of a small lake, dim-lit gazebos perfect for a romantic tryst, and an open-air bar at the edge of the hill overlooking Newhome.

On the grounds, figures moved here and there, dressed in comfortable, casual clothes. But the way they moved—the furtiveness, the caution—told Matt they were Mecha Corps like themselves, or high-ranking Union military.

An otherworldly beautiful receptionist greeted the trio and called a pair of friends to show them to their rooms. Matt looked disappointedly as Michelle and Soto were escorted away down separate wood-paneled halls, and he was directed down yet another. He'd hoped to have a room closer to hers.

At his door, Matt's host pressed a wood-and-aluminum access card into his hand, and invited him to call her personal number there for anything. She was a slim, blond-haired woman with sky-blue eyes, attractive in a mathematically perfect way. Matt was too tired to play to her act. All he wanted to do was sleep. He thanked her absently, and she gave him an understanding smile in return.

His room was huge, at least a hundred square meters in size. On one side, a wall of glass framed Newhome like a photo. Another wall of pale wood unfolded into a full bar, and an inset wallscreen showed neutral scenes of

Eridani nature. The bed was so large that eight people could comfortably sleep in it, and the bathroom alone was larger than any quarters Matt had ever been assigned.

"Definitely a bribe," he said to himself. But at the moment, it didn't matter. The bed was perfect, like falling into a cloud.

Matt woke the next day to his Perfect Record. His father's gift, and his curse—the ability to seamlessly recall every single moment of his life.

In his memory, Matt was grappling with Rayder on Jotunheim, the lost planet of the HuMax. Rayder held Matt's Mecha in an agonizing grip, dangling Matt over the edge of a chasm cut into the planet's burning core. *"Who made the HuMax?"* Rayder asked, his violet and yellow eyes burning with superhuman passion. *"None other than your precious Union."*

The Union hiding evidence of HuMax survival was one thing, but the Union creating HuMax? He couldn't believe it. The Union was formed as a response to HuMax aggression. The Union had saved humanity. Everyone knew that.

Just a trick to save himself, Matt thought. And it still didn't work. In his moment of triumph, Rayder had let his guard down. Matt Merged with Rayder's Mecha and toppled his adversary over the edge, ending the Corsair's dreams of Union domination. And avenging his father's death.

The memory should have been a happy one, but Matt sat up in the too-soft bed, shaking with angst. All that time chasing Rayder, intent on ending his life. That had given him clarity and purpose. Rayder's death had cast his whole future into disarray.

It was nearly noon by the time Matt made it to Pleasure Dome Restaurant. It was raised one story above Mecha Corps' Shangri-La, with a panoramic view from the gray-green sea to the broad, undeveloped valleys to the west of Newhome. Fluffy cirrus clouds cut broad swaths in the deep blue sky, making the whole scene look like an overly retouched image.

Around him, couples and small groups sat at tables and talked in low, polite tones. Matt was terrified. This was the kind of place he'd only read about. Where you had to have manners. Where there were protocols and pleasantries. He had no idea how to behave. He'd never been to a place like this before.

He picked up a leather-bound book and scanned a menu printed on real paper. He didn't know what most of the dishes were. What the hell was a club Reuben? Or steak Tataki? The brief descriptions below the menu items were flowery and vague. Coming from Union Insta-Pak rations and "what we got is what you eat" in his refugee days, it was overwhelming.

The pounding in his skull swelled to a new crescendo. Matt gripped his head, willing the Mesh hangover a swift exit. He didn't belong here.

A waitress came to take his order. Another pretty girl. This one less otherworldly, with close-cropped black hair and a single silver earring, in Eridani's sunburst crest.

"Coming down off Mecha high?" she asked, giving Matt a friendly smile. They were probably paid to be friendly, Matt thought.

"Mesh hangover," he said.

"Is that what they call it now?" she asked. "We have some local herbal tonics that help ease the pain."

"You're a Mecha pilot?"

The woman's eyes skittered away. "No."

Then how would you know if they worked? Matt wondered. But he didn't need to bite her head off. She was just doing her job. He let her talk him into an evil-tasting glass of bile-colored liquid, and sat sipping the awful stuff. He looked in vain for Michelle and Soto, but they never entered the lounge.

What he did see were other people, looking at him. At several tables, heads nodded in his direction, making their companions take quick glances at him. Some of them were assessing. Some of them were scared.

Matt caught fragments of conversation: "Mecha star." "Big shot." "Show-off." They were talking about him. Despite the Union and the Corps' careful communications, word had gotten out about him—the first Demonrider.

After lunch, Matt made himself explore the resort. It was beautiful, in that parklike way that overly designed spaces have. It reminded him a little of Aurora, the planet where he had gone to school.

Matt ignored yelled invitations to join a half dozen others in the lake-sized pool, and walked quickly past the bar, where only the most hard-core drinkers sat in the middle of the day.

Inside, he found an arcade, filled with virtualities. They used simplified versions of the Mecha interface suits and viewmasks. Matt ignored the whispers of the people around him as he connected into one called *Mecha Corps: Final Adventure.*

Matt burst out laughing. It was just another rescue-the-ambassador scenario, running through the maze of a Union city to battle Corsairs armed with conventional weapons. There was no Mesh high. Nor was there a single challenge. He'd done more intense exercises at training camp. It couldn't even compare to his time on Keller—

Fighting those weird Corsair Mecha.

The thought still unsettled him. Corsairs weren't supposed to have Mecha. No other interstellar governmental organization besides the Union had biomechanical Mecha. Everyone knew that.

Matt stripped out of the game suit and went back outside to the pool, nursing his gut-twisting unease. No matter what the Union said, Corsairs had Mecha now. Mecha such as he'd never seen, with a weapon he'd never experienced. Were they a result of Rayder's capturing Hellions less than a year ago? Could they have cracked the code so fast, when even Union labs couldn't unravel Dr. Salvatore Roth's technological secrets?

Matt shook his head. It seemed as though his life was nothing but questions. And it was clear the Union wanted him here at the resort so he wouldn't have any desire to ask them.

The next few days were like walking through a dream. Matt's Mesh hangover slowly abated, but the need to get back into the Demon grew. He found himself sketching little stick-figure Demons on the napkin fabric in the Pleasure Dome Lounge.

Some days he met Michelle and Soto for breakfast; some days he didn't. Even through their Mesh hangover, they both had that intent, serious Mecha Corps look. They didn't doubt they were doing what was right and good. Even after Jotunheim and the Union cover-up, even after Keller and all the unresolved questions.

Shangri-La offered a whole range of Newhome tours, via land, air, or sea. Matt went with Michelle and Soto to the Capitol Plaza, hoping to recapture that sense of awe he'd felt when he first arrived on Earth and saw the ruins of Cape Canaveral.

Capitol Plaza was impressive. Ringed by towering skyscrapers and placid canals, it was more like a park than a plaza. Roman pillars fronted the grand entrance of the Congress Hall, above which was inscribed the Union motto: IN UNITY, ADVANCEMENT. IN DISCORD, DECAY.

But the neoclassical buildings, massive monuments, and parklike grounds didn't impress Matt. Even the festive crowds of tourists, clutching Union starburst flags, didn't change his mood.

The only thing that stirred his feelings was a massive, dull black slab of vitreous stone, as big as a football field. Set away from the other buildings among rolling hills of carefully cultivated Earth bluegrass and poplars, the slab was deeply scarred by fusion exhaust. On its side was a number: 100.

Platform 100. Built to mark the landing place of the first shuttle from Earth, carried here inside the first Displacement Drive asteroid ship. Launches from Platform 99 on Earth were what built the asteroid ship and started the Expansion.

At Platform 100, Michelle stopped and stared for a long time, her smiling face turning somber.

"What's the matter?" Matt asked her.

Michelle shook her head. "Just thinking about how far we've come."

Matt nodded. Michelle was from Earth. This had special meaning for her. He remained silent and let her look. Maybe she was thinking of her parents, forever bound in their Earth jobs.

Back at the resort that evening, Matt found Michelle sitting alone in the Shangri-La open-air bar, at a little table overlooking Newhome Valley. She looked wistfully out at the valley as an untouched glass of white wine sat in front of her. From this angle, the thin ribbon of the space elevator sliced a neat diagonal into the darkening sky. The passenger module was visible as a tiny pinprick of light, far up the ribbon.

"Waiting for someone?" Matt asked.

Michelle jumped, then turned and shook her head. Her eyes seemed to look through him, at something very far away. "No. Just . . . passing the time."

"Waiting to go back?"

A sigh. "Just enjoying my time here, right now. You should try it sometime."

You're enjoying it because this is all part of Mecha Corps, Matt thought. The reward for good corpspersons who don't ask too many questions.

But, for once, he was able to push that thought aside. It was okay. Michelle was all-in. She'd always been all-in. It's what she was.

"Have you thought about . . . are you going to be Mecha Corps the rest of your life?" Matt asked, finally.

Michelle looked out across the city for a long time before responding, "Probably. But for the moment, it's nice not to have to work so hard for a while. Don't you get tired of working sometimes?"

No, Matt thought. But was that true? Not really. He was living his life at a dead run. He didn't have time to think about what he was doing.

I don't want to think about what I'm doing. There are already enough questions.

"I don't know," he told her, finally.

Michelle focused on him. Her blue eyes were still and clear, fixed on his own. She was waiting for something. Waiting for him.

"Would you like to have dinner with me?" Matt asked.

Michelle's eyes widened. "Are you asking me out? On a date?"

Was that what he was doing? Since Mecha Training Camp, to the hidden Mecha Base and through all their experience together in the Corps, their lives had been too breakneck to even think of dating. But now—

"Yes. I am."

Michelle stood up, smiling, and offered Matt her arm. "I thought you'd never ask."

Matt took her arm. This was it. His chance.

Michelle grinned up at him. For one moment, the world was perfect. "It's just too bad we have to eat that—well, whatever that stuff is they're feeding us at the Pleasure Dome."

Matt nodded. It was supposed to be haute cuisine, but he'd never developed a taste for it. Not as a refugee.

There had to be other places to eat. The Newhome tour shuttle had passed through a number of little townships on the way up to the resort. They had to have restaurants.

"Who said we have to?" he asked her, explaining his idea.

"I don't think we're supposed to leave," Michelle said.

"We just did, this morning."

"I mean, besides the tours."

"You took out the universe's greatest supervillain, but you'll follow the rules now?" Matt teased.

Michelle laughed. "You're right."

"Come on," he said, offering his hand. She took it and let him lead her through the grounds, out the gate, and down the smooth concrete roads to the nearest cluster of houses and apartments. It turned out to be a small village, with a main street, a market, a little touristy art gallery, a bar, and a single restaurant named From the Earth.

Matt and Michelle shared a grin at the name and went in. As promised, the place featured a whole slew of old-Earth-type foods, heavy on the hamburgers and fries. Soon the two were diving happily into old-fashioned plastic baskets of grease-soaked food, under the be-mused gaze of the owner of the place.

"Much better!" Michelle said. "I was wondering who I'd have to kill to get a burger in the Corps."

Matt nodded. Even he knew what hamburger was, though the refugee ship version was made from vat-grown meat. The Corps was heavy on Insta-Paks and gloppy stuff that wouldn't fly away in zero g.

"This is fun," he said.

"You're finally enjoying yourself?" Michelle asked, her eyes glittering in the low light of the restaurant.

"It's good being here. With you."

Michelle beamed, magnifying her beauty tenfold. Matt smiled back at her, feeling, just for a moment, as if he belonged. Maybe there was a future with her. With Mecha Corps or not.

"We should do this every night," he told her.

Michelle nodded. "Yes!" Then her expression dark-ened, and she added, "Not tomorrow."

"Why?"

Silence for a long time. Then: "I'm seeing Kyle."

Anger flared red-hot in Matt. Kyle Peterov. The Eri-dani senator's son and former Mecha pilot. The guy who'd stolen Michelle away from him. The guy who'd tried to kill him, in the grip of Mesh rage. Of course he'd be here on Eridani. Probably working in a comfortable job Daddy had arranged for him.

"Don't be angry," Michelle said. "He called, and I—"

"Had to fly back into his arms," Matt finished for her.

Michelle flushed. "We're just friends. I don't see why you hate him so much."

"How can you see this guy? He's the reason the Cor-sairs probably have Mecha."

"Matt, that's not fair. He was captured by Rayder—"

"And *we* killed Rayder. Without him."

"You can't blame him for the Mecha on Keller. They don't even look like Hellions. And who's to say they haven't been working on Mecha for years? It's not like it's a secret the Union has them. We just have to make better Mecha now."

Matt clenched his fists, struggling with his rage. "So it's all forgiven with him now? Just pick back up where you've started, is that it?"

Michelle dropped her eyes, her mouth set in a thin line. "You're starting to make me feel like I have to make a choice."

"We all have to make choices. I try to make good ones."

Michelle reddened. She pushed her plate away and stood up. "We should go."

Matt saw his chance flying away. His whole future with her lay in ruins, like a nuclear wasteland. "I'm sorry," he said, standing.

Michelle gave him one last murderous glance and headed for the door. After paying the owner, Matt followed her back up the hill to the resort. She didn't even glance back at him as she stomped off to her room.

Matt stood in the hall, his fists clenched into white balls of pain. His last words echoed in his mind. *"We all have to make choices. I try to make good ones."*

Yeah. Right.

The next morning, Matt had a breakfast visitor. Which was fine. His food was tasteless, and he dreaded seeing Michelle again. He looked up to see a familiar person, wearing full Mecha Corps uniform. Colonel James Cruz, former leader of Mecha Base.

"Can we talk, Captain?" Colonel Cruz asked.

Matt studied the man. His craggy face. His carefully

combed silver hair. Was that what he would become, forty years from now?

"Talk away," Matt told him. "Sir."

"In a less public place, perhaps?" Colonel Cruz asked.

Matt shrugged. It didn't matter. He let Colonel Cruz lead him to a small meeting room, with a single window that looked out onto the grounds.

"I'm here for two reasons," Colonel Cruz told Matt. He pulled a small velvet case out of his breast pocket and opened it. Inside was the oak-leaf insignia of a major in the Mecha Corps.

"First, congratulations, Major Matt Lowell. For valor and bravery in action on Keller, I'm pleased to—"

"Valor and bravery?" Matt blurted, unable to stop himself. "We overpowered them a thousand to one. They weren't even ready for us."

"Regardless, Major, you were decisive."

"What were those Mecha on Keller?" Matt asked.

Cruz's eyes narrowed. "I'm not at liberty—"

"Nobody is supposed to have Mecha, except the Union."

"I can't discuss confidential information—"

"Tell me, or you can close that case and walk away," Matt said, his hands shaking. He felt as if he'd stepped outside himself, and was watching from far away.

Cruz ground his teeth. "Are you threatening a superior officer?"

"No. I'm saying that if you don't talk to me, I'll continue doing my part for the Mecha Corps as a captain and Demonrider. Hell, send me back now. But I don't want any more bribes. I want answers. I think I deserve that."

Cruz nodded, sighed, and shook his head. Finally he said, "We suspected the Corsairs had something, but we were as surprised as you were on Keller. ACCs are one thing. This is another. A new faction. I don't know a whole lot more about the Mecha, but I'm told it's not purely biomechanical. It's more like an automated sentry, with very, very good system disruption software."

Matt sat back, his mind churning. That jibed with what Peal had said. If the damn silver Mecha weren't so fragile, or if there were more of them, they'd be a formidable enemy.

"What about the people? On Keller?"

Cruz shook his head, but his eyes darted away.

"They were working with the Corsairs," Matt said. Not a question, a statement.

Cruz wiped his face with his hand. "Corsairs can be persuasive when they need to be."

"How?" Matt howled. How could anyone join forces with those—those animals?

Cruz shook his head, but said nothing.

"And the second reason you're here?" Matt asked.

Cruz nodded. "Concurrent with your promotion, I am authorized to offer you a singular post at Mecha Training Camp, optimizing a new team for a special mission critical to the stability of the Union. Time is of the essence."

Matt raised his eyebrows. "Any more details?"

Cruz shook his head. "I can give you none until you agree to take the mission. The only thing I can say is that this is absolutely critical, and you will be rewarded for your participation."

"Publically recognized?"

"Rewarded," Cruz said firmly.

Matt nodded. So it was another mission like Rayder. Another impossible objective. Or something the Union needed covered up like whatever they were protecting deep underground on Keller. It was one of those things he should ask Soto about. He should tell Michelle. He should sit and think and maybe even sleep on it.

We all have to make choices, Matt told himself. Thinking of his abject failure last night. Thinking of Michelle, getting ready for her date with Kyle.

"When do we start, sir?" Matt asked.

3

CAMP

Back on Earth. Backwater Earth.

They wouldn't waste space elevators on Earth, Matt thought as he shuttled down to one of his old haunts, Mecha Training Camp.

Formerly Cape Canaveral, Mecha Training Camp now looked like an ancient ruin set among gray-green swamp. Overgrown, crazed concrete runways alternated with low-roofed, utilitarian buildings and the pockmarks of rusted gantries at the edge of the sea. Matt knew about the underground, high-tech base beneath the facade, but that didn't change the fact that the Earth was a neglected, timeworn planet, eclipsed by the more prosperous worlds of the Union.

Matt's Perfect Record had unreeled that first day when he met Michelle Kind and Major Soto. Soto handing him the flak jacket. Michelle charging up the first hill.

Matt closed his eyes. He'd left Eridani without telling either Michelle or Soto. Maybe he should have.

The shuttle touched down north of the training camp, on a new runway near an inland bay. To the south lay Cochran's Cove, the mock city where Matt had done his first Mecha Cadet exercise. The shuttle pilot directed

Matt to a group of low buildings, their cinder-block sides peeling paint, but with a new stainless steel plaque reading ADVANCED MECHAFORMS EXTENDED TRAINING, FACILITY 1.

Matt opened the door to find Dr. Salvatore Roth, the father of modern biomechanical Mecha technology and general manager of Advanced Mechaforms, Inc., the company that produced Mecha exclusively for the Universal Union. He sat in a small, unadorned room, his back to Matt as he studied a wraparound nonphysical projection screen. On the screen, body images swept from green to yellow and red and back again. Over Roth's shoulder, darkened one-way glass looked out into a larger chamber, where a dozen cadets in milky interface suits and viewmasks were cabled up to silicone wire looms hanging from the ceiling.

Matt frowned as his Perfect Record brought back more memories. Dr. Roth had probed Matt much the same way he was doing with the cadets right now. Matt wondered just how much Dr. Roth knew about him, and about his talents.

"You're not HuMax," Roth had told him. Cold comfort, in the wake of Rayder's destruction. And Matt wouldn't put it past Dr. Roth to use a convenient lie, if it served his needs. Matt still didn't know what the origin of his genetic gifts were, even if Roth said he wasn't HuMax.

"Dr. Roth—" Matt began.

Roth held up a hand for silence. Matt snapped his mouth shut and waited, arms crossed, until Roth looked up from his screen. His eyes showed no expression at all, as if they were made of stone.

"This is what you will do, Major Lowell," Dr. Roth said. "You will take this group of Demon Adepts—"

"Adepts?" Matt cut in.

Roth pursed his lips in irritation at the interruption, then continued. "Adepts are select individuals in my improved training regime."

"An improvement from throwing cadets in a Demon and hoping they don't die?" The words just popped out.

Roth's face compressed into a deep scowl, but he continued without comment. "Your task is to optimize the performance of the Adepts, with the goal of deploying a team of three to four Demons at the earliest possible date."

Matt sighed. "And good morning to you, Dr. Roth."

Roth just stared at Matt. Any semblance of humor or sarcasm was always lost on the imperturbable general manager.

"Why not deploy us?" Matt asked.

"Us? Be more precise."

"Me, Major Soto, Captain Kind."

Roth waved an annoyed hand, as if swatting a fly. "Additional Demon resources must be developed. Also, your team requires downtime to optimize long-term usability."

We're tools to him, nothing more. But what could Matt do about it? He'd accepted the assignment. He had to carry it through. "What do you want me to do?"

"I have already stated the top-level goal. In detail, we expect you to observe, instruct, and interact with our adepts in order to increase their Mesh efficiency and Merge capability, as determined by ongoing monitoring. You will select three to five best-performing members for a time-critical, high-priority mission. I must stress that time is of the essence."

Matt sighed. "Why me?"

Roth stared at Matt for several seconds without speaking. "Your record speaks for itself. You were first to master the Demon. You helped Major Soto move successfully from Hellion and Demon, which I believed impossible. Also, arguably, you are the factor who enabled the final Merge at Jotunheim."

Matt shivered, remembering his epic battle with Rayder and his HuMax companions—now conveniently swept under the rug by the Union. The less said about Jotunheim, the better. Media like UUN and UCN repeated the same comforting stories: Geos was rebuilt, the memorials were placed, the nameless heroes selflessly gave their all for the Union, and beyond that, the citizens didn't need to know.

Reward. Not recognition. Colonel Cruz's voice came back, echoing hollowly.

Did that mean this was another chance to go up against the Corsairs? The HuMax? Maybe even that new Corsair faction that the colonel had mentioned? Matt shivered in sudden anticipation. But questions still resonated louder.

"How were the Corsair Mecha able to hold us down on Keller?"

Roth just looked at Matt neutrally, but didn't answer.

"How did they immobilize the Demons? What were those Mecha?"

"We are investigating their system disruption technology as we speak," Roth said, his words clipped.

"What if they use it again?" Matt pressed.

"We expect to have a countermeasure available shortly."

"And the Mecha? I've never seen anything like that—"

"It is not a derivative of my biomechanical technology," Dr. Roth interrupted, his expression finally twisting in anger. Or was he hiding something?

"Then what is it?"

"We believe it is advanced conventional technology, but as before, the particulars are not important to your mission."

That was it. Roth was hiding something. The Mecha were closer to his than he wanted to admit. Maybe even taken from the same tech base. After all, Rayder had had control of the Union Hellions for some time. Maybe he'd passed on the information.

"Then how did the Corsairs make Mecha? Are they working with the Taikong? The Aliancia?"

Roth's expression hardened. "You have a choice. You may train our adepts, or you may return to a standard Union-supervised Mecha Corps team, to execute assignments they see fit. Of course, their view of your capability may change if you refuse this opportunity."

Matt nodded. Nothing more than a tool. A broken tool.

"Let's get started," he told Roth.

The ten adepts studied Matt suspiciously, like a class sizing up a new teacher. Matt felt suddenly self-conscious, in his crisp blue Mecha Corps uniform with new-minted major's insignia. Should he have dressed down like Soto, to be more on their level?

The adepts all wore the milky interface suits of Mecha Cadets, with their name displayed prominently on their upper chest, along with a new, unfamiliar graphic: a crouching Mecha, similar to the Advanced Mechaforms logo. Its tiny head and vestigial horns tagged it as a Demon.

Behind them, ten Demons hulked against the overcast Florida sky. Their bright red bodies were virtually the only color between the gray sky and the muted brown-green of the soggy land. Three targets, black-and-white bull's-eyes, had been set up a kilometer down the field.

What did they know about him? Matt made himself meet the stares of his protégés. They waited patiently, saying nothing. What would Soto do?

"Okay, let's see what you've got," Matt said, pointing at the Demons.

The adepts nodded, some of them grinning. They immediately broke ranks and scrambled up the extended ladders to their Demons' cockpits. Pilots' chambers irised shut, and the Demons, shuddering, stood to attention.

"Sink or swim? You've been taking lessons from Dr. Roth?" came a familiar voice, behind Matt.

Matt started and turned. Behind him stood Jahl Khoury, holding a colorful slate. He wore his Mecha Corps Auxiliary sergeant's uniform, with a new bar Matt had never seen before: tiny, alternating silver and black bands. Jahl was Peal Khoury's brother and geek-in-arms, and he'd been in the same Mecha Training Camp group as Matt.

"Jahl! Where'd you come from?"

Jahl waved at the low testing building behind them. "I've been working with the fresh meat. Dr. Roth neglected to give you this." Jahl waved the slate. "You'll need it to monitor their Mesh Effectiveness."

Matt nodded. "How much training do they have?"

"They've been trained specifically on Demons from the start. But . . ." Jahl trailed off, grinning.

"But what?"

"You'll see." Jahl handed Matt the slate.

On the screen, ten sets of readings bounced from forty-one percent to fifty-six percent Mesh Effectiveness. Matt grimaced. Fifty percent was the threshold for use. Some of these kids couldn't even move the damn things. And none of the ME numbers were stellar. Matt wasn't surprised to see two of them standing rooted in place while the others stumbled around like drunks.

"You can give them commands through here," Peal said, pointing at a comms button on the slate.

"Is it even worth it?" Matt said, gesturing at the Mesh Effectiveness.

"Your call. They've had a ton of time in the optimization room, though."

Matt frowned. Maybe this was just the test-day jitters. He'd take them a little further. He hit the comms button and said, "Demons, line up in groups of three and fire at the targets, using your MK-160s and popcorn rounds."

The Demons obediently shambled into two groups of three, and one group of two. Two Demons remained immobile, twitching now and again. Matt shook his head. Even the ones that moved had crappy coordination. He didn't need a slate to see that.

"What about us?" a cadet's voice came through the slate. One of the Mesh Effectiveness boxes illuminated ELIZE ROBBE, 43 PERCENT. "The ones who can't move. Uh, sir."

"Have you ever managed to achieve stable Mesh above fifty percent?" Matt asked her.

"Ye-yeah," Elize said, breathing heavily. "It's just—it's like there's something in the way. Sometimes I can get past it, sometimes I—like now."

Something in the way. The ghost in the machine, the presence Matt had felt in the Mecha, so many times.

"Are you fighting it?" Matt asked her.

"Yes, sir," she said, through a ragged breath. "As hard as I can!"

"That's your mistake," Matt said. "You can't fight it. It's stronger than you are. You have to get closer to it. Accept it."

"But it hurts," Elize protested. "It's all pain, like knives, and . . . hate!"

And dust and static, and talons razoring through your mind, Matt thought, remembering his first time in a Mecha. Elize was probably cowering in the gray nonspace of Mesh, staying as far away from the presence—the neural feedback, the reflection of a cadet's own fear, Dr. Roth said. Matt wasn't so sure.

"Go to it," Matt said. "Walk through the pain. Accept it. When you accept it, you can control it."

But was that true? Matt wondered. That voice, that thing in the Mecha—it seemed all-powerful. Was it simply biding its time, waiting to take control?

"Yes, sir," Elize said. Her open comms passed through a gasp and a series of whimpers. Matt closed his eyes. Why was this so hard?

Suddenly Elise's Mesh Effectiveness shot up to fifty-three percent, and her Mecha rocked forward and began to move.

"I—I think I've—it hurts, but it's different now," Elize said.

"Good. Continue."

Elize's Mesh Effectiveness continued to climb, peaking at sixty-one percent. Now she ranked at the top of the adepts. Chatter from the others showed that they saw it too.

"That's it," she said, taking some smooth steps forward. "I can't—I can't make it go higher."

"That's good progress for now, Cadet," Matt said. "Join the others and start the exercise."

"Thank you, sir!" She ran over to stand with the group of two.

The other Mecha still wasn't moving. Matt switched the comms to his channel, and could hear only sobbing. The cadet didn't even respond to his commands.

Matt sighed. "Cadet, stand down," he said. "Return to—" He looked at Jahl for help.

"Conditioning."

"—conditioning. You'll get another chance."

The Demon powered down and the cadet marched, head down, past Matt and Jahl to the low building where Dr. Roth worked.

"Begin firing drills, Cadets," Matt told the rest.

"Adepts," one cadet cut in. The slate identified her as Norah Posada Gracia.

"Adept is a title that's earned," Matt shot back.

"How?" she asked. "Sir."

"You could take a lead from Elize. Her Mesh Effectiveness is higher than yours now."

"I don't need to give in to it!" she shot back. "I can fight!"

"Sir," Jahl added.

"Sir," she said. Her Mesh Effectiveness chart shuddered higher, before peaking at sixty-three percent. Matt could only imagine the battle of wills between Norah and the thing in the machine.

That was what Kyle did, Matt thought. He never accepted it. He fought it. And in the end, it broke him.

"You'll do better if you accept it," Matt told her.

"I'll do it my way, sir," Norah said, as if through gritted teeth.

Matt shook his head. It would have to do for now. Best to see what they could do. He had the nine adepts cycle through the firing drills, then had them do some simple hand-to-hand combat.

The adepts sucked.

There was no other way to put it. They couldn't target, they couldn't shoot, they spent minutes switching from the MK-160 to Fireflies and back again. Under the overcast Florida sky, vast swaths of soggy ground erupted all around their targets, with only a few rounds hitting their marks. Mecha grappled ineffectively with Mecha, like two drunks wrestling outside a bar. The deep booms of their biometal bodies clashing together echoed hollowly across the land, like defeat.

As the cadets grew more weary, their Mesh Effectiveness scores decreased. Two, then three Demons dropped out of the exercises. Eventually only five stood standing, and three wavered at the very edge of fifty percent.

"That's enough," Matt said, calling all the pilots out of their Mechas. They stood in front of him, wobbly, in interface-gel-coated ranks. Their eyes shone with the lingering effects of Mesh high. They'd be hungover tomorrow. Brutally.

"How'd we do?" one of the adepts called out, a slightly pudgy, short man with shoulder-length hair. His interface suit identified him as Jie Teng. He'd been one of the better performers. His Mesh Effectiveness hadn't dropped below fifty-eight percent through the entire exercise.

"Not as well as I expected," Matt said.

"Who are you to judge?" another adept called out, a young woman, almost painfully slim, with high cheekbones and buzz-cut black hair. Norah Posada Gracia.

A slim spike of anger shot through Matt. *I'm the guy who took down Rayder,* he thought. Though he couldn't say that. But what could he say? *I was the first to use a Demon? The first to Merge? Still the best at Mesh?* It sounded like empty boasts.

"I'm the person Mecha Corps chose to train you," Matt said. "That's all you need to know."

Norah crossed her arms and grumbled, but said nothing more.

"I heard you were on Keller, sir," another cadet said. Matt didn't catch his name tag.

"Among other operations," Matt told him. That stirred some more muttering among the cadets. This time, some of it even sounded respectful.

Like Soto, when I heard he'd fought at Forest, Matt thought. Maybe the Union would tart up Keller into some famous Mecha battle, a turning point in Union history where only the might of the Mecha Corps had stopped an unspeakable Corsair ground invasion on a colony world. Maybe the easy victory they had, or the fact that Keller was working with the Corsairs would never get out. Or maybe Union helping Corsairs was just the beginning. How many people knew that Corsairs could be HuMax? How did that all fit in?

"Dr. Roth wants a progress report," Jahl said, interrupting Matt's thoughts.

"Already?"

Jahl nodded at his slate. "Dr. Roth has spec'd three to five days as an optimal training and selection time."

"How would he know?" Matt spat.

Jahl shrugged. "I didn't say I agreed. But he has shared his estimate with Mecha Corps Command."

So that's what they'd be expecting, Matt thought. That meant no break for the adepts tomorrow. They'd have to work through their hangover. If they were even able to move at all.

But how the hell would he get them up to snuff in just a couple of days? They didn't have time for weeks of training, like when he worked with Soto.

Then Matt had a sudden flash of insight. *Sink or swim. Turn it on its head.*

"Tell Roth we're moving forward with the five adepts who maintained Mesh through the whole exercise," Matt told Jahl.

"You don't think that some of the others deserve a chance—" Jahl began.

"They do. Just not here. We don't have time."

Jahl nodded. "Yes, sir," he muttered at Dr. Roth's image on the slate.

Matt grinned.

The five adepts who made it through the exercise would go again tomorrow. And this time, there'd be a surprise.

The five adepts had interesting histories. The buzz-cut woman, Norah Gracia, hailed from Paradise Lost, a refugee Displacement Drive ship, just like Matt. But she hadn't gone to Aurora University like Matt. She hadn't gone to any college at all. It was unlikely she'd be able to. Her disciplinary records, spotty as they were, had her in detention, and later in the brig, for much of her time on Paradise Lost.

Another, Mikey Kerr, was a survivor of Highland, a rich precolony world that had just been established when the Corsairs attacked. Mikey had lived a year by himself, completely alone, on Highland before being rescued. Again, like Matt's time on Prospect after the Corsair attack when he was a child. Matt had spent two weeks in the lonely tunnels under the surface, after burying his father in the wind-whipped sand outside.

Jie Teng was the son of a tech magnate on Geos, an open genemod, but one without the signature violet eyes. Like Matt, whose genetic gifts from his father were well hidden.

Elize Robbe was from Forest, a solid Union world, and was once counted as one of the smartest students in Union Grade 6, after coming up with a solar optimization system for the planetary ecosystem. A prodigy on many levels, she also counted a "photographic memory"

as one of her skills. Matt found that coincidence especially chilling. Was she a genemod too—one like him?

Finally Marjan Veluszic, whose records were as blank
as a broken slate in the years before his observation for
Mecha Training Camp.

So many echoes of myself, Matt thought. Hidden
pasts, refugee status, last person standing, genemod. Like
looking in a shattered mirror. Did any well-adjusted, up-
and-coming Union citizens ever become Mecha Corps?

Probably not, Matt thought. Not unless it was someone like Kyle, where it was all for show. Quick stint in
Mecha Corps, great showing for a senator's son, a check
mark on the way to being a senator himself.

And even then, Kyle hadn't exactly been stable, had he?

Matt shook his head, sitting alone that night in his
little Mecha Corps apartment. Maybe he should call Michelle. He had plenty of units for the über-expensive
FTLcomm connection. Maybe he should burn some of
them.

No, Matt thought. *Play this out. Then decide.*

He went over the adepts' histories one more time,
even though he remembered every word. Trying to put
together the puzzle, looking for clues to a bigger meaning.

But the meaning, if any, eluded him.

Matt was waiting for the adepts that next morning,
standing tall in his own Demon, as rain sheeted down on
the grim gray-green land. Sensory feedback meant he
felt the trickle of water down his back, running along the
Demon's serrated spine. He felt the chill gusts of morning air, and the sodden ground beneath his feet. Inside
the Demon, he was the Mecha. There was no separation
between him and what he rode. It was an amazing feeling. The best feeling in the universe.

Matt's heart beat double time as Peal and the adepts appeared. He'd told Peal to get them suited up and get them started with their exercises. The five adepts moved slowly, slump-shouldered, grumbling from Mesh hangover and the ill weather. If any of them noticed the sixth Demon as they made their way to their own Mecha, they didn't give any indication. Matt held himself perfectly still, all external systems off, as if the Demon was unoccupied.

As the adepts suited up, their Mesh Effectiveness lit on Matt's internal viewmask, showing as floating tags over the Demons. Not surprisingly, it was lower than the day before. But all of them managed to activate the units. Matt let them take a few shambling steps before he sprang to life.

The closest Mecha was Norah. She managed to half turn before Matt was on her. He slammed into her Mecha full-force with a resounding metallic clang, taking her Demon's feet fully off the ground. For what seemed like an eternity, the two Demons flew through the air. Then Norah impacted on her back with a whoop Matt heard through the comms. Her Demon slid thirty, forty, fifty meters before coming to a rest at the end of a soggy dark furrow in the Earth, already filling with water.

"Wh-wha-what the hell was that?" Norah sputtered as the comms lit up with exclamations from all the adepts.

"That's combat," Matt said, on COMMS→ALL. "You never know what's going to happen."

"You bastard!" Norah screamed, struggling under Matt's Demon. Her Mesh Effectiveness had gone up to sixty-seven percent, but Matt countered her blows effortlessly.

"Good," Matt said. "Fight me, don't fight the thing in the machine!"

"I'll fight you both!" Norah yelled, thrashing to throw his Demon off.

"An enemy of an enemy is my friend," Matt told her.

"Not that . . . thing!"

"The time to fight the ghost in the machine will come, but accept it for now," Matt said, softly, quietly, the words spilling out of him. Almost as if something were feeding him lines.

Yes, something said. Something not him. Matt smelled ancient dust, acrid with decay, and felt a prickling over his skin, like static. His own ghost in the machine.

That's not a reflection of my personality, Matt thought.

All of you. All you are. Momentary images flashed in Matt's mind's eye: ripping Norah's Demon's arm off as she lay prone and helpless, tearing into her chestplate.

Matt closed his eyes. *No. Not now.*

The thing in his Mecha receded from his mind, as if agreeing with him.

Norah thrashed hard, almost bucking Matt off. Her Mesh Effectiveness hit the seventies for the first time.

"He can't take us all!" Norah screamed over the comms. "Come on, guys, help me!"

Four Demons converged on Matt. He grinned, watching their Mesh Effectiveness. Every one of them was climbing as their adrenaline and determination kicked in. They spiked through the sixties and into the low seventies.

Matt waited until the lead two Mecha were almost on him, then sprang off Norah and triggered his thrusters. He shot a hundred meters into the air as the two Mecha collided shoulder to shoulder, where he'd been just a moment before. Elize's and Mikey's Demons resonated like a bell, and collapsed in a tangled heap on Norah's Demon. Norah struggled to push them off.

Another Demon triggered its own thrusters and soared toward Matt—this one tagged MARJAN. But Marjan's Mecha went wide, its rearside thrusters firing intermittently. Marjan struggled frantically as the Demon headed back toward the ground. He barely managed to keep from landing headfirst in the muck.

"Don't try too hard," Matt told them. "You're all still babies."

Growls of rage came through the comms as two more Mecha launched themselves at Matt—Norah and Jie. Norah made it all the way to Matt's perch in the sky and grappled with him. But she didn't know anything about aerial combat. Matt fended off her blows with ease. Undeterred, she lashed out at him, harder and faster, her arms blurring. Matt nodded in satisfaction. Her Mesh Effectiveness was seventy-five percent.

Matt used his thrusters to push Norah back down to the ground. She crouched as if collapsing under his thrust, then used all her strength to throw Matt off with a powerful shove. Matt laughed as he staggered back and tried to keep his balance. She was strong. This was fun. A little more—

Norah's fist fairly blurred as she caught him with an uppercut. Faint pain sizzled on Matt's chin, and his vision went fuzzy as sensors strained with the impact. Matt's Demon went down on its butt.

Norah's Mesh Effectiveness peaked at eighty-one percent. Matt grinned. Perfect. It was going just as he had hoped.

Norah was on him again, fists pistoning as she shouted incoherently. The other Demons piled on, tearing at Matt. In contact with them, he felt their thoughts through the neural interface: anger and fear, twisted around the unnatural rush of Mesh high. Rising higher into irrational rage.

Uh-oh. Their Mesh Effectiveness was spiking, but their emotion was taking it out of control. If he didn't stop them, they might end up like insane like Kyle . . . or dead like Ash.

"Stop!" Matt cried. The five Demons ignored him, their minds clamoring even more loudly for his blood. "Disengage! That's an order!"

Something like distant laughter, with the smell of static and dust, came as a response.

The ghost in the machine. The thing Roth didn't want to talk about. It was riding them, taking them out of control. And enjoying every second of it.

"Shut them down!" Matt shouted, to COMMS→P. KHOURY.

"I can't!" Jahl told him. "I'm not at that access level!"

Shit. Norah's Mesh Effectiveness was in the nineties, and everyone else's was in the high eighties. The cacophony of their minds was so loud Matt couldn't tell where he ended and they began. He tried to physically throw them off, but they kept him pinned.

"Get Roth!" Matt yelled.

"He's offline!" Jahl said.

No choice. He had to stop them now. There was only one choice: Merge.

Even though he'd never Merged with more than two other Demons before. Even though each additional Demon added exponentially to the Merged configuration's power.

If he succeeded, what would stand on the surface of the Earth? A towering red colossus, burning bright with infinite energy? A thing capable of tearing the planet apart?

It didn't matter. *Merge,* he thought.

Matt's Demon ceased to be a singular entity. Its biometallic muscles liquefied and flowed like syrup, melding with the five Demons that surrounded him. Fragments of their panicked thoughts beat at Matt's consciousness: *What's happening! I can't. No, I can't! Pull away! Get off me!*

But Matt was stronger than them. He drew them in. Into himself. As he drew the thing in the Mecha. He would use their power, as he used the ghost in the machine's.

Now I see, Elize thought, relaxing. She dreamed of technologies Matt only barely understood, great orbiting antimatter generators that could spawn entire new worlds.

What do you see? Matt asked.

Magic, she thought. And that was all Elize needed. Her mind settled down into a solid beat, in time with the Mecha's biomechanical systems.

It is all based on force and pain, thought Jie. *This. The Mecha. You. Your entire life.*

You don't need to follow my path, Matt said, sending Jie images of Jahl and his own accomplishments. Jahl and Jie were similarly entwined with technology. Jie understood and nodded, slipping into sync with the Merged Mecha.

I want nothing to do with you! I am nothing like you! Norah yelled. But she softened. Her mind echoed with long, desperate chases down cold, dark, weightless halls, like Matt's earliest years.

Your time will come, Matt told her. *You can fight all your battles in a Mecha, even the ones in your own mind.* He showed her the death of his own father.

You are nothing like me, she thought, but the thought was soft-edged, more tentative. Her mind spun like a perfectly balanced engine in time with the merged Demon.

You think you're the chosen one, Mikey thought, his mind unsettled and angry. Matt saw Mikey riffling through his own memories, his anger building at Matt's accomplishments.

I don't think anything. I don't even know what to do with the rest of my life, Matt thought, showing him the disastrous date with Michelle. Mikey laughed out loud and relaxed, falling into the overall rhythm.

I refuse you all! Marjan's thought was a scream in the darkness. He sent dagger-edged images of fire and destruction, obscuring any memories of his past. The Merge they worked for wobbled at the edge of instability. If Matt let it go, Marjan would drag them all down into a hell only Kyle had seen.

No choice. Matt opened his mind to all of them and let his Perfect Record unspool the memory of his first Merge. The one that ended with Ash dead and Kyle insane.

Brute force doesn't make you a Demonrider, Matt told them. *Try to control too much, and you might end up losing everything.*

Elize and Jie faltered, swimming in amplified emotion. The Merge sputtered like a flame starved of oxygen.

DeMerge, Matt thought.

The six Demons lay, separate once more, under the leaden sky.

The next day, the adepts stumbled out to the field, more hungover than ever. They looked as if they hadn't slept in a week: hollow-cheeked, sunken-eyed, with the dull stare of people who only wanted the nightmare to end.

But when they got in their Demons' cockpits, not one of them had less than seventy-seven percent Mesh Effectiveness. Matt watched them, fluid and smooth, as they wrestled and fought mock battles, ran endless rounds through the targeting bull's-eyes, and flashed through the sky like lightning.

Maybe that was all they needed. A challenge.

Or maybe, just maybe, some of his skill had rubbed off on them in the Merge.

When they were done for the day, Dr. Roth made an appearance. He was dressed in a rumpled lab coat, and he blinked at the setting sun as if suspicious of its light.

"You and your team leave tomorrow," Roth told Matt.

4

UNCHARTED

Most Displacement Drive ships were little more than converted asteroids, but UUS *Helios* was the jewel of the Union fleet.

Completely encased in meter-thick steel armor and shock-absorbent scaffolding, with giant fusion engines and reaction pits for maneuvering, it was ready to go into battle anywhere, against the heaviest fire. Matt, Michelle, and Soto had ridden the still-incomplete *Helios* to do battle with Rayder. Now its list of victories were longer than any other Union ship.

Now Matt lay outside on UUS *Helios*'s smooth steel surface, watching the stars change with every Displacement. But the cold steel beneath him was unsettling. Without the crunch of asteroid rock underneath him, without shards to throw and to watch spin out into infinite space ... something was missing. He couldn't even feel the Displacement Drive charging and discharging. When they Displaced, there were only the shifting stars to note their passage.

But the stars were spectacular. They were far beyond the edge of the Union, in a thick part of an arm of the Milky Way. Stars clustered together in brilliant arrays, like precious gems on black velvet. So close they had color—young blue-white stars, middle-of-the-road white-and-yellow suns, bloated orange-and-red giants. It was an amazing view, one he was happy to see directly, rather than piped down to the bridge's screens.

But it also meant they were far past the edge of the Union. The last time he'd gone this far was out to Jotunheim, the hidden capital planet of the HuMax. Where was this assignment taking them?

Matt didn't know. He didn't know much at all, other than that they were shipping out for "a developing situation, with input to be given regarding objectives at key points."

That wasn't like his previous missions. There was always a brief. This was empty, all data redacted. Colonel Cruz had stopped answering his questions about the mission. He just stared through Matt, as if looking at something far away.

Echoes of those questions pattered in his mind.

"Are we going up against the Corsairs?" he'd asked.

"It's possible," Cruz had said. *"Not enough information at present."*

"Is this another HuMax mission?"

A pause. Then a strange sigh. Cruz's eyes were hard, determined.

In the end, all Matt knew was that they were going far out—maybe farther out than Mecha Base, set in the middle of a protoplanet eight thousand light-years from Earth—and that they expected trouble. A lot of it.

"Isn't it dangerous to be out here?" a voice grated through Matt's comms as a space-suited figure came to lean over him. In the dim starlight, he caught the hint of a face. Elize.

"Get down!" Matt said, sweeping her feet. Elize yelped as she fell slowly in the microgravity toward the deck. She whirled her arms, trying to get her balance.

"Let yourself fall," Matt told her. "Staying near the surface is safest."

Elize stopped struggling and fell toward the armor plating of UUS *Helios*.

Smart, Matt thought. She didn't need a dozen explanations. "The Displacement field is probably ten or twenty meters off the surface, but it's best not to take chances."

Elize came to rest beside him. "Then why are you out here?"

Because there weren't any NO EGRESS AT DISPLACEMENT signs, Matt thought. But he didn't tell her that. He just pointed up and said, "Look."

Elize drew in her breath as she saw the stars for the first time. Really saw them. Not on a screen, not through a tiny window. Right there, the grand panorama of the universe.

A Displacement happened just at that moment, and the stars shifted fractionally in the sky.

"Wow," she said, after a time.

Matt let her watch for a while in silence. Elize was an interesting person. She'd been pestering him the entire time about how he learned to use a Mecha so well, asking for more tips on how to use hers, bugging him about the real ramifications of their Merge, peppering him with ten thousand technical questions about biomechanical tech he couldn't answer.

"I . . . I can't analyze this," she said, after a long time. "I have to just look."

"Sometimes looking is enough."

"You say the most profound things."

Matt laughed. She was clearly interested in him, but he never got any kind of sexual vibe off her. More like a disciple.

Great, he thought.

"Look," Matt said. "It's not profound. It's just, well, hell, I don't think I'm half as smart as you. You'd give Jahl a run for his money."

"'A run for his money'?" Elize sounded confused.

"Old Earth expression." Something else he'd picked up from Michelle. His Perfect Record turned back to her. That last night. His stupid explosion about Kyle. What if he could turn the clock back and redo that one moment in time? Would he be here, on the UUS *Helios*, again, heading for a mission on the edge of nowhere?

"Where are we going?" Elize asked, after a time.

"I don't know," Matt said.

"You're mission leader. You should know."

Matt shook his head.

"I didn't think the Union extended this far out."

"It doesn't. Not even . . ." Matt trailed off.

"Not even what?"

Matt sighed. Why not tell her? She was Mecha Corps, as of today. "Not even Mecha Base."

He told her about Mecha Base, buried deep in the heart of a forming planetary system, the perfect hiding place for the Union's most advanced technology. Perfect until Rayder figured out where they were.

Had they moved Mecha Base? Matt wondered. He realized he had no idea. He'd been moving so fast, for so long.

"You really don't know anything about the mission?" Elize pressed.

"I know that I'm expected to follow orders, and you're expected to follow my lead."

Elize didn't say anything for a while. Matt imagined her frown. She didn't like to follow orders blindly. Nor did he. He wondered if she would challenge his authority.

"What will it be like?" Elize asked, finally.

Matt shook his head. If it was anything like their time on Jotunheim, battling Rayder and the HuMax . . .

But that was insane. Nothing was like that. Nothing could be like that, ever again. And even Matt could see they weren't heading to Jotunheim again.

But Elize wasn't asking about that. She was asking about fighting in the Demons. In space. She'd never done that. She'd never been to Mecha Base. He was taking a totally raw team into a totally unknown place, for a completely unspecified mission.

Matt laughed.

"What's so funny?"

"It seems like we're always doing the impossible."

Matt felt a hand grasp his own. Through the thick space suit fabric, it was as cold as the steel beneath him. "You helped me, and I'll help you," Elize told him.

"Do the impossible?" Matt asked, turning to look at her.

Elize was already looking at him. In the dim starlight, her dark blue eyes glittered like black diamonds.

"Of course," she said, as if she did it every day.

"Don't think you know me," Norah said, later that day. Matt looked up from his Insta-Pak rations in the UUS *Helios*'s mess hall and regarded her. Norah's brow was drawn down in deep furrows, beneath her close-cropped black hair. Her eyes narrowed in anger.

"Haven't you told me that before?" Matt asked.

"I just want you to know, after that mind fuck of yours, that Merge or whatever you call it, you still don't know me. You think you know me, because you were a ref too. Yeah, boo-hoo, that and five units will get you a nice coffee. You don't know what I had to go through to get to training camp, and don't think you ever will."

Matt's Perfect Record dredged up instants of time

that had passed while they were in Merge. Norah gripping an antique gunpowder pistol as a hulking man bent over her, grinning. The blinding report. Tribunal. Thousands of hours of digging time while everyone congratulated her actions. The simple mind equation of weapons equals power, and the most powerful weapon is Mecha.

But those were fleeting glimpses. She was right. It was easy to take that and weave a whole story from it. It would be a lot harder to get to know her.

She knew the story of Matt's father. He could tell her the rest. But she'd dismiss that. Norah was a core of anger, surrounded by purpose.

"I don't care," Matt told her.

"What?" Norah rocked back. She'd expected him to be conciliatory.

"I don't care if you don't like me."

"I never said—"

Matt raised a hand. "I don't care if you have issues. I don't really even care what your agenda is. What I care about, Sergeant, is two things."

Norah glared at him, her slit eyes still furious, her mouth working angrily.

"First, that you'll do what I say, when I say it, without hesitation."

Norah squared her shoulders. "Of course. You're my commanding officer!"

Matt held back a smile. She was reacting exactly the way he figured she would.

"Second, don't assume you know me. You don't know me, or enough of me, even though you're a ref, and even though you've had a tough life. You have no idea what I went through after training camp."

Norah blinked. She hadn't expected her own words to be thrown back at her. Her expression cycled from rage to hard assessment. Eventually she nodded. "Yes, sir."

Matt nodded. Norah studied him awhile longer.

"Is there anything else?" Matt asked.

"No, sir," Norah said, and double-timed away.

Matt sighed. He could have handled that better. But what was he supposed to do? Coddle them?

"She really likes you," said a familiar voice.

Matt looked up. Jie Teng stood at the edge of Matt's table, holding a just-opened Insta-Pak. His piercing violet eyes reminded Matt of Mecha Auxiliary sergeant Lena Stoll, whom he'd worked with in Mecha Training Camp and on Mecha Base. She'd been the first open genemod Matt had met. It had been a shock back then.

"You're not antigenemod, are you?" Jie continued as Matt studied him.

Matt laughed again. How could he be, when he was genemod himself? He still didn't know the extent of his father's gifts. But Jie knew that, through Merge.

"Is that a yes or a no?" Jie asked.

"No," Matt said, motioning for the other man to sit. He seemed so harmless, in a chubby and happy kind of way. It was hard to take Jie seriously, mostly because of the way he looked.

And yet he was the son of a major Geos tech entrepreneur. He'd been genemodded for a reason. What advantage had Jie's father given him?

"No, you're not antigenemod or no, you don't like genemods that much?"

Matt shook his head. "Your parents chose to make you that way. It wasn't your choice."

Jie looked down at his Insta-Pak and didn't answer for a while. When he did, his voice was low. "I wouldn't change anything," he said.

"You must have been bullied. Cut out."

A nod. "And worse."

"And you'd still choose to be genemod?" Matt pressed.

Another nod. "We can't move forward, just as we are."

Matt clenched his fists. That's what the HuMax had thought. Dangerous thinking that had almost destroyed all of humanity.

"What's your gift?" Matt asked.

"Longevity," Xie said.

Matt sucked in his breath. The holy grail of HuMax tech, the stuff people dreamed about—and would pay any amount of money for.

"How long will you live for?" Matt asked.

Xie shook his head. "Nobody knows. Some say the HuMax could do a hundred and fifty, two hundred years. But they were cut short, weren't they?"

Matt nodded. On the surface, it seemed like such a trivial thing, to live longer than normal. But if it enabled Xie to continue actively learning over decades, or even hundreds of years, that was an amazing advantage. Over the long term, Xie could set himself up very, very nicely.

Over the long term.

"Why'd you join Mecha Corps?" Matt asked.

Xie looked confused. "What do you mean?"

"You might get killed!"

Xie laughed. "Of course!"

"I don't get it."

Xie leaned forward conspiratorially. "Major, can you imagine how exciting it is to potentially snuff out a couple hundred years of life?"

Matt shook his head. No. No, he didn't. He didn't even know what it meant to look forward to a few decades. Of any kind of life.

Matt found Marjan and Mikey in the Demon Docks, going through drills. Beneath their hulking Demons, Jahl Khoury watched readouts on a slate.

"Restless?" Jahl asked as Matt walked up. The two Demons were running through simple weapons checks.

"Is it safe to run the Mecha in here?" Matt asked.

Jahl pursed his lips. "We have permission from Colonel Cruz."

"You didn't answer my question."

"Nor did you answer mine."

Matt bent over the slate and studied the colorful readouts. Marjan's and Mikey's Mesh Effectiveness hovered in the high eighties, solid and stable.

"At least they have good control," Matt said.

"Yeah, they have a synergy that almost rivals yours. Since the Merge, that is. What did you do to them back on Earth?"

"Just Merged," Matt told Jahl.

Both Demons suddenly turned toward Matt and Jahl, hunkering down in an aggressive stance. Matt's heart skipped a beat. From this perspective, Demons were things of nightmares.

"He did nothing," Marjan's voice grated from the slate. "We do this by our own hands, not this so-called Mecha superman's."

"He didn't do a damn thing except ambush us," said Mikey.

The Demons took a step forward, their Fusion Handshake ports glowing with deadly blue power. Matt's guts twisted in fear. Even if Mikey and Marjan's Mesh was stable, they couldn't control their emotions in Mesh. They might spool up, out of control.

"May I remind you that you're addressing your commanding officer?" Jahl barked.

"An officer earns respect. He doesn't simply command it. Isn't that so, Major?" Marjan asked, through the comms. His Demon reached out as if to grab Matt.

Colonel Cruz's voice bellowed over the comms. His

PERSONAL/CONFIDENTIAL icon flared on the slate. "That's enough, Adepts! Stand down!"

"That's not fair, we're just having some fun!" Mikey said.

"You've now earned the right to sit on the bench for our upcoming exercise," Cruz told them. "Major Lowell, I recommend you send them in only if you need assistance."

"But, sir!" Marjan protested.

"Sir, we didn't mean nothing, sir," Mikey chimed in.

"Ah, so I'm 'sir' now. Your attitude is unbecoming Mecha Corps. I repeat, I am recommending you sit out the upcoming mission."

"Sir, please!" Marjan cried.

"It is up to Major Lowell to decide on my recommendation, or to determine if you should have any additional disciplinary actions," Colonel Cruz added. "However, my recommendation will go on record."

Marjan's Demon stood and saluted Matt. Both of the giant Mechas looked down at Matt expectantly. Matt licked his lips. Could he safely leave them behind on this mission? He didn't have enough information, beyond the enigmatic deploy-and-wait-for-more-orders instructions. But he wasn't going to say that in front of his adepts, or in front of Cruz.

If Cruz recommended it, he must know what to expect, Matt thought. *Or at least I hope so.*

"Agreed with your recommendation, Colonel," Matt said. "As long as I can have the assurance they will be ready to back us up if needed."

"We will hold all Mecha at readiness on final Displacement," Cruz said. "They will be ready."

Matt nodded. "Agreed."

The two Demons stiffened, but no sound came from Peal's slate. Their Mesh Effectiveness readings wavered, but never fell out of the eighties, as their emotions ran wild.

"Acknowledge your orders, Adepts," Cruz told them.

"Acknowledged," Mikey said.

Several beats later, Marjan's rough voice added his own "Acknowledged."

Matt waited in his Demon, deep in the rush of Mesh. Deeper perhaps than he'd ever been before. The imaginary talons of the thing inside the Mecha scratched at the surface of his mind as the smell of dust and the prickle of static came sharply to his senses. At this point, he almost welcomed it. He had it under control.

Maybe it's not a ghost in the machine at all, Matt thought. Roth insisted it was a reflection. And maybe it was—a reflection of himself.

Matt studied the Mission Brief projected in his view-mask, searching for meaning. Nothing had been added since they deployed from Earth. It still read:

ORIENTATION/MISSION BRIEF
Version 0.0.1, 22.04.2322
GENERAL INTELLIGENCE
System 0195-GX7A-1023 is (redacted).
ENVIRONMENT REVIEW
Planet 5 of System 0195-GX7A-1023 is semi-habitable, with a frozen surface overlaying liquid oceans beneath.
OFFWORLD: (redacted)
ONWORLD: (redacted)
CURRENT SITUATION
Developing. Union military intelligence will advise as necessary.
OBJECTIVES
Deploy to specified markers and await orders.

KEY TEAM
COLONEL Cruz, UUS Helios Strategic Command
MAJOR Lowell, Mecha Corps Leader (Special)

And that was it.

Matt scanned the readings from his team. All were stable, with Mesh Effectiveness in the seventies and eighties. Marjan and Mikey were stable, not spiky at all. Was it possible they'd gotten past Cruz's admonishment?

I hope they see some action, Matt thought.

"Prepare for final Displacement," Colonel Cruz said on the public channel, his voice oddly hushed.

Matt switched the focus on his viewmask to the UUS *Helios*'s external sensors, which showed a close-packed star field with multiple tags indicating stars within one to three light-years. One of them had to be tagged 0195-GX7A-1023, but he couldn't see it.

The stars changed. In front of them, a star jumped to the fore, shining with pinpoint-pure white radiance. That meant they were still far out within the planetary system. Cruz was really being cautious.

"Hold for spectral recon," Cruz told them on the public channel.

Matt's heart echoed in the gel-filled chamber of the giant Mecha, beating the seconds away. Ten, twenty, thirty. Nothing changed in the star field. No messages came from the bridge. Matt began to think this was just a formality, that they were just being overcautious.

"Prep for—" came an unfamiliar voice from the bridge, tagged COMBAT INTELLIGENCE. Before he could finish the sentence, he was cut off by a deep, reverberating boom from the comms.

Impact shock rattled through the Mecha Dock's expanded steel decking. On Matt's viewmask, the external view tracked several new objects, which moved blindingly fast across his POV. Each was tagged HEAVY-MATTER PAYLOAD.

Four more of the heavy-matter rounds hit the *Helios*. The ship reeled and sensors went offline, patchworking Matt's POV. Damage assessments began scrolling on-screen.

"Orders to deploy, sir?" Matt shouted at Colonel Cruz.

"No! Hold! We're not in close enough!" Cruz snapped. Then, off-mike, "Helios gunners, target at will with heavy-matter guns."

The *Helios* hammered as its own guns came online. New tags swarmed outward in Matt's POV. Small points of brilliance marked where they took out the enemy heavy-matter rounds. Others sped on, presumably toward the source of the bombardment.

"Hitting us so far out. That means they've compromised the deep-space defense systems," Colonel Cruz told Matt, his PRIVATE comms icon flashing. "That means they have everything, planet on out. You should expect to take fire as we Displace into orbital deployment range."

"Yes, sir," Matt said. "Who are 'they,' sir?"

Cruz's comms icon snapped off without an answer.

Tags traced the UUS *Helios*'s heavy-matter rounds to their targets. It was like watching the universe's slowest virtuality game. Eventually red markers flared at the HEAVY-MATTER EMPLACEMENTS and listed them as DE-STROYED.

"Targets eliminated," Combat Intelligence told them. Hold for additional assessment." Thirty seconds passed. Sixty. No other heavy-matter payloads came their way.

"System secure," Cruz reported. "Prepare for planetary Displacement."

As UUS *Helios* Displaced into orbit around Planet 5, it rocked under heavy fire. Matt's Demon had to grab a railing to stay in place. Dust clouds filtered out from the raw stone walls of Mecha Dock, just beyond the expanded steel grating. The asteroid was taking a real pounding, despite its extensive armor.

Outside, Matt's screens showed a crazed white snowball of a planet, together with a half dozen tags that showed orbital gun emplacements. Smaller, faster-moving tags tracked the assault coming at the UUS *Helios*: heavy-matter payloads, clouds of Sidewinder missiles, even the matter/antimatter beam of a Zap Gun, piercing dark space like a pillar of flame.

A Zap Gun? Matt thought. That was Union technology. Had the Corsairs captured a major Union base? Or did they have antimatter annihilation technology now too, as well as Mecha?

There wasn't any time for that. "Permission to deploy, Colonel?" Matt barked into the comms.

"No! Hold!" Cruz said, shouting off-mike to get the heavy-matter artillery back online and rotate to target their own Zap Gun. "We didn't expect—they moved the platforms—smarter than we thought."

"We can help!" Norah said.

"Adept!" Matt cautioned.

"We'll—" Cruz swore as the Zap Gun beam found the ship again. On Matt's damage reports, armor plating evaporated, exposing the core asteroid. "We'll soon have this under control."

"Sir—" Matt began.

"No!" Cruz yelled. "They're smart, Major. They're hitting us hard, but they're not targeting the Mecha Dock. They're waiting for you to come out."

"Sir, we can deploy through alternate—"

"Last time: No!" Then, softer: "Let us do our job. Then you can do yours."

Raw black space lit with the fury of the *Helios*. Multiple antimatter beams speared out, cutting swaths through the torrent of destruction aimed at the ship. They converged first on one orbital emplacement, then another, turning each into a soundless orange fireball.

Soon there was only a single orbital platform left. It redoubled its Zap Gun fire, finally scoring hits on critical UUS *Helios* systems. The FTLcomm transmission array ablated in a blinding white firestorm. The maneuvering pits took a hard hit, blowing them out of shape as the surrounding ceramic exploded into vapor. Even the Mecha Dock doors were struck. The massive steel armor glowed dull red, orange, shading into yellow and slumping toward a molten pool, before the UUS *Helios* managed to focus on that last platform.

The Mecha Dock doors quickly cooled, groaning and squealing as their tortured shapes vented air into space. They were only orange-red when Combat Intelligence came back on the comms.

"Planetary orbit secure," the bland voice said. In the background, Cruz cursed.

Cruz himself was soon back on the comms, feeding Matt a new set of coordinates on the planet's surface. "Deploy as soon as Mecha Dock doors become functional. Assemble at the location provided. Wait for orders. If engaged, use all weapons to destroy the enemy."

"They weren't trying to destroy the *Helios*," Matt said, spitting out the first thing that came to mind.

Cruz said nothing for a long time, but his comms icon

remained lit. He switched to a private channel, CRUZ →LOWELL. "I said they were smart."

"They were trying to capture us?"

A pause. Then: "Yes."

"How could they—even with Union weapons—how could they expect—"

"Prepare to deploy, Major," Cruz interrupted.

Matt ground his teeth. "Who's the enemy?"

Cruz growled, "Prepare to deploy."

That's all you need to know, Matt thought, anger rising. All the stuff about the military he hated came rushing into his mind: drills, following orders, going in blind like this. Don't worry about why they were trying to capture a Union warship, don't think about who you're fighting, just do what we tell you. Like a machine. Something to be turned on, used, and disposed of again.

He had graduated top of class at Aurora University. He could have been a top executive at one of Eridani's largest firms by now—or at least on his way up. He didn't need to be here. His father was avenged. His true mission was over. And he knew the Union hid the whole truth from its citizens.

So why do you keep doing it?

And in the yawning space of his mind, he finally admitted: *I don't know why I do any of it anymore.*

When I get back, I'm going to find out, Matt told himself. He'd get with Peal and Jahl and investigate Keller. And 0195-GX7A-1023. He'd dig into the Union and the Corsairs. The Mecha. Even the HuMax.

That's my new purpose, Matt realized. *To find out what's really going on in the Union.* So there'd be no more of these crazy missions, no more Kellers, no more Jotunheims. Maybe that would be enough to fill the empty space where revenge used to be.

Matt forced himself to breathe deeply, calm and regular, as the Mecha Dock doors cooled. Because if his enemy was really smart, they'd be waiting when the Mecha came out.

Two minutes later, the Mecha Bay doors ground open. The last wisps of atmosphere exhausted into space, taking rock dust and haze with it. The raw metal of the doors framed the snowball world. Shades of white and blue mixed with off-gray, in feathery fractal patterns all over the surface of the planet. There was not a single mountain range, not a hint of vegetation. Just a frozen ball of ice.

Matt shivered. It wasn't a human world. Not a place anyone would live. And yet the briefing hadn't listed any resources or strategic importance. Why did the Union have such heavy artillery around it?

"Adepts Norah, Elize, and Jie, enable Zap Guns and deploy," Matt said.

Matt pushed off the scaffolding and stopped himself at the edge of the door. Even with the power of the Zap Gun coursing through his Mecha's arm, it would be stupid to just go charging out. The three others came up beside him, the jaunty visors of their Demons almost questioning.

"Sir?" Elize asked.

"If they're smart, they'll be waiting to slice us to bits."

"Orbital space is secure," Combat Intelligence droned.

Yeah, like they don't know a trick like playing dead, Matt thought.

"Continue your mission, Major," Cruz added.

Matt frowned. There was nothing he could do. It wasn't as if he could rip a section of Mecha Dock scaffolding off the walls and wave it out the doors, trying to draw fire. The only thing he could do was try to ensure the success of his mission.

"Go out in twos," Matt told the adepts. "Back to back, weapons ready."

"What, sir?" Jie asked.

"In case one of us gets roasted," Norah said. "Come on." She grabbed Jie and turned him around so they were back to back. The two jumped off into space.

Matt half expected to see the two red Mecha disappear in the brilliance of a Zap Gun beam, but nothing happened. The bright white sun painted them in high contrast as they drifted away from the UUS *Helios*.

"I guess it's us," Elize said. She went back to back with him and they jumped off. Matt tensed as the UUS *Helios* fell away. With the wraparound perspective of the viewmask, it was as if he were floating naked in deep space. The close-packed stars were a gaudy display above the perfect white planet. Inside the Mecha, he heard nothing except for his mechanically assisted breathing and the faraway beat of his heart. It would have been a beautiful moment if he hadn't been worried about being vaporized.

"What a place," Elize said.

"Can the chatter, Adept," Matt said.

"Oh!" Elize's teeth clicked together.

As they fell toward the planet, Matt scanned his sensors. No enemy tags. The only thing in his POV was the coordinates he'd been given, another featureless point near the planet's equator.

Just over the horizon from their target, local temperatures read twenty degrees C higher than the background. A power plant of some kind? A downed warship?

But if that was the case, where was the Displacement Drive asteroid that had brought it here? Warships didn't end up in deep space by themselves. Matt strained with the Demon's Sensory Enhancement, but even its magnification was far too weak to resolve anything at the hot point.

"I have some abnormal temperature readings on the surface, sir," Norah said.

"Got it," Matt said.

"Weapons, sir?"

"If so, they're not firing at us."

"It's near our objective, sir," Norah pressed. "Maybe *at* our objective."

"Understood. Now please clear comms, Adept."

Norah's comms icon blinked out. Matt ordered the adepts to go into formation and prepare for reentry. He felt the powerful changes ripple through his own Demon as the thrusters re-formed along his back and the Mecha became a slim, delta-winged shape to help them down through the planet's nitrogen atmosphere.

The four Mecha arrowed down. In the thin air, heating was minimal. It felt like a feather, brushing Matt's chest, as they descended. Almost comforting. Toward the end, faint warmth lit his front side.

The four Demons used thrusters to slow as they descended: sixty thousand meters, forty, twenty. Details resolved on the surface: frigid blue channels, cutting deep into the white ice toward the hidden oceans, miles below. Fractal patterns radiating from the channels, slightly darker than the base ice. Here and there, wisps of methane clouds obscured the surface, as sharp winds scoured the landscape. There wasn't a single living thing in sight.

Five thousand feet. Two thousand. All quiet.

"Prepare to land," Matt told the adepts.

Their Demons unfolded, blasting thrusters to slow their descent. Clouds of white water ice blew up, instantly subliming to vapor in the blaze of the Demons' fusion exhaust. Soon they stood on the surface ice, each in a little pit made by the heat of its thrusters.

"Team is down, Colonel," Matt told Cruz. "Awaiting orders."

Cruz's comms icon lit, but before the man could say anything, a hail of Fireflies arced at Matt's Demons—followed by their source, a battalion of Hellions.

Union Mecha. On this frozen world at the edge of nowhere.

5

HIDDEN

As the chrome black Hellions flickered at Matt and his team, his thoughts went into overdrive: Hellions? Union Hellions? Yes, they were unmistakably Union Mecha—Matt had trained first in Hellions, and he'd recognize them anywhere.

But Union Mecha weren't just left lying around on any world, especially one so far out from the Core. Especially not a full battalion. That meant this was an important base. But did that mean the Corsairs had captured a strategic Union world, and compromised all of its technology? If so—

The Fireflies hit. Matt's POV whited out as force feedback through his interface suit left him gasping for breath. He flailed as he flew backward through the air. His Demon crunched down hard on its back, digging shiny gouges in the planet's surface ice.

Matt shook his head. Fireflies didn't have a punch like that!

"Heavy matter," Jie gasped. "They're using heavy matter in their Firefly rounds."

Matt scrambled to get up as his vision cleared. The Hellions were on them now, moving blurring fast, almost as if the Hellions' Rayder had been modified to remove their limiters. Almost. They were damn fast, but not Rayder fast. It was almost as if they simply had very, very good pilots.

Matt barely got to his feet before three of the Hellions barreled into him, their razor talons slicing painfully at his arms. Their fusion ports glowed dull orange as they charged Fireflies for another assault.

The rest of the Hellions attacked Matt's team, clinging to them like lampreys. Norah screamed in frustration and tried to target them with the Zap Gun, but the big weapon was useless in close quarters. Xie beat at his attackers, trying to dislodge them, but the nimble Hellions avoided his grasping hands. Elize hit the ground and rolled, triggering her own Fireflies. The Hellions danced away from the smart rounds, which exploded harmlessly in the sky. Their brilliant light strobed the scene below, rendering the battle in jerky freeze frame.

Smart, Matt thought. *Get in close so we can't use our Zap Guns or Sidewinders.* They moved too fast for Fireflies too. Which left—

"Fusion Handshake!" Matt yelled. "Use it!"

"What's that?" Xie asked.

Ah, shit. They didn't even know the slang yet. What the hell was it called? "CQFA! Close-Quarters Fusion Annihilator! Now!"

Matt's vision went white as another round of Fireflies came down on him. This time it didn't come back fully. Jagged pieces of his POV were covered in gray pixels, and the dreaded countdown began: REGENERATION COMPLETE IN 32 SECONDS.

The Hellions were on him again. Their fusion ports glowed in orange puzzle pieces in his POV. They'd wipe out the rest of his visual sensors, and then they'd take him apart.

Matt enabled his Fusion Handshake and grabbed for the Hellions. They skittered away like roaches, comfortably ahead of his grasp. He flailed again, but he simply wasn't fast enough. Through the working parts of his visual sensors, he saw the others having the same problem.

He was going to be taken down by old-style Hellions!

Matt triggered his thrusters and leapt for the sky, but the Hellions only strengthened their grip as he ascended. Their fusion ports were angry orange now. Only a matter of moments before they destroyed the rest of his visual sensors. If he could only get ahold of them—

—or not. Matt remembered the trick they'd used, back in the asteroid soup of the condensing planet. If he couldn't knock his Hellion attackers off, he could still use the Fusion Handshake.

Fifty meters up, Matt held his hands out in front of him, aiming at the melee with Xie, Norah, and Elize.

Now, he thought, and triggered a Fusion Handshake.

Pure power exploded down his arms. A blue shock wave shot out in front of him, expanding outward in a cone of compressed plasma.

It hit the Hellions on the ground like a hurricane. They blew off the Demons as ice geysered up from the surface in great sheets. Clouds of water vapor billowed, obscuring everything below.

Matt flew backward and landed on his back, knocking his own Hellions loose. Before they could come back at him, he raised his hands again and triggered another Fusion Handshake. The Hellions disappeared in a hail of ice and water vapor. Matt slid backward along the ice for a hundred meters before stopping.

"Use your Fusion Handshakes like this!" Matt said. "Aim arms-out to keep them away, then get a grip on them and let them have it!"

The three Hellions came back at Matt like wraiths

emerging from the steam. This time he was ready for them. He put his arms out, faking another defensive Fusion Handshake. As they swung toward his side, Matt grabbed a Hellion at the last second and triggered the close-quarters annihilation wave.

Power surged down his arm. The Hellion went rigid as the fusion shock wave hit it. Electrical discharges arced into the air from its visor, talons, and joints. The whole thing rippled like water, then crumpled inward and fell limp.

Good, Matt thought. One down.

REGENERATION COMPLETE, his POV said as his vision flickered back to a hundred percent.

The two others came at him. Matt triggered thrusters and leapt over them, grabbing each one by its visor as they passed underneath him. Two more Fusion Handshakes later, two more Hellions lay smoking on the ground. They slowly disappeared into a pool of meltwater, as former steam fell as snow on the scene.

Matt surveyed the battle. Norah had two Hellions down and was grappling with another. Xie had one down and two were dancing around him, trying to avoid his outstretched hands. Elize was down on the ground, with three Hellions on top of her. They triggered another burst of Fireflies, and Elize's Demon convulsed. Her visor shattered and crumpled inward, visual sensors smoking.

Matt moved without thinking, charging forward with his hands out in front of him, triggering a Fusion Handshake. The shock wave shoved him backward, his Demon's feet cutting channels in the ice. But the Hellions assaulting Elize's Demon tumbled off. They scrambled to their feet and paused, cat-still, to look back at the battle scene. After a moment, they fled back in the direction they'd come.

Regrouping, Matt thought. Most likely at the heat source.

What waited for them there? More Hellions? Demons? Or something even stranger, cooked up in this bizarre Union base on the edge of nowhere?

Matt went to Elize and helped her up as Norah and Xie dispatched the remaining Hellions. She flailed against him, until the contact between the Demons allowed his thoughts to filter through.

"Major Lowell?" Elize gasped. "I'm sorry! I can't see!"

"What's the regeneration counter read?" Matt asked her.

"Regeneration indefinite," Elize said. "Reconfiguring visual sensors for partial capability."

Shit. Reconfiguring was bad. Real bad. That meant it could be hours before she got her sight back. Even then, it might not be the same ever again. And Matt couldn't send her blind back to the UUS *Helios*.

"What's the matter, sir?" Norah asked, coming up behind him.

"Watch the horizon," Matt said. "Let me handle this."

"Yes, sir," Norah grated. But she turned obediently and motioned for Xie to take a position opposite her.

"What can I do, uh, sir?" Elize said.

"Hold a sec." Matt bent over to examine her visual sensors. Her entire visor was cracked open, exposing eight orbs that might once have looked like eyes. Now they were blobs of gooey metallic ooze, surrounded by shredded biomechanical muscle. As he watched, metal flowed and re-formed, and one "eye" slowly regained its shape.

Matt shivered. Mecha were damn near magic technology. Much higher technology than the Union supposedly condoned and regulated.

"I see something!" Elize shouted. "I'm getting, um, looks like heat sigs. False-color imaging."

"Enough to fight with?"

"No, sir."

"Still no numbers for regeneration?"

"No."

Matt swore. He could Merge with Elize. That would probably give them full visual function. But would they be able to work through Elize's waves of emotional confusion? It was too much of a risk.

"Report, Major," Colonel Cruz's voice grated over the comms.

Matt sighed, then rapped out, "Enemy Hellions encountered at the coordinates specified. Nine neutralized, three escaped toward heat signature noted in descent. One Demon down with visual sensors except heat sigs offline, unknown regeneration time."

"Send the damaged Demon back to the ship," Cruz ordered.

"Heat sigs aren't enough for her to navigate back to the ship," Matt said.

A pause. Then: "I'll send down our backup squad for a pickup. In the meantime, proceed to the heat signature and eliminate the remaining Hellions and their pilots, as well as any and all other hostiles."

Matt frowned. Cruz was sending down Marjan and Mikey. It made sense, but it felt bad. Really bad. He didn't want them at his back.

"What hostiles, sir?" Matt asked. "Corsairs?"

Another pause, this one longer. Then Colonel Cruz replied in a low, rough voice, "Hostiles are anything that moves."

Anything that moves. Matt's stomach did a flip-flop. What was he being sent in to do?

"Sir, can I ask—"

"You have your orders, Major. Carry them out."

Matt clamped his lips down hard on his response. The whole thing smelled bad.

"Acknowledge your orders, Major," Colonel Cruz growled.

"Acknowledged, sir," Matt said, choking on the words.

They left Elize behind with orders to ascend blindly into the sky in the event of any Hellion attack. Theoretically, Marjan and Mikey would be able to intercept and guide her back to the Helios. Theoretically.

"I'll be fine, sir," Elize told him. "My visuals are coming back online, a little. I may even be able to join you—"

"Go back, Cadet," Matt said, his voice sharp and on edge. Elize noticed it. The head of her Demon cocked to one side, as if she wanted to ask him what was wrong.

"Move out, team," Matt told Norah and Jie.

"Overland or by air, sir?" Norah asked.

Matt frowned. In his POV, the location of the heat source was now clearly marked with a big red OBJECTIVE tag, just over the edge of the horizon. An expanded aerial map put it the middle of one of the blue ice fissures.

That meant two things. One, they were probably dug in to the fissure. Two, on this billiard-ball-smooth planet, they'd be going into battle without cover. There were no mountains or ridges to protect them.

Flying in meant the three remaining Hellions would hide below the edge of the fissure and pick them off as they passed overhead. It also meant they'd be flying directly over whatever weaponry they had hidden in the chasm.

On the other hand, overland meant the enemy would easily sense their approach, and be able to pop up at the least convenient moment. Still, it meant not having to deal with any potential artillery.

"Overland," Matt said. "Be prepared to go skyward when I give the order."

"Yes, sir," Norah rapped out.

"Understood, sir," Jie said.

Matt sprang to life and shot off toward the objective at a dead run. His clawed feet ripped the ice, sending up a rooster tail of shards as his ground speed climbed: eighty, a hundred and twenty, two hundred kilometers an hour. The other Demons came to run by his side, powerful red legs pistoning in sync.

The ground blurred past quickly, an endless plain of gray-white under a blue-black sky. Matt lost himself for long moments in the rhythm of Mesh.

Soon tags swarmed in front of him. They were coming over the horizon, in view of the fissure. At first, it was only a line of slightly darker blue-gray against the ice, bleeding background heat into the chill atmosphere. Then it resolved into something with depth—Matt could see the far edge of the ridge, glittering in the sunlight. Together with a hint of something, glowing with warm light, built into the fissure itself. Thin metallic ribs arced over the surface of the glowing object. Through its semi-transparent surface, Matt could see hints of movement within.

What the hell? Matt thought. It looked almost like an environmental dome. But why would they have a dome like that, way out here?

He didn't have long to be puzzled. A new angry red tag popped up in front of him, at the same time two others appeared at his side. The Hellions. Brilliant Fireflies arced at the Demons.

But this time, he was ready.

"Fire thrusters!" Matt said, shooting into the sky.

Norah and Jie followed, their fusion flares blasting the ice surface to clouds of water vapor. Fireflies sparked through the clouds, jagging upward to follow the Demons. Matt waited until they were close enough to see the individual fusion flames.

"Go down now!" Matt shouted at his team. "Aim at the Hellions!" He flipped in midair and fired thrusters skyward, almost blacking out in the savage g-forces. Even suspended in magnetorheological gel, his vision went red.

Matt accelerated downward toward the closest Hellion. The Fireflies turned to follow. The tiny rounds sputtered, their heavy-hydrogen fuel almost exhausted. It would have to be enough.

The Hellion saw what was coming and froze. Matt grinned in guilty delight. He must look like an avenging angel, descending in wrath with falling stars as an escort.

Fifteen meters from the Hellion, Matt hit the thrusters one last time, full-on. This one did knock him out for a moment. His vision disappeared down a tunnel, and there was a second of silence.

When he opened his eyes, his Demon was lying about fifty meters away from the edge of the ravine, and there was nothing left of the Hellion except smoking wreckage.

More Fireflies impacted on Jie's target in a pillar of flame. The Hellion jerked spasmodically and collapsed, melting into the ice. Jie landed hard next to it, stumbling to get his balance.

Norah's reverse-Firefly attack had gone wide. She grappled with the untouched Hellion, holding the struggling Mecha's visor with one hand. Her arm and hand glowed bright, actinic blue, and the powerful boom of a Fusion Handshake rattled the surface ice like a drum. The Hellion's visor and chestplate folded inward, venting a puff of atmosphere from the pilot's chamber like a dying gasp.

The three Demons stood alone on the freezing world, with the thin shriek of the wind their only companion.

"I just—I just killed someone," Jie said, his voice thick with remorse. "In a Hellion. Are they Union Mecha? Was he one of ours?"

"You're just now realizing this?" Norah cut in.

"Can someone please tell me if I just killed a Corsair, or Mecha Corps?" Jie's voice choked through tears.

"Can it!" Matt yelled, feeling terrible. He had the same doubts. "We have our orders. And we'll get through this, one way or another."

"Yes, sir," the two adepts said.

Matt breathed deeply, willing his heart to slow its thunderous beat. Everything was upside down, as if he were free-falling over an infinite dark plain. Here he was, fighting the Union's own Mecha. And this was only the beginning.

Next was whatever was down that fissure.

Matt crawled cautiously to the edge of the ravine. The fissure was heavily reinforced with metallic struts, its edges deeply gouged by industry. In the center squatted a massive construction of steel and semitransparent duraplas, almost a full kilometer long. The top section of the structure ballooned up, held in place with the metallic ribs Matt had seen earlier. Matt's enhanced sensors showed an interior temperature that suggested a climate fit for people, and residual oxygen leakage indicated that the thing was pressurized.

Next to the structure, a flat expanse of steel with thruster burns served as a rough spaceport. At one end of the spaceport stood a twenty-meter-diameter air lock. Big enough to admit Demons. Or conceal more Hellions.

But that didn't make sense. Why would they hold Hellions back? The rest of the fissure didn't hold any visible weapons.

"We can just blast the roof, sir," Norah said.

Matt turned to look at her Demon. It had joined him at the edge of the fissure. Jie hung back, as if still shaken by the battle. His claim about not caring about his long life was long gone.

"Our orders are to kill anything moving," Norah added. "It seems like the easiest solution."

"Easy doesn't make it right," Matt told her, his bile rising. This wasn't a mission. This was extermination. And he wasn't going to simply close his eyes and take the easy way out. Not anymore.

To Norah and Xie, he rationalized, "Easy also isn't definitive. What happens if the structure is full of pressurized chambers? Blow the roof off and they wouldn't even notice."

"It limits their movement," Norah said. "And makes them more likely to freeze to death."

"We'll go in through the air lock, Adept. Why don't you lead us down and unlock it?"

"Yes, sir!" Norah said, her voice thick with sardonic respect.

Norah fired thrusters and descended into the fissure, trailing long waves of fusion heat. Matt half expected her to take fire, but the chasm was cold and dead. Not a single weapons tag floated in his POV. No life signs wrapped in space suits. Nothing. After the Hellions, it was almost too quiet.

Matt motioned for Jie to follow Norah. Jie's Demon blasted off and descended to join her on the fusion-scarred spaceport decking. Norah advanced to the air lock, taking a position to its side.

Matt fired his thrusters and descended into the fissure. Diffuse sunlight made the sheet ice walls glow sky-blue against the dark metal of the scaffolding. It was almost like descending into a clear blue ocean. Peaceful. Almost serene.

And that wasn't the only thing that was peaceful. The spaceport was unscarred by Firefly or Sidewinder fire. There weren't even any telltale dimples from depleted-uranium rounds. If this facility had been compromised by Corsairs fighting the Union Mecha, they'd been awfully discreet. There was no sign of a struggle at all.

When he reached the other two Demons, Norah was bent over the air lock's control panel. It bore the logo of United Technologies. That was a Union contractor.

This is a Union installation.

Matt rocked back, shivering with a strange sense of unreality. A Union installation? Out here? Why did they send him to a Union facility? What the hell was inside?

Norah finished her work at the control panel. The CYCLING light flashed red and the doors shivered, dislodging flakes of ice. After long moments, the doors cracked open, exhaling a pale puff of residual atmosphere.

"Get back," Matt told them, stepping to one side of the doors, Zap Gun ready.

Norah and Jie ducked to the other side. Matt waited patiently as the doors rumbled fully open. Dim work-lights illuminated a space filled with scarred yellow plastic pressure crates. Matt ducked his head for a better look.

Matt's POV jerked and rolled as his visor rocked back. Stitches of depleted-uranium bullets *spanged* off his hide as a dim figure inside struggled to tame the bucking gun.

Matt blinked, finally getting a good look at his assailant. His mouth dropped open in amazement. The gun was an MK-16, full Hellion issue. But it wasn't a five-meter-tall Hellion holding it. It was a person. *A thing.*

Something three and a half meters tall, its body wrapped head to toe in carbon-fiber weave. Goggles the size of tea saucers covered its eyes, and a crude breathing pipe hooked to an oxygen tank on its back vented white oxygen at every bad weld.

The — thing — wasn't wearing a space suit at all. It was holding itself together with mechanical binding, and sucking on a raw oxygen tank. Matt's mind reeled. What the hell was it?

That's when he noticed its eyes. Violet-and-yellow HuMax eyes.

HuMax.

More fire came from a dozen figures in space suits. They were all HuMax. Some wore real Union space suits, bearing the seal of UARL, Union Advanced Research Labs. Some wore baggy rescue suits. Some were wrapped like the giant thing, taking their chance in the near-vacuum outside. Some had no choice but to be wrapped up in the makeshift suits, with bodies grown grotesquely out of proportion. One had four arms.

All held weapons. Most were MK-1s, but one pair operated another MK-16. The din of gunfire was oddly high-pitched in the thin atmosphere, and the impact of the depleted-uranium slugs was distant, almost painless. The HuMax creatures advanced grimly, squinting against the reprisal they knew was coming.

They're desperate, Matt thought. *They're protecting their home.*

That was why they had attacked the Demons the moment they hit the ground. That was why they'd done that desperate stupid move of trying to capture the *Helios*. They wanted out. And when they couldn't get out, they were forced to protect their home, by any means necessary.

But — HuMax in a Union installation? Grotesquely transformed HuMax, at that? What did that mean?

"Permission to open fire, sir," Norah said.

Matt whipped around on her. She'd exchanged her Zap Gun for an MK-160. The gun was comically huge against the pitiful weapons of their attackers.

"Hold!" Matt yelled, stepping in front of her. They weren't in danger from the HuMax's weapons. There was no way such a pathetic force could overwhelm three Demons.

"Our orders—"

"The hell with them!" Matt cried, his eyes leaking tears.

He remembered his promise, just before the mission had started: *I'll find out what's happening. I'll drag it into the light.*

That was his new purpose.

Matt's Perfect Record played back an image from his past: Merging with the HuMax city of Jotunheim, and being gifted with their knowledge of the Expansion.

Biometal calls to metal, he thought. *Everything seeks to Merge.*

Matt plunged his Mecha talons into the air-lock control panel, feeling the shock of electricity mixed with the thrill of data. Ropes of biometallic muscle Merged with the conduit, chasing it to its origin. Deep down, to the Union computer beating at the heart of the installation. A very well-guarded computer. Because this was UARL, the most advanced Union technology branch. The same people his father used to work for.

Deep in Mesh, Matt's mind met the computer. It responded with suspicion and a challenge. But its secrets were poorly hidden; a note made by a Union scientist on an insecure line revealed the pass code, and Matt was soon inside, drowning in data.

In the space of milliseconds, everything was laid bare. And Matt's whole life changed forever.

*   *   *

Code-named UARL: Arcadia/Progress 001, it was one of the Union's most secret development programs, intended not only to study HuMax, but to breed and improve upon them.

Starting fifty years ago with forty-one "founding stock," the Union scientists worked to decode the HuMax's genetic makeup and isolate their beneficial traits. The first result of that research was a refined genetic code base—one still deemed too risky to deploy to the general Union population.

Matt reeled. Not only had the Union been working with HuMax, but they had completely mapped and cataloged their genome. If that knowledge had been released, families could have selectively chosen even more amazing genetic enhancements for their children.

"Except everyone would have chosen everything." Dr. Roth's voice came back to Matt. *"That's what humans do. Tick all the boxes on the options sheet. And then you're back at HuMax. And HuMax are uncontrollable."*

It got worse.

UARL documents referred to "most secret" founding Union data from the "initial HuMax development program." That data went back over two hundred years, and included coordinates of known HuMax settlements like Prospect. Performance data rated HuMax variants by hardiness, efficiency, reliability, and effectiveness. It was like reading an engineering report on a new piece of machinery.

Matt's mind reeled. Rayder had been telling the truth. The Union had created the HuMax!

Their gruesome research continued to this day. The giant carbon-fiber-wrapped hulk was described as an "Enhanced HuMax Type/+size+strength+longevity." The one with four arms was an "Enhanced HuMax Type/+appendages+versatility." There were dozens of others, from +empathy+perception to +durability/partial-vac-capable. Video showed the artificial wombs where the HuMax were grown, the tests on the screaming violet-and-golden-eyed children, and the reams of observational data on the adults in every type of situation, from combat to sex (forced and consensual).

And it showed the postnatal experiments. Some of the HuMax weren't born with enhanced capabilities. Their genomes were rewritten by retrovirus after they had reached adulthood. Sweating, screaming superhumans struggled against their carbon-fiber bonds on sterile stainless steel tables as UARL scientists watched. A snippet of one scientist's report leapt out at Matt: "resequencing allows for more variations to be studied in a shorter period of time relative to pure breeding programs, with relatively low mortality load."

Matt squeezed his eyes shut, trying to hold back the tears. Everything he was told was a lie. The Union had made the HuMax, it studied the HuMax, and it continued its invasive research, even at the cost of lives.

Only heavy doses of soporifics in the water supply had kept the HuMax under control. At least until one of their genetic rewrites rendered a couple of the HuMax insensitive to it.

That was what precipitated the revolt: first, turning off the drug feed, then taking over the remote research facility. The HuMax captured the researchers and demanded they arrange passage off the world. But, remote as it was, and secure as it was, Planet 5 was served only by Union military and the Mecha Corps.

There was no way out. The HuMax used the FTL-comm to try to reach help, but they were at the edge of any human exploration; no one came.

Except the Union, of course. The Union, via Matt and his kill squad.

When UUS *Ulysses* appeared, they tried to capture it. A last, desperate measure to save themselves. An impossible task. Of course they'd failed.

And now my orders are to ensure their total defeat. To kill every one of these beings.

Everything he believed, up in smoke. Every thought about the valorous Union, shredded. Matt retracted his Demon's talons from the control panel.

Disobeying orders was treason, plain and simple. He had to kill the HuMax if he wanted any future with Mecha Corps.

Kill them, said the voice in his Mecha, veiled by static and dust. *Kill them all.*

But the voice was far away, distant. His mind was whirling with the implications. This whole thing was a setup. The Union knew he was the best man for the job. After all, he'd taken out Rayder. His father had been killed by a HuMax. He was the final solution.

Reward, not recognition, Matt thought, remembering Colonel Cruz's words. But no reward would erase the Perfect Record of this massacre if he went through with it.

Matt stood and placed himself between the HuMax rebels and his team. "Stand down," he told Norah and Xie. "Hold fire."

"Sir, our orders are to eliminate anything moving," Norah said, her MK-160 twitching.

"Do not fire! That's an order!"

"Yes, sir." Norah's gun barrel descended toward the floor. Her Mecha's posture indicated irritation.

"What are your orders, sir?" Xie asked.

"Pull back. This area is secure."

Reluctantly, the two giant Mecha backed away. The peppering of depleted-uranium bullets on Matt's backside abated. Behind him, the HuMax glanced at each other uncertainly, not sure about this new development. Matt turned to address them. Maybe there could be some kind of resolution to this beyond killing.

Colonel Cruz's voice boomed in Matt's ear: "Major, status report!"

"Completing my mission, sir," Matt told him.

"Don't lie to me! We've been monitoring your status!"

"And you still want me to kill them all, sir?"

"Yes. Proceed!"

Matt sighed. His future, elusive as it had been, went up in flames. He simply couldn't do it.

I'm not a tool, Matt thought. *I'm a person.*

And for once, it was time to make a good choice.

"No," Matt told Cruz.

"Are you refusing a direct order?"

"Yes, sir. I'm afraid I am, sir."

Cruz's voice snapped off his private comms with a clipped curse. His comms icon immediately popped back up on the COL. CRUZ→TEAM channel.

"This is Colonel James Cruz," his voice boomed. "New orders. I am removing Major Lowell from command. Disregard any further orders from him. Mr. Lowell, return to the *Helios* immediately."

A short pause. "Full team, proceed with orders to eliminate all life-forms at objective."

6

ROGUE

"Step aside," Norah said, aiming her MK-160 straight at Matt's visor.

Behind her, the air-lock door framed an icy world sliding toward night, with long shadows casting the fissure into deep dusk.

In that moment, Matt felt everything as if outside himself. The desperate HuMax lab subjects behind him, fighting to protect the last thing they had. Norah in front of him, sighting down the barrel of the MK-160 and a posture of grim purpose. Xie standing next to her, looking around uncertainly, his rifle still pointed at the floor.

Matt sighed. He could go back to the UUS *Helios* and face the Union. Given the deep-cover nature of the mission, there would certainly be a court-martial—and he'd lose every chance to get the answers he sought.

But that's the only choice, Matt thought. What else could he do? Try to convince his team to stand down, after being given a direct order from Colonel Cruz?

Or fight next to the HuMax rebels? That was even crazier. Why would he fight to protect the race that murdered his father? The race that almost brought about the end of all humanity?

Matt turned to look behind him. The HuMax rebels had stopped firing. They could tell that when one giant robot was holding a gun on the other, something significant was happening. They watched the three Mecha with wide violet-and-yellow eyes, even as many of them died from exposure in their leaking, jerry-rigged space suits.

Kill them, a voice rasped again, like static in Matt's mind. *Make your space. Rule them all.*

"Move." Norah's voice rasped through the comms as she motioned with her MK-160.

"What are we going to do now?" Michelle had asked him, a million years ago.

"Save the universe," Matt had told her. *"From whatever it needs saving from."*

Even the Union, the voice rasped. And in that moment, it made sense. Even though Matt knew the pain and insanity that gibbered behind it.

Matt holstered his own MK-160 and held up his hands, as if surrendering. He stepped away from the HuMax and headed for the air lock. His footfalls echoed like rifle cracks in the thin atmosphere.

Norah swiveled her gun to point at the HuMax. Xie still pointed his at the floor.

At the air lock, Matt plunged his talons into the control panel again and reached out to grab Norah's Demon's shoulder. His Demon's arm elongated to close the gap between the two Mecha as Xie recoiled in surprise. His claws dug deep into Norah's shoulder. Her angry, panicked thoughts flooded into him as she yelled in surprise over the comms.

What are you doing! Not in my mind again! No! Stop!

Matt pulled Norah back toward his Mecha, bowling her off her feet. He dragged her into Xie's Demon and heard the sob of his thoughts. Once all three Demons were in contact with each other, Matt thought, *Merge.*

No! No! Can't Merge! Norah screamed.

Why? Xie asked.

Matt's talons flowed into Norah's shoulder as Xie's tangled arms melted into the other two Mecha. Their thoughts beat at him, panicky and confused.

Stop Merge and hold, Matt thought. Their transition slowed and ceased. The Merge slowly began to reverse. Matt struggled to keep it stable, but he could only slow the process. They'd soon deMerge, and he'd lose control over Norah and Xie. He'd have to be quick.

First things first, though. Matt cycled the outer air lock shut and began pressurizing the dock. The atmospheric readouts climbed toward green, as the HuMax's makeshift space suits slowly stopped outgassing.

Let me show you, Matt told Norah and Xie, channeling the summary of the Union's HuMax research project to the two other pilots.

At the same time, he opened the air lock's inner doors so they could see the interior of the Union research installation.

It looked like videos of old-time prisons, pre-Expansion stuff from Earth. Floor-to-ceiling rows of cells flanked either side of a sterile plaza. Utilitarian walkways passed by every cell. There were no bars, but large, clear windows ensured that the cell's occupants had no privacy. Some were heavily scarred. Others were pristine. Overtop all, the ribbed translucent ceiling glowed faintly purple in the dying daylight, casting a pallid glow over the entire scene. From some of the cells, yellow-and-violet eyes looked down on the air lock, quivering in terror.

You see? Matt asked the other two pilots. *You see what they've been doing?*

It's horrible, Xie thought, his mind sending overtones

of revulsion and panic. He was genemod himself. Was this where his enhancements came from? If so, how was he truly any different than these people here?

We have orders, Norah thought, her mind clamped desperately around a grim idolization of the Union. *There are other reasons. We don't know everything.*

That's what I thought, Matt told her.

I am nothing like you! Norah screamed in her mind, suddenly pushing him away. Matt's talons came out of her shoulder. She was now connected to him only through Xie. Matt was losing control.

Norah, Matt thought. *Just look—*

Depleted-uranium slugs stitched across Matt's torso, needle pricks of pain. Matt looked up. Inside the Union installation, in the broad plaza, stood two Imp Mecha, carrying old-style MK-14 rifles.

Matt frowned in grim memory. Through his childhood, his most prized possession had been an Imp Mecha model. He used to hold it at night as his refugee ship dropped off to sleep, and dream of using an Imp to wipe out the man who killed his father. His first exercise in Mecha Training Camp had been against an augmented Imp. It seemed he couldn't escape them.

Compared to the Demons, the Imps were tiny, primitive things, titanium space frames and aerogel armor, with tiny slits of duraplas for the pilot to peer through. Purely mechanical technology, with a weak fusion core. They were still used widely in industry and on frontier worlds because of their durability, but they were no match for a Hellion, much less a Demon. This was just the last-ditch effort by the HuMax to protect their home.

We're taking fire! Norah screamed in his mind, her brain twisting and bucking like an animal aflame.

Before Matt could react, she threw off the last vestiges of his Merge and scrambled to her feet, drawing her

MK-160 in one smooth motion. She charged into the hail of depleted-uranium fire, her head down.

"Stop!" Matt shouted.

Norah brought up her giant rifle and pressed the trigger. Muzzle flashes strobed the plaza. One of the Imps rocked back in the impact of the fifty-millimeter slugs, spraying titanium and aerogel armor shards. The other reversed course and scrambled back toward the rear corridor it had emerged from. Norah charged forward and pumped more slugs into the first Imp. In the enclosed space, the reverberation of her gun was immense, like thunder. The fallen Imp quivered and lay still.

Matt tried to go after her, but he was still Merged with the control panel. *DeMerge!* he thought desperately. His hand emerged from the metal, but the process seemed immensely, painfully slow. Xie still cowered where he'd fallen, his Demon trembling in confusion.

"I'm out," Xie mumbled over the comms. "I'm out of this. Leave me out of all this. Please."

As Matt came free of the control panel, the second Imp entered the tunnel, turned, and launched a half dozen old-style Streaker antipersonnel missiles. They hissed at Norah's Demon. She ran straight at them, never faltering. She batted away two aimed at her visor in great greasy fireballs. The rest impacted and exploded on her Demon with no effect. She ran trailing flame, her MK-160 thundering destruction. Depleted-uranium slugs annihilated the door frame where the Imp had launched its missiles. But the Imp itself was long gone, down a tunnel of ice. Norah slammed into the tunnel entrance and thrashed at it in anger. Her Demon was too big to fit into the three-meter-tall tunnel.

Matt launched himself at her. He had no idea what he'd do when he reached her Demon, or what the future held. He only knew he had to protect these innocent people. The rest would follow.

Norah whirled to aim at him. Matt tucked away his MK-160 and withdrew his Zap Gun. Norah scrambled to match him as he tore across the plaza.

Could he shoot precisely enough with the Zap Gun to disable her Demon? Without killing her? Without taking the whole facility out? Matt clamped his teeth together grimly and aimed.

A bright flash from overhead blinded Matt as a thunderous *crack* reverberated through the facility. Instinctively he ducked and rolled, bringing his Zap Gun up toward the source of the light. A brief hurricane plucked at his giant Mecha, whistling past his ears.

Two red Demons, riding pillars of antimatter thrust, descended through a gaping hole in the ceiling of the Union research lab. One carried a third Demon around the waist. Behind the Mecha, stars had begun to glitter in the deepening dusk.

Around them, the contents of the facility fountained out as the atmosphere blasted out of the roof. HuMax in makeshift space suits were sucked off their feet and flung into the deadly-thin atmosphere of the frozen world. Others gasped and thrashed on the floor, trying to breathe. Air streamed out of two hundred closed cells, screaming like claws on glass in the thin atmosphere. Some of the cells had been barricaded with sealant. Most hadn't.

Marjan, Mikey, and Elize had arrived.

Marjan came at Matt like an arrow. A giant red arrow, a demigod of hell. For long moments, Matt could do nothing but think, *It's all over* as the HuMax writhed and died in the tenuous atmosphere outside. He was only dimly aware of Norah and Mikey, aiming their Zap Guns at the opposite blocks of cells.

Marjan slammed into Matt. His cockpit rang like a bell, and Matt's Demon hit the plaza floor hard, banging his visor against the steel decking. In that moment of contact, he felt everything: Marjan's dark thoughts of rending and tearing Matt's Demon to bits, his murderous hate for the show-off who'd shamed him in the Mecha, his satisfaction with Colonel Cruz's orders to ensure the complete destruction of the hidden Union installation and everything inside it.

Marjan swiped at Matt's Demon's visor with his claws. Matt brought an arm up, blocking him at the last moment. Marjan's Demon's hand glowed with blue-white fusion power as he struggled to find a grip for his Fusion Handshake. If Matt let him lock on, he might be done for.

Dazzling light filled the chamber as Norah and Mikey unloaded with their Zap Guns. Cells vaporized on either side of the two struggling Demons, showering them with red-hot spatters of molten aluminum. Walkways flashed yellow-hot and crumpled into a tangle of twisted metal. Matt imagined he could hear short, high-pitched screams as the HuMax were wiped out, one by one.

"No!" Matt screamed, and bucked Marjan off him. He fired thrusters and went full-force at Norah. The reflection of the incandescent Zap Gun beam in her visor cast a jagged highlight along its mirror surface, as if she were smiling.

Matt hit Norah before she could react. Her Zap Gun fire went wild, slicing through the remaining cells. Metal girders and duraplas sheets collapsed and pelted the Mecha with razor-edged debris. Matt batted it away as he dug into Norah. She struggled to bring her Zap Gun around and aim it at him.

Behind them, Mikey continued the wholesale annihilation of the opposite cells. His job was almost complete; the entire north side of the complex slumped in on itself, ready to crumple. Deep blue ice showed through holes in the structure. Where the Zap Gun touched the ice, it billowed clouds of white steam, which instantly froze into snow and fell inside the complex.

Norah's thoughts were a reflection of Mikey's and Marjan's. She was enjoying this. She would enjoy it even more if Matt toppled with the Union installation. To her, he was the one thing holding her back. She had faith in the Union and its orders.

Matt shoved her Zap Gun away as it sputtered to life again. It shot upward through the remaining cells, slicing through the metal like butter. The cell block collapsed outward, crashing to rest on the ravine outside. The rest of the roof slammed down around them. The few remaining HuMax in their jerry-rigged space suits disappeared under the debris.

Matt screamed silently. *Dead. All dead.* He couldn't help them. He'd completely failed.

Marjan hit him again, wrapping his hand around Matt's head. For a moment, Matt's POV was completely filled by the glowing blue Fusion Handshake port. He could count the ribs in its dispersion modifier, and he saw the power cycling up to firing potential.

I could let it end here, Matt thought. *What place do I have in a Union that condones operations like this? In a Union that, in some ways, might be worse than the Corsairs?*

Save the universe. However we can.

Red-hot anger surged through Matt. He couldn't just let it go. He had to keep trying. And there was only one way he could stop Marjan now.

Merge, he thought.

For an instant, the three Mecha melded together. Matt felt Norah's familiar panic, but she couldn't stop the process. Matt was too strong.

No, Marjan thought. And he pulled away.

Marjan's Demon's hand emerged from the beginning Merge. Then his leg. Marjan's Demon struggled against the mass, and pulled itself almost completely free.

Matt reeled in shock. How could Marjan resist the Merge?

Gloating satisfaction came in waves from the other man. *I've been practicing,* he thought. *You're no longer the master.*

Marjan's Demon thrust its talons into the proto-Merge of Matt and Norah's Demons. It tore through Matt's biomechanical flesh like a knife. Matt screamed inside his viewmask.

Merge, Matt thought, putting all his force into the command. His Demon quivered and pulsed, trying to comply, but Marjan's Mecha remained stubbornly separate.

Do you know where my hand is now? Marjan thought, dry like dust and crackling like static.

DeMerge, Matt thought, trying desperately to scramble away. But he remained stubbornly attached to Norah. He sensed her grim amusement. Behind him, Mikey finished wiping out the rest of the cells. All the HuMax were dead. Every single one.

My hand is wrapped around your pilot's chamber, Marjan thought. *And my Fusion Handshake is charged and ready.*

Surrender or die, Matt thought. Except Marjan didn't expect him to surrender. Didn't want him to surrender.

It was over, no matter what he did now. He'd failed.

Matt caught the flash of a red shape out of the corner of his eye, blurring fast. His cockpit rocked as a new figure hit the three Mecha, hard. Marjan's thoughts went instantly from gloating satisfaction to immense surprise. His grip on Matt's biometallic innards slipped.

Desperately, Matt bucked as hard as he could, thinking, *DeMerge!* Norah's Demon melted away from him as Marjan's hand popped out of his chest, triggering a Fusion Handshake in free air.

Matt flew backward from the blast. He came to a clanging halt on the shattered wreckage of the south cell block.

Tags in his POV told the story. The thing that had bowled into them was Elize's Mecha, its visor still only half-mended. She'd turned to Matt's side!

Matt didn't have time to celebrate. Mikey came at Elize, pinning her with a grip around her neck. Norah and Marjan stood and fired thrusters, accelerating his way.

"Go!" Elize cried through the comms. Then she turned to her attackers and said, "I give up! Repeat, I surrender!"

Matt crouched, preparing to fire his own thrusters and head into orbit. But a new warning flared in his POV: THRUSTER RECONFIGURATION INCOMPLETE: DISABLED (90 SEC).

What the hell? A leftover from his partial Merge? Matt didn't have time to think. He had to get out of there.

He whipped around. Behind him was the tunnel the Imps had emerged from. Too small for a Demon. But if he changed form, the way they did when they flew in space, maybe he could do it.

Transform, Matt thought, charging at the tunnel. His Demon hunched over and changed as he moved, elongating and narrowing. His body streamlined, arms reaching out in front of him to become grappling hooks, head and pilot's chamber moving forward in his body. His legs melded into a sinuous tail that propelled him along like a snake.

Matt's snakelike Mecha shot into the tunnel, just as

the other two Mecha came up short. Marjan beat the entrance to the tunnel and tried to ram through, but his Demon's bulk wouldn't fit. And, apparently, he couldn't transform as Matt had just done.

Two hundred meters into the tunnel, it terminated at a closed steel air lock. Its cycle light glowed red, indicating it had been depressurized. Matt's snakelike Mecha rose so he could peer through the window in the door. The air lock beyond was closed. He could see only hints of a larger space beyond through the tiny windows on the other side. His POV showed a significant heat signature from the room, though. That meant it was probably still pressurized.

Which meant there might be someone in there. Someone—or something.

Still, it wasn't as if he had a choice. The tunnel didn't go anywhere but to this air lock.

"Lowell, it's over," Colonel Cruz's voice came over Matt's comms. "Return to the surface to be escorted back to the *Helios*."

"So it's no longer 'Major,' is it?" Matt asked.

Silence for a while. Cruz hadn't been expecting that. When he came back onto the comms, his voice was lower, more reasonable. "What are your other options? Stay there and starve? There's no other way out of this system."

"Same for the HuMax," Matt said.

"Return to the surface."

"And have Marjan rip me apart?"

"That was regrettable. I'll ensure your safe passage back."

"To a court-martial," Matt added.

"For internal review. It would probably come to that, yes. But again, what else will you do?"

I don't know, Matt realized. The thought was oddly

freeing. Yes, he could go back. He could go through the trial. He could spend the rest of his life on Keller.

Or in a place like this. *You're a genemod too. What would the Union, or even Dr. Roth, give for carte blanche to study you?*

Matt shuddered.

One thing he could do: investigate that room. He put Colonel Cruz on mute, wrapping himself in chill silence.

Matt opened the first lock door and nosed his Mecha in. The lock was just large enough to hold the giant Demon, with it curled in on itself like a boa. He started the pressurization cycle and waited for the interior doors to open.

They revealed a large, cylindrical space, with a high domed ceiling. Inside, chrome bars and green hospital curtains sectioned off the floor space, with the outer walls fronted by glass-walled offices.

A medical facility, Matt thought. Probably where they did the genetic work on the HuMax. He could only imagine how nightmarish a place it must have been.

The problem was, this looked like another dead end. No corridors led away from the dome. There was no way out.

THRUSTER RECONFIGURATION COMPLETE, Matt's POV showed. He sighed. A lot of good that would do him. He stood, transforming seamlessly back into the Demon's standard humanoid form.

In the chamber, the chrome tubes holding the drapes swayed slightly. An Imp burst out and ran at Matt. It carried an MK-14, but it didn't raise it to fire. Its antipersonnel missile launchers were empty, just gaping holes along the sides of its torso. It slammed into Matt's torso and beat his Demon with the MK-14. Through the tiny slit-window to the Imp's pilot's chamber, Matt saw the sketchy outline of a man's head.

The Imp was clearly out of ammo. Matt plucked off the struggling Mecha with one razor-taloned hand and held it out at arm's length. He let it struggle awhile longer; then when it was clear it wouldn't stop, he disconnected its fusion power pack.

The Imp stopped moving. Matt set it down on the floor as the lid to the pilot's chamber flipped open. Inside was a HuMax with graying hair. He glared up at Matt's Mecha with eyes that burned with murderous rage, then scrambled out of the cockpit and retreated into the drapery.

Matt followed. He found the man standing in front of a hospital bed where a young woman sat, shaking her head woozily. Even in a shapeless hospital gown, she was beautiful, with regally high cheekbones and short flame-red hair. Her eyes, like the man's, were gold and violet.

The woman was the first to notice Matt. Her eyes went wide and she scrambled off the hospital bed. The man turned and stood in front of her, his arms out in the universal gesture of protection.

Matt sighed sadly. There was nothing the HuMax man could do to save her, for all his superhuman abilities. Against a Mecha, he was powerless.

Matt triggered his external comms and said, "I'm not going to hurt you."

The two winced at the booming voice of Matt's Mecha. The man didn't move or say a word.

And why would they have any reason to believe him? Everyone was dead. Everyone except these two. And as soon as the other Mecha came, they'd be dead too.

"Are there any other ways out of here?" Matt asked, gesturing around the dome.

"I'll not help you hunt the rest of us!" the man spat.

"I . . ." Matt trailed off. *I'm not like them anymore. I've gone rogue.* But how did he say that, in a way that would convince these HuMax?

"They're probably already dead," Matt said.

"Monster!" the woman screamed.

Matt couldn't contradict her. He hung his head. "Look. I know you won't believe me, but I'm—well, I'm hiding too. Hiding from a court-martial. So if there's any other way out of here, I'd really like to know."

The man bent low and muttered something to the woman. Something like *I think there was one fighting against the others.*

"There's nothing except this lab," the man said. "This is the end."

Matt shook his head. Trapped. Until the other Mecha managed to transform themselves.

Bright light, like lightning, lit the duraplas dome. A pillar of flame traced a lazy figure eight in the ice outside the dome. A sound like distant thunder rolled over them.

"What was that?" the woman cried.

With a groan, Matt realized exactly what it was: his former team, probing the ice with their Zap Guns. They were out on the surface, shooting down into the ice.

"More Mecha," Matt said. "Shooting at us."

"Why?" she asked.

"Because I wouldn't kill you," Matt told her.

As if in answer, another pillar of brilliant white light exploded, this one closer. Thunder boomed even closer as the ice outside the dome fractured, splintering the light into rainbows.

"What do we do?" the woman asked.

And that was the question, wasn't it? What could he do? Stand there and wait to be vaporized or try to take on three other Demons at once? Or—

"Get in the Mecha," Matt said.

"What?"

Matt irised open the pilot's chamber and pushed himself through the magnetorheological gel. Surfacing, he pulled his viewmask aside and looked down at the two HuMax from his vantage point on the giant Mecha's chest. He thrust an arm out of the cockpit and waved.

"Get in," he said, kneeling so his chest touched the floor. Handholds opened on the Mecha's skin, leading up to the cockpit access.

The two held back, leaning close to talk to each other. Without his enhanced senses, Matt couldn't hear what they were saying.

A third Zap Gun beam lanced the ice, even closer than the last two. Half the dome lit with the brilliance of an atomic explosion, nearly blinding Matt. Even the HuMax covered their eyes.

"Now or never!" Matt yelled.

The man pushed the woman ahead of him. She scrambled up the front of the Mecha with surprising speed. The man paused at the base of the Mecha's chest and looked up, as if suddenly uncertain.

The woman reached the pilot's chamber. She pulled herself over the edge and paused for an instant. Her gaze flickered from Matt to the depths of the magnetorheological gel, back to Matt. Her eyes were a little larger than a human's, and her violet-and-gold irises were intensely colored. A complex series of emotions passed over her face in a handful of seconds: relief, anguish, shock, betrayal.

"Get in!" Matt said. Calling down to the man: "Come on!"

"I'll drown!" the woman shouted, pointing at the gel.

Another Zap Gun beam hit, this one the closest yet. The entire dome went white and groaned under the close call. When the beam passed, the screech of escaping air filled the chamber.

"You'll be fine!" Matt said, and pulled her in. She splashed in the pink murk and spluttered.

"Respirator!" Matt said, pointing at the emergency air. Without a viewmask, she wouldn't see anything, but she'd at least be safe.

The woman pulled the respirator on and gave Matt one last distrustful look before pushing herself as far away as possible from him. The three would have a tight ride in the cramped pilot's chamber.

Matt looked down. The man was halfway up the Demon's chest, moving fast. Good. They'd both—

The world disappeared in light. Matt's eardrums popped, first inward from the pressure wave, then outward as the air exhausted from the circular dome in a terrific gust. They'd been hit glancingly by a Zap Gun beam, but that was enough—the chamber was compromised!

When Matt could see again, the man simply wasn't there. He caught a glimpse of something rising on the column of air through the Zap Gun's blasted channel. The woman next to him splashed and cried out, her voice almost ultrasonic in the thin atmosphere. Matt's eyes bulged as he whooped out all of his air. His head spun. Near vacuum. He'd be unconscious in seconds.

"Get down," he tried to yell. The words came out as a single squeak. He pushed the woman down into the gel, snugged on his viewmask, and triggered the cockpit iris. Everything went dark, then lit in the Mecha's POV. Next to him, the woman thrashed and screamed through her respirator. Her fists beat at him, surprisingly strong in the viscous gel.

Matt turned and grabbed blindly, catching her by the shoulder and neck. She grappled with him, her hands finding his neck. Matt bent low near her ear and screamed, hoping she would hear:

"If you want to get out of here alive, stop fighting with me!"

The woman ceased struggling and sobbed something, maybe something about her father. Was that who the man was?

"There was nothing I could do," Matt yelled.

The woman just shook her head and cried. Matt turned back to the front of the Mecha, where his POV showed Marjan's Demon emerging from the channel his Zap Gun had cut.

Matt didn't hesitate. He drew his own Zap Gun, aimed it at the ceiling, and triggered its irresistible force. The lab exploded in white clouds of water vapor. Behind him, Marjan tumbled backward into the channel he'd just cut.

Matt's Zap Gun blasted through the ice. Steam vented upward, clearing the remains of the dome.

Matt followed the steam upward, firing his thrusters full force. Up through the thin atmosphere, up away from the icy world. To orbit.

But where, he wondered, *will I go from there?*

7

EHILE

In orbit over Planet 5 of the nameless system, Matt's Demon transformed into a streamlined shape, a red arrow with thrusters on the back and Firefly ports forward. It looked like a pre-Expansion vision of a spaceship, a grand vessel for transporting passengers and cargo from star to star.

Except for one problem, Matt thought. *Without a Displacement Drive, I'm not going anywhere.*

Especially here. His POV showed no familiar tags, no named systems at all. Every star was nothing but a catalogue number, every planet just a numeric appendage. They were so far out none of the empires of humankind had claimed a single foothold.

Even if they were close to the Core of the Union, it wouldn't matter. The only interstellar travel humanity had was via the Displacement Drive, and the Displacement Drive required a mass of ten billion metric tons or more to work. So, unless Matt found a spare antimatter reactor, a Displacement Drive, and a convenient asteroid, his flight was soon going to end.

Behind Matt, new tags appeared, above pinpricks of fusion exhaust:

DEMON 021: AD. NORAH GRACIA
DEMON 007: AD. MARJAN VELUSZIK
DEMON 012: AD. MIKEY KERR

His adepts were coming for him. Worse, he was sandwiched between the UUS *Helios* and the Demons. They would soon be in firing range.

Could he hold the adepts off? Possibly. Maybe he could even defeat them. But then he'd have to conquer the entire *Helios* in order to make it home.

Do whatever it takes, make your own time at all costs. The thought was like a whisper in his mind, only half heard. The scratchy voice of the Mecha.

I have to agree, came another thought.

Where the hell did that come from? Matt wondered. That other voice was clearly outside himself.

You can hear my thoughts? Sudden panic overlay the second voice. It wasn't the voice of the Mecha. It was something new.

Who are you? Matt asked.

I am 076-50-035A, came a thought, sudden and crisp. Overlaid was an image of a woman's slim wrist and a 2D bar code tattoo.

You're the woman I rescued?

Yes. Hate raged through her as flickers of those final moments in the dome came to Matt. Information unfolded: The man in the Imp was her father. Both of them were HuMax subjects. She'd lived her entire life in the Union's chill laboratory. He'd been trying to protect her as she had just been—

Matt cringed as the memories came, sharp and fast. This woman had been selected for one of the Union's genome-rewriting projects. She'd been injected with the reverse-transcription virus, and had been unconscious until Matt had arrived.

The genome rewrite had just started. She was changing now as she hung beside him in the Demon's magnetorheological gel.

Changing into what? Matt wondered.

Fear, overlaid with ironic mirth, was his answer.

I don't understand, Matt told her.

I don't know how I will change, the woman thought. *The Union doesn't give us a map to our new genetic code.*

Matt bit his lip, imagining this beautiful woman turning into one of the four-armed monsters . . . or something even more terrible.

Don't pretend to care about me, she told him.

I can't pretend, Matt thought. *This is mind to mind.*

In response, he got only chill suspicion. Of course. Why should she trust him? He was Mecha Corps, in service to the Union.

Or was he? How could he say he served the Union now? He sensed this woman, this 076-50-035A — watching him, observing his reactions.

What's your name? he asked her.

0-76-50-035A.

Don't you have a real name? I'm Matt. Matt Lowell.

We are forbidden to use informals.

Wow. How far did they go to dehumanize them?

It's okay, Matt told her.

You're trying to trap me, she thought. *You'll use this in my files when you take me to another lab.*

Matt laughed out loud. *There's nothing left of the lab,* he told her. *And I don't have any idea where to go. Go ahead, take a look.*

Matt opened his mind more fully to her. For long moments, something like a warm breeze flowed through his head. When it was done, the woman was still suspicious, but her fear had ebbed a little. She could see they were both outcasts now.

I'm Ione, she told him.

Ione who?

Ione O-3-5-A.

Matt sighed. Ione would have to do.

He glanced at the three pursuing Mechas at his back. They were closer now. The tag for the UUS *Helios* was still over the horizon. He hovered in between destruction by Zap Gun and destruction by heavy-matter weaponry. Unless he simply surrendered.

If you surrender, they'll kill me.

Matt shivered. She was right. And more than likely they would kill him too. Cleaner than any court-martial. The valiant hero dying in battle, so sad.

Are there any other Union installations in this system? he asked her.

We know only the Home, Ione thought.

Matt nodded. How could she know? In any case, it was ridiculous to think there was any other place of refuge in the desolate system.

Helios popped over the horizon of Planet 5, a dark speck against the distant sun dazzle. Tags in his POV tracked the tiny dot, calling out its distance in ever-decreasing numbers. At his current speed, he'd reach it in nine minutes.

A single bright thread flashed away from the UUS *Helios.* Matt jumped. Was it launching missiles at him? But his forward view was clear of tags. No missiles rocketed at him; no heavy matter was coming his way.

Another tiny flash, this one brighter. Matt frowned. What was happening? Was the *Helios* engaging another orbital emplacement? That didn't make sense. They'd captured those before the exercise even began. And there was no tag—

No. Wait. There was another tag in Matt's POV. It was simply buried behind the *Helios*. Matt used his Enhanced Sensory Array to zoom in. The speck of the *Helios* grew to the size of a coin, glittering in the chill sunlight of the unnamed sun.

Off the *Helios*'s planetward side was another dark, lumpy disk, bristling with antennae. Its tag read DISPLACEMENT DRIVE SHIP (ORIGIN UNKNOWN, WEAPONS UNKNOWN).

Another Displacement Drive ship? Matt's heart pounded. Was it a way out of here?

Missiles flashed from the unknown Displacement Drive ship and arced at the UUS *Helios*. At the same time, heavy-matter rounds from the *Helios* hit the Displacement Drive ship, rocking it visibly. Great gouts of gray dust fountained up from its surface. Unlike the *Helios*, this ship wasn't armored—it was just a simple converted asteroid. It wouldn't last long under the *Helios*'s bombardment.

Why wasn't it Displacing out? Matt wondered.

Too old, Ione thought. *Waiting to recharge.*

What do you mean? You know this ship?

Called on FTLcomm. Friends finally heard us. But friends came too late.

Friends?

You know them as Corsairs, Ione told him.

A Corsair ship? Matt's stomach turned over. Corsairs working with the HuMax? Like Rayder, all over again?

They didn't know of us until the revolt, Ione thought. *But they know of HuMax.*

Matt's Perfect Record brought back the Union records from his Merge with the computer. The HuMax had used the FTLcomm. And they'd finally reached someone.

More heavy-matter rounds hit the Corsair Displacement Drive ship. Antennae and sensors vaporized, shards sparking in the sunlight. The poor ship wouldn't last long.

Would it last long enough to recharge its Displacement Drive and flee? That was the real question. It obviously didn't have a fast-cycle drive like the *Helios*. How long did it take to recycle? The older ships could take ten or twenty minutes.

Suddenly everything was completely clear. He tucked his visor down and pushed his aft thrusters into redline, rocketing at the Corsair ship. Hopefully it would last long enough for him to arrive.

As Matt landed hard on the Corsair ship's surface, he knew that one of two things would happen. Either his comms would light with Cruz's icon, for one last offer. Or they'd—

HEAVY-MATTER WEAPONS TARGETING, Matt's POV screamed, in bright red letters.

—try to blow him out of the sky.

So that's how it is, Matt thought. The Corsair Displacement Drive ship was still intact, but it had taken heavy damage. Its comms arrays were scoured off the surface, and its single heavy lock jetted wispy streamers of air.

Matt drew his Zap Gun and aimed it at the *Helios*.

HEAVY-MATTER WEAPONS LOCK, his POV showed.

Alarms shrilled in Matt's ears as the *Helios*'s went off. For a moment, Matt actually saw the hazy dark matter, rocketing his way. He fired his Zap Gun straight into the middle of the mass.

All of space went white around him. Shock waves battered his Mecha, and he tumbled over the surface of the Corsair asteroid in a haze of dust and rock shards.

But he'd hit the heavy-matter rounds and neutralized them. His Zap Gun beam had also sliced neatly through a section of the *Helios*'s armor, exposing the shock-absorbing scaffolding beneath.

But now his adepts were less than a minute away from him. ANTIMATTER WEAPON TARGETING flashed from the three Union loyalists. No matter where he went, one of their guns would follow him.

Good run, almost made it, Ione thought. At the back of her mind, she imagined a future where another Union rebel like Matt actually succeeded in freeing the HuMax and getting the word out.

"No," Matt said. He scrambled toward a deep pit in the surface and aimed his own Zap Gun at the incoming adepts. Maybe he could take one of them out—

The stars changed.

Suddenly there was no UUS *Helios*. No Demons. Nothing in the star-speckled sky at all.

The Corsair ship had finally Displaced.

He was safe. For now.

Matt lay on the surface of the Corsair ship for long minutes, content simply to rest for a while. The close-packed stars above were still beautiful, even if they were half covered by red REGENERATION countdowns. Ione seemed content to leave him alone as well, though her mind still swirled with undercurrents of unease.

Matt jumped when a proximity alarm flared to life. New tags floated in his POV. Three people in mismatched space suits had come out to the surface of the asteroid and were approaching his Demon cautiously.

Corsairs.

They moved in the shuffle step of people familiar with microgravity. One carried a large weapon that was longer than the person was tall. Matt wasn't familiar with the model, but his viewmask tagged it as a PORTABLE FUSION CANNON.

That wouldn't be good. Assuming the guy could hit him, that is. The heavy gun fought the space-suited figure's every move. Shooting it would probably give him a one-way ticket out of the asteroid's gravity well into deep space.

Matt pushed himself up to sit so he could get a better look at them. The three men scrambled to hide themselves behind rocky outcroppings. Matt almost laughed. They'd thought he was incapacitated.

But how was he going to talk to them? He set his comms on WIDEBAND➔ALL and opened his mouth.

And suddenly realized: *I have nothing to say.* What could he possibly tell them?

Don't shoot, I'm with you guys now?

Come on, we're all in this together?

Take me to your leader?

Matt toggled the comms off and sat in silence as the three figures struggled with the gun.

Tell them the truth, Ione thought.

Matt sighed. She was right. He turned the mike on again and said, "This is Major Matt Lowell, former Universal Union Mecha Corps, surrendering."

It was like taking a knife in the guts.

It's the right thing to do, Ione thought.

And I made a vow to start doing a better job at doing the right thing, Matt thought. That didn't mean it wasn't painful, though.

Matt jumped when his comms crackled to life. A new comms tag showed UNKNOWN➔M. LOWELL.

"Major Lowell, why would we believe you?"

Matt shook his head. "Did you see any of the battle at all? The Union, coming after me? Shooting at me? I'm half-wrecked."

"And you could still shatter this ship like a walnut if I let you in the locks."

Matt sighed. "Who are you?"

"I'm Hector Gonsalves, captain of the independent

ship *El Dorado*. And now that we've made our introductions, I'd ask you to push off into space."

Shouts erupted behind the captain's voice. "But it's a Demon! Do you know what that's worth?"

Gonsalves shouted them down.

Of course. They'd want his Mecha. What a prize for the Corsairs! He thought of telling them they could have it, then clamped his mouth shut on the words. That was stupid. That was giving away too much. But he could play on their greed.

"I protected your ship," Matt said. "Surely that deserves some repayment, like transport back to a colonized world."

Captain Gonsalves didn't say anything for a long time. "I saw what you did. That doesn't mean it wasn't staged."

"I risked my life to protect you!" Matt cried. "Was the *Helios* firing on me staged?"

More silence. Finally: "What use do we have for a Union rebel?"

Matt pushed down rising anger. Outside, on the asteroid's surface, the man with the antimatter rifle was still trying to get it aimed at Matt. The two others struggled with him, pushing down the heavy barrel.

"You can shoot at me and lose three crew members," Matt said. "Or you can let us in and we can talk like humans."

"Us?" Gonsalves said. "There are multiple pilots?"

"Myself and one survivor. From the lab."

Gonsalves swore softly, but didn't reply. Finally: "Put him on."

"I can't. She's on the emergency respirator. No comms."

Gonsalves said nothing at first, then barked orders off-mike. The three men outside looked up, as if listening to their own comms. That made sense. Gonsalves was safe somewhere deep in the asteroid, and his crew was outside tending to the monster.

Finally Gonsalves came back on the comms. "Is the survivor HuMax?"

"Yes."

"Okay. This is how we'll do it, Former Major. You will proceed to the main space dock five hundred meters from your current position. My men will maintain anti-matter rifle targeting on you at all times. If you do anything other than walk, slowly, I won't hesitate to blast you out of existence. I have plenty of spacecraft to pick up my men."

Matt did as he was told. Two of them men walked backward ahead of him, cradling the heavy rifle. One led the way, casting nervous glances back.

At the spaceship dock, the doors were warped by heat and jammed with rocks and dust. They ground only three-quarters of the way open before groaning to a halt. Matt had to duck to fit through the lock.

Inside, small spaceships of almost every imaginable type covered the walls. There were Aliancia Fuegos, Tai-kong X-10s, even a Union Rhino and a handful of converted freighters. All bore the Corsairs' thousand-daggers shield. Matt stopped in the middle of the dock and waited for the doors to cycle. After an age, the battered steel doors slammed shut. Soon his external sensors showed a breathable, but thin, atmosphere.

Matt triggered the cockpit iris and surfaced, pulling off his viewmask. He helped Ione up to the top of the cockpit. She pulled off her mask and wiped the pink magnetorheological gel off her face. Blazing violet-and-gold eyes flashed at Matt.

She was down the side of the Mecha and holding on the steel scaffolding before Matt was even out of the cockpit.

The three men flanked Ione and Matt as he came to join her on the scaffolding. She stared at his white, skin-tight interface suit, as if seeing him for the first time. Which, he realized, she was.

A small interior air lock opened and another man floated out to greet them. He was a heavyset, dark-colored man just starting to go gray, with a small goatee of salt-and-pepper hair. He wore a sober olive green suit with no identifying badges or medals at all. He stopped five feet away from Matt and Ione and looked them up and down.

"Former Major Lowell?" the man asked, looking at Matt.

Matt nodded. "Captain Gonsalves?"

"Yes. I'd offer to shake hands, but let's see where we land first."

Matt nodded, his face heating. He bit off a sharp reply.

"And this is?" Gonsalves said, nodding at Ione.

"Oh-76-50-035A, sir!" Ione barked.

Gonsalves shook his head. "Ah, our ever-efficient Union. What did they do to you, poor girl?"

"Her name is Ione," Matt said.

Ione looked at Matt suspiciously. He held her gaze, thinking, *With me, you're a person, not a number.*

"So, what do we do now, Former Major?" he asked. "Do you swallow your pride and say, 'I'm a Corsair now'?"

Matt ground his teeth. At that moment, he hated Gonsalves more than anything. To break it down into those terms, to make him say something like that, not knowing his past . . .

But what other choice did he have?

"I'm a Corsair now," Matt said.

PART TWO

VILLAIN

"Those who make peaceful revolution impossible will make violent revolution inevitable."

— John F. Kennedy
President of the United States

"In the silence of space, we make echoing choices."

— Petter Corolis
Union Prime (2220–2228)
Founder of the Freecycle Party

"THE SPACE BETWEEN"—Holes in Humanity's Empire

(Excerpted from long-form video documentary by G. James Gellschaft)

VO:

. . . whether Union or Aliancia, Taikong or Corsair, we're all familiar with charts showing the relative cubic volumes of these domains.

(insert graphic showing Universal Union stars in blue, Taikong in red, Aliancia in green, Corsair in gray)

Looking at it this way, the Union dwarfs the rest of the interstellar governmental organizations, with over two times the volume of its closest neighbor, the Taikong Lingyo. This is especially true when we count the Union's newest Colony-Candidate worlds.

(graphic expands to show additional volume at the edge of the Union, farthest from its IGO neighbors)

Impressive, isn't it? In the span of only three hundred years, humanity has expanded to control a volume of almost thirty million cubic light-years.

(graphic transitions to show only two single white stars to represent their separate but united systems, lonely pinpoints of light)

But this statistic hides the fact that we in no way control all of these thirty million cubic light-years; we pop from place to place using our Displacement Drives, with cumbersome routes based on gravity-well velocity relative to the destination.

(overlay of a Displacement Drive ship disappearing in one system and reappearing in another)

We don't explore the space between the systems; indeed, it's not even feasible for us, at this time, to explore many worlds of our own galaxy, since they do not align with the galactic mean rotation.

(diagram shows a system canted to an angle off the galactic plane)

And without exploring those spaces, we do not control them.

(diagram shows the space between worlds, expanding out to show the relative cubic volume between them—it is mind-bendingly huge)

So, in reality, our empire is better seen as points of light.

(transition to historical footage: an antique jet plane, flying over flat cropland)

In the past, our ancestors referred to the space between the East Coast and West Coast of the United States of America as "flyover country"—relatively unimportant for the megabusinesses of the era. However, this flyover country largely fed and clothed the same people who disdained it. And, unlike our Space Between, flyover country could be explored.

(transition to historical footage of Expansion-era Displacement Drives)

How much of our history has been written by the routes our primitive Displacement Drive ships can take? And how much will be rewritten once we discover a reliable way into this unknown space?

8

ALIANCIA

Matt and Ione's debriefing with Captain Hector Gonsalves wasn't a debriefing at all. Matt didn't really know what it was.

The Union military, even a relatively loose unit like the Mecha Corps, operated on the razor's edge of discipline. You knew that after a mission, you'd be given exactly one hour to shower off the magnetorheological gel and get back in your dress uniform. Then you'd report to a sterile stainless steel conference room, strap yourself down on a Velcro-bottomed plastic chair, and wait for the mission leader and Mecha controller to report. If there were fatalities, they'd spark up the FTLcomm and turn on the nonphysical displays, so fuzzy images of higher-ups in the Union Army and Mecha Corps could glare down at you from their chilly offices on Eridani. You knew they'd spend two or three hours with you, reviewing every decision and giving you feedback on how they'd do it better. Debriefings were Matt's least favorite part of the Mecha Corps, but he'd mastered the art of looking as if he was listening, nodding in the right places, and having a decent answer ready when they asked their nonsensical questions.

But Captain Gonsalves didn't operate like that at all. After laughing hard at Matt's declaration that he "was a Corsair now," he and two of his biggest guards escorted Matt and Ione up to his captain's chamber. Or at least Matt thought they were guards. Except for a single red strip of cloth on one sleeve, they wore no uniform or decoration. One was clothed in a tan digger's coverall, and the other wore tattered jeans and a black T-shirt.

They floated through rough-hewn rock tunnels, patched here and there with shiny black blobs of sealant. Some still stank of long-chain polymers—fresh wounds from the engagement with UUS *Helios*. Hector brought up the front, moving with the practiced ease of someone who had grown up in zero g. The two guards brought up the rear. Matt glanced at Ione, but she didn't meet his gaze. Her eyes were wide, glassy, and fixed straight ahead.

In shock, Matt thought.

The captain's chamber was another rock room, but this one was clearly appointed by someone who was comfortable living in microgravity. There was no ceiling and no floor. Rich wood cabinets ran along the short walls of the room, and the exposed stone was acid-etched with intricate, intertwining patterns. Screens divided a free-sleeping scaffold and a rudimentary zero-g kitchen from the rest of the space. Polished aluminum handholds and footbars radiated out from a central space where a 3-D holotank showed their position in a relative star field. It was notably devoid of tags, except for their current velocity and vector.

Captain Gonsalves went to one of the cabinets, pulled out a large, plush towel, and threw it at Matt. "You might need this."

Matt caught the towel, but made no move to wipe the remaining magnetorheological gel out of his hair.

Gonsalves turned to Ione. "Can I offer you anything? Food? Water? A drink?"

"Alcohol?" she asked, looking both fascinated and repulsed at the same time.

Gonsalves grinned. "Of course."

"Water is fine," Ione said. She watched in fascination as the captain flipped himself upside down to reach a tap and bulb in the zero-g kitchen, and gripped the handrail even tighter. She wasn't used to microgravity. She wanted to orient herself, like the Union military.

Gonsalves came back, handed her the drinking bulb, and hooked a foot around a rail. "Okay. First let's figure out what the shit all this is. Let me guess the basics. Mr. Former Major here was sent by the all-knowing and ever-benevolent Union to clean up its nasty little mess. And by clean up, I mean kill everyone in the place."

Matt opened his mouth, irritated by Gonsalves's look of smug satisfaction. Then he closed it. Gonsalves was right. His thoughts beat slow and stupid, as Mesh hangover began to clamp down on his mind.

"I refused the order," Matt said. "Sir."

Gonsalves laughed. "No 'sirs' here. People call me 'captain' because I call the shots on this ship. Beyond that, there ain't much in the way of salutes and sirs. No pomp and circumstance. Not any more than there absolutely needs to be."

Matt crossed his arms and said nothing. Did Gonsalves want him to believe they weren't a heavily militarized group of terrorists? What was he playing at?

Gonsalves continued. "So you deserted your team and came to join the big bad guys in the sky, the terrible Corsairs?"

Matt tensed. "I was team leader."

"Not very bright on the Union's part, putting a potentially disloyal leader on this mission."

Matt started. But Mecha Corps never expected he could be disloyal, given his history. On paper, he was the safest choice.

"HuMax killed my father," Matt said.

Hector's smug look faltered a little. "HuMax?"

"Yes."

"I find that very hard to believe," the captain said.

"I killed Rayder," Matt said.

Gonsalves stared openmouthed at Matt for several seconds, then rocked back, bellowing laughter. He couldn't catch his breath for almost a minute afterward. When he was done, he wiped tears from his eyes and patted Matt on the back, like an old friend. "Oh, that's good. Real good. You're a riot."

Matt realized how stupid it sounded. Like something out of a low-budget melodrama. Even the Union wouldn't admit the mission ever happened. He could never prove it.

"Is it true?" Ione asked. "A HuMax killed your parent?"

Matt nodded.

"And you tried to save us. Save me," she breathed, her voice husky and low.

Gonsalves shook his finger at her, like a man admonishing a child. "Don't swallow the whole line, my dear," he said. "Anyone who can claim they killed Rayder can make up some real whoppers."

"Who is Rayder?" she asked.

Gonsalves shook his head. "Someone we're better off without."

"You didn't follow Rayder?" Matt asked.

The captain snorted in disgust. "Hell, no. His faction never made even a twentieth of the Confederacy. Of course, we got tons of other crap factions out there. But let's get back to this. Okay. Secret Union lab, supposed Union defector. Are there any other Union bases out here Beyond the Between that we need to know about? Anything we're going to get surprised by on our way to Tierrasanta?"

"Tierrasanta?"

Gonsalves frowned. "I'm asking the questions, Former Major."

"We went straight to the system, no stops or detours," Matt said. "So there could be additional bases, but I don't think the Union would group, uh, things like this together."

"You didn't go into any other systems? Not even for velocity matching?"

Matt shook his head. "The UUS *Helios* has maneuvering thrusters."

A nod. "Right. It's one of those damn new warships. It doesn't have to slug around in gravity wells like we do."

Matt remembered the orbital velocity matching they'd had to do on older ships: laboriously detailed, iterative Displacements into gravity wells of gas giants, so they could precisely set the big asteroid into an orbital velocity and vector at arrival. He'd forgotten how difficult it could be, being spoiled by the Union's newest generation of Displacement Drive ships.

It must have been even more work for Hector Gonsalves, with this ship's old-style, slow-recharge Displacement Drive. Why had he gone to the trouble to come all the way out here to save Ione and the other HuMax?

"What were you going to do with them?" Matt asked, nodding at Ione. "If we hadn't gotten there first?"

"Well, obviously we were going to roast them on a spit and chew the succulent flesh off their bones," Hector said, leering at Ione. "Or at least the ones we couldn't sell as doxies or slaves."

Matt stared, wide-eyed. He couldn't tell if Hector was joking or not. The man appeared dead serious.

"That's what your Union would have you believe, right?" Hector continued.

Matt nodded.

Hector shook his head. "Well, there are Corsairs who would do just that. Maybe worse."

"It would still be better than staying there," Ione said softly.

"You can't possibly mean that," Hector told her, his expression crumpling with concern.

"I mean it." Ione wouldn't look at them.

"What did they do to you?"

Ione shook her head, but said nothing. The silence stretched out, only the low hum of the Displacement Drive charging as a background.

"You didn't answer the question," Matt said. "What would you do with them?"

Hector sighed and cast hooded eyes at Matt. "It's never so simple. Our explanations probably won't be satisfying to someone who lives with the nanny Union wiping their ass."

Matt's head twisted in Mesh-hangover headache as rage fired in his belly. *I grew up as a refugee,* he thought. But Captain Gonsalves didn't deserve to know that. Instead, he said, "Try me."

"Talent is valuable," Captain Gonsalves said. "And HuMax are some of the most talented people out there. Some would remain with us. Others—we'd exchange with other factions—"

"For money," Matt said.

"Of course for money!" Gonsalves snapped. "Or ships, or machine tools, or food, or whatever the hell else we need."

"Like slaves."

"Like football superstars!" Gonsalves yelled, his face

turning bright red. Ione's eyes darted from one man to the other, her expression tightening in concern.

Gonsalves saw it. He bit down on another remark, and instead said, "Look, Former Major, you don't have to like the way we operate. But this is the way it works around here. There's no safety net. If you don't like it, you can step out right now."

"I bet you'd like that," Matt said, drifting deeper into Mesh hangover. This one was going to be bad. How long had he been in the Demon?

"It'd be easier. I wouldn't have to spin you to the crew."

"Sell me. Sell my Mecha." Matt's words were suddenly slurred. He had to get to bed. Better to sleep off the hangover than try to tough it out awake.

"Small market for Mecha," Gonsalves told Matt. "And the factions using it, well, I don't think you'd like them. And they may already have gone past that clunker."

"Demon is great! Try me. Greatesh Mecha pilot ever." Matt's eyelids fluttered as the headache beat deeper into his brain.

Gonsalves suddenly looked concerned. He bent over Matt and thumbed up one of his eyelids. "What's the matter with you, kid?"

"Not a kid. Mesh hangover . . ."

Gonsalves pursed his lips and nodded. "The illustrious Union. Just pay your bills, don't break any of the rules, and never mind the secret labs, or the addiction of your best and brightest to a destructive technology."

"Union isn't like . . . uh . . ." Matt trailed off. His vision had gone dark and blurry at the edges. What had he been talking about?

Gonsalves smiled. "I thought you were a Corsair now."

Matt nodded. Why not? Corsair, Union, HuMax, all fine. He stared down a long, dark tunnel. Sounds seemed to come from very far away. Someone leaned over him, someone with bright violet-and-gold eyes.

"Beautiful," Matt said, and passed out.

When Matt woke, he was alone in Gonsalves's room, wrapped in a sleep net.

Matt pulled himself out of the soft synthetic mesh, his head pounding like a runaway antimatter reaction. He'd passed out from Mesh hangover. Passed out! He'd never done that before. Why was this so bad? Because he'd shared the pilot's chamber with Ione?

Matt went to the door and tugged at it, half expecting to be locked in. But the door popped open, revealing rock tunnels.

Across from Matt's door, a red-sleeved guard hung casually off a handrail. He looked up as Matt emerged.

"Am I under arrest?" Matt asked.

The guard shook his head and muttered into his slate. Gonsalves's squeaky voice came back from it.

"Hang out," the guard said. "Captain'll be back in a minute."

"And if I don't?"

The guard shrugged. "Then you'll get lost."

Matt waited. After a few minutes, Captain Gonsalves came down the corridor, trailed by Ione.

"Why am I under guard?" Matt asked as they came up.

"For your own protection," Gonsalves said. "I still have to figure out how to spin this to the crew. We don't normally go picking up Union military, you know."

"Former military. I'm a defector."

Gonsalves nodded. "Traitor there, traitor here, goes the saying."

Matt reddened, his head pulsing tripletime. "I'm

not—I wouldn't be—" A traitor. That's exactly what he was. He'd turned his back on the Union.

But the Union didn't deserve his loyalty.

"They broke my trust," Matt said. "I don't owe them anything."

Gonsalves nodded. "That's a good start. But we're going to need a lot more spin."

Ione put a slim hand on the captain's green suit jacket. "He deserves a chance."

"The crew ain't exactly friendly to the Union."

"I will protect him," Ione said.

Gonsalves bellowed laughter, then quickly sobered. "I forget. You probably *could* protect him."

Ione colored. "I can't change what I am."

Gonsalves looked at Ione for a long time. Then he sighed. "You sure?"

Ione nodded.

Gonsalves sighed. "Your call. We'll see how it goes."

Matt just looked at Ione, wondering what he should say to her. Thank you? But he'd saved her life. And she was HuMax! Ione returned his gaze, her violet-and-gold eyes confident and intense.

Matt turned to Gonsalves and asked, "What are my duties, sir?"

"Duties?" Gonsalves asked. "I don't command any more than I have to. That goes double for Union defectors. But there's plenty of work on the job boards. You better just hope they'll give the Union kid a shot."

Matt nodded uncertainly. What mattered now was getting some food. Anything would be fine. Anything to help his murdered head.

Ione took him to the mess hall first, which was labeled, rather playfully, as ROBERTO'S RETREAT, A FINE DINING ESTABLISHMENT.

Fine dining evidently meant mismatched tables bolted haphazardly to cracked native stone, with a long buffet featuring powdered eggs and soy bacon, glopped together with an unidentifiable gravy to keep it on the plate in microgravity. That was fine. Matt dug in, surprised at his hunger.

"Is it good?" Ione asked when he was done.

"Good enough," Matt said, looking around. Roberto's Retreat held only a few crew members, and none of them paid the pair more than passing attention.

"Thank you," Matt told her. The words felt right. "For promising to help me."

"You deserve your chance."

"So do you."

Ione looked away, her eyes brightening with tears. Matt reached out to take her hand, but stopped himself before he touched her. Two voices warred in his head: *She's HuMax. She's a person.*

"I'm sorry," Matt said.

"For what?" Ione asked, not looking at him.

For everything, he thought. But that wasn't him. That was the Union. What could he say? He said the first thing that came to mind. "What's going to happen to you?"

Ione started. She knew exactly what he was talking about. The genetic modifications, now starting to take place deep in her body.

"Thank you for not telling the captain," Ione told him, after a time.

"That's not an answer."

A head shake. "I don't have any answers."

"Can you . . . feel it?"

"I feel hot, but that's all," Ione told him.

And later, what happens? Matt wondered. But he couldn't chase that idea right now. He was here, on a

Corsair ship, with a HuMax. So, back to the old question: What the hell are you going to do?

Matt grinned sadly. He had no idea. None at all.

"Are you all right?" he asked.

For several long moments, Ione just looked at him. Not quite a blank look, not quite an accusatory stare. Almost respectful. As if she was thinking, *You almost treated me like a real person there.*

Then it was gone. She looked down at the table and asked, "Are you?"

Matt laughed. It was a fair question, after passing out yesterday. He probably still looked gray.

"It's a side effect of using the Mecha," he told her.

Another odd look. *Then why do you use them?* she was asking. But too polite to ask it out loud. Or too scared.

Matt made himself stand. "I have an idea," he said. "Let's take a tour. See how our new home works."

Ione broke into an open, happy smile. It was the first time he'd seen it. It transformed her face. She was even more radiantly beautiful this way. Matt made a promise to try and keep her smiling.

"Yes, I agree," she said.

Ione paid for their meal at Roberto's with cash the captain had given her. Even more bizarrely, it wasn't on a card but in old-fashioned plastic bill form.

Matt asked her where they were supposed to get more money, but Ione seemed confused by the entire concept. He decided not to press.

They went first down to the Displacement Drive core, which was accessible by a completely unguarded shaft. Anyone could drop down right on top of the fusion reactor, radiating blast-furnace heat in the big hollow inner chamber of the *El Dorado*. One bored engineer looked up at their arrival, and seemed only too happy to break his routine and show them the finer points of charging and discharging their antique Displacement Drive. The ship could only manage a Displacement every seventeen minutes.

Back up the corridors, they saw the dorms they were expected to sleep in. Coed, of course. Two bored crew members lay on their bunks and played video games. Like the engineer, they didn't have any problem showing Matt and Ione the finer points of reserving their own beds. Ione chose a bunk above Matt, near the walls in the back. She brushed rock chips off the top of the mesh cover. The chips spun off in the microgravity, falling slowly toward the floor.

Matt squinted at his surroundings. The crew didn't seem to care about them at all, despite the captain's mutterings. He didn't know whether to be relieved or worried. Shouldn't someone be at least curious?

Nearer the surface, the exterior viewing rooms were all barricaded off, still not vacuum-worthy after their battle with the UUS *Helios*. They discovered three other restaurants, the yawning spaceship dock, and a half dozen weapons emplacements, all but one of which were also sealed against vacuum leaks. At the last weapons emplacement, three technicians argued heatedly over the old-fashioned Taikong laser. Or at least Matt thought they were technicians. They wore no uniform, but they also didn't wear red armbands. And they had that totally absorbed, I-know-I'm-right geeky tone he knew all too well from Peal and Jahl.

One of them, a pudgy black-haired kid who couldn't have been more than nineteen, noticed them first. He sniffed the air and wrinkled his nose. "Hey, you smell something Union? It just got rank in here."

Matt held up his hands. "Just leaving," he said, grabbing a handrail and turning Ione around.

But the three were fast. They caromed off the ceiling and came down all around Matt and Ione. The chrome wrenches they carried suddenly looked very heavy.

"Yeah, the captain's crew choices are pretty crap, but this is the crap of the crapper," another one said. He was a skinny, mousy-haired guy with a still-glowing slate peeking from an oversized shirt pocket.

"We don't want any trouble," Matt said, looking for an easy way out. But the guys were clearly used to micro-gravity. The corridor was short and they covered it at all levels. There wasn't an easy way through.

"He has a nice pet," the first one said, coming in close to touch Ione's cheek.

"Hey!" Matt said, grabbing the guy's arm. The kid wailed in pain and brought his ratchet up to strike.

Before it hit, Ione grabbed it and twisted it out of his hands, her hand moving in a flash. The two others paused for a moment, then moved in with their own weapons. Ione elbowed one in the chest and knocked the wind out of him. But the impact sent her spinning as well. The last guy's swing almost caught her on the forehead.

If you're going to fight, fight to win. Matt brought his leg up and kicked the last guy away, and dodged a jab from the first pudgy kid. Ione caught her spin and came back like a flash, kicking the remaining techs hard in the groin, one-two, with legs that almost blurred as they moved. The two men screamed in pain and crumpled as the last guy backed away.

HuMax. Superhuman. But for how long?

"Let's get out of here," Matt said, shoving Ione ahead of him. She led the way to a corridor intersection a few hundred yards away, then grabbed a rail and put her head down, her eyes tight shut.

"What's the matter?" Matt asked.

Ione's eyes snapped open and she looked up at him,

her pupils darting from side to side. "I—should I—should I have done that? I—the Union—"

For once, Matt didn't think. He took the terrified girl in his arms and hugged her close. She tensed against him, then relaxed. She was very warm, very soft, and Matt heard the faint, rapid patter of her heart. She smelled of new jumpsuit and fear-sweat and cheap shampoo.

For the first time, Matt could almost imagine—

What? Falling for her? For a HuMax?

They had nothing in common. He couldn't imagine her upbringing. He couldn't imagine what her life had been like. And he had no idea what the genetic rewrite would turn her into. But, in that moment, it didn't matter.

"Thank you," he said.

"For what?"

"For taking them out."

Ione nodded, not pushing away. Matt made himself end the embrace and hold her at arm's length, just so his spinning thoughts would stop their dizzy march.

"It was okay?" Ione asked him, her eyes darting across his face again.

"It was exactly the right thing to do," Matt told her.

"It was the dumbest-ass thing you could've done!" Captain Gonsalves thundered. "Now I've got a ship full of Union- and HuMax-haters on my ass!"

"No, he doesn't," said a woman in a featureless gray jumpsuit.

They were on the bridge, such that it was. External viewports were welded shut with steel plate in the aftermath of the battle. Half the instrumentation was still dark. But one large holotank still worked, and that's what Hector Gonsalves, the woman in the jumpsuit, and a half dozen other crew members were gathered around. Tags showed the vector velocity of the *El Dorado* relative to Tierrasanta. They were diving into the gravity well of a gas giant, trying to get a closer match to their destination.

"Yes, I do!" Gonsalves yelled. "This is the calm before the storm. They'll roast me at breakfast!"

"No, they won't," the woman said, an ocean of calm. She was fiftyish, with graying hair and a slim, almost ascetic figure. She turned finally to look at Matt and Ione. "Don't mind him. He doesn't like the Union. Everyone knows that tech crew are a bundle of dicks."

"Come on, Anne!" Gonsalves protested.

Anne pursed her lips. "They are dicks." She held out a hand. "I'm Anne Raskin."

Matt and Ione introduced themselves and shook her hand. Anne went serious. "You guys should still be careful. Sleep together?"

"What?" Ione and Matt asked in unison.

"In close bunks, I mean," Anne corrected.

"Yeah." Matt glanced at Ione. Her face was red.

"Keep it that way. For a while anyway. Who's sponsoring you, our captain?"

"Sponsoring?" Ione asked.

"They'll be working," Captain Gonsalves broke in. "Go to the boards first thing tomorrow, pick something you're qualified for. Not weapons or ships. Internal. Still plenty of repairs to make."

"Yes, sir," Matt said.

"No sirs here!" Gonsalves snapped, but he seemed to be in a better mood. He let them watch the rest of the velocity-matching maneuver, then even gave them some tips on the highest-paying jobs.

That night, Matt and Ione made it a point to hang out as long as possible in Roberto's Retreat, until the crowd had died down and the ship had drifted off to a quiet place. Matt didn't know what he could ask Ione about her life, without stepping into a minefield of bad memories. So he spent most of the time answering her questions about the Union, about his life, about himself. He wasn't sure how much of it made sense to her, but she watched him with apparent interest.

When they got under the covers, it took him forever to go to sleep. All he could do was stare at the bare steel of the bunk above him, knowing Ione was there.

But in the next week, as they made their way to Tierrasanta, it became more of a routine. Matt and Ione took jobs together, doing a lot of the grunt work of slopping plastic putty into cracks, hauling broken stone, and replacing bent reinforcements from their big battle. They got some hard stares and nasty comments, but nobody openly engaged them.

And, as they worked, they learned the reason they were going to Tierrasanta. For all their repairs, there was a ton of work they couldn't do. They needed to go into a full Displacement Drive dock for more permanent fixes. There was even a betting pool on how broke the captain would be when he got the bill. Some of the more morose crew members speculated that it might be enough to bankrupt him.

Captain Gonsalves wasn't angry, Matt realized.

He was scared.

9

TECH

From orbit, Tierrasanta was a mix of dun-colored rocky continents with olive green bands of vegetation and calm, deep blue seas. The continental mass was far larger than Earth, with only fifty-five percent of the planet covered in ocean. Only a few wispy white clouds wreathed the planet, and two tiny polar ice caps looked almost like an afterthought.

It could be any of a dozen Universal Union frontier worlds, Matt thought. A fringe planet valuable in terms of resources or strategic position, but too marginally Earthlike to merit full inclusion in the Union Congress.

It had taken the *El Dorado* three attempts to match their velocity to a proper Tierrasanta orbit. Three attempts, each with a half dozen Displacements. But now that they were in a stable orbit, the repair ships swarmed in.

Matt watched through one of the remaining portholes as they clustered around *El Dorado*. The ships were huge scaffolded structures, with utilitarian gray-white cargo boxes bolted along their length. On either end, bell-shaped fusion ports provided thrust. Along their length, cranes and zero-g manipulation arms sprang from the scaffolding. Some were already at work on the *El Do-rado*. The faraway grind of steel on stone filled the ship.

Maybe the bankruptcy talk was overblown, Matt thought. Everything seemed to be moving right along.

Still, it didn't hurt to be sure. Matt took every job he could in the spaceship dock. His Demon still hung on a rack, a hulking red humanoid figure, polished and perfect against the backdrop of battered ships. It wasn't as though Matt had to worry about any of the *El Dorado*'s crew getting into it. The Demon was keyed only to Matt's neural interface.

But they could sell it wholesale, a little voice whispered in Matt's mind.

And who wouldn't want a chance to dismantle some of the Union's most prized technology? Matt wondered. Captain Gonsalves's dismissal of the Mecha market didn't sit right with Matt. If he was really hurting for money, he'd find a buyer.

After all, there was nothing stopping them from simply pulling it out of the dock with a winch. Maybe they'd already sold it. Maybe that's why the repairs were going so smoothly.

After the first couple of days above Tierrasanta, Matt started wearing his interface suit under his worker's overalls. The damn thing was hot, and the tight silicone ripped at every regrowing body hair he had. But it would warn him if they were tampering with his Demon. If they tried cutting into the pilot's chamber, or if they hooked it up to a winch, it would let him know.

This is crazy, Matt thought as he worked on welding the scaffolding in the spaceport dock.

No. It wasn't. He was just protecting his interests. It made total sense. Matt looked up at the shining red giant once again and licked his lips. Maybe he should just take the Mecha himself. Head down to the planet. Make his own deals. He could get in the cockpit on his break. Even just Meshing for a while—

Mesh. Matt groaned. He longed for it. That amazing high, that feeling he could do anything. That's why he was fantasizing about taking his Demon. He just wanted to get inside and Mesh for a while.

Then why don't you? that little voice asked.

Because I don't need it, Matt told himself. *I'm not addicted.*

Yes, you are. That voice again. That grinding, screechy voice, almost like the ghost in the machine was talking to him, here outside the Mecha.

No!

Just give in. Get in the cockpit. You'll feel better. It's your Demon anyway. Do what you need to do. You're a God inside it. The voice beat at him, growing more and more insistent.

"Are you all right?" Ione asked.

"I'm not!" Matt yelled. Snapping back to reality, he saw that his plasma torch had cut halfway through the expanded-steel decking he was supposed to be repairing. Ione had put down her wrenches and come over to see to him.

"Sorry," Matt said, pulling the torch up and snuffing the plasma. "I—I'm more tired than I thought."

"You're not sleeping well," Ione told him. "I hear you tossing and turning all night."

Thinking about my Demon. "If you're up to hear me, how come you aren't tired?"

"I don't need as much sleep as you do," Ione told him with an impish grin.

Her mood had improved remarkably in the past week. Whatever process was at work rewriting her genome had yet to manifest. *Maybe her father was wrong,* Matt thought. Maybe she was never treated. Or maybe the transformation had already taken place, and it was too benign to notice.

"Then you should do something else," Matt grumbled, unable to keep the irritation out of his tone.

"Sometimes I do," Ione said.

Matt opened his mouth, then closed it. He didn't want to ask. He wasn't her keeper. They were together by chance, nothing more.

"Shit work, that," Anne Raskin said, passing by on an overhead handrail. They'd learned Anne had grown up Union like Matt. She didn't say much more, except her parents had raised her on Geos.

"Yeah, sorry!" Matt called.

"Try to keep your mind on your job," she called back.

"Yes, sir!" Matt said, unable to stop himself.

Anne's yell of "No sirs here!" echoed through the spaceship bay. All eyes turned to look at Matt. He reddened and sparked up the torch again to fix his error.

But even then, he kept looking up at the Demon.

Matt took a loading job down on Tierrasanta. He told himself it was so he could see another world, an Aliancia world. The Aliancia was supposedly the sleepy backwater of interstellar governmental organizations, a place where a few bribes would buy you a life away from the rules and regulations of the Union. His refugee ship had traded with some Aliancia worlds, but he'd never had enough spare money to go down to the surface. He'd never seen one.

But was that the only reason he went down? A little voice kept whispering to him, *Because you're farther away from the Demon.*

And it did keep him at arm's length from the Demon. Didn't that prove he wasn't addicted? Didn't that show he could let it go?

Says the guy still wearing his interface suit, that little voice said.

Matt shook his head. It wasn't addiction. It was just a logical precaution.

Being down on the surface was interesting. Tierrasanta, on first glance, looked a little like a Union colony world. At least until you noticed how old the port city of La Malinche was. Low, native stone buildings stretched out for several kilometers from the main spaceport, with a cluster of midrise skyscrapers standing at the edge of a broad river. The city had grown for decades, maybe over a century, spreading far from the first landings without a Union-style master plan.

La Malinche's spaceport itself was like any other. Kilometers-long runways of fusion-glassed soil stretched out in a patchwork pattern to accommodate horizontal shuttles, while a wide, black-blasted patch served VTOL craft. Large warehouses and hangars backed up to the city, served by an ancient rail line that snaked deep into La Malinche.

In addition to the *El Dorado*'s landing shuttles, there were a dozen brightly colored craft bearing the red, white, and green Aliancia stars, and a gigantic VTOL lander that might once have been Taikong, but was now so modified that its origin was beyond recognition. It bore the Corsairs' thousand-dagger crest. Powerloaders swarmed around the thing night and day, busy with an immense load of cargo from La Malinche. Their operation far dwarfed the *El Dorado*'s. Matt wondered which Corsair faction they were.

His curiosity spiked the next day when the *El Dorado*'s ground crew had to pick up some specialized transmitting electronics from a warehouse near the immense Corsair ship.

The interior of the warehouse wasn't the usual neat

rows of packaged gear; it was more a grab bag of everything from the latest FTLcomm antennae to ancient flatscreens, all placed haphazardly on giant racks that stretched fifteen meters to the ceiling. Surplus and reclaimed gear. That wasn't unusual. But one of the items was.

Matt stopped stock-still at the end of one of the junk corridors. In front of him stood a Union Mecha Corps Hellion, its chest unfolded and one of its arms partially disassembled. Carbonized blast scars marred its blackchrome finish, and its biomechanical skin was peeled back from the side holster that would normally hold a Zap Gun. The Zap Gun itself was gone.

A Hellion? his mind screamed. Hearing that the Corsairs had Mecha was one thing. Seeing a pinnacle of Union-funded technology piled among racks of surplus tech junk was a punch in the gut.

A dark-skinned woman came out of the Hellion's chest cavity and sat on the stairs to the cockpit, her head bent low over a glowing slate. She wore a white jacket that was smudged with dirt and pale red hydraulic fluid, and her hair stuck out in crazy spikes from what was once a carefully pulled-back bun. She glanced up at Matt once and went back to her slate, almost as if she had never seen him.

Metallic footfalls came down the corridor behind Matt. He turned—and jumped in shock. Two more Mecha were headed his way. But these weren't Hellions, Demons, or anything he'd ever seen in the Corps. They were multisegmented, dull silver, with four arms, like the strange things he'd seen on Keller. They were flanked by two men in formfitting gray uniforms, with a Corsair thousand-dagger insignia on their chest.

Instinctively, Matt dropped behind the end of the racks, prepared to fight. What were those things doing here? Were they from that other Corsair ship?

"Already?" the woman on the Hellion stairs called out, looking up at the pair of Mecha.

"Afraid so, Dr. Lira," one of the men said.

"Another four hours?" Dr. Lira pleaded.

"Not a chance. Boss wants this loaded now."

"Two hours?" She looked back longingly at the cockpit.

"Now," the man said, his voice firming.

Dr. Lira sighed and jumped off the stairs. A young man, also wearing a dirty white coat, came out from behind the partially dismantled arm, holding a strip of biomechanical muscle.

"Make sure you leave all the parts, Doctor," the Corsair said, his voice hardening.

"Of course." She nodded at the kid, who tossed the biomechanical strip inside the Mecha's chest.

The researchers stood aside as the two silver Corsair Mecha flanked the Hellion, picked it up, and carried it down the corridor and out into the spaceport. The men followed the Mecha. They headed straight toward the giant VTOL transport, where they quickly blended in with the rest of the Powerloaders that swarmed around it.

Those aren't Powerloaders, Matt realized.

Seen at a distance, they looked like Powerloaders, but every single one of those things was the silver-segmented Mecha. Entire platoons of the things.

What kind of Mecha were those? And what was that faction?

A sigh made him turn. Behind him, Dr. Lira and her compatriot were watching wistfully as the Hellion disappeared up into the belly of the Corsair transport.

"Who are they?" Matt asked.

Dr. Lira started, as if seeing him for the first time. "Who are who?"

"The Corsairs that just took the Hellion."

"They're Corsairs. I don't know. Wait—you know what a Hellion is?"

Matt frowned. Shit. He'd said too much. He grabbed at the collar of his coverall and zipped it up even farther, to make sure it covered his interface suit.

"We've gone up against the Union," Matt said, standing up straight.

"What do you know about Hellions?"

Matt made himself laugh. It sounded forced and artificial. "I know they're hard to kill. Are you trying to come up with a better way to kill them?"

Dr. Lira shook her head. "No. They're—they're really odd technology. It's a blending of nanomachines and artificial neural structures, at its base level, but I have no idea how it's all coordinated."

Interesting, Matt thought. He opened his mouth to encourage her to talk more, but she interrupted him before he could get started.

"And there's a neural interface to the pilot too," she said. "I can't see how that can be safe. They've had that Hellion in the warehouse for six months, and all the hawks have been saying, 'Use the damn thing to defend La Malinche!' But I don't want to know what would happen to the pilot."

Mesh, wonderful Mesh, Matt thought. "You've had this thing for six months?"

Dr. Lira pouted. "And we only got permission from the bureaucrats to study it a week ago. Now they've gone and sold it to the Corsairs, and we haven't got half the answers we need."

Sold it. Sudden spikes of fear jolted through Matt. Just as they could sell his Demon. Maybe they'd somehow disabled the warning systems. Maybe it was already gone.

No. He couldn't think that. Not now.

"It looks like that faction already has Mecha," Matt said, nodding at the Corsair VTOL ship outside. "I wonder why they need a Union piece."

"Are you kidding?" Dr. Lira said. "Where do you think they learned how to make the Lokis?"

"Lokis?"

"Those things," she said, nodding at the silver Power-loaders.

"What faction are they?" Matt asked.

"I told you, I don't know. Maybe the Cluster, maybe Last Rising. Why? What faction are you from? Don't you have Mecha?"

Yes, Matt thought. *We have one.*

"No," he told her.

Matt paid the cancelation fee on his loading job and went back to the *El Dorado* on the next cargo carrier, squeezed between two-meter-high plastic containers of raw soy protein. His mind chanted terrible thoughts: *My Demon's gone. They've already sold it. They only agreed to let me go down on the surface because they wanted to get rid of me. I'll never see it again.*

But his interface suit told a different story. His Demon hadn't been compromised. Its systems still reported back FULLY OPERATIONAL. READY TO DEPLOY.

But maybe they'd figured out how to spoof it. Maybe they'd had help from the other faction, which was clearly much more technologically advanced than the crew of the *El Dorado*.

But as they approached, he noticed that the repair ships had stopped their work. The arms were retracted, and no space-suited figures swarmed near the big rock of the *El Dorado* anymore. Had they run out of money? The repairs were scheduled to take three more days. The quietude was both reassuring and troubling.

When they arrived in the spaceship dock, Matt stopped stock-still, his breath going out of him.

His Demon was gone.

Matt shoved through the cargo containers before they'd even docked and pushed his way to the air-lock doors. They'd done it! Stolen his Demon! Red, acid-burning spikes of anger flared through him as he waited for the locks to open. The other passengers stayed away from his clenched fists and flushed face.

Matt flew out the air-lock door and nearly collided with Ione and Captain Gonsalves. In a flash, he grabbed a handrail for leverage and kicked the captain hard with both feet, sending him flying down the corridor.

"Matt!" Ione shouted, and dove for him. But Matt had already pushed off in pursuit of the captain. He reached the man as he hit the opposite wall and grabbed a handrail. Matt swung hard at his face, but Gonsalves ducked. Matt's hand glanced off the hard rock wall, skinning his knuckles and sending a bolt of pain through his arm. The captain yelled something at him. Matt didn't care. He wound up so he could hit him again.

Matt's arm was caught. He yelled and whipped around to strike his attacker. It was Ione. She grabbed his arms and pinned him to the floor. Matt couldn't do a damn thing except scream to get his Mecha back.

"Stop it!" Captain Gonsalves yelled, pulling himself up. "Your Mecha's still here. Damn crazy Union addict!"

"We should have told him," Ione said.

"Yes. We should. The Cluster should have gone to another planet to reprovision too. And he should have stayed down on the surface awhile longer."

Matt screamed and bucked, but Ione and the two men held him securely.

"We relocated your Mecha," Captain Gonsalves said. "The Cluster—"

"Liar!" Matt yelled.

Gonsalves pursed his lips, then continued. "The Cluster wanted to come by for a visit. We couldn't let them see your Demon, so we moved it to the, uh, secure cargo dock."

"You're lying! Show me!"

Gonsalves grinned. "If I'm lying, how can I show you? Now, do you want to listen to reason, or do you want to fight some more?"

"You sold my Mecha! To finance your repairs!"

Gonsalves's expression darkened. "I don't think so. Especially since the Cluster's motto is 'if they have one piece of tech, they probably have more, might as well take it all.' No way I'm going to have them annex the ship."

"He's telling the truth," Ione told Matt.

Matt shook his head. It kinda fit together. Made sense. But—

"Show me!" he said.

Gonsalves sighed. "I'll do better than that. I'll see you take it for a spin."

"I don't need to Mesh!"

"I disagree," Gonsalves said.

A security team joined Ione and dragged Matt down through rough, dusty corridors to the other side of the asteroid ship. Captain Gonsalves followed. They came to a dead end, solid rock. Matt knew exactly what was going to happen. They'd kill him now, and that would be the end. He thrashed against his captors and succeeded in getting one arm free. Ione, flash-quick, helped them get ahold of Matt again.

"You sold me out!" he yelled.

"Oh, please," Captain Gonsalves said. He did something on his slate, and the rock wall pivoted aside. Beyond it was a conventional air lock. Through the window,

Matt saw a shadowy space, lit by pinpricks of orangish sodium lamps. Something large and red hulked inside. His Demon!

"Let me in!"

They cycled the lock and took him out into the large space. Racks for cargo, largely empty now, lined the interior walls of the dock. A larger pair of steel doors on one side of the dock warned EXTERIOR EGRESS-NO LOCK!

A smuggling dock, Matt thought. But it was just a whisper next to the other thoughts churning in his head. Because inside the dock was his Demon. Matt's heart pounded. Everything was okay. They were telling him the truth.

"Let him go," Captain Gonsalves said. The security goons let Matt loose, and he pushed away from them to float toward the giant Mecha.

"Get in the damn thing," Gonsalves called. "Don't come out until you can act human again."

"I'm not addicted!" Matt yelled back at him.

Laughter was his only answer.

It didn't matter. What did they know? It was his Mecha, and if he was addicted, maybe that was just fine. He irised open the pilot's cockpit and dove in, not even bothering to remove his jumpsuit. It didn't matter. Matt snugged on the viewmask and closed the iris, feeling the warm magnetorheological gel flood the chamber.

Mesh, he thought.

Warmth exploded inside him. It was like being taken apart and reformed into another being—a being with atomic energy in its veins. Matt shivered in pure pleasure. He could do anything. Be anything. He could break through the dock doors and be free. He could rule Tierrasanta like a king.

Matt forced his rushing thoughts to slow. Yes. He could. And deep within non-Union space, he'd probably quickly meet a Corsair faction like the Cluster. Maybe they had enough tech to take him on. Better to stay here and play defense.

Matt sighed. Everything that Gonsalves said rang true. He'd been out of his mind.

Addicted.

"So, are you ready to hear how you can help us?" Gonsalves said when Matt came out of the Mecha.

The security guards were gone, but Ione still watched him steadily with her yellow-and-violet eyes. Those enchanting eyes.

"Help you?"

"Yes. Despite your addiction, you aren't a complete idiot," Gonsalves said. "You called it before. We're out of funds. I stripped the secure dock, I hocked my own stuff, I sold bonds to all the crew, and we're still in a pinch."

"I won't sell the Demon," Matt said.

"That's not what I'm thinking about."

"Then what is it?"

"The Cluster is here. They're one of the two or three richest Corsair factions. They could pay for our repairs out of the change they find in their couch."

Matt shook his head. The phrase meant nothing to him.

"Old Earth expression," Gonsalves said.

Like Michelle. *Easy as pie.* A pang of regret and loneliness pass through Matt. What was she doing right now? Enjoying a stay on Eridani? Or wiping out more innocents in the name of the Union?

Gonsalves saw his reaction. "What's the matter?"

"Thinking of someone," Matt told him. "Someone from Earth."

Gonsalves blinked. "Earth native?"

"Yes."

The captain sighed, and his eyes went blurry and unfocused, as if he were looking at something far away. "I've always wanted to visit Earth."

"It's a backwater."

"It's our damn home!" Gonsalves exploded. "The origin. Where we started. Doesn't that mean anything to you?"

Matt held back a chuckle, remembering the hot and smelly Cape Canaveral swamps. "Why don't you go?"

"Because the Union controls it!" Gonsalves said. "Why do they have a right to monopolize Earth?"

Matt shook his head, surprised at Gonsalves's heated outbursts. It was like seeing a small piece of his soul. "What do you have in mind?" Matt asked.

"For what?"

"For me."

Gonsalves blinked. "Yeah. You. Here's the idea. The Cluster would pay good money to have a chat with a real live Mecha Corps officer."

Matt started. A chat? More like an interrogation. They'd want Union secrets. And he wasn't ready to simply sell the Union out.

"No," Matt said.

"They wouldn't have to be real answers," Gonsalves said.

"I can't do it."

Gonsalves went red. "You've seen what the Union has done. And you still want to protect them?"

"No."

"Then why not?" Gonsalves asked.

"I don't want another Geos." Rayder's attack. Five million dead. Even if the Union was experimenting on HuMax, their civilians didn't deserve to be slaughtered.

Gonsalves winced. "Yeah. I hear you. But I'm out of

options. Either I find some more funds or we're going to be parted out right here where we sit."

Matt shook his head.

"You don't understand, do you? If they take us apart, they'll absolutely get your Demon. And you. And Ione. And whatever else they want."

Matt frowned. That was a problem. And he couldn't just get in his Demon and set out on his own. There were too many question marks. "What's to stop them from taking me with them?"

"We do it on Tierrasanta, under the protection of the Aliancia. Even the Cluster won't chance their heavy-matter guns."

"You've thought this through."

Gonsalves gave Matt a thin, sad grin. "I've had a lot of time to think about it."

Matt sighed. "No other choice?"

"None."

How bad could it be? Matt wondered. He could pick and choose what he would tell them. And when it came to Union defense, he didn't really know that much. He knew even less about Mecha tech. And maybe this would be his chance to ask about those segmented Mecha. The Loki.

"A half hour. No more."

Gonsalves blew out a big breath, all the tension leaving his body. "Thank you. I'll get it set up."

They shuttled Matt down to La Malinche and took him on a train to a large government building, where the Cluster had set up a conference room. A magistrate of the Aliancia courts and his retinue sat as observers on one side of a large oval table, and Captain Gonsalves and his armed guards sat at another.

The Cluster had sent only one man. He walked into

the room, exchanged pleasantries with the Aliancia and with Captain Gonsalves, then went to sit next to Matt. He was a thin, dark-skinned man with deep brown unblinking eyes. He wore the same formfitting uniform as the two Corsair Mecha handlers, but with an additional gray stripe on his shoulder.

"Thank you, Major Lowell, for talking with us," he said mildly, extending a hand. "I'm Petr Volinsky, ranked subcommander in the Cluster."

Matt made himself shake the subcommander's hand. His grip was firm and his hand was cool. The man displayed little emotion, and his eyes fixed Matt with a calm stare.

"I see you wore your Neural Interface," Petr said. "That will make this a lot easier."

"What do you—"

But that was as far as Matt got. The subcommander extracted a small black box and slate from his pocket and pressed a button, and suddenly the conference room disappeared.

Matt stood on an endless gray field, dimly lit by an unseen sun. His heart thundered as he whipped around, trying to figure out where he was. He tried to yell, but he had no voice. He raised his hands, but he couldn't see them. His body wasn't there! He was nothing, just a disembodied mind.

A familiar warmth stole over Matt, soothing and uplifting. Things stirred in the gray mist, things that smelled like dust and crackled like static. Talons scraped the surface of Matt's mind.

Mesh. The subcommander had somehow placed him in Mesh.

That little box must be some kind of mental interface. Matt's soundless scream echoed only in his own mind as the talons raked harder.

Don't struggle, said a grating whisper. *Your mind is very interesting. Many things here.*

Of course! His Perfect Record! If they were Meshed with him, they could pull any information they wanted. This wasn't an interrogation; this was a way to suck his mind completely dry.

Matt thrashed against the talons. Their cold touch retreated from the surface of his mind, then plunged deeper. Memories spun toward the surface: working with his father on Prospect, and his trip back to the planet as a cadet.

Jotunheim. They could find the location of Jotunheim, the former HuMax capital. The wonders they could find there. They didn't care about any Union defenses or Mecha Corps strategy—they were going for the ultimate repository of that fallen civilization's superscience.

Matt grasped the coordinates away from the scratching claws of the Corsairs' mind-control. Angry screeching reverberated in his mind.

Give the coordinates to me! Give them now!

No! Matt fled over gray fields, frozen now with chilling ice. Cold, hard blades slashed harder at his mind. It would have the answer in a second.

But if it was connected to him, he was also connected to it. Maybe it was like the thing in the Mecha. Something you couldn't fight—but that you could subsume.

Matt thrust the coordinates down into the deepest jumble of his mind, feeling a momentary flash of a million dark emotions—rage at his father's death, desire for Michelle and Ione, righteous anger against the Union. He grabbed at the talons and ignored the razor pain as he took it in. The thing dove hard into his mind and tried to grab at the coordinates, but Matt had it now. He fed it every irrelevant thing he could: terror at his first training at Mecha Camp, old sayings from Pat, his refugee boss, painful images from Ash's death.

The thing screamed and recoiled. Matt grinned as it struggled against him, shredding through the weight of his memories. Brilliant, blinding pain raced through his mind.

Give me what I want!

But Matt wouldn't let it. He took his jealous anger at Kyle and flung it at the entity, screaming as it sliced through his feelings. The thing was deep in his mind now. It was hard to tell where he ended and it began. It was only a nanometer away from the information it desired. Close, so close. Its voice shrilled with glee.

Confirm—

Flash. He was sitting back in the conference room, amid the babble of angry voices.

"—no unadmitted technology aids, we told you!" the Aliancia magistrate yelled at the subcommander. Captain Gonsalves's security men stood, pointing stubby Aliancia J-40 pistols at the Cluster's man.

Petr held up his box and slate. "It is off."

"This is a civilized discussion, not a mind rape!" the Aliancia magistrate grumbled. "Either you converse with this man or you leave."

"If it is civilized to wear a neural interface, it is civilized to use technological aids to facilitate discussion," the subcommander said mildly.

"You will give the neural interface to my staff if you wish to continue," the magistrate said as two new men flanked Petr.

The subcommander smiled and stood. "That will not be necessary. Thank you for your time, Major Lowell."

Matt just blinked up at the man, brutal afterimages from his Perfect Record scattering his thoughts. Done? He was done? It didn't make sense.

"The monetary part of the contract is binding, whether you terminate the discussion early or not," Captain Gonsalves said.

Petr nodded. "It has already been made good. I wish you an excellent day, Captain."

Matt watched, stunned, as the man walked out the door.

What the hell was that technology?

And—even more frightening—had he gotten the information he'd come for?

10

BETWEEN

Captain Hector Gonsalves's secret home, Esplandian, was one of the most bizarre places Matt had ever seen.

At one time, Esplandian had been just a large oblong asteroid, twenty kilometers on its short axis and thirty-three kilometers on its longer side. Ejected from a solar system a few billion years in the past, it had found its way to the dead, dark space between stars, where Displacement Drive ships almost never passed.

By dumb luck, an early Displacement Drive ship had detected it in the first days of the Expansion, but had never thought to add it to the catalogue of systemless objects in deep space. No real wonder; in those days, such a mass was too large to turn into a Displacement Drive ship, too small to be a meaningful gravity well, and too far from the nearest sun for easy solar power.

And that would probably have been the end of the wandering rock if Hector Gonsalves's great-grandfather four times removed hadn't been on the ship that found the asteroid. Because, twenty years later, he returned to claim the mass for himself, not as a ship but as a home.

The story was that he'd foreseen the HuMax rising as a threat to humanity, and wanted a safe harbor away from the early colonies at the dawning of the Expansion. Or at least that's what Hector told them as they approached the giant asteroid on a cramped shuttle filled with crewmen from the *El Dorado*.

Matt only half listened, staring at the amazing thing before him. Over the last two hundred years, Esplandian had been hollowed out, built up, and refitted into a small city in space.

Buildings made of native concrete and steel stuck out of the asteroid at crazy angles, with warm yellow light streaming through ten thousand pinprick windows. At one end of the asteroid, a sprawling junkyard of spaceships covered the native stone. Matt picked out battle-scarred Taikong freighters, utilitarian Union transports, and ancient open-scaffold ships bearing the flags of dead Earth nations. Most had been cannibalized for parts. On the other side of the asteroid, open space docks hosted a similar bizarre array of functional spacecraft. Across the middle of the rock, some enterprising souls had rearranged boulders to approximate the Corsair thousand-dagger flag.

"... and that's the only reason they call my brother, Federico, 'mayor of Esplandian,'" Captain Gonsalves was saying when Matt tuned back in. "Our family founded this place and built it to the fifty thousand souls you see today."

Matt suddenly understood a lot more about why Captain Gonsalves was a Corsair, and why his particular faction operated the way it did. In some ways, Captain Gonsalves was more of a refugee than Matt ever was. He wasn't just displaced from his home planet. He'd never had a planet at all. Esplandian was his entire life. But he wasn't really a Corsair in the sense Matt had been taught to understand them.

"Where are we?" Matt asked.

"In the Space Between," Hector told him. "Where nobody would look for us. Hell, where nobody would expect us."

"I mean, relative to the Union."

Hector laughed. "That's the real funny part. We're actually just beyond the Union Core, at the interface with Aliancia Space."

So close! Their location unnerved Matt. That was closer in to Eridani than many of the Union colony worlds. If the Union had known about Hector's Esplandian, they would have wiped him out long ago. They wouldn't even bother with Mecha, since there was nothing to preserve here. They'd just send a warship and slice it to pieces.

Another laugh. "I know what you're thinking. But no worries."

"We're near the Union?" Ione asked, leaning against Matt as if for comfort.

Hector shook his head. "A few billion kilometers of Space Between is better isolation than a thousand light-years. There's no reason for them to ever come here. They're interested in worlds on convenient routes, not rocks in the middle of nowhere."

Matt hoped Hector was right. It was unsettling being so close to the Union. It was also frustrating. It reminded him of his pledge to find out what was really going on with the Union . . . and fix it.

At the time it had seemed almost possible. He was Mecha Corps, one of the most highly trusted cadres in the Union military establishment. He talked to people like Dr. Salvatore Roth and Colonel James Cruz. Hell, he'd been on an FTLcomm conference with the Union's prime!

Now, stuck in the middle of the Space Between, on a ragtag Corsair asteroid, what the hell could he do about the Union? Nothing.

And maybe that's okay, he told himself. *Live your life. Let the Union deal with their own problems. Stay hidden, and make your mark here.*

But what about Michelle? Soto? The billions of other innocent people who trusted the Union implicitly? Did they deserve to be kept in the dark, not knowing what was going on around them?

And even more importantly—what did the future hold, even if he stayed hidden? There was still the mystery of the Corsair Cluster and whatever mind-interface tech they'd used on him. Captain Gonsalves was apologetic, but completely unhelpful. He knew little about the Cluster, other than that they were technologically aggressive. He didn't know what the segmented Mecha were, and he didn't seem to care too much about them. They were as removed from his world as a nanosemiconductor factory was from a miner on Keller.

Matt's knuckles were white on the aluminum brace pole of the Corsair shuttle as they docked. He'd spent most of his years bent on a single purpose: avenging his father's death. Would he ever find his new compass?

The docking bay was filled with families welcoming their sons and daughters back, vendors hawking fast food, and currency exchanges that listed the types of barter items they were looking for. Matt stopped stock-still in the melee, overwhelmed by the press of humanity. Esplandian was warm and humid and smelled of algae and body odor. It was like stepping back into a refugee ship. For a moment, he wanted to turn around and get back in the shuttle and ask the pilot to take him anywhere, it didn't matter where. This was too much like his past. It triggered too many painful memories.

Ione walked several steps ahead of him before turning and looking back quizzically. Captain Gonsalves clapped Matt on the shoulder, almost sending him flying in the microgravity.

"Why don't we talk for a bit, Former Major?" he said, nodding at Ione to include her.

"About what?"

"A job."

"There aren't job boards here?" Matt asked.

"Of course. But this might be more interesting."

Reluctantly, Matt nodded and let Captain Gonsalves drag him to a bar that overlooked the docking bay. The proprietor nodded familiarly at Gonsalves and led them to a small, private room in the back. A faded photograph hung over the head of a battered wood table. It showed a pudgy, dark-haired man in a U.S. Space Authority uniform.

Gonsalves nodded at it. "Pedro. My great-great-great-great-grandfather. Or close enough. Founder. You'll see photos of him a lot around here, but it's not like we goose-step around saluting them or anything. People here just like him, and what he created."

Matt shook his head. He had no idea what the captain was talking about. "What's the job?"

Gonsalves sat down at one end of the table and motioned for Matt and Ione to sit.

"Relax. Have a drink." He pulled a bottle of dark whiskey out of a cabinet and then took three drink bulbs from it. Ione looked at hers and wrinkled her nose.

"I don't want a job I have to get drunk for," Matt told the captain.

Gonsalves laughed. "You Union drones. Every one with a steel girder up his ass. This is just a pleasantry. If you don't want it, fine."

Matt crossed his arms and waited.

Gonsalves glared at him, then blew out a breath. "I

was only partially kidding about your Demon being our defense. What do you say about using that thing for us?"

Matt shook his head. "I think I'd rather go to the job boards."

"This pays better."

"And?"

"And you'll be working for the Founding Family."

"Which means?"

"Respect, prestige, confetti at your funeral. Come on, man! You need a new home. We can be that for you. And don't try to say you don't need to get in that thing from time to time. Why not use it for us?"

Matt licked his lips. Captain Gonsalves's mention of his need to use the Demon had immediately spiked his heart rate. A little voice whispered, *Yes, you need it. You know you need it. There's no better feeling in the world. You can do anything in your Demon.*

"What about Ione?"

A little smile. "Ione can't run a Mecha, as far as I know."

"What happens to her if I take this offer?"

"I can use the job boards," Ione said.

Matt shook his head. Too many times, he'd seen her ready to punch ACCEPT on a job that was clearly sketchy. She'd never lived in the real world. For all the abuse in her past, she didn't know how cruel people could be.

"Your job will provide plenty of income for the both of you, if that's your wish."

"With her own room?"

Gonsalves laughed. "Do we look like a rich world? Families room six to a hundred square meters. You'd stay together."

"But—" Matt began.

"Plenty of privacy, if that's what you want."

Ione opened her mouth, as if to speak, then seemed to think better of it. "I can use the boards."

"No!" both Matt and Gonsalves said, in unison.

Tears glittered in Ione's eyes. "I—I don't need your help."

Matt put his arm around her waist. It was amazing how natural it felt. Ione let him hold her for a moment, then shrugged him off.

"I want to do this," he told her.

"So you'll take the job?" Gonsalves chirped, grinning.

Matt sighed and nodded. Only half hating himself.

Matt spent the next few days getting acquainted with his new home. He and Ione were given a "luxury apartment" in one of the newest concrete towers. Matt supposed it was luxurious compared to a refugee ship. Forty square meters, finished polished stone, with two sleeping areas and a reconfigurable main room. It was clean and competent, but nowhere near inviting. One small window looked out over gray asteroid rock and dust, dark in the dim starlight.

Most of the asteroid was given over to agriculture. Over the past two hundred years, forty percent of its interior had been hollowed out. Fusion tubes ran down the length of the space, illuminating microgravity-tolerant plants within the cylindrical space. Half of the jobs in Esplandian were in or around the farms. Planting, harvesting, weeding, waste recycling, and food processing were the local industries. Completely understandable with fifty thousand people to feed. After one fly-through of the damp, fetid space, Matt was very happy he'd taken Gonsalves's offer.

The asteroid's age had a lot of other ramifications. Since the earliest days, Humans and HuMax had lived together on Esplandian. Its population was almost ten percent HuMax today. There was even a HuMax town, where HuMax bodybuilders and acrobats displayed feats of strength and dexterity that humans could only imagine. Oddly enough, HuMax weren't highly represented in the technology or entrepreneurial side, though.

But there were HuMax doctors. It didn't take long for Matt's curiosity to get the better of him. He talked Ione into seeing one.

Dr. Arksham had a compartment deep in the asteroid, near the constant hammering of the diggers. The space was large, fastidiously clean, and well lit with modern antiseptic lighting. Only a small steel plaque announced the doctor's name and specialties:

DR. UVE ARKSHAM
HUMAX & HUMAN PHYSICIAN
SPECIALIZING IN EPIGENETIC COMPLICATIONS

The doctor was an older man with silver-gray hair and bright violet-and-yellow HuMax eyes. Other than a slight stoop, he was in amazing physical condition, with sleek musculature that spoke of hours upon hours of time in the gravity centrifuge. He looked from Ione to Matt and back again, before giving her a tentative smile.

"What brings you here today?" he asked.

Matt looked at Ione, but she wasn't paying attention to him. She stared around the office, her eyes wide and fearful. She took a step back toward the door.

Of course, Matt thought. This was like going back to Planet 5.

"It's all right," Matt told her. "If you want to go, we don't have to do this."

"I—" Ione's eyes locked on his for a moment, before skittering around the room again. "I don't know."

"What's the matter?" Dr. Arksham asked.

"She's had a tough life," Matt said. "This may not have been such a great idea."

"I can go?" Ione said.

"If you want."

Ione drew a shuddering breath and nodded. "I think I can do this. If you stay with me. There are no weapons, at least."

"Weapons?" Arksham exclaimed.

Ione nodded. In fits and starts, with help from Matt, she told the doctor the story of her life on Planet 5 and the experimentation that had been done on the HuMax. Dr. Arksham's expression hardened with almost every word, but he didn't seem surprised at all. When Ione got to her own genetic retranscription, she broke off, tears flowing freely. Matt pulled her close and let her cry, finishing the story for her.

"You're the famous defector," Dr. Arksham said, looking at Matt.

Matt nodded. The word still hurt.

"How does the truth feel?"

"Not good."

"Cold reality is better than warm fantasy," Dr. Arksham said.

Matt nodded. Impulsively, he asked, "Do you hate us?"

Dr. Arksham raised an eyebrow. "Hate you? As in HuMax hate humans, or Corsairs hate Union?"

Matt shook his head. It was a stupid question. He shouldn't have asked it.

"It's all the same level of idiocy," Arksham continued. "There's no gene for evil. There are only people. Some good, some bad."

Matt couldn't think of anything to say. After his growing up knowing HuMax were monsters and Corsairs were the enemy, Dr. Arksham's low-key common sense seemed almost surreal.

"As for you and your decision to defect?" Arksham continued. "I'll say only one thing: good for you. It takes a strong person to see the truth. And stronger to act on it."

Dr. Arksham had Ione get up on the exam table and went through his usual doctorlike things, running tests on a slate with displays too complex for Matt to understand. When he was done, he sighed.

"You have a fever," he told Ione. "Thirty-eight point five Celsius."

"That doesn't sound bad," Matt said.

"HuMax body temperatures are cooler than human norm, so she's running two and a half degrees above basal temperature."

"And?" Ione asked.

"And that's all, so far. Whatever genomic alteration method they're using, it's very, very subtle. Not virus-based at all. I can't detect it. We're either looking at prions or—" The doctor broke off and shook his head. "Or nothing. Nanomachines are fantasy."

"So she might just have a fever?" Matt asked.

Dr. Arksham shook his head. Very slowly, as if speaking to a very small child, he told Matt, "HuMax don't get sick."

Don't get sick? No colds, no flus, no cramps and pox? Matt frowned. He didn't know that about HuMax.

"Then why are there HuMax doctors?" Matt asked.

"When HuMax were made, humanity wasn't so concerned with, well, what they used to call the 'end-use conditions.' When we get old, all sorts of nasty epigenetic-based abnormalities crop up."

Helluva price to pay for not getting sick. Matt looked at Ione, but she just returned his gaze steadily.

"So, what does her fever mean?" Matt asked.

"It means something is going on. Something very much not normal. Something profound. I'm sorry."

"What's going to happen?" Ione asked.

Dr. Arksham looked away. "I wish I knew."

"How long do I have?"

A quick head shake. "I wish I knew that too."

The days slipped away with endless regularity under the unchanging star-speckled black sky. No work to do, no duties to perform. The asteroid never fell under attack. Hector Gonsalves assured him the time would come, but Matt wondered how long he'd pay Matt and Ione to do nothing.

Matt watched retransmitted UUN news and tried to ignore the growing itch to get back in the Demon. He wouldn't let his withdrawal symptoms go as far as they had gone the last time, he told himself. But that didn't mean he had to run back to the thing every day.

Watching Union news was like seeing transmissions from another universe. In the Union's world, all was right and proper. The Unicrats had won big in the elections, on promises to expand the Core Worlds and increase funding to even the most far-flung colonies. The Corsairs were mentioned only as a distant threat, easily countered by the valiant Mecha Corps. Again and again, the Union repeated the same lies: only the Union had Mecha. Mecha were the surgical instrument protecting the Union from the predatory Corsairs. No force could stand against Mecha.

Boy, will they get a surprise if the Cluster follows in Rayder's footsteps! Matt thought. With mental interface technology and hundreds of those segmented silver Mecha, they'd cause total panic if they ever hit a Union world. In time, they might even build up enough of an advantage to take the Union down. But that wasn't the way to right Union wrongs. Dictatorship under the Cluster would be no better than the current leadership, if they routinely used mind rape in their interrogations.

Beyond that, the media was dead boring, except for the football from Eridani, where the game always seemed to be a point of planetary pride. Ione watched the news and some of the games with him for long hours without comment.

Then, one night when Matt was drifting off to sleep, she said, from the other side of the room, "I don't understand your world."

"It's not my world anymore," Matt said.

"Your people."

"They're not my people," Matt protested.

But was that true? He still watched their propaganda. His every thought revolved around how he could fix what was wrong with the Union. Why did he care? Good people were right here, all around him. Maybe better people, overall, than a culture that condoned the torture of people like Ione.

"I'm sorry," he told her.

"For what?"

Matt shook his head. He had nothing to be sorry about. He was the hero here.

Or was he? Would it have been better to let Ione die than be turned into whatever she was going to become?

"About my people," he told her.

Silence for a while. Only Ione's soft breathing, and the almost-inaudible wheeze of the ventilators.

"My people have done worse. I've heard the stories."

It was Matt's turn to lie quiet for a time. Who really started the war? he wondered. Humans, when they created and consigned HuMax to brutal lives on frontier worlds? Or HuMax, for using violence to change their fate?

"We're all just people," Matt whispered. "Why can't we act like it?"

There was the soft rush of covers on the other side of

the room. Ione came to look down at him, her face a charcoal sketch in the starlight from their window. Her lips pressed softly against Matt's.

He tensed, a thousand thoughts arcing like lightning in his mind. *She's HuMax! She's sick! She's—she's—*

Matt kissed her back, hard. *We're all just people.*

After what seemed like an endless and perfect time, Ione pulled back. Her eyes sparkled in the reflected starlight.

"I could go back to my bed," she breathed.

"You could," Matt said, and pulled her closer.

The next day, Matt and Ione shared a late breakfast. Her hand was soft in his as they drifted into Pedro's Mess, the cafeteria-style eatery near their apartment. Matt half expected to see amused glances from Esplandian citizens, but nobody even gave them a second look.

Just people, he thought. Good people.

But something still ate away at him. A funny idea that had come to him while lying awake in the early morning, listening to Ione's soft breathing. A big idea. One that might change everything for everyone.

After breakfast, Matt went to see Captain Gonsalves in his office. It was a cramped little room much like his quarters in *El Dorado*. Etched rock walls, expensive wood furniture, and a holotank showing Esplandian, *El Dorado*, and a handful of ships near the giant asteroid. Hector's brother, Federico, was also there, a slightly older, fatter, and significantly more stressed-looking version of the captain.

"I finally meet the latest stray you brought home," Federico said to Hector, crushing Matt's hand in a strong grip.

"He's more than a stray."

Federico laughed. "You could never resist a sad story."

"He has an important role in the defense of Esplandian and *El Dorado*," Hector protested.

"About that," Matt said. Both men turned to him, as if suddenly remembering he was there. "Are you really secure, hiding out here at the edge of the Union?"

"Yes," Hector said, without hesitation.

"You aren't worried the Union might find you someday?"

"They haven't in two hundred years," Hector shot back. "Why would that change?"

"Technology. Technology always changes. What happens when they work out a new kind of deep-space sensor and find your hiding place?"

Federico shot a tense glance at Hector, who pretended to ignore him.

Matt pressed on. "If they find you, they aren't going to care about the nuances of good Corsairs and bad Corsairs and independent Corsairs. You're Corsairs, and you're too close to the Union. You know what they'd do."

Hector gripped the edge of the desk and looked down, not speaking. Federico licked his lips but said nothing.

"And you know how it'd come out. You won't have a chance against a team of Demons, even with me leading the charge."

"So why don't we let you go now, Former Major, and save some of the public funds?" Hector said, trying for levity.

Federico put a hand on his brother's shoulder. "What would you suggest we do, Mr. Lowell?"

"You can't outfight the Union," Matt told them. "So you have to change the Union."

Federico and Hector both looked at each other and bellowed sudden laughter. "Change the Union? Tell me how that'd work."

Matt grinned. He'd thought a lot about that. They had recognized his value as a Demon pilot, but they hadn't thought about his value as an information resource. All the incredible places he'd been. All the stuff he was forbidden to talk about.

"First, we'd go to Jotunheim," Matt said.

"The HuMax capital world?" Federico asked. "The location was lost in the Human-HuMax War. Everyone knows that."

"My father found it," Matt said. "He worked for the Union Advanced Research Labs. And I've been there."

Hector laughed. "Kid, you and I have to go fishing someday. You have the best stories—"

But Federico was studying Matt intently, as if weighing the truth of his words. He cut off his brother. "What if it's true?"

"It's a real place," Matt said, struggling to keep his words even. "There's a huge city there, with technology beyond the Union. Beyond the Cluster."

Hector and Federico shared a grim look. "Dealing in tech is messy. You'd trade with the Cluster? Last Rising is worse."

"We'd use it for ourselves. We can show everyone the Union created the HuMax!" Matt's voice rose as he saw his chance slipping away.

Federico chuckled. "Everyone knows that."

"Citizens of the Union don't!"

"You don't get it," Hector said, shaking his head sadly. "Meddling in Union business isn't part of our charter."

"Even when the Union will eventually meddle with yours?"

Silence in the room for a time. Finally Federico said, "Where is this planet?"

"You aren't thinking—" Hector began.

"Just getting info."

Matt went to the holotank and punched in the coordinates his father had hidden for Matt's eyes alone, all those years ago. The false-color points of light blurred by, finally centering on a binary system of a miniature black hole and a pale white dwarf star. Floating tags called out the gravity well and radiation profile for the system in angry red.

Federico leaned forward and pointed at the tags. "Would *El Dorado* take that pounding?"

Hector shook his head. "Doesn't matter. That's a five-, maybe six-week trip. One way."

Matt's stomach sank. With their slow-recharge drive, it would take forever to get there.

Federico shook his head. "Out for twelve weeks? We can't do it."

Hector nodded. "Sorry, Former Major. My brother's right. We have shipments to make, and other responsibilities. And I don't think anything less than one of the Union's armored ships could last long there—" Hector broke off, looking at the entrance to his office with a horrified expression.

Matt turned to look. In the doorway hung Ione. Her face was flushed and blotchy, alternately bright red and pale white. Sweat streamed down her temples, and dank locks of hair crawled down her cheeks. Dark sweat stains gathered at her neck and armpits. Drops of her perspiration had peppered her simple light blue blouse.

"Matt," she breathed, grabbing the doorway, her eyes rolling back in her head. Her grip slipped off the door frame, and she floated into the room.

Matt shot to Ione and caught her in his arms. Her entire body was sodden, and she was hotter than any human being he'd ever touched. She shivered in his arms and her eyelids fluttered open.

"It's okay," Matt told her. His voice was strange and

high-pitched; it seemed to come from very far away. Maybe because it was drowned by the other voices screaming in his head: *Is this my fault? What's going to happen now? This changes everything!*

"Not okay," Ione rasped.

"I'm sorry!"

"Don't be," Ione told him. "All just . . . people. Worth it for that."

Matt couldn't say a word. He could only look into Ione's bloodshot gold-and-violet eyes, sparkling with admiration for him.

"I'll get you to the doctor," he said, flying out the door, down the hall, down any hall, with Ione pulled tight to him.

"Hope I remember you," she said softly.

"You will!"

"Hope I don't become . . . a monster."

"You won't!" Matt yelled. "You won't!" Hoping it was true.

11

HIT

The rough rock tunnels of Esplandian rocketed by as they rushed Ione down to Dr. Arksham. When they reached him, he took one glance at her and barked, "Cooling!"

Arksham's assistant rooted through a jumbled mess in a closet and came up with a large, semitransparent bag. They shoved Ione in, strapped her down, and plugged it into a power supply. The plastic immediately began to chill, sweating droplets of condensed water. Ione moaned and struggled, her eyelids fluttering.

Arksham did a bunch more doctorlike things and frowned at the readings on his slate. Matt wished he'd taken a premed course or two back on Aurora.

"What's happening?" Matt asked.

"What do you think? Your Union friends' genetic rewrite is starting!" Arksham snapped, not looking up from his slate.

"They're not my friends!" Matt yelled.

Arksham's gaze came up to meet Matt's. A momentary flash of anger passed through his HuMax eyes. Then he frowned and shook his head. "Right. Sorry. It's just . . ."

"Just what?" Matt wanted to grab the old superman and shake him.

"Just that we have to keep the fever down. And stay calm. We can manage her while she's in this state."

"What happens when the rewrite is finished?"

Arksham sighed. "I told you. I don't know. But I can try to keep her from being killed by the process."

Dr. Arksham's assistant helped bundle Ione onto a table and strap her down. Matt watched helplessly, wondering what he should do. It felt like his fault—but he'd already done everything he could to make it right. Why did he feel so guilty? Because of his association with the Union?

Or something else? Guilt for leading her on, for not breaking contact with her as soon as they'd been rescued?

No. That wasn't it. He didn't know what was in his future. It was as likely as not that Ione was part of it.

But was this someone he actually wanted to spend the rest of his life with? If this was really love, would he even be having thoughts like this?

Or was love actually a spinning jumble of emotions, feeling so deeply so many things, something he couldn't really analyze?

I'm stuck again, Matt thought. *Like with my father on Prospect. The day he died. Am I going to lose someone I love—again?*

"Is there anything I can do?" Matt asked Arksham.

"Unless you picked up a medical degree since I saw you last, no."

"I could—"

Arksham pushed Matt toward the door. "Go."

Matt stopped himself at the door frame, looking back at Ione's bundled form. Dr. Arksham saw the direction of his look, and his expression softened a little. "I'll let you know if anything changes."

Matt nodded and drifted off down the hall. He had no

appetite for lunch, so he went up to see Hector again. The office was closed, with a sign that read BACK TOMOR-ROW.

Matt thought briefly about hunting down the captain, or his brother, but he realized that was just a dream. No matter how much he talked, they simply didn't have the capability to go trolling for superhuman technology on the edge of explored space.

Matt made himself stay away from Dr. Arksham's office, but he couldn't get his mind off Ione. His dinner sat untouched; his Union news spooled past unwatched. When he finally fell into a fitful sleep, it was interrupted by dreams of Mecha Base, rocking under the continuous impact of debris from the Maelstrom it was hidden inside.

Boom.

Big hit. A really big rock. There shouldn't be anything that big in a stable orbit. Maybe they'd strayed from their ideal parabola.

BOOM.

Even bigger. Nothing that big should hit them. Ever. Matt had a sudden vision of Mecha Base shattering under the impact.

Matt's eyes fluttered open. His ears still rang with the last impact. It took him a second to realize where he was. On Esplandian, the Corsair asteroid. Night. His room was dark. Ione was at the doctor's. Strange red light flashed on his internal comms screen.

Strange red light? Matt sat up. In their external window, a large cloud of dust rose over the rough surface of Esplandian. It rolled against a block of brightly lit windows, glowing with internal light. Above the dust was the irregular outline of a new asteroid. This one wasn't any simple Displacement Drive ship, though. Half covered with armor plate, and crisscrossed with scaffolding, it was clearly a warship.

It wasn't a dream.

Esplandian was under attack.

"Mr. Lowell! Former Major! Wake up, it's time to earn your keep!" Captain Gonsalves's voice screeched through Matt's flimsy apartment door, over the pounding of his fist.

Matt ducked as Captain Gonsalves's security team exploded through the door, shattering the opaque plastic.

Gonsalves looked Matt up and down, noting his interface suit. His expression went instantly from total panic to serious concern, the chameleon feat of a man used to managing people.

"You need to be on a ballistic shuttle to *El Dorado*," Captain Gonsalves said, pushing Matt out the door.

"Who's attacking us? What do they want? How many are there?" Matt said as the rough stone corridors blurred past. They were heading down to the main docks. "I saw an armored asteroid! Is it Union?"

"Probably Last Rising, don't know, the one you saw ain't the only one, and probably not, in that order," Gonsalves said. "So far, it looks like they're just making sure we're paying attention. I'm sure we'll hear about the glorious opportunity to join their faction shortly."

They continued down to the docks, taking a shortcut through a small tunnel bored perpendicular through the main shafts.

Matt's Perfect Record parsed Gonsalves's answer, and he shot back. "Last Rising? Are they like the Cluster? How many ships total?"

"First two questions: probably, and worse. We think there's four ships. All armored."

"Last Rising is worse than the Cluster?"

Gonsalves nodded. "The Cluster doesn't go in for the

big hammer so much. But I hear they like to brag. If they talked about you, Last Rising might have come around to see if our Mecha pilot came with a Mecha."

"Who the hell is Last Rising?"

"A new faction. Real powerful. They move into a system, put the hammer down, and next thing you know, everyone's singing their praises. Like they're all brainwashed. Bad, creepy fuckers."

Matt nodded. Corsairs, just like in the Union movies. It was almost a relief. "It won't happen to us."

Gonsalves laughed. "Love your spirit. But what's one Mecha going to do against four Displacement Drive ships?"

Matt grinned. "You'd be surprised."

"I'm gonna buy you lobster dinners for a year at Rodrigo's if you can turn this around."

They plummeted into the main dock. Matt and Gonsalves were packed into a small pod that looked almost exactly like a standard escape vehicle—except for the heavy-duty fusion rocket stretching five meters out its backside. Dense foam sandwich seats smothered Matt as the hatch closed.

The idea was to shoot the pod across to a matching fluid-damped receiving dock on the *El Dorado*, as fast as possible, so the Corsairs wouldn't notice—or, if they did, they wouldn't have a chance to react.

Acceleration slammed Matt back painfully in his seat. His skin stretched and puddled against the sandwich cushions. His vision went instantly gray, before he slid into the complete darkness of blackout.

Next he knew, the hatch on the pod was opening. His ears rang and his vision didn't work quite right. It was like seeing through red haze. Captain Gonsalves's sandwich cushions unfolded, exposing a bruised and unconscious man.

"Captain!" Matt yelled. Gonsalves didn't respond, so Matt pulled him along out into the corridors. The lights were low; the *El Dorado* was still in idle mode.

"Did you get the number of that truck?" Captain Gonsalves said, rousing, as they reached the secure dock.

"What?"

Gonsalves waved a hand. "Old Earth saying."

"We're here," Matt said, cycling the lock.

"Here where?" Gonsalves looked blank. The trip had hit the older man a lot harder than Matt. Matt made himself speak slowly and simply.

"We're on *El Dorado*. I'm gonna go out in the Demon. When I use the Zap Gun, the EM noise will probably cover your powering up."

Captain Gonsalves nodded, still looking confused.

"Power up," Matt said. "We'll need your firepower."

"Esplandian has firepower too."

"Call your brother. Get it online. All of it." Matt shoved Captain Gonsalves toward the bridge and launched himself toward his Demon.

"Let's turn this around," Matt said, under his breath.

I'm home, Matt thought as the rush of Mesh took him. For long moments, nothing mattered—not the Corsairs, not Ione, not even his uncertain future. He was whole and complete, and the warm sun of Mesh illuminated every part of him.

An UNKNOWN comms tag flashed bright red as Captain Gonsalves's voice took Matt out of his reverie.

"New info," Gonsalves told him. "The Corsairs haven't detected that damn ballistic shuttle we just took, or, if they have, they're ignoring it. But now they're jabbering the standard demands: *join the party, you're going to love being part of us, open your hatches to our boarding party, submit or die.*"

"Sounds like a wonderful offer," Matt said, still happily buoyant.

"I'll stick to the little rock my grandfathers made," Gonsalves said, his voice low and bitter.

Matt nodded. He understood that. Gonsalves just wanted to live a simple life, not hurting anyone. Didn't he deserve, well, just to be left alone?

Unbidden, a powerful memory came welling up from his past. Running down the dusty corridors on Prospect as his father grumbled about his work. Work seemed so complicated. Impossible. Matt wanted nothing to do with it, ever. He just wanted to remain free the rest of his life.

But life isn't like that, is it?

Matt switched his Demon to external sensors. New overlays appeared in his POV. They showed the relative position and mass of the *El Dorado*, Esplandian, and four UNIDENTIFIED MASSES. But that was all it could show him. Just a wire-frame view, a positional sketch.

"I'm going to take a direct look," Matt told the captain. Using the Demon, he cycled the locks manually and crept out onto the surface of *El Dorado*.

The lock was positioned facing Esplandian's dock, which meant he wasn't immediately visible from the position of the Last Rising ships. Matt shuffle-walked over the surface until he could poke his visor over the horizon.

Two ships were immediately visible, both partially armored asteroids with massive scaffolding for strength. Neither bore any sigils, flags, or insignias. Presumably there were also two warships on the opposite side of Esplandian.

Total overkill. One would be enough to crush the asteroid if they wanted to. Which meant they wanted to capture it.

A whip-thin line of white light flashed from one of the ships to Esplandian. Vaporized orange-red dust clouds fountained up from the surface. One of the tallest buildings rocked visibly, shedding sheets of concrete and steel. When the beam was gone, a large crater glowed dully next to the building.

We can take this down anytime, they were saying. *Give up now.*

"*They're getting insistent,*" Gonsalves said over the comms.

"Are you powered up?"

"Yes!" Gonsalves's voice firmed.

"What about your brother?"

"Probably hiding under a desk," the captain said. "For now, I have your back. Esplandian'll come online when the firing starts, Federico or no."

Matt grinned. So the captain was the real captain, and the mayor was the figurehead when the captain was away on missions. Gonsalves was a leader of more than he ever let on.

Two more lines arced out from the Corsair ships, cutting figure eights around a pair of tall structures. The brilliant beam glanced one of the residential buildings, which flickered and went dark. Air jetted from the damaged side in snow-white jets.

Matt's anger went white-hot. Enough screwing around! It was time to teach those Corsairs a lesson.

"Do it!" Matt yelled, leaping off *El Dorado* and pulling his Zap Gun in one smooth motion.

Matt pushed his thrusters to full, targeting the nearest Corsair Displacement Drive ship.

Fire, he thought.

The Zap Gun exploded with energy, erasing his view of the ship ahead. A wire-frame diagram showed deep hits on the scaffolding and armor. Matt kept shooting through the intense light, targeting the ship's docks.

ANTIMATTER WEAPON TARGETING, his POV screamed.

Matt reversed thrusters and shot back beneath the bulk of Esplandian. On the other side of the asteroid, two more Displacement Drive ships drifted. Matt sighted down the barrel of the Zap Gun and squeezed the trigger as fast as it could recycle, laughing at the immense power shooting down his arm. Spaceship docks vaporized, scaffolding melted and ran like water, and deep gouges scarred the Displacement Drive ship's armor.

This was it. He was invincible. He'd take them out all by—

ANTIMATTER WEAPON TARGETING. LOCKED, Matt's Pov screamed, changing instantly from targeting to locked. Matt pushed his thrusters past redline, but it was too late. His world went completely white, and he roared in the electrifying pain.

RIGHT LEG FAULT. REGENERATING: 107 SECONDS.

Matt dove for the cover of Esplandian's dock. As he popped out the other side, he had to smile. *El Dorado*'s heavy-matter guns were landing heavy impacts on two of the armored Displacement Drive ships. Armor dimpled and caved in as rock disappeared.

Esplandian's own heavy-matter guns finally came online and pounded the armored Corsair ships. They actually heeled over from the impacts.

Bright threads lanced out from the Corsair Displacement Drive ships, hitting the *El Dorado* hard. Its unprotected rock melted to orange-red slag instantly as hot gas and vapor billowed up from the points of impact. Shiny new comms antennae and observation cameras sagged and disappeared in the blaze.

Matt went full-power toward the closest Displacement Drive ship. It swelled ahead of him as his POV screamed ANTIMATTER BEAM WEAPON TARGETING.

But Matt was too fast this time. He zagged unpredictably as he came closer, using all the g's his side thrusters could give him. They never locked.

Matt fired his Zap Gun at point-blank range down the yawning mouth of a spaceship dock, grinning in delight as red-hot molten steel and stone exploded out its mouth in response. Matt kept firing deeper and deeper into the dock. Eventually he'd reach deep enough inside the ship to hit the Displacement Drive's antimatter power supply, which would be its end.

Something moved in Matt's POV. He turned to look. A swarm of bright, metallic objects shot at him from the other Displacement Drive ship.

Fighters, he thought. But they didn't move like fighters. They moved sharp and fast. And the tags that hovered over the oncoming cloud didn't say UNIDENTIFIED SPACECRAFT. They said UNIDENTIFIED MECHAFORM.

And for a moment he froze.

What was coming at him wasn't a platoon. It was a swarm. A seething, hungry mass of Mecha, hundreds of them, in all shapes and sizes. Most of them were like the silver, segmented Mecha he'd seen on Keller and with the Cluster. The Loki. But Matt also glimpsed vaguely humanoid shapes, as well as wormlike and spiderlike forms. And they weren't all silver. Some were dark and sleek, their reflective bodies and mathematically perfect curves recalling the design of a Hellion. Not quite a Hellion, though. Some were only three or four meters tall. Some were almost as big as a Demon. Some had multiple arms, legs, or wings.

Not just Mecha, but a whole plague of Mecha, Matt's mind gibbered.

Only the Union has Mecha, a sardonic little voice retorted, smelling of dust, prickling like static.

Matt bit back manic laughter and moved. If those Mecha had the same system-scrambling algorithm he'd come up against on Keller, he was done. He didn't have Michelle to Merge with. He didn't have a team to lean on. It was just him.

Matt knew his only chance was to concentrate them in one area so he could take them out en masse. He forced his Mecha to redline speeds, shooting between the *El Dorado* and Esplandian. Glowing red craters pocked the surface of each rock.

"We're getting hammered!" Captain Gonsalves cried through the comms. "Federico wants to surrender."

"Do you?" Matt asked.

"Do we have a chance?"

"Maybe!"

"Maybe?" Gonsalves howled.

"Best I can do!" Matt yelled back.

The Corsair Mecha followed Matt down between Esplandian and *El Dorado*. For a moment it looked like a perfect setup. Matt flipped himself over to face his pursuers and aimed his Zap Gun.

That was when his rear POV lit with warnings.

More Mecha. Another swarm like the first. They'd already figured what he was going to do, and moved to hit him from the rear. He didn't think he could take both groups out before he was engulfed. And he couldn't get around them to target the armored Displacement Drive ships. He was stuck between two rocks and the Mecha swarms.

"What's got more power? Esplandian or *El Dorado*?" Matt yelled at Captain Gonsalves.

"Esplandian has antimatter—"

That was all Matt needed to hear. He dove hard toward Esplandian, thrusters scorching and spitting molten biometal. The Mecha swarms followed.

It was a stupid idea, a desperate idea, but it was all he had. Matt hit the docks hard, instantly sprinting toward a control panel. Behind him, Mecha shot down from the star-studded sky. They hit the decking with hard clangs. Silver Lokis swarmed toward him, blindingly fast.

Matt reached a control panel. The closest of the Mecha swarm were only a hundred meters away. With one arm, he fired his Zap Gun at the horde, blasting Mecha instantly to incandescent gas. He thrust his other arm deep in the panel, thinking, *Merge.*

Matt focused his entire force of will on Esplandian. This was more than a Merge. This was his last hope. If he could reconfigure Esplandian's systems to provide both raw power and processing capability, he had a tiny chance to win.

Matt's mind expanded with Esplandian's systems. Time seemed to slow as he *became* the semisentient processors beating at the core of the ancient asteroid.

Matt dove deeper, into the antimatter core of the asteroid. Huge power beat there, waiting to be unleashed. Matt closed circuits, forged new ones, and channeled the fury of the antimatter toward the surface, toward his Mecha.

But on the dock, his Zap Gun couldn't vaporize all the Mecha; some were too fast, and some had zero-permeability coating. They pressed closer, even as he gunned more desperately. He had only moments before—

The first Loki impacted with Matt, almost knocking him away from the panel. Explosive images cascaded through his mind. His arms and legs jerked as if he'd touched a live wire. This Loki had the same system interrupter as the ones on Keller!

Merged with the semisentient processors of Esplandian, Matt realized what the system interrupter was. All he needed were the countercodes.

Matt caught a glimpse of mathematics, differential equations and probablisitic loops nested sixty levels deep. It was based on a pseudo-random spread-spectrum key. The other Mecha were immune because they could receive the key. Matt just had to tune in to the same transmission.

Paralyzing pain lanced through Matt's chest. He screamed and beat at the raw rock of Esplandian. A single, javelin-sharp arm of a giant spider Mecha stuck deep into his chest panel, pinning him to the rock. He was lucky it hadn't hit the pilot's chamber.

Matt struggled through the pain and pushed the Loki off him. A new warning lit in his POV.

ANTIMATTER WEAPON LOCKED.

Matt glanced up. One of the armored Displacement Drive ships had repositioned itself to get a clear bead on him.

He hadn't won. He'd lost. Everything. Again.

Just like that day on Prospect.

12

GHOST

Matt snapped awake, weightless and shivering. The shattering pain of Mesh withdrawal thundered through his head as he winced against the dim light.

He floated near the center of a small stainless steel cell. Tiny blue pin lights in one wall provided a chill glow, while the impassive eye of a camera lens reflected his every move like a fun-house mirror.

The door was a faint round line, with a three-centimeter-tall slot set into the middle of it. The slot gave Matt a view of a long, dark corridor, lined with many more of the slotted round doors.

Matt's interface suit was gone. All he wore was a thin, bright red jumpsuit.

Captured, Matt thought. This was a Corsair brig. A Last Rising brig.

But that made no sense. He should be dead. There was no reason to keep him alive.

Unless they needed a pilot for the Demon.

Was his Demon still intact? Matt searched his aching memories for an answer, but his Perfect Record couldn't reach beyond the moment he was hit dead-on with antimatter.

Matt's breath quickened and his heart beat faster at the thought of his Demon being destroyed. How deep did his addiction go? Were there more stages to withdrawal? Could he die from it?

You should be asking yourself, "What happens if they have your Demon intact, and expect you to pilot it for them?" a little voice whispered to Matt.

Matt shivered. That was the real question. Would he fight for them, as he'd fought for Esplandian?

Could he flip sides again?

Can you afford not to?

Matt sighed and searched the surface of his tiny cell one more time, but it was as featureless as it looked. The only way out was through the circular door.

Matt sighed and turned to address the camera. "Okay, I'm awake." His voice echoed hollowly in the metallic space.

The camera's opalescent glass lens didn't even twitch. But somehow, somewhere, Matt knew he was being watched. He had to be. They wanted him for something.

"What do you want?" Matt asked.

Still no response. Matt's cell was almost deathly quiet. Even the hiss of the ventilators only echoed in from the corridors outside.

"Come on!" Matt said, and slapped the wall next to the camera.

But its glittering eye just stared back at him.

Many hours later, as Matt was drifting off to uneasy sleep, they came for him.

Matt heard them coming down the corridor outside long before they arrived. Ten fingers, four hands, two strong men slapping on the hollow aluminum railings outside. They didn't chatter as they came closer, and their handgrips were paced in a regular, metronomic pattern, as if they were machines programmed for a job rather than human beings.

Men acting like machines. Men become machines. The thought was sudden and certain.

How can I know this? Matt wondered.

But he was sure of it. Since he had woken, his thoughts seemed to rush at light speed. He could take tiny fragments of data and correlate them with the experience stored in his Perfect Record to understand things in a flash.

Dr. Roth's words came back to Matt: enhanced inference to the point of precognition.

Was that what this was? Matt had never felt so clear. Every small sound spoke volumes. Even the lack of sound. The men outside didn't speak to each other at all. They didn't tell jokes, or talk about last night's game, or even complain about the job.

They weren't here just to do a job. They were controlled. Mind-controlled. And in a gut-churning instant, that reminded Matt of someone else from his past.

But that was impossible—

Shadows fell across the slit in his door. Matt flattened himself against the wall next to it. Maybe he could surprise them as they came though.

A small fish-eye lens poked through the slot in the door and turned to regard Matt.

"Prisoner away from the door," a man's voice said, in a bored monotone.

Matt didn't move.

"Prisoner away from the door, or incapacitating spray will be used."

Shit. Matt pushed himself away and turned to face the circular orifice.

The door clanked open and folded outward. Two men peered in at him. Both wore tightly tailored dark gray shirts and pants, with no decoration other than a small silver bar on their chests. One man was dark-haired and slim; another had mousy, receding hair and an average build. Their eyes were odd—not HuMax, but simply notable by their lack of engagement. The men looked through Matt, rather than at him.

Mind control. Like with Kyle Peterov, the Mecha pilot captured by Rayder, the general in Shadows. The man Matt thought he had killed.

"Take me to your leader," Matt said, suddenly sure who it must be.

He followed the human drones down corridors lined with cell doors. Not a sound came from within any of the cells, but dim shadows moved behind many of the grim slits.

Were these people from Esplandian?

What had happened to Captain Gonsalves? Ione?

Eventually they came to a longer hall, where sparse traffic moved along the handrails. Most of the Last Rising crew were clad in the same dark gray outfit as Matt's guards. Some wore a more decorated version, with two chest bars.

A few wore civilian clothes like Matt. Only the ones in civvies paid him any mind as he passed. A startling number of them had yellow-and-violet HuMax eyes.

A caste system where the more valuable members were under less mind control. Matt's mind raced. His future was clear. Accept or be forced to accept.

The men escorted him to a heavy steel pressure door marked BRIDGE. There were no door screens, no palm-print-based genetic access locks, just a camera eye like the one in his cell.

The two guards paused and waited. After a few moments, the door groaned as its locks were retracted, and it swung inward on a small, featureless chamber with another pressure door on its opposite side. A protective air lock.

Matt barked a laugh. "Can't be too careful, even with mind control."

The two men didn't answer. Matt waited as the first door shut behind them and the other door cycled.

It opened to reveal a conventional bridge: nonphysical displays over multipurpose consoles, with people hunched over systems diagrams. All of the console wranglers wore a different uniform, sleek deep black with a single red stripe on their chest. Aluminum handrails ringed the displays and consoles. A single captain's chair rose above the level of the ship's functional controls. It was currently unoccupied.

Slit windows at the front of the bridge showed a star field and the glittering lights of Esplandian. The residential blocks appeared to be largely intact.

Matt sighed in relief. The giant asteroid hadn't been completely destroyed in the battle.

"Matt!" a familiar voice called. Matt turned to see Captain Hector Gonsalves entering the bridge from a small room off to one side.

"Hector?" Matt asked. The man looked exactly the same as he had when Matt last saw him. He still wore a casual gray suit. Not a single hair was out of place.

Gonsalves grinned at his reaction. "Yes, of course, who else would it be?"

Matt's heart skipped a beat. There was no way Gonsalves should be smiling. He was already under their control.

"Hector—but—what about Esplandian?"

Hector laughed. "It's all a big misunderstanding."

"Misunderstanding?"

"Yes."

"But they attacked your asteroid!"

Hector waved a hand, as if batting away a fly. "You have to keep an open mind."

"And you chose to join them?"

"Of course." Hector's expression was open and child-like. "You will too, once you understand what they're trying to accomplish. They're going to unify all the Corsairs. Exactly what you were beginning to talk about! Take on the Union."

Matt only half heard Hector. "What about Ione?"

"The girl is fine," said a new voice. "Except for the genetic rewrite your Union has inflicted upon her."

Matt looked up to the source of the familiar voice. It was exactly what his accelerated Perfect Record had told him. Anger rose, twisting his guts and reddening his face.

"You should be dead," Matt said.

It was Rayder.

Two meters of perfect HuMax, with dark, close-cropped hair and a chiseled face like something off a classical sculpture. He wore an all-black uniform devoid of any decoration, under a simple gauntlet of dark body armor. His belt held a small dagger and a Taikong P-06 pistol. His intelligent yellow-and-violet eyes fixed Matt with an unflinching stare.

The HuMax who had killed his father. The man whom Matt had cast into the molten core of Jotunheim.

"Dead?" Rayder said, smiling, amused. "More a ghost, soon to return to my old haunts."

"I killed you."

Rayder chuckled. "You forget the first rule of dueling: always ask to see the body."

"I—how—" Matt stumbled over his words as his Perfect Record fed back a thousand painful images. The day Rayder struck Prospect, where Matt's father worked for

Union Advanced Research Labs. Rayder accepting Matt's father's data slate, then killing him in cold blood. Matt's ill-fated charge in the powerloader.

Rayder's one chilling line, as he spared Matt's life: *"Bravery must have its reward."*

And those years, all those years, Matt had spent plotting to avenge his father's death. In the instant that Rayder spared him, he'd made Matt what he was. He'd twisted Matt into a machine, bent only on revenge. A broken machine once that revenge was accomplished.

But his father hadn't been avenged. Rayder still lived!

Rage spiked in Matt. He screamed and lunged at Rayder. His guards caught his arms and held him back.

Rayder didn't even flinch. If anything, his sardonic grin widened. "I expected a warmer welcome. You seem to have embraced the HuMax, if your companion is any indication."

"Where is she?" Matt struggled against his captors, but they held him tight.

"Safe for now. That is, until the Union's genetic rewrite works its way through her system."

"Cure her!"

Rayder laughed and came to sit at the edge of the captain's platform, as if he and Matt were having a friendly chat. "She's that important to you?"

"Yes!"

"You side with HuMax now? With Corsairs?"

"Yes!"

"Then it will be only a small step for you to join me."

"I—" Matt began, then shut his mouth so hard his teeth clicked together. Join Rayder? How could he even think that?

"I know you're confused," Rayder said, his voice almost kind. "But you'd be joining Captain Gonsalves, who voluntarily joined us, when we explained to him what we plan to do."

"Rayder's going to unify the Corsairs," Captain Gonsalves told Matt. "If we're unified, we're the balance to the Union."

"You're mind-controlled," Matt cried.

Captain Gonsalves chuckled, as if amused by the suggestion. "Of course not!"

"Why don't you just mind-control me?" Matt asked Rayder.

Rayder looked away briefly. "Programming is for lower-level functions. I want your willing cooperation."

But something in his tone wasn't right. Matt's accelerated thoughts matched his tones to ten thousand individual memories in an instant. Rayder was lying.

Maybe he's already tried, Matt thought. *Or at least tried as much as he trusts. He doesn't want to spoil you.*

Yes. That headache wasn't just Mecha hangover. It was Rayder's programming as well. Whatever was behind Matt's Perfect Record might have given him some immunity to Rayder's mind control. It might even have triggered his ability to infer and understand at a glance.

"I don't believe you," Matt said. Best to play the game. Get more info. Compute the probabilities.

A momentary flash of anger passed through Rayder's eyes. "Why not? You are the only person ever to fight me to a draw. You have extreme innate talents, especially with respect to Mecha."

Matt frowned. "You have your own Mecha now."

A nod. "We've taken Dr. Roth's work much further than he anticipated."

"You or the Cluster?" Matt asked. They had the same Mecha on Tierrasanta.

Rayder shook his head. "The Cluster are good for

only one thing: intelligence. Our people there helped determine your whereabouts."

"They work for you?"

"They work for me, whether they know it or not," Rayder said, sounding bored. "My informants exist throughout every Corsair faction, and our strength grows in the Taikong and Aliancia domains. My unification is unavoidable."

"Keller. That was you."

Rayder nodded. "By proxy, yes."

Matt's racing mind laid it all bare. Rayder's programmed minions existed throughout the Corsair factions, an invisible network of power. Eventually they would rise, as one, and change the face of the universe.

"Is joining me so different than the changes you have already undergone?" Rayder asked. "You've turned your back on your Union. You've embraced HuMax as human. This is simply the next logical step."

It all sounded so reasonable. So compelling.

"You killed my father," Matt told Rayder.

"And you yourself have made no mistakes?" Rayder asked.

People did make mistakes. Matt made tons of them. And what happened in the past shouldn't define the future.

But it was also completely wrong.

Joining Rayder wasn't the same as joining Captain Gonsalves. It was like joining the Union again. The Union held HuMax against their will and did terrible experiments on them. They had no choice in the matter.

Rayder was the same way. His programmed masses didn't choose to be that way. There was no way Gonsalves chose mind control, and Matt didn't believe that any rational being had ever chosen to have their will controlled by another person.

Just like the Union. Both had decided that their ends justified their means, no matter how terrible they were.

The decision was clear. Even more, Matt's path was crystalline. *Save the universe*. He knew what that meant now. It meant balance and freedom, in all human spaces.

"No," Matt said. "I'll never join you."

For just an instant, Rayder looked genuinely surprised. "You know what you're saying?"

Matt squared his shoulders. "Yes, I do."

Rayder sighed and shook his head. He stood up, went to his captain's chair, and sat down in it. When he looked up, his expression had hardened. "I'm tired of this. Accept my offer."

"No," Matt said. "I'll kill you. This time for real."

Rayder nodded and stood. "Then try to do so. Now."

13

WILLPOWER

Matt shivered, chilled by the cold resolution in Rayder's eyes. Take on Rayder right here, right now, barehanded.

Everything integrated into Matt's Perfect Record to give him a complete understanding of the situation: Rayder's tight jaw, and the corded muscles in his neck, the way he stood, slightly hunched, waiting for Matt to come at him. The glittering anticipation in his slitted eyes. Rayder was furious. This was no act. The HuMax superman was ready to beat Matt to death.

Which was exactly what would happen. There was no way Matt could win against Rayder, strength versus strength. Desperate stats raced in his head: HuMax were two to five times stronger than humans, in terms of both physical strength and speed. HuMax endurance was fifty percent greater than human.

Matt's heart thundered, and his breath came in shuddery gasps. All of his accelerated thought ended in a single conclusion: *I'm going to die today.*

"I'll get in any Mecha and take you on," Matt told Rayder.

Rayder smiled, a slow, sad smile full of menace. "Are

you so addicted?" Rayder removed his Taikong pistol and handed it to Captain Gonsalves, who took it without changing expression.

"I'll take on your entire Mecha fleet in my Demon!" Matt said, his voice rising in desperation.

"If you are to kill me, you will do it here and now." Rayder unstrapped his dagger and handed it to Gonsalves as well. He reached for the clasp of his body armor, popped it off, and hung it over his captain's chair.

"A HuMax against a human isn't a fair fight."

Rayder laughed. "Life is never fair. You play the hand you're dealt."

Matt swallowed. Despite his laughter, Rayder was as angry as ever. Matt wasn't going to talk him down.

"I hope you don't mind if I broadcast this to my Last Rising command," Rayder said, nodding at the camera eyes that extruded eagerly from the bridge's walls. "Such entertainment as this is not to be missed."

And used, Matt thought. His death would be used as propaganda when Rayder went against the Union again. He'd been hiding, rebuilding his power, but it was only a matter of time before he hit the Union—this time decisively.

Good. Let them cancel each other out, Matt thought. But his accelerated thought told him it wasn't that simple. Calculations raced—the number of Mecha he'd gone up against, how large Rayder's organization had to be to spare four Displacement Drive warships on Esplandian, the interior of the ship and size of crew. Rayder might win. Would probably win. And humankind would fall before him.

Matt's death could be the death of freedom itself.

The bridge doors opened, and a stream of men and women wearing civilian clothes came floating in. Every one of them had violet-and-gold HuMax eyes. They gathered around the walls of the bridge, jockeying for the best positions.

"It doesn't hurt to have a few eyewitnesses as well," Rayder said.

Of course. Rayder wanted to gloat. He'd invited his most trusted HuMax companions to watch the show.

"What about them?" Matt said, struggling to keep his voice even. He nodded at Gonsalves, the guards, and the HuMax spectators, who were all waiting eagerly for the show.

"They won't interfere," Rayder said. He waved a hand, and the two guards released Matt.

No choice. He had to go through with it. And somehow, he'd have to win.

Matt took a quick look around the bridge. It was clean and bare of ornamentation. There was nothing he could use as a weapon—not even a single forgotten coffee bulb or worklight in sight. The spectators and crew were unarmed, and the guards' sidearms were snicked away into biokeyed holsters. Even if Matt could grab one, he'd never be able to use it.

He'd always been taught, *If you have to fight, get in the first shot. Fight dirty.* Nice guys ended up in the hospital.

Nice guys ended up dead.

But there was no chance of getting the first shot. Rayder stood tense and ready for him. There was no cover, no element of surprise. No matter how Matt came at him, he'd be ready.

Matt's racing mind ran the probabilities in detail, instantly piecing together all the pieces from his Perfect Record—every fight he'd been in, every brawl he'd seen, every contest of strength he'd glimpsed in passing on a screen.

Turn away: Rayder would be on him in a moment,

slamming Matt's head against the aluminum railing of the bridge hard enough to bend the hard alloy. Go straight for him: Rayder would catch him and snap his neck in one swift motion. Dive under him, hoping for a dirty shot: Rayder's pistoning fist would cave in his skull.

But . . . Rayder's magnetic soles held him in place on the bridge. He oriented himself to the floor like a person born and raised in gravity. And Matt had never seen him fight in microgravity. Maybe, just maybe—

Matt leapt toward the ceiling, far above Rayder's head. The bright lights of the bridge came up fast. He swung from a fixture and risked a backward glance.

Shit! Rayder was less than a meter away. Cords stood out in his neck, and his lips skinned back from his teeth in murderous rage.

Matt's stomach sank. Rayder was fast, insanely fast. Matt coiled and kicked hard at Rayder's face, but Rayder grabbed his leg before he could react. Rayder's fingers dug into his calf like the armor talons of a Mecha.

Rayder ripped Matt from his perch and threw him down at the bridge floor. The room blurred by as Matt flailed in midair. He hit hard on his shoulder. Agony shot through his neck and down his back.

Rayder descended on Matt like an avenging angel. Matt grabbed a rail support to dodge. Too late. Rayder hit Matt like a hammer, pinning him to the floor with his strong legs.

His fist flew down at Matt's face. Matt's right eye flashed bright red, and something like an atomic explosion went off in his head. His neck snapped back agonizingly, shooting electric pain across his shoulders and down his back. Matt's forehead glanced off a bridge railing. He heard someone howling in pain. It took him a while to realize it was himself.

Matt caught a glimpse of Captain Gonsalves, standing

impassively with Rayder's gun, knife, and armor. If he could get to them—

Crack. Another blow landed on Matt's face. Matt's head snapped to the other side. Rayder's grinning face blurred by. Matt's world went red as blood pooled in his eye. Droplets flew off his face, to paint the bridge floor.

This is how it ends, Matt thought. *The next blow will crush my skull against that rail. And that would end the short career of Matt Lowell, former Mecha Corps, now hired security for a backwater Corsair faction.*

Wait. The rail.

Matt arched his back and snapped his head to one side. Rayder's fist flew past his face, only grazing the skin on his cheek. Matt swore he heard the whistle of parting air behind it.

There was a dull bonging noise. Rayder's fist had missed Matt and struck the bridge railing. He'd hit it hard enough to knock the upright out of its welds. Rayder's hand oozed blood, and the clean white bone of one knuckle protruded from his hand. Rayder's face crumpled in pain, and his legs spasmed, releasing Matt.

Matt scrambled out from under the HuMax, grabbing the broken rail and flinging himself at the bridge door. He had to run. It was the only chance he had. If Rayder pinned him again, he was dead.

Matt reached the bridge door and swiped desperately at the door screen. It only flashed red. The doors remained closed. No way out. He was locked in.

A low growl and the rustle of clothing signaled Rayder's return. Matt jumped for the ceiling, not sparing the time to look.

Too late. Another blow sent new crescendos of agony shooting through Matt's gut. Kidney shot. He'd be peeing blood tomorrow. Matt whirled in midair, the room wheeling around him.

A shadow loomed on one side of him. Matt crouched down into a ball, increasing his spin. Rayder shot through the space he'd occupied moments before, his face a rictus of rage.

I dodged him, Matt thought, in an instant almost giddy.

Rayder grabbed a blazing ceiling light and kicked Matt with both feet. This one caught him in the chest like a sledgehammer. Matt went flying back down into the bridge, his lungs whooping to catch nonexistent breath. His head struck an aluminum console with a crack, and warm blood flowed into his hair. Matt wheezed thimblefuls of air into his lungs. Captain Gonsalves stood above him. The man stood and watched impassively, with a far-away look in his eyes.

"Help," Matt wheezed.

Gonsalves's face compressed in concern, but he didn't move to help Matt.

But behind Gonsalves . . . Rayder's door. His ready room? It didn't matter. Matt moved, using all of his strength to leap for the door. Muscles tore in his legs in his last desperate move. Rayder came down on the bridge and swiped at Matt with his crushed hand, spraying warm blood. But he missed. Matt's trajectory was set.

Matt shot through the door, catching its edge with one hand and slapping the interior door screen's CLOSE icon with another. If it was keyed only to Rayder—

The door slammed closed behind him. Something heavy thumped against its hard steel. Rayder.

Matt hammered the LOCK icon. He was in a small, spare room, outfitted with a large nonphysical projection display, two fixed chairs, and a table. Beyond the table, a large, thick window looked out onto the Last Rising Mecha Dock. Beyond, rows upon rows of the silver Mecha covered every wall of the space.

The Mecha Dock!

Better yet, a hatch surrounded the window. This was Rayder's escape route!

Matt shot at the window, palming the hatch to cycle. If the Mecha Dock was in vacuum, he was dead. But he was dead anyway.

The hatch popped open, hissing as the air pressure equalized. Matt's ears popped. But it wasn't vacuum. The Mecha Dock was pressurized!

Matt leapt through the lock. Toward Mecha. Toward freedom.

In the Last Rising Mecha Dock, scaffolding covered every wall and extended out into the center of the space. Thousands of silver Lokis and hundreds of the dark-colored, smaller-than-Hellion Mecha hung from the racks, waiting to be used.

And, in the middle of them all, Matt's Demon towered over all of them.

It had survived. Matt thought. It wasn't destroyed.

But Matt noticed small differences: its joints were simpler, and it had lost a dozen of the ridges that ran down its back. The Demon had been badly damaged in the battle. It hadn't been able to resume its exact form.

Matt didn't care. He whooped with joy and lunged at the giant Mecha. It was the most beautiful thing he'd ever seen. In a flash, he was at the pilot's chamber opening.

But the iris was closed. Matt keyed in the emergency code again and again. The iris didn't even twitch.

Shit! He wasn't wearing an interface suit! No wonder it wasn't opening. The Demon didn't know its pilot was outside.

Matt went down the rows of black Corsair Mecha, but none were open. Nor could he figure out how to open them.

Something—anything—Rayder would be here soon. Matt shot deep into the docks, where the detritus of construction still lay. A single Powerloader sat slumped against the loose rock and shards of an unfinished tunnel.

Matt threw himself at it. But the battery pack was dead. The machine would be nothing more than a coffin.

Air locks clanked open, sending cavernous echoes through the Mecha Dock. Rayder's voice called out into the space: "Face me like a man, and end this now."

Matt slipped out of the old Powerloader, straining to get a glimpse through the expanded steel decking. Rayder was there with full entourage: Gonsalves, spectators, and a half dozen floating camera eyes.

Matt's hand brushed a pile of rubble, and the big rocks shifted. It was only a small grinding noise, but it was enough. Rayder's head snapped around, and his yellow-and-violet eyes fixed on Matt through the decking.

Rayder's face twisted in amusement. He barked harsh laughter. "You return to your childhood weapon?"

Matt froze. A weapon, any weapon, was all that mattered. What could he use?

"I still remember the look in your father's eyes as I shot him," Rayder said. "He looked like you, right now."

Matt's face flushed, hot with rage. "You made me this way!"

"Your father made you. I only shaped you."

And yet still Rayder didn't make any move. Matt frowned. What was Rayder trying to do? Draw him out?

Yes. Matt's racing mind saw it all. In a space this large, Rayder would be at a disadvantage if he moved first. He wanted a clean, quick kill. And he'd taken precautions. He now wore his knife and pistol.

"Bravery must have its reward," Matt said. The words

Rayder had told him when he left Matt behind on Prospect.

"And what a reward it is," Rayder said. "To face me alone on this day. Your name will live on. You will be the man who challenged the gods."

"You're no god. You lost to the Union. You lost to me, on Jotunheim." Maybe he could taunt Rayder into acting first.

"Gods lose battles all the time," Rayder said. "What makes them gods is that they never stop fighting."

"No," Matt said. "That's what makes them idiots."

Rayder's face darkened, but he only advanced calmly to the edge of the scaffolding. Matt shrank back into the shadows behind the old Powerloader, his hands slipping against the hard chunks of asteroid rock.

"This is how it ends for humanity," Rayder said, sticking his head over the edge of the scaffolding to look Matt in the eye. "Crouching in the shadows."

But in that instant, it all came together. The perfect moment. The summation to all his days on refugee ships, tossing rocks out of their gravity wells and thinking of the day he'd get his revenge.

Matt grabbed a baseball-sized piece of the asteroid rubble and flung it at Rayder with one smooth, practiced motion. Pain arced through his bruised collarbone. But his aim was good. The sharp chunk of stone flickered out across the hangar and caught Rayder on the forehead. A pink spray of blood colored the air as the HuMax cursed and staggered back.

In an instant, Rayder's expression turned to murderous rage. He threw himself over the scaffolding and launched at Matt. Now his knife was out in plain view, a sharp and deadly sliver of steel a full twenty centimeters long.

This is it. Matt's heart hammered in staccato pace as he visualized what he had to do.

What you have to sacrifice, he thought.

When Rayder was only five meters away, Matt jumped at the other man. He'd need maneuvering room. It required precise control and microsecond reflexes.

Rayder's hand whipped up as he approached. Matt faked in one direction. Rayder's knife followed him like a laser. Then, at the last moment, Matt brought his own arm up, leaving his midsection unprotected.

Rayder took it. His knife flashed up and plunged deep into Matt's gut. Fiery, incapacitating pain shot through Matt's entire body as he bellowed in agony. It was the end of the world—the end of everything.

Matt gathered his strength and brought his other hand up. In it was a head-sized rock. It hit Rayder right in the temple. A hollow *tock* reverberated through the hangar. Rayder's eyes rolled and lost focus, and his spasming hand missed a grab at Matt's clothes. Rayder hit the rubble hard as Matt continued to float off into free air.

Matt's entire shirt was soaked with blood. The spreading warmth was almost comforting over the radiating pain. If he could just rest for a while, just a while—

No! It wasn't over. Not yet. Matt doubled over, his slitted eyes picking out Rayder's position. Red blood ran down the HuMax's forehead in great gushers. But he'd already staggered to his feet. He leapt again.

Rayder shot at Matt, his furious eyes focused on only one thing: erasing this one human from the universe. Matt looked helpless as he drifted into the big Mecha Dock. Rayder had all the advantage.

Rayder knew it. Triumph lit his expression as he shot across the last three, two, one meters to Matt. His arms reached for Matt's neck. One twist, and it would be over.

Wait, wait, wait, Matt thought. *Now.*

In a single smooth movement, Matt pulled the knife

out of his gut and brought it up hard into Rayder's midsection. Matt's vision went red and black through the pain, but he forced himself to shove it hard, up through the stomach and into Rayder's heart. Hot blood fountained over Matt's hands as the knife found its target.

Rayder spasmed in surprise, grabbing at the knife embedded in his body. He pulled the knife from his heart and swiped at Matt wildly. The knife went wide. Rayder's eyes fluttered as he pitched forward. He was losing blood fast. Fist-sized red globules floated slowly down toward the deck in the microgravity.

Matt pushed away from Rayder. The HuMax caught his leg. He might be weakening, but he was still strong. The two tumbled in the cavernous Mecha Dock.

Rayder went for his Taikong pistol. Matt was barely able to knock it away as Rayder fired. The round *spanged* off the steel scaffolding like a gong.

Matt's head reeled. He saw as if looking down a dark tunnel. He was losing blood himself. This damn superman could still kill him!

No. He wouldn't let it happen. He wouldn't let what had happened on Prospect go unavenged. He was no longer that little boy. He might not be a god, but he was man enough to do this one thing.

Matt used all his remaining strength to kick Rayder in the face. The gun popped out of Rayder's hand. Matt caught it and pointed it at Rayder's head. He pulled the trigger.

Nothing happened.

"Keyed . . . ," Rayder rasped through blood. His red smile was a terrible thing. Rayder tried to twist the weapon out of Matt's hands.

Keyed. Biolocked to Rayder. Matt's mind was no longer speeding. It slugged through the simple equations as the world dimmed. What an adversary. Rayder had almost thought of everything. Almost.

"Take it," he told Rayder, putting the gun in the Hu-Max's hands. Rayder grabbed at it frantically. But he was weak. Matt flipped the gun over, under Rayder's chin. His hands wrapped around the other man's. Through the blood, Matt put his finger over Rayder's own and squeezed the trigger.

The explosion seemed oddly muted. Gore erupted from Rayder's neck as the back of his head flew away in red-and-white fragments.

"There's your reward," Matt said, before passing out.

14

KING

Matt came to under bright lights and soft, faraway sounds. Next to him, a bank of monitors showed an outline of his body, with areas shaded green, blue, and yellow within. An angry orange line slashed his belly, right where he'd taken Rayder's knife.

But he felt no pain. No pain at all. Matt moved his hands to feel his wound, but his arms moved slowly, as if weighted down. Liquid sloshing noises accompanied his motion.

Matt looked down. He was lying in a tank of clear fluid, completely naked. White threads shot through the gel, connecting with Rayder's knife slash. Only a vague pink scar showed he'd ever been injured.

Matt explored his injury gently with his fingers. It didn't even hurt. He was completely healed.

More Jotunheim technology, he thought. More rewards Rayder had reaped from that secret HuMax world. Better even than the Union's Accelerated Recovery.

But—why had they saved him? He'd killed their leader.

Was it possible Rayder was still alive? Could they resucitate him using this seemingly magic technology? What if they were resurrecting him for another cage match, this one in a real arena? Matt's heart bleeped a little faster on the monitor.

A medic stuck her head through the door and floated over to see him. She wore the gray Last Rising uniform with two bars on her chest.

"How do you feel, sir?" she asked.

"I—" Matt paused. Sir? What was that about? A trick? Or was it possible they were grateful he'd killed Rayder?

"Can you get me out of here?" Matt asked.

The medical technician's brow furrowed. "I can, sir, but the healing process is only ninety-eight percent complete."

"But it won't hurt me to get out now?" Matt asked.

"You'll have a scar."

Matt nodded. That was okay. He needed a reminder of his battle.

"Get me out of this thing," Matt said.

"Yes, sir," the tech said. She went to the screen and punched in a long series of instructions. The gel drained from the cylinder and the top half of it retracted backward. She pulled towels out of a cabinet and came to dry Matt off, working with cool efficiency.

"Rayder is dead, right?" Matt asked, taking the towel from her.

"Yes, sir."

"Can I see the body?"

"Of course, sir." The girl drew out a slate and spoke softly into it. After a few minutes, two other uniformed medical staff people came down the hall with a zero-g stretcher. They set it in front of Matt and watched as he unzipped the bag.

Rayder's blood-clotted face. His head, half gone. Rayder was dead. Matt blew out a big breath and dismissed the two staff members with the stretcher.

"Where's Captain Gonsalves?" he asked the first technician.

She looked confused. "Who?"

"One of the men from the asteroid you captured."

She nodded. "Convert H. Gonsalves, yes, First Class Programming. I am only second class. I don't know where he is."

Matt frowned. None of this made sense yet, but she seemed to be willing enough to follow his orders. He didn't want to dive too deep into it yet. Best to look for Gonsalves the last place he'd seen him.

"Take me to the bridge."

She frowned. "Sir, I must remain at my post. However, you may freely move about."

Stranger and stranger. Matt stood and pushed off for the door. Then he caught himself and turned back to the technician.

"Can you bring me some clothes, please?"

"Yes, sir," she said, with the same efficiency.

Matt chafed at the Last Rising uniform. It was dead black, with no adornment, just like the one Rayder had worn. He tried to explain to the med tech that he wanted his interface suit back, but she didn't seem to understand.

Nobody paid him any mind in the main corridor of the Last Rising ship. When he arrived at the bridge, the doors cycled even before he could approach the camera.

The bridge hadn't even been rebuilt yet. Technicians still worked on replacing the broken railing.

Captain Gonsalves stood comfortably by the captain's chair, watching the navigational screens. Esplandian still glowed dimly outside the slit windows. The Last Rising ship hadn't moved at all.

Captain Gonsalves looked down and locked eyes with Matt. "Welcome back, sir."

Weird. "I thought there were no 'sirs' here."

Gonsalves paused, and his jaw worked, as if he was biting back his first response. "There were no 'sirs' in *El Dorado*, or in Esplandian. But in Last Rising, there is the right of succession and allegiance."

"Sucession and allegiance?" Matt shook his head.

"Allegiance to Mr. Lowell, successor to Rayder, sir," Captain Gonsalves said.

Allegiance to me? Matt's mind whirled. He gaped at them. He'd killed Rayder—

—to become their new leader?

"Allegiance to Mr. Lowell, sir," chimed the guards and technicians, in unison.

Seven Corsairs met Matt's gaze, patiently awaiting his orders.

Matt slumped against a bridge rail, his mind swirling in surreality. "You'll all do anything I say?"

"Please wait until the succession order has been fully transmitted to the fleet and outlying agents, sir," one of the navigators said. "Otherwise, you may not be recognized as the Last Rising's Ultimate Arbiter by second- and third-class citizens."

Matt's stomach churned. They weren't playing. He'd inherited Rayder's entire organization. And they would slavishly follow anything he ordered them to do.

All of them.

The enormousness of it hit Matt like a hammer. *If I wanted to be an emperor, I have the power now.*

It was too much to take. "Don't follow me!" Matt cried.

The technician blinked in confusion. "You are not going anywhere, sir."

"No! I mean, don't do what I say. Release everyone from mind control!"

"It is impossible to refuse your orders, sir. I'm afraid your second statement makes no sense."

A hand fell on Matt's trembling arm. Matt jumped. It was Hector Gonsalves. His expression looked both troubled and sad.

"The programming is too deep in the second- and third-class staff, sir," he said. "I understand your meaning. Unfortunately, I can't comply with either the first or the second statement."

"Stop calling me 'sir'!"

"I can't, sir."

Matt groaned. Captain Hector Gonsalves, formerly such a strong leader—now reduced to this.

"You're aware you're mind-controlled?" Matt asked.

"Yes, sir."

"Can I order you to release yourself from it?"

"No, sir."

"There's got to be a way to reverse the process!"

Hector shook his head. "I'm not sure, sir. I can check with the medical technicians."

"Please do so!" Matt cried.

But, he realized, why would they have a reversal procedure? Rayder didn't care about anything other than controlling his hordes. Matt knew the Union doctors had succeeded in bringing Kyle Peterov out of Rayder's mind control once they'd returned to Mecha Base, but he didn't know what they'd done, or how complex the procedure had been.

"Is there anyone serving under Rayder who isn't programmed?" Matt asked.

"Not to my knowledge, sir," Captain Gonsalves told him.

"How big a force does Rayder command?"

Gonsalves shook his head. "I don't know the full extent, sir."

"It depends on the metric, sir," one of the technicians said. "By direct measurement, Last Rising is one hundred fifty-three thousand persons approximately, sir. If you include planets and colonies on which Last Rising is a de facto controlling government, we are approximately one hundred sixty-five million citizens. This excludes the approximately fourteen thousand agents in rival IGOs."

A hundred and sixty-five million people. Matt's head swam. It wasn't a gigantic number in terms of the Union's billions, but it was enough to make Matt shiver with dread. Was he now responsible to all of those people, as their new Ultimate Arbiter?

It was too much to take. Being their leader was worse than being their enemy, Matt thought.

"If, however, Mr. Lowell is interested in the fighting force he can command, we must factor in the approximately one thousand five hundred piloted and fifty-five thousand autonomous biomechanical Mecha. This force is easily the superior of any interstellar governmental organization, sir."

Wait. Had the technican just said what he thought he said?

"Your Mecha force is greater than the Universal Union's?" Matt asked the tech.

"Yes, sir."

Matt shook his head. That was unbelievable. For one faction of the Corsairs to move past the Universal Union in Mecha forces in a single year—it seemed impossible.

One single, driven, desperate faction, Matt's mind whispered. They wouldn't care about pilot addiction, neural buffers, or any of the parameters the Union had forced on Dr. Roth. It was entirely possible they were ahead of the Union in technology and firepower.

"What about Esplandian?" he asked Gonsalves, who was bent over a screen, talking with a medical team.

"It's currently in sorting and programming mode, sir."

"Stop! I mean, cease operations. Release all citizens of Esplandian who haven't been mind-controlled yet."

"Sir, that could cause conflict," Captain Gonsalves told Matt. But, deep down, did his eyes suddenly spark with a tiny fleck of hope?

Unfortunately, Gonsalves was right. If they simply released everyone right now, the Esplandians would use every cutting laser, Taikong pistol, and field machete they had to massacre the Last Rising personnel.

"Ignore that last order," Matt told Gonsalves. "Cease mind-control processing, but hold the rest of the population in secure areas."

"Yes, sir."

Matt nodded at the screen. "If there is a way to reverse programming, begin applying it to the Esplandian citizens first. If there isn't, put all medical resources toward developing a reversal procedure."

"Reversing programming may be dangerous, sir," Captain Gonsalves told him. "Last Rising citizens may not continue to follow you after the procedure is complete."

Matt turned to Captain Gonsalves, laughing. "Good!"

The equipment the Last Rising used for programming looked like old-fashioned imaging gear, but it was coupled with an injected psychoactive substance that was sealed in biohazard-secure packages. The doctors muttered about "applying inverse patterning in the active state," and promised to have the results of testing back to Matt as soon as they could.

Matt had a technician to take him on a tour of the Displacement Drive ship as he waited for word on the reversal procedure.

The Last Rising's flagship, *Helheim*, was impressive even in the context of a Union battle-hardened Displacement Drive warship. The fact that it had been built in less than a year made it even more stunning.

It wasn't finished, of course. Work continued as Matt followed the gray-suited technician through the ship's corridors. Groups of diggers worked around the clock, widening and deepening the tunnels within the asteroid, while riggers welded stainless plate on steel scaffolding to strengthen the ship.

Even unfinished, it was a fully functioning, battle-ready warship. Its heavy-matter weaponry was capable of targeting all eight sectors of approach, and it was augmented by antimatter beam weapons fore and aft. Its power-generation core ran the latest Taikong antimatter reactors as well, for a charge-and-Displace capability almost equal to *Helios*—forty seconds. Combined with armor comparable to anything Matt had seen on a Union ship, *Helheim* clearly had only one purpose: to lead assaults on heavily defended territory.

Matt went down to the Mecha Research cavern deep within *Helheim*, where new forms grew in gel suspension. It was like a scene from Dr. Roth's own labs. The pilotless, autonomous Loki were grown in vast numbers. The black Mecha were piloted, and grown much more sparsely. But there were dozens of other shapes in the tanks. Some were low, flattened discs with six or eight arms, like spiders. Others were long and slim, like centipedes or snakes. Still more were hunched and heavily armored, looking strong enough to withstand a full Zap Gun strike. And in between all of those types were one-offs, ranging in size from only a couple of meters across to hulking giants as large as Matt's Demon.

What the Union's been doing to HuMax, the HuMax are doing to Mecha. Experimenting. Tweaking. Changing.

Matt's slate chimed. It was Gonsalves and the doctors.

"We have results, sir," one of the doctors said.

"And?"

"We have processed twenty subjects through the test reversal procedure, sir. Nineteen showed no significant effects. One is restrained in a psychotic state."

Great, Matt thought.

"Keep at it," he told them.

Matt went to visit Ione on Esplandian with Gonsalves at his side.

The asteroid was still a mess, barely functioning with a skeleton crew of mind-controlled Esplandians. Whole blocks of housing had been turned into holding cells for the population awaiting processing. Mind-controlled Esplandians had a full-time job shuttling food through a series of security locks that separated the apartments from the rest of Esplandian.

The crew also had to tend to the needs of the entire asteroid, as well as repair the damage from the battle with Last Rising. Matt saw lots of exhausted faces among the mind-controlled crew as they shambled through the motions of their jobs.

It hurt Matt to think about what they were going through, but there was nothing he could do about it. *Helheim* was busy repairing their own damage, as were the three other Last Rising ships.

When Matt arrived, Ione lay sweating on a gurney, strapped down to its stainless rails. Her face was flushed, and the straps had rubbed the skin at her wrists raw. She'd been left there alone!

Anger shot through Matt like an electric current. "Where's Arksham?" he snapped at Gonsalves.

"He's awaiting programming in the residential blocks marked as temporary holding cells, sir," Gonsalves said.

"So you just left her here?" Matt exclaimed, pointing at Ione.

"I'm sorry, sir, but nonfunctional staff are given lowest priority." Gonsalves looked genuinely sad.

So they would have left her here to die! Matt grabbed Gonsalves by the lapels of his suit, wanting to slam him against the hard stainless walls of Dr. Arksham's office.

Gonsalves didn't resist. He just looked apologetically at Matt and waited for his punishment. He was only a messenger. In some ways less than a machine. Matt blew out a long breath and let Gonsalves go. "I'm sorry," Matt said.

"For what, sir?"

Matt shook his head. Gonsalves wouldn't fully understand, not while he was still programmed.

"Get Dr. Arksham out of the residential block," Matt ordered. "And get him back in this office!"

"It may take some time, sir."

"Do it now!" Matt snapped. He went to bend over Ione. Her breath came slow and steady, despite the heat radiating from her body.

"I'll save you," Matt said. "I will."

When Gonsalves came back with Dr. Arksham, the man shot a single angry glance at Matt before going to work, attaching Ione's intravenous feed and stuffing her into a cooling bag again.

"What's going on?" Arksham asked as he worked. "Am I to take from your attire that you've made another conversion of convenience, and now salute Rayder?"

Matt looked down, suddenly remembering the uniform he was wearing. His face reddened in embarrassment. He had to get some real clothes.

"I killed Rayder," Matt told Arksham. "He's dead."

The old man looked over his shoulder at Matt, his eyes deeply skeptical. He studied Matt for several seconds before seeming to come to a decision. "If that is true, congratulations. At the moment, please forgive me if I don't shake your hand."

"It is true. And I will make this right. Just as soon as . . ." Matt trailed off.

"As soon as what?"

"As soon as we figure out how to reverse Rayder's programming." Matt explained the problem to Arksham. The grizzled HuMax listened patiently, his expression softening slightly as Matt told his story.

"Not a clue," Arksham said. "Doesn't sound like any technique I've come across."

Matt nodded. The closest thing was Kyle. If he only knew what the Union had done to reverse the process—

Wait. Pieces fell into place with almost palpable thunks. Matt turned to Gonsalves.

"A technician said that Rayder has fourteen thousand agents at other IGOs. Are any of these deployed in the Universal Union?"

Gonsalves studied his slate. "Five thousand one hundred of them, sir."

Matt started, then bellowed a laugh. Five thousand Corsair agents in the Universal Union? Congress would come apart at the seams if they knew!

"Find out if any of our agents have access to Mecha Corps captain Kyle Peterov's medical records, specifically a procedure he'd undergone on Mecha Base." It was possible they were sealed too deeply, but it was also possible that was the shortcut they needed.

"Will do, sir," Gonsalves said, and headed out the door.

When he was gone, Matt went to sit beside Ione's bed. The medical readouts were incomprehensible to him, except the most basic. But he saw her vital signs were still in the green, and the display appeared to indicate she was still being nourished intravenously.

"It'll be all right," Matt said, taking her hand. It was warm, very warm. Calluses from her hard work in *El Dorado* still felt rough on his fingertips. But her hand was limp. She didn't respond at all, didn't make a sound.

"It'll be all right," Matt said again, his voice high and tight. It was very loud in the still room.

Was he trying to convince Ione?

Or himself?

Even with Kyle's medical records, it took an entire week to work up a process to reverse Rayder's programming. Rayder had refined his process significantly from the first time they went up against him. How significantly, Matt didn't know, until he requested access to Rayder's private files and was eagerly given it.

Rayder had stolen amazing amounts of technology from Jotunheim—much of it after Matt and the Union had left him for dead. An automated safety process of the long-dormant HuMax city had sucked him in before he burned up in the core of the planet, and robotic medical systems had brought him back to health. It was an unthinking reflex of the grand city, something Jotunheim would have done for anyone falling through the shaft.

But what it let Rayder do, more importantly, was to gain access to the deepest level of surviving HuMax technology, without the Union discovering him. He'd brought advanced mind control with him when he finally came to the surface, months later. Its first deployment had been on a Union Displacement Drive ship, which he'd used to escape Jotunheim.

Rayder had also brought Mecha tech out of Jotunheim—and, adding to Matt's rage, much of it was based on a fragment of Matt's own Demon, rather than HuMax technology. Some HuMax tech was blended in to create both the segmented silver Mecha and the black humanoid ones, but the majority of it was Dr. Roth's.

I gave Rayder the key to Mecha, Matt thought bitterly.

At the same time, how could he blame himself? Matt wondered. He was a pawn of the Union, just as Gonsalves was a pawn of Rayder.

No more. Never again.

But there was more. Much more. The mind-control process was clearly Rayder's crown jewel, but the autonomous Mecha with the Mesh-scrambling system interrupter was another important by-product of his time alone on Jotunheim. If Matt hadn't killed him, Rayder would have been in a position to take on the Union directly in a matter of months. With his web extending through the most powerful Corsair factions, and even into the highest echelons of the Union—one of Rayder's agents was a high-placed aide in the Union Congress—the outcome might have been the complete overthrow of the Union.

The rest of the tech that Rayder had brought into his personal archives was nearly incomprehensible, though. Much of it read as madness. However, Matt was able to surmise it was these shrouded conversations that led Rayder's agents to dig on Keller.

At least a third of it was text transcriptions between Rayder and another party identified only as "Contact." Contact's replies were heavily stilted, in a manner that suggested many layers of machine translation after hard encryption:

> RAYDER: The key biomechanical principle is an advanced magnetorheological application, allowing transformation of form without losing integrity?
>
> CONTACT: No. Not. Imperfect/oddly affected thinking/language.
>
> Biomechanical/transformative equals molecular/ nuclear analog of lifeforces/communication. (reference to translation animation 0.105-03; imagery indistinct and not interpretable—support note.)
>
> RAYDER: Nanotechnology?
>
> CONTACT: No not no again not increase understanding! Imperfect analog/representation; higher level forces in play/in work. Life not perfect. Biotech approach perfection of form/thought/life.
>
> RAYDER: You're not suggesting a metaphysical interpretation?
>
> CONTACT: Physical metaphysical same/undifferentiated. Different acting in simplistic mass-based existence.

There was much more in that vein, complete with blurry diagrams that seemed to show molecular recombination. Matt shook his head. That was pure nanotech, and everyone knew nanotech didn't really work. It was one of humanity's lost dreams. Even the heights of the Expansion hadn't produced true nanotechnology, other than pure biological processes.

But if that was true, what were Mecha? How did they work? If it wasn't true nanotech, then what was it?

In their lust for power, was the Union using the same source as Rayder? Was this really magical technology from some unknown source? Were they covering up even more than Matt suspected?

Of course they were. Why did he even bother asking himself anymore?

When the mind-control reversal process was complete, they tried it on Rayder's crew first. Crew members released from programming looked around in a state of confusion, and were able to recall more details from their life before Rayder's mind control.

But when asked where their allegiance lay, every single one of them pointed to Matt and said, "Matt Lowell, sir!"

Rayder's medical staff pointed to comparative brain scans, displayed on large nonphysical screens, and pronounced them significantly changed, and in line with unprogrammed brains. The process worked, they insisted. Every part of Rayder's control had been removed.

"Residual imprinting," Dr. Arksham told Matt, when he next went to see Ione.

The poor woman was still deep in the throes of fever. Her eyes had sunk down in their sockets, darkened by the virus burning its way through her system. She hadn't suffered any physical changes, but her hand was slim and bony, almost anorexic.

"Will she survive?" Matt asked.

Arksham sighed. He'd softened toward Matt of late, as his real concern for Ione was apparent. "I'm doing everything I can."

"Tell me."

A head shake. "Impossible to tell."

"Don't lie to me."

"I'm not lying to you. I'd tell you if I knew." Dr. Arksham crossed his arms. "I thought you were interested in the apparent failure of the mind-control reversals."

Matt nodded. "Yes. Yes. Residual imprinting, you said?"

"Might be. Or it's really failing. Why don't you try it on Hector or Federico? You'll know then."

"And if it doesn't work, and I turn their brains to mush?"

Arksham barked a laugh. "There are plenty of people on Esplandian who'd say it wouldn't make a difference."

"Not funny! Hector is a greater leader than he could pretend to be, and Federico is damn sharp."

"I know. I'm sorry. But you have to look at the facts. The scans show the programming has been removed. It also shows there's no damage to the person's mind. The reversal process can't hurt Hector."

"Unless there's something we can't image, something we can't measure," Matt said.

Arksham crossed his arms and shook his head. "No. Now you're going mystical on me. The process works. The person's brain is unharmed."

Matt frowned, but said nothing.

"You'll never know if it works unless you try it on someone you're familiar with," Arksham continued.

Matt gave in. He had to know. He asked Gonsalves to come down to the chamber in *Helheim* where Rayder's doctors had hacked one of the programmers into a reversal machine.

Gonsalves lay back on the working slab. But as the hood came down, something sparked in his eyes. He looked at Matt—really looked at him—and nodded.

Or at least Matt thought so. Maybe he had just imagined the whole thing.

Five minutes later, the hood came off. Gonsalves blinked and opened his eyes. "All hail Matt Lowell, successor to Rayder," Gonsalves said.

The world seemed to collapse around Matt. "It didn't work," he said, to the doctors, to the room, to anyone who'd listen.

"Mr. Lowell will lead us to the prosperous future as the ultimate arbiter!" Gonsalves continued.

"He's worse!" Matt said. "You made him worse!"

The doctors clustered close, muttering about their scans and readouts.

"We will all follow the former major into the glorious new age!" Gonsalves cried, his voice rising.

It was useless. Gonsalves was as programmed as ever, shouting propaganda about—

Wait. "Former Major?" Matt asked.

Gonsalves's face broke into a huge grin, and he barked laughter. "Gotcha!"

"Asshole," Matt grumbled.

Gonsalves turned serious. "You were so worried the deprogramming wasn't working, when all the numbers pointed right. You just couldn't accept that these guys would choose to follow you of their own free will. Of course I had to have a little fun with that."

"You scared the hell out of me."

Gonsalves grinned. "Good. Builds character."

"What was it like? Being mind-controlled?"

"It's hard to describe," Gonsalves told him, his face twisting in troubled memory. His cavalier attitude had simply been his way of dealing with it, Matt realized. "It's—it's not painful. The ideas were always my own. But there were walls around them. I just couldn't think certain things."

"And you called me 'sir,'" Matt reminded him.

"That's the scariest part!" Gonsalves cried. "Seriously, you did the universe a favor by killing that crazy fucker. Now let's get everyone deprogrammed and see where the chips land."

"What if most of them want to go out on their own? Or want to be Rayder themselves?"

"I bet most of them will still choose to follow you," Gonsalves said reassuringly.

"Why? I won't have mind control."

"Exactly," Gonsalves said. "Because you don't."

PART THREE

TERRORIST

"Where liberty dwells, there is my country."

—Benjamin Franklin
American Patriot

"This Expansion leads us outward to our fate, our destiny."

—President Samuel Mayflower
Last President of the United States of America

COMPARISON OF BIOMECHANICAL TECH-NOLOGY

Advanced Mechaforms vs. Corsair Sample

Version 0.4.4.3—ONGOING

CONFIDENTIAL: UARL ONLY/NOT FOR DISTRIBUTION

SUMMARY: This assessment is based on de-construction of sample of a 2-gen Mecha from Advanced Mechaforms, Inc., aka "Hellion" and one captured pilotless Corsair Mecha, aka "Loki."

SUPRA-LEVEL FINDING: Both the Hellion and Loki samples display advanced materials technology similar to that proposed by (ARCADIA—FURTHER IDENTITY REDACTED).

SUPRA-LEVEL INFERENCE: Both Dr. Roth and at least one Corsair faction are obtaining working knowledge from (ARCADIA) or off-shoots thereof.

SUPRA-LEVEL RAMIFICATIONS: If this supposition is correct, the implications to the Union are extreme. Dr. Roth does not operate under the same constraints as the Union's (ARCADIA POLICY DOCUMENT—REDACTED). In addition, if (ARCADIA) is in communication with others beyond UARL, additional technology leaks may be present.

DETAILED FINDINGS: (REDACTED)

15

PLAN

From space, Forest didn't quite live up to a name suggesting vibrant greenery. Its tiny continents were dull olive and sand, striped with areas of darker green along mountain ridgelines. Slightly smaller than Earth and mainly ocean, Forest's largest landmass was only about the size of Australia.

The rest of the planet was broken up into island chains, stretching gracefully across the deep blue ocean. These chains were dark green, and it was here that Forest took its name—from the kilometer-high pseudo pines that were part of its rich island foliage.

Now we see how good our intelligence is, Matt thought as they began reentry into Forest's thick, humid atmosphere. Forest was a prized Union world. They were going straight into the heart of the beast.

"They've accepted the entry codes," Anne Raskin called back through the open door to the pilot's cockpit.

Matt nodded. "Good."

Matt and Anne were coming down in a captured Union shuttle, coincidentally the same model as the one that had taken him down to Mecha Training Camp on Earth. Matt's Perfect Record replayed that moment in intense detail, as if on command. He'd been so excited, and so proud.

Look at you now, Matt thought as the shuttle windows began to glow orange from atmospheric friction. *Plotting to topple the Union.*

But that wasn't really right. It wasn't toppling. He was more trying to achieve an awakening. Awakening to what the Union could be, and allowing everyone to have the freedom to realize their dreams. Even if they were different.

The scream of the atmosphere rose to a peak, then deepened as the shuttle slowed. Soon the tiny windows cleared, and Matt saw an island chain ahead of them, against the still-curved horizon.

"We're cleared to land," Anne announced.

Matt nodded. The UARL access codes they'd gotten from Last Rising's intelligence network were the key to their success. Rayder's foresight and ingenuity had paid off again. Without his informants, they'd have no chance of dropping in on a Union planet undetected.

Their cover story was a UARL pop-and-drop, allowing the *El Dorado* to retreat as soon as the shuttle was launched. Gonsalves's Corsair ship wouldn't stand much scrutiny. All it would take is one bored FTLcomm ops with some time on their hands to check their orders.

But it wasn't as if Matt had any choice. He had to do this in person. Proxies wouldn't work. At best, they'd be killed. At worst, they'd be shipped off to Dr. Roth to have their secrets squeezed out of them.

Matt blew out a shuddery breath, as the enormousness of the whole plan came back to him again. And so much of it wasn't a plan at all. More like playing by ear.

The bump of the shuttle touching down roused Matt from his thoughts. He leaned to look out the window, and got his first glimpse of where Forest first got its name. The landing strip had been carved into gray granite mountainside, and on either side of its stone expanse were towering pseudo pines, fifty to five hundred meters tall. The gigantic trees blurred by as the shuttle slowed to a stop.

Anne opened the door for Matt and lowered the steps for him, as if he were a real Union dignitary. She wore a Mecha Corps Auxiliary uniform, while Matt wore a plain black business suit, its lapel marked by a silver Union one-and-twelve-stars insignia. His holopaper documents, ID tattoo, and slate tags all called him out as Dr. Dexter Nantes, a UARL researcher with Multi-Max security clearance. All of it would bear some scrutiny, but the Last Rising techs had waffled when pressed on how much.

Matt stepped out of the shuttle into the bracing air. It was crisp with the smell of growing green plants, but it smelled nothing like an earthly pine forest. Instead, the pseudo pines had a cloying, musklike undertone.

At the end of the runway, utilitarian facilities had been hacked into the side of the mountain, and a broad exercise field of raw stone stretched into the distance. On it, two Demons grappled with each other, their bright red dulled by distance and haze. Around them, a half dozen Hellions looked up at the fighting Demons, like kindergartners watching their teenage brothers brawl. Matt grinned involuntarily as he watched them.

"See something you like?" Anne asked him.

"A little less familiarity, and 'sir' would be appreciated," Matt snapped. "Hellions and Demons both have sensory enhancement."

"Yes, sir!" Anne was suddenly all-business.

They walked in silence to the gatehouse that guarded the mountain facility. A small plaque on its side read:

ADVANCED MECHAFORMS, INC.
MECHA TRAINING CAMP 03
A UNIVERSAL UNION DEVELOPMENT

Matt tried to hide a frown. Despite being dressed down by the Union after the near loss of Mecha Base, Dr. Roth's corporation still had top billing. How deep did his hooks go into the Union?

Very deep, the Last Rising operatives told Matt. So deep that much of the information was redacted, even at Multi-Max security level. The Union had an entire team devoted to examining Roth's technology and his motivations. Every six months, they reported the same thing: Roth is unknown and therefore dangerous, but also indispensable.

I could tell them one thing they don't know, Matt thought. Delving into Rayder's records, Matt had found that Roth had spent several years exploring fringe space outside Corsair territory before he founded Advanced Mechaforms. He showed up in many Corsair colony records. He'd even negotiated with one of Rayder's lieutenants at the time, seeking passage to HuMax worlds as yet unknown by any IGO.

He'd been searching for something, out here on the fringes of human expansion. Had he found it? Had that been the basis of all of his Mecha technology?

There were whispers of other HuMax worlds beyond Jotunheim—Mu and the Seven Cities of Gold, lost tech wonderlands beyond the imagination. But was that wishful thinking, or were they real places?

Unfortunately, Matt was only sure of one thing: he didn't know.

Forest was one of three new Mecha training camps. The one on Earth had been deemed too limiting to meet the needs of an expanded Operation Pushback, so new training camps had been opened on worlds throughout the Union. The Union knew the HuMax and Corsairs were getting stronger, so they were pressing Roth to build and train an army.

And kill more cadets, Matt thought, remembering the two deaths in his own group. Out of thirty candidates he'd entered with, only four had made it to full Mecha Pilot status.

"ID and purpose of visit?" the guard at the gatehouse asked them. She wore a Mecha Corps Auxiliary uniform, thankfully of a lower rank than Anne's sergeant stripes.

Matt and Anne presented their holopaper IDs, which the guard ran under a scanner. Matt's heart beat double time until the machine chimed green. Matt took both sets of IDs back from the guard and turned to walk through the gate.

"Purpose of visit, sir?" she snapped.

Matt froze for just an instant. Then he remembered who he was supposed to be. Dr. Nantes would never take an ounce of crap from a lowly Mecha Auxiliary.

"Did you miss my UARL credentials?" he growled back.

The woman flinched. "No, sir, but—"

"Or my clearance?"

"No—"

"Then perhaps you were unaware my security level has de facto carte blanche access to any facility of the Union, especially a *contractor* installation," Matt said.

"Go right in, sir," the guard told him, looking down.

Matt glared at her a moment longer, then turned and walked crisply toward the office. The two Demons were still grappling on the exercise field, but now they were getting past the level of simple exercises. One of them used its thrusters to do a backflip over the other, then kicked it so hard the other one went skidding across the field with a metallic screech.

On a whim, Matt turned and headed toward the field instead.

"Where are we going?" Anna asked.

"Sir!"

"Where are we going, sir?" she repeated.

Matt grinned. "You'll see."

By the time Matt reached the exercise field, the victor Demon was helping the fallen one up. Both turned to look at their two visitors, which caused all the Hellions to turn and look as well. Silhouetted against the rapidly falling sun, the troop of razor-edged Mecha were suddenly like golden colossi, ready to strike terror into passing merchant ships. Matt shivered, momentarily unnerved. If he wasn't right about who was in the Demon, he might regret his impulsive detour.

The victorious Demon seemed to look at Matt for a long time. He swore he could see its biomechanical lenses, hidden deep under its visor, widen for just an instant.

Then it jogged to the edge of the field, where Matt and Anne stood. Anne squealed a little bit as the ringing metallic footfalls made the stone beneath their feet quiver. It knelt down, casting its shadow on them.

On the Demon's chest, the pilot's chamber irised open. A figure emerged and descended the ladder, wiping magnetorheological gel from his eyes. Clad only in a skintight interface suit, he was like a classic statue, perfect in proportion.

Matt grinned. "Major Soto."

Soto's eyes widenened in recognition. He took two faltering steps forward. "Matt—"

Matt cut him off, fast. "Dr. Dexter Nantes."

Soto blinked, swallowed, and his expression hardened.

"It's now Colonel Soto, Dr. Nantes."

"Colonel Soto. Congratulations on your promotion."

Soto nodded. "Congratulations on your balls."

Matt jumped, then stifled a laugh. "We have Union clearance to examine any installation—"

Colonel Soto cut him off. "I get it, I get it. Let's go somewhere we can talk."

Matt nodded. The hulking figures of the still-active Demons hammered the point home. No doubt, they were listening with sensory enhancement up to full. No doubt, their records would eventually be examined.

"Lead on, Colonel."

Soto took them inside the facility, which was constructed of drab gray concrete tilt-up walls bolted directly to the hollowed-out section of mountain. Rows of small, square windows looked out over the incredible vistas below, where the pseudo pines gave way to olive-colored grassland and wild rivers cutting through dark native stone.

Soto led them down to a door covered in aluminum mesh, at the end of a long hallway. He opened the door and motioned Matt and Anne in. Matt paused, looking into the room. It contained only one desk and an FTL-comm set, and the room was lined with the same aluminum mesh as the door.

"Not a brig, I assure you," Soto said, reading Matt's mind.

Matt shrugged and stepped in, with Anne following. Soto was last in the door. He went to close it, but the sound of running footsteps down the hall made him pause. He waited while a slim, dark-haired woman wearing a Mecha Auxiliary uniform slipped in: Lena Stoll, Matt's first Mecha controller.

As Matt opened his mouth, she held up a hand. "Wait." She closed and locked the door, then went around to the back of the FTLcomm system and disconnected it from its power and network lines, carefully capping the sockets.

When she was done, Lena stood and went straight to Matt, enveloping him in a big hug. Matt tensed, then softened and returned her embrace. He suspected she'd always been attracted to him, far more than her emotionless visage could express. But at the same time, it brought back memories of Ione. Matt pushed Lena gently away.

"Something I should know?" Anne asked, watching Matt and Lena with amused eyes.

Lena broke the hug and glared at Anne. "You're not Mecha Auxiliary." She turned back to Matt. "You're supposed to be dead!"

"First things first," Matt said. "I assume it's safe to talk here?"

"Faraday cage," Major Soto said, banging on the metal mesh that covered the whole room. "This was a UARL lab before they repurposed it for Mecha Corps."

"They use it to talk to Dr. Roth now," Lena said. "Small chance they'd use FTLcomm to listen in, but I've disabled it in any case."

Matt nodded. "It's good to see you all again."

Soto came and clapped Matt on the back, nearly knocking him over. "Same here, kid! What the hell happened to you?"

"What's the Union's story?" Matt asked.

"You were leading a standard operation when you lost contact with the rest of your team," Lena said. "They searched for you for two weeks, then announced you lost. They suspect internal Mecha system failure, rather than overwhelming force."

"Dr. Roth isn't happy with that explanation," Soto added.

Matt grinned. Of course Roth wouldn't be. He loved his Mecha more than anything.

"When was the last time you had a Demon outright fail?" Matt asked. "Beyond regeneration?"

Soto shook his head. "So what really happened?"

Matt opened his mouth, then suddenly realized that whatever he said was going to sound completely insane. In this crowd, that meant *get it out now*.

Matt took a big breath and said, "I've joined the Corsairs. And I want you to join me."

The room went completely silent, as if everyone was holding their breath.

Soto nodded, just once, and went to sit in the single chair behind the table. He opened the desk drawer and drew out a small 2111-model pistol. Matt tensed, and Anne started.

Soto didn't point the gun at them, though. He put it on the table, sat back, and put his arms behind his head.

"You'd better be a damn good salesman," he told Matt.

Matt started where he should have, trying to keep his eyes off the implied threat of the gun on the desk.

He told them what he'd found out about the Union, showing security footage that was a condensed version of his assault on Planet 5. Seeing the bright, three-dimensional images of the HuMax being slaughtered only heightened the pain of Matt's Perfect Record. The most terrible thing was that he knew exactly how many HuMax had been subjected to the program, and exactly how many atrocities had been visited on them by the Union.

Soto watched impassively, flinching only when the Demons came through the roof of the facility. Lena leaned forward intently, as if studying the scene, but her usually impassive eyes narrowed in sympathetic pain as the HuMax died. Perhaps thinking, *I'm a genemod too. Could they do this to me?*

When it was over, there was another silence in the room for a long time. Eventually Soto shook his head.

"This could be faked."

"It isn't," Matt shot back.

Soto looked at the floor, as if unwilling to meet Matt's eyes. "The Union must have a reason for doing . . . what they're doing."

"Yes. They're continuing the research they started a long time ago. The Union created the HuMax."

Soto's eyes snapped up to meet Matt's. "Now I know you're insane. There's no possible way—"

Matt pressed on. "They're also looking for more Hu-Max technology they lost in the Human-HuMax War."

Soto shook his head violently. "I don't believe it."

"You were at Jotunheim. What became of it?"

Soto clamped his square jaw down hard, but said nothing.

"You were on Keller. What were they digging for?"

More silence.

"You're here on Forest, training new cadets. What are they ramping up for? More ragtag Corsairs? Or are they shooting for an army big enough to take down all the Corsair Mecha out there, and the HuMax they've lost control of?"

Soto shook his head and said nothing, but his expression was deeply troubled.

"Let me show you something else."

Matt ran another clip, this one of Esplandian. It wasn't the best video in the world, or the most coherent, but Matt knew it was showing Soto something he'd never seen before: a neutral Corsair outpost.

Matt let it play through the Last Rising attack, and his

fight with Rayder. At Rayder's first appearance, Soto sat straight upright. "He's dead!"

Matt held up a hand, and let the video play. The rest was too much. Soto didn't need to know about mind control, the Last Rising intelligence network, or anything more.

When it was done, Lena was the first to speak. "What are you going to do with this?"

Matt grinned. "Same thing I always thought I was here for: save the universe."

Soto barked a hard laugh and then looked embarrassed. "Seriously."

"First, I want to see if you'll join me."

"On the basis of a couple of videos—"

"You know it's more than a couple of videos." Matt turned to Soto, there at his side. He'd stood with him a year ago in front of the Union Prime via FTLcomm as she explained they'd have to sweep the whole thing under the rug. He knew there were secrets. More than secrets. Deep, dark, buried things, orchestrating all the happy public relations to keep the Union on an even keel. Or worse.

If anyone would join him, it would be Soto.

Soto looked to one side, then the other, his face twisted in a rictus frown. It was as if he was trying to deny the whole thing with a gigantic shake of his head.

Finally Soto's eyes rose to meet Matt's. "You believe in these . . . Corsairs?"

"I believe in people having a right to their freedom. And I believe they deserve not to be lied to by the people they trust to lead them."

"Mikey and Marjan were here last week," Soto told Matt. "If you'd been here when they were—"

"It would have been bad."

"They would have recognized you! What would you do?" Soto still didn't look at him.

"I'd escape."

"And if you couldn't?"

"I'd do whatever I needed to do," Matt told him.

Soto's eyes finally rose to meet Matt's. "You believe so much—in Corsairs?"

Matt just nodded slowly. Anne began to speak, but Matt put a hand on her arm to silence her.

"Why are you taking this kind of chance?" Soto asked.

"Because I need you. It can't be just me." And a decorated hero of the Union was one of the most important allies he could have.

"What do you expect me to do?"

"Same thing you're doing here. I just thought you might like doing it for the right team."

"Corsairs don't have Mech—" Soto began, then bit back his words.

"We have Mecha. A lot of them like you've never seen before."

More silence. In the Faraday-shielded room, it was total and absolute.

"You've had your doubts," Lena said, her soft voice suddenly loud. Everyone turned to look at her.

"Lena," Soto said.

The sergeant came to put her hands on Soto's shoulders. She looked him in the eye, and waited until he met her own.

"You don't like this assignment. Admit it."

"Lena, I . . ." Soto trailed off and looked at Matt, almost as if for support.

Got him, Matt thought, his heart hammering hard with excitement.

"I know about the new training camps," Matt said.

Soto nodded. "Bag of shit, they are. Knocking these kids through in half the time, man with knife versus shark-style."

"You weren't easy on us," Matt said.

"They don't care here. Dead, insane. Doesn't matter. We're losing nine out of ten. Three out of ten dead."

Matt frowned. "I thought Roth was under additional oversight."

"He is. But it's not about cadets. It's about the big goal. They're mobilizing for a bigger operation than Pushback, but I don't know much more than that."

Time for the offer. "Come and train our guys. I'll give you as much time as you need."

Soto shook his head, his eyes bright and uncertain. "How can I trust you?"

Matt nodded. Time for the third video. He showed them the programmed Last Rising crew, and the ongoing release procedure. Soto watched the video twice, then looked up at Matt with new respect.

"You're doing this?"

"Yes. I am."

Soto looked at Matt with an expression of mixed awe and distrust. He seemed completely unable to speak.

"If you don't go, I will," Lena told Soto. She turned to Matt. "I assume you need Mecha controllers on your staff."

"Lena, hold on!" Soto snapped.

She turned to him. "You've had your doubts. It's time to do what's right."

"Can I think about it?" Soto asked Matt. "Come back in a week—"

"The Union's going to review the records here, match up their faces, and come asking hard questions," Lena said. "It might not even take a week."

Matt nodded. For all he knew, the Union was Displacing warships into orbit right now. "It's now or never, Major."

"Colonel," Soto corrected.

"Actually, if you join us, you won't have a rank. Or we can make one up."

Soto looked shocked. "What are you, then? Prime? President?"

Matt laughed. "I haven't even thought about that yet."

Soto stared long and hard at Matt, as if trying to decide whether or not he was kidding. Finally he nodded. "If you want me, I'm your man."

Sergeant Stoll stepped forward. "I volunteer as well, sir."

Matt grinned. "There won't be any 'sirs' where we're going."

Lena and Soto both looked completely confused, which caused Matt to break into laughter again.

Just before they left, though, Soto put a hand on Matt's shoulder and bent close to say, low and serious, "If I don't like what I see when we get there, you won't live thirty seconds."

Back on Esplandian, Soto stared up at the grand array of Mecha, his mouth hanging open. Their firepower had swelled as the integration of Last Rising personnel continued. Dozens of Aesir, their Hellion-like Mecha, stood in ranks on either side of the dock, their smooth black curves a stark counterpoint to the rugged rock walls. Matt's Mecha pilots trained in Aesir, except for the handful of captured Hellions and Matt's lone Demon. Deeper in were racks of silver-segmented Loki.

"It's not polite to stare," Lena Stoll said, giving Soto a sidewise grin.

She'd opened up during their transit on *El Dorado*, asking Captain Gonsalves tons of questions about his home, his vocation, his ship, his political philosophy, and Corsair economics. Gonsalves had seemed thrilled to have her as an audience, and went on for hours.

Matt's slate chimed, again and again, as they toured the docks. Matt looked at the screen and sighed. Everyone knew he was back, and there were a thousand decisions to make. He knew why Federico didn't want the leadership job.

Soto looked over his shoulder at the slate. "You really are their leader, aren't you?"

"He told you that," Lena said.

"How should I know?" Soto looked genuinely pained. "Nobody even salutes anyone here!"

Captain Gonsalves, who'd come up to join them in their tour, laughed. "The kids do, when they're playing Corsairs versus the Union. But only when they're playing the evil Union."

Soto's face compressed in brief anger. Then he sighed and addressed Matt. "So, what percentage of the Corsairs do you lead?"

"I don't know," Matt admitted.

"You don't know?"

"We don't have a complete census," Matt explained. "Hell, we don't even know how many of the Last Rising crew will join us as we release them from their programming."

"Most of them," Gonsalves said. Anne nodded in agreement. "I'd say, all told, the Esplandian Nation will end up being about a third of the Corsairs."

"Esplandian Nation? Is that what you're calling it?" Soto asked.

"I guess so," Matt said. "I hadn't really thought about that either."

Soto frowned. "Names and symbols are important, Matt. Esplandian isn't bad. If I remember right, it's a fictional land in Spanish legend. That will connect to a lot of the Union—and, more importantly, it makes the Aliancia predisposed to like us."

"We have good relations with the Aliancia," Gonsalves said.

"But what flag do you fly?" Soto said.

"Flag?"

"You're not going to use the Corsair thousand-daggers flag, or Rayder's symbol?"

"I hadn't thought about that either."

Soto stopped Matt with a hand. "You'd better start thinking about it! This stuff is important. The better you present yourself, the better chance the Union will accept it."

Matt swallowed and nodded. Soto was right. He couldn't just play it by ear. A lot more had to be added to the plan. Which meant even more decisions.

Soto seemed to realize the weight he was laying on Matt's shoulders. He looked around and changed the subject. "So, where are these kids you need trained?"

16

LUCK

Soto and Stoll fell into Esplandian life as if they'd been born on the asteroid.

Soto worked with the Last Rising Aesir pilots, grumbling at first about the differences between the Aesir and Hellions, then finally conceding that yes, maybe the Aesir's weapons systems (a single micromissile that straddled the line between Fireflies and Seekers, and a single antimatter annihilation weapon built into the right arm of the Mecha) were simpler and easier to master than the Union Mecha. Unfortunately, the Aesir also lacked neural buffering, so they were as addictive as Demons. Documentation on their Merge ability was sparse, but it seemed that they fell somewhere in between a Hellion and a Demon in overall capability.

Matt stuck to his Demon, in the few times he went out. The Aesir were no match for it. He could take out an entire squad by himself.

But add the Loki to the equation, and things got dicey. Their neural disruption capability edged the balance of power to the Aesir. Matt was always able to prevail in the end, but Soto had a simple, blunt explanation for that:

"The kids are crap," he told Matt. "They have way too much to unlearn. They've probably been programmed in some way or another their whole lives."

Matt told Soto to see if anyone from Esplandian wanted to try the Mecha. Soto posted the job, but he was surprised to see very few takers even at "hazardous duty" pay grades.

"They know about the addiction," Gonsalves said. "They're not willing to throw their lives away for an infernal machine."

"It's only a mental addiction," Soto grumbled.

"Is it?" Gonsalves asked. "Unless he was just being dramatic, I saw Mr. Former Major here pass out from withdrawal."

Soto looked away.

"There are ways to manage it," Lena Stoll said. "We can minimize the risk. All Mecha Auxiliary once piloted Mecha, and we do not require Mesh."

"But you *want* it," Gonsalves said.

"Desires can be damped," Lena said, almost as if she were emphasizing her impassive demeanor.

Gonsalves sighed. "It's a rough chance, no matter how you paint it."

"We'll bring in new pilots from other Last Rising worlds," Matt said.

Soto groaned. "Which will be just as shit as the ones we have here."

"There's an ace in every team," Matt told him. "It's your job to find them."

"Great," Soto said, bitingly sardonic. But Matt knew, deep down, Soto was enjoying the challenge. He'd find the aces. And he'd train them.

And, with any luck, they'd be ready before the Union struck them first.

*　　*　　*

One eighteen a.m. Dr. Arksham's office was completely silent, except for the low rush-and-tick of Ione's respirator.

Matt sighed and rubbed his eyes. Ione's cheeks were deeply sunken, her eyes almost lost in their sockets. Her life support's coolly glowing screen showed all bodily functions optimal: breathing at sixteen breaths per minute, blood oxygenation within normal limits, and pulse at a strong sixty-five beats per minute. But those healthy numbers were a fiction, something imposed on Ione by the machine. Without the respirator and cardiac maintenance, she'd already be dead.

"You really care about her." Dr. Arksham's voice came from the doorway. Matt jumped and looked up.

"Yes," Matt said. "I do."

Arksham came to lean over Ione. He put a palm on her forehead, even though the screens read her exact temperature to two-digit precision: 40.13 degrees.

"Why?" Dr. Arksham asked.

Why do you care for her? That's what Arksham was asking. Matt thought of a thousand instant answers. Planet 5. The injustice. The Union.

"Maybe I'm part HuMax," Matt said, finally.

Arksham shook his head. "What do you mean?"

Matt spent the next fifteen minutes giving Arksham a brief account of his life, focusing on his father's genemod tricks and his Perfect Record. He even explained how the Perfect Record had seemed to expand into a frenetic probability calculator when he'd fought Rayder.

When Matt was finished, Arksham nodded. "Genemod. I should have known. I wondered how you were able to beat Rayder."

"Have you heard of anything like—like what I experienced?"

Arksham shook his head. "No. Never. Your Perfect

Record sounds like it betters even a typical HuMax memory. You don't know what genetic sources your father used for your genemodding?"

"No."

"We can find out, if you'd like."

Matt jumped. "How?"

"I'll have our Last Rising intelligence network run a sequence on you."

"Do it!" Matt's heart pounded. After all these years, after Roth's dismissing him as "not HuMax," maybe he'd finally have an answer.

Arksham took a blood sample from Matt and ran it into a compact chrome instrument. When he was done, the machine chimed.

"What now?" Matt said.

"Now we wait. This machine just does the sequence. Last Rising techs do the cross-reference."

"How long?"

"A few days, maybe more."

Matt sighed, and looked again at Ione. Arksham saw the direction of his gaze and said, "Yes. I've had them run her genome too."

"What did they say?"

"Whatever the rewrite is, it doesn't cross-reference."

"Will she recover?" Matt asked.

Dr. Arksham looked at Ione for a long time. When he spoke, he didn't turn to face Matt. "You should worry about yourself, not her. This plan to 'change the Union' is suicidal."

"Someone has to do it."

Arksham shook his head and stood up to pace. He said nothing for a very long time. Finally he stopped and turned back to look at Matt.

"A long time ago, a famous man—I forget his name—

said something like 'The measure of a good idea is how hard it is to ram it down people's throats.'"

"Aiken," Matt said, suddenly remembering his American Principles class in Aurora University. "It didn't quite go that way, but I know what you mean."

"You really think you can change the Union?" Dr. Arksham asked.

"'If at first the idea is not absurd, then there is no hope for it,'" Matt quoted.

"Who's that?" Arksham asked.

"Einstein."

A nod. "An excellent quote." But Arksham just shook his head and looked even more troubled.

"What's wrong?" Matt asked.

Arksham fixed him with tired eyes. "For all Einstein's ideals, they still built the atomic bomb."

Matt nodded. "And we learned to stop using them to wipe out worlds wholesale. Change is possible."

Arksham sighed. "I just hope your change doesn't start with a war."

Matt's breakfast with Soto and Lena was interrupted by priority comms from Gonsalves, beeping for attention on his slate. Matt turned on the video and saw Gonsalves down in Esplandian's docks, overseeing the unloading of supplies from Tierrasanta.

"What are we short on?" Matt asked, anticipating Gonsalves's emergency. It was normal to come up short on important supplies, but Anne Raskin was usually the person who reported it to him.

"We're not short. We're plus."

"Plus what?" Matt said, irritated.

"I think you need to come down here."

"Why?"

Gonsalves grinned. "Just come on down."

Crap, Matt thought. Between the late nights and the constant grind of leadership, he didn't want to play any of Gonsalves's guessing games.

"Tell me."

"No," Gonsalves said, his grin getting bigger. "Just come down. And smile. This is a good plus."

Matt grumbled, but he knew Gonsalves wouldn't drag him away for no good reason. He left his breakfast behind and went through the corridors to the docks, with Soto and Lena in tow.

When he got there, he found Captain Gonsalves talking with two slim, dark-haired men wearing casual Aliancia attire. Two very familiar men.

"Peal?" Matt cried, pulling himself along the rail faster. "Jahl?"

Peal laughed and waved as Matt approached. Jahl just nodded, grinning. Matt brought himself to a halt only a meter away from the pair, his mind going a thousand miles per minute. Peal and Jahl, the wunderkind of Hyva. Former Mecha Cadets. One a full Hellion pilot. For long moments, all he could do was stare at them.

"He looks confused," Peal said.

"Surprised," Jahl added.

Peal nodded. "After all, how can we possibly be here?"

"Yes, a real problem for their security, he's thinking."

Matt frowned. They were right. If Peal and Jahl could find him, could the Union be far behind? Was there a Union warship parked outside Esplandian?

No. Gonsalves wouldn't be standing there comfortably, watching in good humor. That meant Peal and Jahl had—

"You defected from the Union?" Matt asked.

"Like we loved it there so much," Peal said.

"No big surprise," Jahl added.

Matt nodded. Peal and Jahl had been "invited" to Mecha Training Camp as an out for some highly illegal hack work they'd done on Hyva. They'd never really been good obedient Mecha Corps—they'd looked at their status as a way to get deeper into the Union systems.

"How did you find us?" Matt asked.

"It wasn't easy," Peal said.

"Don't worry, the Union is too stupid to put it together," Jahl added.

Peal frowned. "For now."

"The probability that they will do the deep-cover research necessary to determine this location is very low—"

"But nonzero." Peal cut his brother off.

Nonzero. Esplandian's docks seemed suddenly chill, and Matt shivered.

"Essentially zero for the hacks at UARL," Jahl argued.

"But you have to admit—" Peal began.

Matt rolled his eyes. If he let them continue, they'd argue for hours. It was what they did. He cut Peal off. "Why the hell are you here?"

"And it's great to see you too," Peal said.

"You know what I mean!"

Jahl saluted. "We are here to join your great and valiant forces, sir!"

Matt reddened, embarrassed. "Don't do that."

Peal elbowed his brother. "Tell him."

"Tell him what? That it's easy to put together fake Union reports about Matt Lowell being lost in a Mecha exercise and the disappearance of Major Soto and Lena Stoll? Or what we found when we unsealed his records? Or that it's just a hop and a jump from that to conclude the Union doesn't have any qualms about using gene-mods like us, any way they want?"

"No. Tell him the important part."

Jahl frowned. "Shouldn't we at least sit down first, have a drink, something?"

"Tell him!"

Jahl groaned, looking visibly uncomfortable. "The Union has expanded Pushback II to include 'unspecified Corsair locations in near-Union space.'"

Matt swallowed, feeling the blood rush out of his head. "They know where we are."

"No," Jahl said.

"But they'll be looking," Peal added.

Captain Gonsalves's grin had disappeared. He cleared his throat. "I think I could go for that drink now."

After shots of vacuum-distilled whiskey in Hector and Federico's private dining room, the full story came out.

It seemed the Union was expanding Operation Pushback II to target specific Corsair factions, including the Cluster, Last Rising, and what they called "nonspecific close-range Corsair incursions."

Peal and Jahl brought comprehensive files with them, and the video and text glowed brightly on the NPP screens in the darkened dining room. The list of resources dedicated to the mission was staggering. Not just *Helios* and *Juggernaut*, but a half dozen new Warship-class fast-recharge Displacement Drive ships. Over a hundred Demons and twelve hundred Hellions were listed as supporting.

"If they find us, Esplandian is dust," Gonsalves said morosely.

"They have to find us first."

Gonsalves nodded, but remained glum. "Not only that, but the Union had noted 'recent upsets in the Last Rising faction, with significant shifts in their overall activity.'"

"So they know I killed Rayder," Matt said.

Peal looked confused. "He died on Jotunheim."

Matt and Gonsalves exchanged glances.

"What?" Peal asked.

"So the Union didn't know Rayder led Last Rising?"

It was Peal's and Jahl's turn to look confused. Matt brought them up to date on what had happened. The duo sat silently as he talked, but their slack expressions spoke of complete amazement. They rocked back when Matt told them about deprogramming the Last Rising members, and his plan to bring the truth to the Union.

"You're a crazy man," Peal said.

"And that's why we love him," Jahl added. But he wasn't smiling. His face was creased deep in a frown, worried.

"We can help," Peal said.

"We already have a team of five thousand informants in the Union."

"Ninety-eight percent of whom are known, and being fed incorrect information," Peal replied.

"By us," Jahl added.

Peal grinned. "Well, not by us anymore. But you understand. Your information is not necessarily accurate."

"We can cross-check it," Jahl said. "Interpolate and synthesize."

"But we can't hack," Peal added. "FTLcomms hacking is tricky. They'll have decaying neutrino trails to back-trace—"

"—unless we use proxies—" Jahl said.

"—but even proxies can be matrixed—"

Matt's laugh interrupted the arguing twins, making them turn and stare at him. He held out a hand. "It's good to see you guys again. Welcome to the team."

Jahl looked confused. "You trust us?"

"We could be working for the Union," Peal added.

"Not a chance," Matt said. "If it was the Union, you would have shown up with a half dozen warships."

Peal laughed. "True. They aren't good at subtlety."

Jahl took his hand. So did Peal. And in that moment, Matt was content. His team was coming back together. What an amazing stroke of luck.

Unless—they actually were working for the Union.

When Peal and Jahl had left, Matt met privately with Gonsalves. "Have the Last Rising analysts look into their back trail. And have them double-check everything they do."

Gonsalves nodded, looking relieved. "Thank you."

But at the door, Gonsalves paused. "Is it worth trusting them?"

"I think they're on the level," Matt told the troubled captain. "And if they are, they're worth our entire team of informants and analysts. They could easily make or break this plan."

"Or we can simply keep our heads down and stay out of Union business," Gonsalves said.

"Do you really think we can, now?"

Gonsalves was silent. Matt used the moment to press his argument. "Yeah. We can keep our heads down. We could hide, and wait while they wipe out all the Corsair worlds. We could sit and watch while they go on to take the Aliancia and the Taikong—"

"They wouldn't do that!" Gonsalves cried.

"You think not?"

Again, the captain had no answer.

"We can wait until the entirety of humanity is Union, and we can watch as they round up all the HuMax and genemod, and do what they want to them. And we can hope they never, ever find us, and keep spinning on this rock in the middle of nowhere. Because if they did find us, there'd be nothing left for us to do. We couldn't possibly defend against a force that big, not even with every Last Rising world at our disposal."

Gonsalves fell silent and leaned back, as if considering Matt's words carefully. "How much do you trust these two?" he asked again, finally.

"Ninety-nine point nine percent."

Gonsalves nodded. "I've taken worse odds. But . . ."

"But what?"

"It's the tenth of a percent that gets you."

Matt put a hand on Hector's shoulder. "Hector, if we don't do something now, we die."

As Matt was drifting off to sleep, he was roused again by the shrill of his slate. *Should turn the damn thing off,* Matt thought, struggling up from his doze.

Matt shrugged off the zero-g sleep harness and blinked up at the slit windows that looked out over Esplandian's desolate surface. His slate's screen spilled chill light in the dark room. Matt grabbed it and scanned the short message.

DR. ARKSHAM: Ione's coming around. Thought you'd like to know.

Matt's heart raced. *How is she? Is she okay?* Why hadn't Arksham told him to come down? He wanted to shout a thousand questions at the slate. But that was stupid. Better to find out for himself.

He threw on the first pants and shirt he could find and rocketed down the tunnels to Dr. Arksham's office. Curious eyes watched as he passed, but Matt didn't care. The only thing that mattered was getting down to see her.

Matt caught himself at the last corridor. What if she was a monster? What if she had been completely transformed? Was that why Arksham hadn't ordered him to come see her?

Matt shook his head. No. Maybe Arksham was just being polite. Maybe he didn't think it was his place to order the leader of Esplandian around. Whatever reason, it didn't matter. He'd have to take that as it came.

He made himself go down the last corridor. He paused for a moment outside the door, trying to get his rushing breath in check. He took a deep breath and opened the door.

Inside, the lights were up full bright, and Matt squinted against the halos. Dr. Arksham and one of his nurses bent over a figure in a hospital bed, still lying prone. A slim hand, free of the cooling bag, rose for a moment, before coming to rest again on the table. She'd moved!

Matt flew closer. Ione's eyes were open, but they were so sunken and bloodshot they almost didn't seem human anymore. Her voice croaked reedily as she tried to speak. Her wrists were so thin they were little more than sticks. She had a long way to go for a full physical recovery.

But she still looked like Ione! Matt's heart surged with hope. Maybe the transformation wasn't as radical as he'd thought, or maybe she'd somehow fought it off.

"Ione," Matt said, coming up beside the doctor and nurse.

"Mr. Lowell, I don't know if now is the time for reunions," Dr. Arksham said. "We have tests to perform, and—"

Ione's eyes found Matt's. "Matt," she gasped.

She recognized him. Matt pushed past the doctor and gave her a quick embrace. It was like hugging a bundle of reeds. "Ione," he said. "I—I missed you."

Ione nodded, her lips turning upward into a painful smile. "I . . . too."

"Mr. Lowell, really, I have to insist," Dr. Arksham said.

"So do I!" Matt snapped. "Give us a moment, will you?"

Arksham looked unhappy, but backed away. Matt took Ione's hand and gave it a light squeeze. Her bones were as sharp as knives. She tried to return the grip, half-heartedly.

"How do you feel?" Matt asked.

"Bad," she breathed, trying to laugh. "But . . . better, I think."

"Yeah?"

"Yes."

Matt's heart soared. She was going to be all right. They could pick up where they left off. They could have a life together.

Ione gripped his hand more tightly. She grimaced and swallowed, as if in pain.

"Are you sure you're all right?"

"Still hurt," she said, voice strengthening.

"We really need to get some real food in her," Dr. Arksham said, his voice firm. "And we need to run tests."

"Of course," Matt said. Arksham was right. She needed to get on her way to recovery. He let go of Ione's hand, but she didn't release her grip.

Matt grinned. She didn't want to let him go.

Ione grimaced again, squeezing his hand tighter. Painfully tight.

"Ione—"

"Something's wrong," she croaked, her eyes going wide.

Arksham and the nurse rushed over. "Where does it hurt? What's wrong?"

Ione shook her head from side to side. "No, no, something wrong, get out, get away!" Her voice rose to a panicked, near-ultrasonic pitch.

Arksham tried to take her pulse, but she batted his hand away. His slate went flying across the room. The nurse tried to pry Matt's hand out of Ione's, but her grip was too strong, incredibly strong. Matt cried out from the pain as she clamped down. Warm blood flowed out of his palm.

Blood? He looked down and gasped. Ione's skin had split open, revealing sharp white spikes. Her bones had turned into razor-sharp weapons, and they ground painfully into the flesh of his hand. The blood that flowed wasn't just hers—it was his own.

"Ione!" Matt yelled.

"Get away, away!" she yelled, thrashing against the restraints that still held her to the bed. She wasn't a weak creature anymore, wracked by disease. She was a whirling harpie, struggling to get free.

Skin stripped back from her other hand, exposing sharp claws. She raked at Dr. Arksham, slashing his face. Red globules of blood flew in the microgravity, spattering the wall of screens on the other side of the room. Arksham yelled and drew back. The nurse recoiled in horror, throwing herself out of the room.

Matt's hand was a throbbing mass of pain. Ione drew him closer to her as she still shook her head in mute negation. Her lips skinned back from her teeth, revealing sharp rows of slashing fangs, set behind her human incisors.

"Ione, please," Matt said.

"No," she moaned. "Can't. Stop."

Her other hand found Matt's shoulder, and spikes dug deep into his muscles. Matt howled and thrashed against her, trying to get free. Ione's claws tore deeper into his flesh, unleashing new crescendos of pain.

Matt couldn't break her grip. Her strength was impossible, absolute. She drew him down into a deadly embrace. Red blood welled up on Ione's hospital gown, and she let out a shrill scream of pain. Matt looked down. New talons had emerged through the skin of her abdomen. They waved hungrily, ready to impale him.

Bang! A sharp report resounded in the small office, deafeningly loud. A small hole appeared in Ione's forehead, and the wall behind her went red with blood and gore. Her hands gave one final convulsive grip, then went slack.

Matt tore his hand out of hers, pushing himself away. He went spinning wildly in the microgravity, hitting the wall opposite with his back and rebounding out into the room.

At the office's inner door, Dr. Arksham held a Taikong P-06 pistol. His hands shook visibly, and his face was a mask of terror. But he'd done what he had to do.

He killed Ione, Matt thought, anger rising. No. He killed the thing Ione had become. The thing the Union had turned her into.

Matt used the handhold to go to Dr. Arksham and take the pistol from his slack fingers. It was still warm from the discharge.

"I—I had to—"

"I know," Matt said. He looked cautiously at Ione's remains. The entire room was spattered in blood, and a faint pink mist hung in the air like fog.

Gone. Ione was gone. Matt couldn't process it. It wasn't happening. Ione was his future. She was his companion, his confidante, his lover.

In that moment, he realized, *I always expected her to just wake up and get better. I thought this would just be a bad dream.*

But it wasn't. Matt felt as if he'd been completely hollowed out, echoing and empty. As if Rayder's chill blade had finished its job and disemboweled him.

But it wasn't Rayder who killed Ione. It was the Union. The fucking Union.

"What—what did they do to her?" Matt's voice was heavy and rough with anger.

Arksham shook his head. "Your precious Union has lots of tricks I've never seen. Like this one. Some kind of extreme combat mode, I suspect."

Matt's anger ramped up into a haze of red. How could they have expected her to survive? Or maybe they didn't. Or maybe the transformation wasn't fatal.

The Union. The Union had taken Ione.

A rustling from the corridor signaled the arrival of Esplandian's red-striped security. They charged into the room, took one look at Ione, and visibly recoiled. One retched and exited the office at high speed.

Arksham came to look at Matt's hand and shoulder. "I can't say I have the tidiest office," he said. "But let's get that fixed up."

"No!" Matt shrugged Arksham off. Ione was gone. The Union had taken her. That was all there was. His other wounds didn't matter. He didn't feel any pain at all.

Matt threw himself out of the office and down the corridor, trailing ruby drops of blood.

17

FLAMEOUT

"This is insane," Soto said as he floated along beside Matt down the central corridor of *Helheim*, the Last Rising flagship.

Matt nodded. "I know."

"The data is probably bullshit."

"I know." The Last Rising intelligence network had waffled about the location, saying it was only the "most probable."

"I'll go in your place."

"You think you have a better shot at it?" Matt turned to look back at Soto. It was still strange seeing him in civilian clothes, though he'd instantly adapted his casual T-shirt and khakis look to his Last Rising command.

Soto sighed and shook his head. Soto knew Matt was the best Mecha pilot they had. And if this was going to work, they'd need every bit of his skill.

They came to the Mecha Dock end of *Helheim*'s central corridor. Looking back down its length, Matt smiled at the changes he saw. The first time he'd floated down the corridor, unthinking mind-controlled crew wearing Rayder's color castes dominated the traffic; only a few technicians were sufficiently free of mind control to even look at Matt. Now it looked like any other thoroughfare in Esplandian, filled with humans and HuMax wearing all manner of clothing, some gathered together in small groups to talk, and some moving purposefully about their work.

I've done this, Matt thought, feeling an instant of pride.

But there was still so much to do.

Matt keyed in his Mecha Dock code and floated into the huge space, followed closely by Soto. Matt's Demon dominated the space, a hulking red skyscraper against the rest of the Mecha. Most of them were Last Rising Lokis and Aesir, but there were a few scattered Hellions as well.

Matt looked up at his Demon, longing to get back in the cockpit. But his Demon would be no good for this mission.

Instead, he floated toward a single Hellion equipped with a streamlined flight pack. Behind it, a chunk of asteroid rock bigger than the Hellion was held in large steel clamps. At the top of the rock was a dark opening, just big enough for the Hellion to crawl inside.

"What happens . . . ," Soto began, then trailed off.

Matt knew what he wanted to ask. What happens if you're detected down there and everything goes sideways? Are you just throwing your life away, in mourning for Ione?

And the terrible thing was: that was partly it. Ione. His Perfect Record tortured him, every minute, with gruesome images of her transformation and demise.

"Then you have a new job to do," Matt told Soto.

Soto nodded, but his expression was pained.

A Last Rising tech emerged from the asteroid hunk and waved at Matt. Matt waved back, his interface suit pulling painfully on his skin. Another reminder this Hellion wasn't his Mecha.

"Five minutes," Soto said, looking at his slate. "You'd better get prepped."

"Yes, sir!"

Soto colored. "I thought there weren't any of those around here."

Matt nodded and pushed off, floating over the steps up to the Hellion's chest cockpit. Inside, raw biometallic muscles wrapped the entire surface of the chamber. Matt wriggled into the harness, plugged in his interface suit's neural connector, and triggered the NPP displays. Compared to a Demon, the Hellion seemed primitive.

"I hope they're right," Soto told Matt as he triggered the cockpit closed.

I do too, Matt thought. But he said nothing as the Hellion folded up like a flower closing for the night. His NPP displays showed Soto quickly retreating to the safety of the dock control room. One corner of the screen counted down the time to their last Displacement—now less than four minutes away.

Mesh, Matt thought. The Hellion's damped neural Mesh was like feeble candlelight next to the Demon's nuclear glow. Matt sighed as his feeling expanded throughout the Hellion. How had he ever been excited about piloting a Hellion?

Matt climbed inside the asteroid chunk. It was a tight fit, even for the relatively small Mecha. He pulled a rock end cap in place over its head, and his screens went dark as he shut out all light.

A brief grinding noise, and Matt's piece of asteroid rocked with movement. Matt knew what was happening: they were moving him in place to the launch doors. Soon they'd slide open. Soon after that, they'd make the final Displacement and fling him out into space.

The countdown on Matt's screen reached fifty-nine seconds. Time for the crazy part.

Power down, Matt thought. The Hellion flashed red-lit warnings. Matt gripped the manual restart and confirmed.

All light disappeared. Matt floated in pitch-blackness. The only sound was a tiny ticking noise, spinning down to silence.

His Hellion was, for all intents and purposes, dead. He'd be going in blind and powerless. But he had to trust Peal and Jahl and the Last Rising informants; he had to trust the *Helheim*'s technician's calculations and their timing. Because the idea was to Displace in, deploy his powered-down Hellion, and Displace out less than forty seconds later, so the orbital sensors had little chance of detecting them.

Or at least that was the theory. Nobody really knew what was going to happen. Nobody knew if he really could reactivate the Hellion as it dropped into the atmosphere, and regain control in time to land. Nobody knew if the Union ACK codes were any good, even if he did get control before planetary impact.

And even if everything went well, Matt had only a single window to meet the *Helheim* again. If he wasn't there, plus or minus twenty seconds, he'd be stranded in Union space.

But that was the only way they had any chance of landing Matt on the Union Core Candidate world of Silver. Their intelligence indicated that the Union still operated a HuMax research lab just outside Franklin, one of Silver's largest cities. If he could get in and expose the Union's secret experiments, he'd have the evidence he needed—

—to avenge Ione—

—to get the truth out to everyone in the Union, and start the process of getting it back in balance.

Silver. Somewhere beneath him, Silver turned, Union sensors searching for any hint of unrecognized activity.

He had to hope that his disguised Hellion was cold and quiet enough to escape detection.

A sharp kick hit Matt hard, bumping him against the back of the cockpit. He cursed and rubbed his head.

This was it. He was committed.

The mechanical timers in Matt's Hellion's protective shell did their job, and the asteroid shard shattered around him, deep in the atmosphere.

Suddenly tumbling, Matt triggered the manual restart and thought, *Mesh.*

The heat of reentry seared Matt's skin as his NPP displays lit, orange and fiery. Fragments of the asteroid glowed red-hot next to him, shading to bright yellow at their leading edge. Below him, the rich continents of Silver spread away like a perspective map, uncomfortably close on the horizon.

Matt righted his Hellion, lit his flight pack, and set his transponder to squawk the Union Mecha Corps ACK code for a routine mission. Theoretically, Silver's planetary defenses would pay no attention to him; he was simply another cog in a greater Mecha wheel. Hellions were openly displayed in all Core and Satellite Union cities now. They were symbols in a larger fight brewing with Demons as its main force.

The ACKs that came back to Matt's signals were routine, simple automated systems disinterested in the whys and wherefores of his mission.

Matt sighed in relief and guided his Hellion to Franklin. The city itself was relatively small, only a half million or so inhabitants, but it glowed like a diamond against the dark night sky. Franklin was being transformed into the Mecha Corps city on Silver. Broad, new-laid fields of pristine concrete flanked two sides of the metropolis, while ranks of Hellions and Demons stood on the practice ground outside the city, where another new Mecha Training Camp transformed cadets into corps.

Matt put his Hellion down in the swamps of a green-tinged lake at the edge of the city, amid fields of tangled green alien plants. Just ahead of him, low industrial buildings marked the edge of Franklin proper, lit by ugly orange sodium lamps.

If their intelligence was right, those nondescript buildings hid a HuMax research lab. Probably not one as grand in scope as the one on Planet 5, but any evidence the Union was experimenting on HuMax would punch a gigantic hole in the Union's party line—and that could open the door to change.

Matt made sure he was recording at max resolution and capacity and moved cautiously forward toward the building. Dim yellowish lights painted windows set high on its facade, but Matt's enhanced sensors couldn't penetrate the thick concrete walls. Only vague heat signatures moved inside.

At the back of the building, more dim light outlined a universal truck dock. The steel roll-up door was fresh painted and pristine. Matt's enhanced sensory array brought garbled fragments of voices from within.

Matt looked at the countdown timer. Less than fifteen minutes to the *El Dorado*'s rearrival. It was now or never. Matt grabbed the bottom of the roll-up door with his Hellion's sharp talons and tugged upward. Its locks gave a brief squeal as they sheared off. The door rolled up effortlessly. Its bang and clatter was shatteringly loud in the still night.

Matt pulled his Hellion through the door. Inside was a large warehouse space, packed with plastic shipping crates. The Hellion's NPPs scanned and tagged the packing codes. They were all processed protein for shipping to industrial food producers.

"Hey! What are you doing in here?" someone yelled. Outside Matt's Hellion, a man wearing a Univeral Foods coverall advanced furiously toward Matt, waggling a finger as if he were scolding a puppy.

"You're not supposed to be here! Damn Mecha, think you own the worlds! Who are you! You'll pay for that door!" The man's litany of complaints just kept coming as his face went scarlet with anger.

Matt had a sudden sinking feeling. This wasn't a lab. This was just another warehouse. Their intelligence had been wrong.

"Hey, you hear me, tell me who you are!" The man now stood only three meters away from the Hellion. He looked up at the big Mecha, totally unafraid. He pulled a slim device out of his pocket. "I'm gonna call the office. You're in big trouble!"

Matt stepped over the man and proceeded deeper into the warehouse. The man ran after him, shouting obscenities. Still, there was nothing but plastic crates of protein. Matt's enhanced senses showed the floor was solid. There was nothing hidden below him. That only left the offices at the front of the building

Matt pushed his Hellion faster, losing the angry functionary in the warehouse. The offices loomed before him. Heat signatures moved behind the thin tilt-up composite walls. Matt grinned. Maybe this was it. He slid to a stop at the facing wall of the office and peered in through the glass windows on top. Beyond were just ranks of cubicles. Some employees had stayed late to play a game of poker. They looked up at the Hellion in surprise as Matt stared at them.

And that was all. The cubicles ended at the glass front of the building, which looked out on a broad courtyard. Matt's enhanced senses found nothing odd.

Wrong.

They were wrong. There were no HuMax here. Nothing here.

"Ninety-eight percent of your network have bad data." Peal's and Jahl's words came back to haunt Matt.

And maybe more. Maybe Peal and Jahl weren't the only countermeasures the Union was using. Maybe none of their data was right at all.

"Gotcha," said a voice behind Matt. A new voice. Not the voice of the yelling man. A big voice.

A Mecha voice.

Matt turned. Behind him stood two Hellions, Fusion Handshakes charged and ready.

It wasn't just bad intelligence.

It was a trap.

No chance for explanation. No chance for anything other than surprise.

Matt triggered his Hellion's flight pack booster. Behind him, the office wall buckled and glass shattered. Matt shot forward and struck the two Hellions like a hammer. His Hellion bucked and rang with biometallic reverberations. The two other Hellions bowled over and went tumbling through protein crates. Billowing brown clouds of powder cascaded out through the warehouse. The yelling man coughed and scampered away from the fighting giants.

Matt accelerated toward the exit, but one Hellion caught him by the arm. He felt its Fusion Handshake charging up to fire. Matt winced. He'd lose the arm. No changing that now.

Then the Fusion Handshake stopped charging. Matt looked down. The Hellion still clung to him, but now its visor looked upward toward his own. It looked almost confused.

Who's confused? a familiar thought came. And in that moment, he knew who he was fighting.

Major Michelle Kind.

Every shattered piece of Matt and Michelle's almost relationship went cascading through his Perfect Record, torturous in its perfection. Seeing her for the first time at Mecha Training Camp. Kyle's assertion that "she will be mine." Growing too close to her for Kyle to control. Holding hands, that one last night after Jotunheim. Trying to save the universe together more than once.

The memories, the feel of Michelle's warm body against his, the taunting memories. It was a brief glimpse of a perfect life, one he could never attain.

Michelle, he thought. *I—I—*

You traitor! she thought, her mind sending waves of hate. In a glimpse, she'd seen him as a part of the Corsairs, as a defector from the Union.

Soto joined me, Matt thought.

Michelle's thoughts paused, just for a moment.

And Lena. And Peal and Jahl.

Doubt. He absolutely felt doubt. Michelle was wondering how much truth was behind his thoughts.

"See?" Matt said, out loud, and sent her images of his mission on Planet 5, and the terrible experiments they were doing on the HuMax.

Michelle softened, just for an instant. And in that moment, Matt saw her mind laid bare. She really did trust the Union. She loved her appointment on Silver. She was a major, and she was going higher. She was with . . . Marjan. Marjan. The new man in her life.

And she just couldn't integrate what he had just shown her.

The Union must have a reason, she thought.

Yes. They created the HuMax.

No!

Matt sent her memories of his battle with Rayder, and his takeover and release of the mind-controlled masses.

The aftermath. Ione, and what the Union had done to her.

But Michelle's anger ramped up, savagely. *You found a lover? A HuMax?* she thought, her mind razor-edged. Her Fusion Handshake cycled up to fire again.

But her grip had faltered. Matt threw her off. She went flailing backward into a tall stack of the protein crates. Gray-brown dust came exhaling out of the warehouse in waves.

From the cloud, a flickering light. Matt rocked back as Fireflies found his Hellion. Sharp flares of pain blossomed on his chest.

And that wasn't the end of the explosion. The flammable dust in the warehouse lit in a reverberant dirty orange fireball. The flame front hit him like a giant fist, pushing his Hellion backward through the warehouse. Matt flailed through plastic crates, spilling more protein powder. The flame front carried him all the way out the roll-up door as the entire building ballooned from the pressure wave. Gouts of dust shot from new-stricken cracks in the tilt-up facade. Wisps of flame shot into the air from the shattered roof.

Matt landed hard on his back, skidding across the blacktop with a wet biometallic screech. Flame billowed out of the ruined roll-up door, passing only meters above his Hellion.

The two Union Hellions flew out of the flames like birds of prey descending on a feast. Matt took one look at their grim, determined visors and knew: Michelle would not join him. Not now. Maybe not ever.

Matt triggered his flight pack and shot toward the sky. Eight minutes to rendezvous. Eight minutes of eluding those Hellions.

And, his screens reminded him, the rest of the Mecha

they were now launching at him—one of which was labeled DEMON.

Matt's thrusters propelled him toward orbit like an ascending rocket. Behind him, his NPP screens showed the Hellions falling behind. They must have had only planetary flight packs on.

One spark kept pursuing. This one was marked with a red icon: a Demon!

Ah, shit, Matt thought. Four minutes and thirty seconds left. What could he do? Straight up against a Demon, he was a dead man.

Matt searched his POV for places to run. But Silver had no moons. Its skies were empty, except for the Union's orbital emplacements.

The brilliant beam of a Zap Gun flashed by Matt's backside, close enough to feel the heat. The Demon pilot was gaining—and he was already within range!

A comms icon flared on Matt's POV: MARJAN VELUSZIK.

"Couldn't stay away, could you, traitor?" Marjan's voice grated over the comms.

Matt smiled, remembering one of Michelle's memories. "Couldn't move into her apartment, could you, loser?" Matt taunted.

Marjan yelled in rage, and additional Zap Gun bolts passed by Matt's sides. These were less targeted, wild. Marjan was losing his grip.

"Did she talk about me?" Matt asked. "I bet she did."

An orbital emplacement loomed in front of Matt. ANTIMATTER WEAPON TARGETING flared in his POV. Matt instinctively jinked away from the emplacement at full redline.

Then he had an idea. It was a stupid idea, an impossible idea. But the whole thing had gone from stupid to impossible. Why stop now?

Matt released the limiters on his flight pack and pushed them to twice redline, ignoring their squeals of imminent destruction. This wasn't about coming back repairable. This was about coming back with his life.

His velocity took him on a wild parabola past the side of the Union's orbital gun emplacement. He had a momentary glimpse of its guns, struggling to track him. Matt pushed his thrusters deeper into redline as he braked behind the emplacement. His velocity dropped like a rock, and he rocketed toward the surface.

The guns on this side of the rock swiveled eagerly. He had only seconds. Matt gave the thrusters all they had.

Bam! Matt impacted on the surface of the rocky emplacement. Dull steel gun turrets poked up all around him. Matt rolled over the surface of the asteroid and reached one of the turrets. Gripping it with both hands, he thought, *Merge.*

Matt's Hellion's hands became one with the turret. Suddenly he was the big gun, an unthinking algorithmic construct on a simple mission: protect the planet. The emplacement was entirely automated. There were no people on it at all, just machines.

In the machine's mind, Matt saw Marjan. Approaching fast, his Zap Gun charged and ready. To the emplacement, Marjan was not a threat, because he broadcast the right Union ACK codes.

As if on cue, a Zap Gun bolt hit the emplacement. Its simple electronic mind registered confusion, but it didn't act against Marjan.

Matt grinned. He could change that. Using the emplacement's own comms, he swapped the ACK codes between Marjan and himself.

Marjan reacted immediately as the guns swung

around to target his Demon. His forward motion slowed fast as his thrusters lit, and he barely jogged out of the line of fire for an antimatter bolt. Marjan retreated away from the emplacement. The guns followed, forcing him farther and farther away.

On the surface of Silver, Matt's screens showed additional sparks crawling toward orbit. More Demons. His safe haven wouldn't survive an assault by them.

One minute, forty seconds left. Could he make it?

You have to, he thought. Matt's NPP screens showed the location of his rendezvous point, a thousand kilometers away.

Matt waited until the heavy-matter guns had reloaded and were ready to fire. He thought, *DeMerge,* and pulled his arm out of the turret. Then, in one quick motion, he blasted his thrusters to full and leapt off the emplacement in the direction of his rendezvous point.

Then, in the same instant, he cut all power except for his screens. Hopefully the interference from the heavy-matter guns had covered his launch. Hopefully he'd drift across space, almost dead, to arrive as the Last Rising appeared.

Of course, if he miscalculated and went a little too far—well, there were lots of stories about finding small orbital shuttles, oddly crystallized and embedded deep within the rock of a Displacement Drive ship.

Matt's heart beat loudly in the tiny cockpit as he drifted through space. Behind him, the Demons converged on the orbital gun emplacement. Brilliant lines of battle sketched in his POV. The clock ticked slowly down: one minute, thirty seconds, ten seconds.

Matt gripped the emergency restart, his lips dry and his breath coming in ragged gasps.

Just outside Matt's Hellion, a gigantic mass flashed into being. Matt swore and restarted his Hellion, looking in vain for a landmark. The *Helheim*'s smooth armored surface was almost completely seamless.

There! In front of him! The Mecha Docks!

Matt shot forward into the dark bay, just as Union antimatter fire rocked the *Helheim*. Orange-yellow explosions lit the docks like lightning, and the air lock itself melted and ran.

Then the stars changed, and there was nothing.

Matt's comms crackled on, the icon reading SOTO.

"Tell me this stunt was worth it," Soto's voice boomed.

Matt sighed. What could he say?

Then he realized what Soto had asked, and he barked a laugh. "Yeah," he said. "It was worth it."

"Then what are you waiting for? Get me the footage, and let's crack the Union wide open!"

Matt shook his head. His Hellion mimicked the motion perfectly. Soto just stared at him, unable to comprehend what Matt was getting at.

"It was worth it," Matt said. "To prove our intelligence is completely worthless."

18

DECLARATION

"Seventeen months ago, a man named Rayder attacked Geos and issued an ultimatum: 'make me prime, or I will smash the Union.'" Matt licked his lips and paused, staring at the glassy eye of the FTLcomm camera. He was alone on the bridge of the *Helheim*, with the exception of two men: Guiliano Soto and Captain Gonsalves.

Matt continued. "You were told Rayder was killed in a daring raid by Mecha Corps personnel. But you weren't told who these corpspersons were. You weren't told many things."

Matt felt sweat beading on his brow, despite the chill of the room. He'd had the techs crank down the temperature to eighteen degrees C, but it didn't seem to help. He didn't like talking to the camera. Talking to people was easier. The tiny, multifaceted lens seemed to be weighing him . . . and finding him wanting.

"I was one of the Corps who participated in that raid. I am also the person who killed Rayder. I am Matt Lowell, first Demonrider and former Mecha Corps major."

The technicians would later insert here a cut scene from Matt killing Rayder, a recording by the villain who thought his triumph was going to be broadcast to his

brainwashed legions. Instead, it would serve a better purpose.

"But I am no longer Mecha Corps. I speak to you now
as the leader of the Free Stars Alliance, a neutral and
independent entity that has no military quarrel with the
Union."

No military quarrel, but certainly a subversive agenda,
a small voice whispered in Matt's mind. He shrugged it
off and pressed on.

"You might ask why a hero of the Union no longer
wears the uniform. It comes back to what the Union isn't
telling you. I've discovered some things about the Union
that I think you should know. For example, the Union's
ongoing experiments in genetic modification."

Matt knew the techs would edit in a brief version of
the Planet 5 video at this point, with extensive attached
archives of compressed data. Hopefully the viewers
would dig deeper into the attachments to see the whole
story: the Union as the source of the HuMax, the ongoing atrocities.

Soto stepped forward. "I'm Colonel Guiliano Soto,
formerly of Mecha Corps. I've known Matt since he was
at Mecha Training Camp. I fought with him against Rayder. I joined the Union from the Aliancia because I believed in what the Union was doing. We need to pull
together, and work as one people. But over the years,
I've seen the hidden agendas, the truth behind the promise. Now I've seen Mr. Lowell's evidence, and I've joined
him."

Captain Hector Gonsalves stepped forward. "And I
am only here today, a thinking man, because of Matt's
overthrow of Rayder's regime. It may sound like a joke,
but if it wasn't for Matt, I'd be a mind-controlled pup-
pet."

Matt addressed the camera again. "If what you've

seen concerns you, contact the Union press and demand
the truth. Contact your Union congressperson and demand the full archives on their genetic modification experiments. Pressure the Prime to release the whole story,
and take action to end genetic experimentation. I want
nothing more than for the Union to fulfill its promise.
But to do so, it must face its past, to create a better future."

Matt held his determined expression for a few moments. The techs would edit the video from there, and
then squeeze-burst transmit it via FTLcomm to their
network's Union transponders.

"How was that?" Matt said as Lena Stoll entered the
bridge, followed closely by Peal and Jahl. In addition to
being an excellent Mecha controller, she was also prov-
ing to be the ideal leader for their flighty duo.

"Better than the first transmission," she said, classi-
cally deadpan.

"So it's still crap?"

Lena didn't react. "Let's hope your earnest tone car-
ries the day."

"He did fine!" Soto boomed. "I just don't think we're
going far enough."

"Calling for open insurrection, or inviting Union
worlds to be part of the Free Stars Alliance, would be a
huge mistake," Captain Gonsalves added, rising to hang
out on a rail. "Then we'd be considered a strategic threat,
inciting secession."

"This is the same thing," Soto said. "We're telling
them their entire government is corrupt and amoral."

Gonsalves shrugged. "It's the principle. People have
hope in change. Even if it's a silly hope."

Matt frowned. Except they had even more tolerance
for the status quo, it seemed.

Their first transmission had hit the Union like a

heavy-matter gun. Major media had erupted about the "new Corsair threat" to the Union hegemony—despite the fact that they flew no Corsair colors, and Matt clearly identified them as the Free Stars Alliance, using terminology carefully stitched together from the Independent Displacement Alliance. Talking heads had painted him as a misguided hero or a rapacious opportunist, standing on the dead body of Rayder to threaten the Union. They played more video of Rayder's attack on Geos than Matt's simple plea asked for.

The few outlets that covered the meat of Matt's content were small and sparse, though lively chatter on the UniNet flared for a week afterward. Nine possible locations of current HuMax experimentation were listed, but the Union citizens who dared investigate found innocent businesses, or a rapid arrest. Their intelligence network couldn't confirm that any of the leads were more solid than their failed one on Silver. One well-funded news expedition found an empty facility, apparently long abandoned. Matt was labeled a crank and a nut, and the buzz on the UniNet began to spin down to its usual low-level mutter about conspiracy theories and political plots.

Net result, zero. No giant revelations. No hint of insurrection, even on the farthest-flung colony worlds. No fires in the street. A few million messages to senators, perhaps, but that was nothing in an interstellar governmental organization spanning billions of lives.

"We have to keep trying," Matt said.

Lena shifted uncomfortably and exchanged glances with Peal and Jahl. Matt frowned. He knew Peal and Jahl were ill at ease with his transmissions, but what else could he do? With no reliable intelligence on Union/HuMax experimentation, they had no other way to make people believe.

"What we have to do is start drinking," Captain Gonsalves said. "Why don't we head out to the Free Stars?"

Soto concurred, and Matt, Lena, Peal, and Jahl tagged along with the group.

The Free Stars was a new bar set deep within *Helheim*, established by some enterprising Last Rising crew who'd repurposed one of the former communal sleeping chambers. Ranks of hard steel bunks had been turned into tables, with chairs set every which way to maximize the space in zero gravity. A long bar had been set up along the back wall, backed by a traditional mirror. Some patrons hung near the bar, not even bothering to use the handholds.

When they were all at a table with drink bulbs in front of them, Lena opened her mouth as if to ask a question, then shut it again. She looked at Peal and Jahl, and they returned her look with nods.

"I know, I know," he told her. "Every transmission increases the chance of discovery of our transponders within the Union. Our effective coverage will shrink. But unless you have other suggestions—"

"Not just that," Peal interrupted.

Jahl shot him a look. "It's by no means certain they have the ability to effectively analyze entangled-pair distortions."

"If we can do it, they can do it too."

"Do what?" Matt and Gonsalves said, in unison.

"We have new tracking techniques in development. Analysis of entangled-pair distortions on the FTLcomms can assist in location of the source," Jahl admitted.

"I thought that wasn't possible if we weren't transmitting directly!" Matt said, alarm rising.

"It's something we've been working on," Jahl said. "Very cutting-edge."

"Does this mean the Union can find us?" Matt said, a sudden chill shooting through his body.

"Some of the research we've been doing here started in the Union," Peal said.

"But the logical connections aren't there," Jahl argued. "We didn't have any idea it could work as a location technique, until just yesterday. The chances the Union would expand on our research—"

"Is small but nonzero," Peal finished.

Lena broke in. "And it's not that simple—"

Matt had had enough. He held up his hands. "Wait. Stop arguing. Do we have a chance of being discovered because of our transmissions? As in, the Union shows up on our doorstep?"

"Even if they extend the research we started to the breakthrough we just had, entangled-pair FTLcomm distortion is nearly impossible to analyze at the level of precision necessary to locate Esplandian," Jahl said.

Matt sighed. Good. But why were they so on-edge?

"However, they may be able to get our range," Peal added.

Shit.

"Of course, they may discount the results at first, since the source will seem too close," Jahl shot back.

"But if they accept the results, it will substantially reduce their search volumetric," Peal said.

"This speculation, of course, is assuming they have our same breakthrough."

Silence fell over the six people at the bar as Peal's and Jahl's verbal jousting sunk in. The stakes were too high. They had to assume the Union would chase down the same answer as Peal and Jahl—especially with a troubling FTLcomms transmission stirring up their media.

Matt shifted uncomfortably on his perch. That was bad. Matt had always counted on losing the odd repeater in Union space, but FTLcomm itself was never supposed to be a problem.

"What if we send the second transmission from a repeater in deep Last Rising space?" Matt said.

"We've been talking about that," Lena told him. "It won't work."

Peal nodded. "One of the principles of FTLcomm entangled communications is that it always reflects the distortion of the original source."

"We'd have to actually do the transmission physically from a remote system in deep space," Lena said.

"Then that's what we'll do."

"Leaving Esplandian vulnerable? And possibly sentencing an innocent system to destruction by the Union?" Lena said.

Matt felt as if he'd been punched in the gut. He could say nothing for a long time. Instead, he sipped his vacuum-distilled vodka and winced at its roughness. The booze was as new as the bar, it seemed.

"How many FTLcomm transmissions can we do and still be safe?"

Jahl and Peal pulled out their slates and bent over the gray-blue glow, muttering to themselves. Matt let them work.

"Assuming they work out the same reverse-processing algorithm we landed on, and they set it at Highest Priority in UARL," Peal announced finally, "maximum may be as high as ten. Minimum could be three."

Silence shrouded the table. Matt shared nervous glances with Captain Gonsalves and Soto.

"So the next transmission after this one, we could be found?"

Jahl frowned. "Like I said, it isn't that simple, and there are a lot of assumptions—"

"But we could?"

Peal sighed. "Yes. We could."

Matt sat silently as Gonsalves and Soto turned to look

at him. At that moment, it seemed as if the entire bar had their eyes on him.

Saying, You're gambling with our lives.

Word from Dr. Arksham interrupted Matt's worries about discovery by the Union. Arksham had his genetic results back. Matt headed to his office, his mind in a daze. Would this finally answer, definitively, what his father's gift really was?

Will I be HuMax? Matt wondered.

Matt barreled into the office. For a moment, his Perfect Record overrode reality and painted the office as he'd last seen it, spattered in blood and gore. Ione's shredded body was still strapped to the table—

Matt closed his eyes, willing back the welling rage. Ione. The Union had taken Ione. They deserved to pay.

They deserve all your rage, a small voice said. Matt started. It didn't even feel like his own thought. It felt— outside, alien. He was hungering to get back in the Demon. The voice was part of his addiction.

In reality, Arksham's office was spotlessly clean. It had undoubtedly been disinfected weeks ago. Matt shook his head and went to the doctor's inner office, where Arksham sat at his desk.

"What am I?" Matt asked.

Arksham raised an eyebrow, as if to say, *No time for pleasantries, hmm?* But he just said mildly, "You're a mongrel."

"Not HuMax?"

"There are similarities. But pure HuMax, with the markers that define it, no."

Not HuMax. Matt nodded, not knowing whether to be relieved or disappointed. "What do you mean, a mongrel?"

Arksham shook his head. "Perhaps a bad term.

There's a ton of old code in your DNA, dating back to the beginning of human genetic modification. It looks like your father mined all the old databases. But . . ."

"But what?" Matt leaned forward.

"But you also have more pure sequences than I've ever seen in a viable genemod organism."

"Pure sequences?"

"Sequences without the junk DNA and redundant viral clutter that fill up the human genome. Entirely engineered parts, crafted to perfection. As if a master engineer was creating a whole new code base."

"My father did that?"

Arksham gave Matt a sad grin. "That's the problem. I don't know of anyone who could have put together these pieces so masterfully, without negative interactions."

"So he found it somewhere in the databases."

Arksham looked doubtful. "I don't think so. There are no referents to large parts of your genome in any of the databases, not even from our Last Rising network."

"Then he got it from the HuMax databases. My father worked with UARL, digging up HuMax history."

A head shake. "HuMax aren't this pure. Never were. He didn't find it in a HuMax database."

Matt frowned and said nothing for a long time. "So, what does this all mean?"

"It means that either your father was the greatest genetic engineer ever known or he found another source, one so buried it doesn't even exist on Jotunheim."

A pure chill worked its way down Matt's spine.

You're not a HuMax. You're a mongrel.

But what was he, really? Had his father found a source nobody else had uncovered, or was it some kind of genetic magic? For all Arksham's analysis, all he'd confirmed was that he was a true mystery.

*   *   *

The second transmission went much like the first.

At first, an uproar. Then Union assurances, coating everything like a confection. Finally separations: Union loyalists, loudly crying for an assault to put an end to the Corsairs once and for all, and Union skeptics, who dug even deeper into Union records—and began to find some corroboration with Matt's message.

Still, even though the ranks of skeptics grew, they were a tiny minority in the grand Union. Their voices shouted on tertiary media, shrill and demanding. Primary media like UUN ignored them, as if they didn't exist.

Of course, Matt thought. UUN was intimately entwined with the Union Congress and military. They'd never say anything against their beloved Union.

And for all the good they were doing, they might as well not be there at all. Peal had charted the rise of skeptics versus transmissions, and even in the best-case scenario, they were looking at dozens of messages before they would even be heard in Congress. They'd be found long before then, and the Union would have every excuse to use its Pushback II resources for one quick, surgical mission.

To excise him. As they had tried to do with Rayder.

Matt lay awake in his Esplandian apartment, looking out the high-set windows at *Helheim*. He knew he should be on the flagship of the Last Rising fleet, but he liked to be here on Esplandian whenever he could. Even though nearly everyone had been released from mind control now, *Helheim* still felt very much like a Rayder vessel.

And maybe that was what he should focus on. Expanding the mind-control reversal process throughout Last Rising space. One more transmission, and they were treading into the danger zone for detection—and without some kind of breakthrough angle, the numbers said they had no chance.

Matt's slate shrilled, lighting the room with its chilly screen glow. Matt rolled over to look at it, and saw a message that both made his blood run cold, and his heart beat a little bit faster.

LENA STOLL: We have to meet. Discreetly.

Matt met Lena Matt at Esplandian's air lock. She'd obviously been waiting for him.

"Have we been found?"

A surprisingly complex set of emotions passed over Lena Stoll's face in an instant. Eventually she shook her head. "Not so simple. Best not to talk here."

"Lead on, my lady," Matt said, trying for levity.

"I was never your lady, and never will be," Lena said, serious again.

Matt didn't know what to say. Eventually he settled for "I'm sorry."

Lena gave him a sad, thin smile. It was one of the most mournful expressions Matt had ever seen. "I don't understand the mechanics of attraction. I just know they don't typically work in my favor."

"Lena," Matt said, reaching out toward her.

"No!" she said, and flung herself down the hall.

Matt followed. What else could he do? And what could he do for Lena? She had Soto. Matt had nothing but an empty space in his heart. Ione was dead. Michelle had turned on him.

Lena led him to a shuttle and set off for *Helheim*. It was a chilly, silent trip. Matt tried to think of something to say, anything. But his mouth was dry, and his words were absent.

In *Helheim*, Lena had her office in the Core tech labs.

Peal and Jahl were there too, their eyes glazed behind NPP displays.

She shut the door and spun one of the displays so Matt could see it. On the screen, a freeze-frame image of Dr. Salvatore Roth stared blankly out at them. It was badly bit-rotted from FTLcomm.

Matt jumped, his heart pounding. "Tell me this isn't live."

Lena shook her head. "Just a message. Not two-way."

"Play it."

Lena nodded. Roth's image jumped to life.

"So the prodigy has decided to set out on his own path," Dr. Roth said. A haughty, sardonic smile twisted his words, but the expression never reached his soulless eyes. "Admirable, in its way, but you're surely aware by now what a fool's errand this is. The Union will find you, as I have found you, and it will crush you."

Matt swallowed. Sweat beaded on his forehead. "He's found us?"

Lena shook her head. "This is a broadwash. He's not targeting us specifically. He's still guessing."

Beads of sweat dripped from Matt's brow. He wiped it away as Dr. Roth continued:

"I am not here to make threats. As you know, I also follow my own path. And I may be able to help you on your own. Specifically, I may be able to provide certain locations that are of extreme interest—and use—to you. Given your failure on Silver, I would expect this to be highly intriguing. If you would like to accept this offer, please meet me at Sangre de Cristo's main port to discuss. Coordinates and date follow."

Roth's image flicked off. Matt stood still for a long time, unsure how to react. Sangre de Cristo was an Aliancia world, closest to the Universal Union. But—

—working with Dr. Roth? Instinctive revulsion flared

in Matt. He still didn't know what Roth had done to him, in those three days he'd been unconscious in Mecha Training Camp. Nor did he know what Roth's final goal was in Corsair space. Their intelligence network had never determined that.

Locations that are of extreme interest. Union labs currently working on HuMax? Could Roth know where they were? His Advanced Mechaforms hooks went deep into the Union. It was possible.

More than possible. Probable.

"You're not actually thinking of accepting, are you?" Lena asked.

"No. I'm not thinking about it." He'd already made his decision.

What other choice did he have?

Sangre de Cristo was less of a colony world. More of an outpost, used by the Aliancia as a base to shuttle rare-metal-rich asteroids back to their two Core Worlds. The sun burned a dull orange, and the world was a barren rock. Only the massive orbiting space station, built out of raw asteroidal steel, was habitable. Displacement Drive ships of the Aliancia and Corsairs hung suspended outside the Sangre de Cristo Station, glowing in the orange sun like rubies strung in a necklace.

Among the Aliancia and Corsair ships, one massive asteroid bore the unmistakable signs of a Union ship: scaffolding and partial armor, and giant antimatter maneuvering rockets.

It wasn't any ship that Matt recognized, though. Not the *Helios*. Not *Ulysses*. In fact, it bore no Union marking, even under deep scrutiny. It just hung there, cool and implacable. *Helheim*'s sensors reported its weapons as inactive; not a single heavy-matter gun or antimatter annihilator was trained their way. If the readouts were to be believed, even the weapons control systems were cold.

"Doesn't mean a damn thing," Soto said, leaning over a technician's shoulder and studying the readouts skeptically. "The Union could Displace in a half dozen warships at any second. This is still a damn stupid idea."

Then why not have them waiting for us? Matt thought. And Soto was missing the even more disturbing possibility that Dr. Roth was building his own Displacement Drive ship, independent of the Union.

"Stupid or not, we're here," Matt said, heading out of the bridge. "Let's do this."

Soto followed, protesting all the way. Matt ignored him, until they reached the dock.

"If you're so skeptical, stay behind."

Soto's sharp features crumpled in frustration. "I'm just trying—"

"If I'm wrong, these people need someone to lead them."

Sudden fear shot across Soto's face. "I can't . . . I won't—"

"You're the best choice," Matt said, and slipped through the air lock. The technicians locked it behind him, so Soto could only pound on the heavy steel.

Matt sighed. He'd made it sound so altruistic, but in reality there were many reasons he wanted to do this alone. What other information could he get from Roth?

And what would he have to agree to, in order to get what he needed?

Lena piloted the shuttle across to Sangre de Cristo Station, cool and efficient. There was no trace of the sad longing he'd glimpsed in her just a few days before. Was that how she felt all the time? Would she ever be able to make a stable connection to her true feelings? Or was her focused impassivity part of her genetic modification, and nearly impossible to overcome?

Matt sighed. He had to let it go. She was a good friend, and a great soldier to have on his side. That was quite a lot. He waved good-bye to her when they were docked, and followed preset markers down a steel corridor into the space station.

Two minutes later, Matt was standing in a spare little meeting room, set with a table and two chairs. There were no windows. The room was buried deep within the space station.

Roth entered after a few minutes. He looked Matt up and down, as if weighing him. Matt refused to look away. After a few moments, Roth nodded and sat at the table. Matt remained standing.

"I'm impressed," Dr. Roth said. "You followed instructions precisely, and you came by yourself."

"Am I to be graded?" Matt asked.

Roth gave Matt a thin, emotionless smile. "Touché. To continue the metaphor, no. You're done with school. You have grown up since I had to drag you back from orbit in the Demon."

Images from Matt's ill-fated First Exercise flashed in his Perfect Record. *Unpermitted Merge! Decouple!* It seemed as if it had happened a million years ago. It seemed as if it had happened to a different person.

Roth has shaped me, Matt thought. Roth could have washed him out, on that one early day at training camp. Instead, thanks to him, he controlled Mecha now, the greatest weapon man has ever known.

But Roth was no father figure to him. Only a cold, calculating politician with his own inscrutable agenda.

"Where are the HuMax labs?" Matt asked.

Roth shook his head, as if disappointed. "So direct. So forthright. Is there to be no give-and-take?"

Matt clenched his fists. His only chance was to use the information he had about Roth's past. "I know you've spent time in the Aliancia. And with Corsairs."

A raised eyebrow. "And you hope to hold this over me? Threaten to tell the Union? Do you think they care?"

Matt's intelligence network's assessment of Roth came swimming back in his Perfect Record. It called him a "necessary commodity" and instructed security personnel to "observe, but not interfere."

"Do you even dare another transmission?" Roth continued.

"We'll continue as long as necessary," Matt said. But his eyes flickered away from Roth's.

The other man chuckled briefly. "We both know that isn't true. The Union will find you if you continue down this path. And they will call on my Mecha to eliminate you."

Matt said nothing.

"But that will destroy what we are both setting out to do: return the universe to balance."

Matt looked at Dr. Roth, openmouthed. Was he actually saying that he had the same goals?

"By making Hellions? Demons? Killing cadets? Addicting pilots?" Matt shot back.

"What better way to curb the Union's rapacious military than to bleed its funds with a perfect tool it cannot replicate? To subvert its most capable citizens with physical addiction to my Mecha?"

Matt rocked back, as if physically stricken. Could that possibly be true? Was Roth trying to bring the Union down—through his Mecha?

No. Impossible.

"I see you're skeptical," Roth said. "But I assure you, we have the same goal: the rebalancing of the Union."

"I don't believe it," Matt spat back.

Roth sighed and spread his hands, as if saying, *I have nothing to hide.* "I understand. But consider my actions to date. I reached out to you. I have come here, at great risk, to meet with you, and discuss how I can further your goals."

Matt ground his teeth. "Or to find out more about us, and report your findings to the Union."

Roth shook his head. "You insult me by calling me a Union stooge."

Matt fell silent. Roth was right. He and the Union had always had a contentious but intertwined relationship. Still, there was something wrong here. Something about Roth. More than his impassive demeanor, more than his severe countenance. Matt had known something was wrong with Roth from the moment he met him. He had his own agenda, and it didn't align with anyone else's — not Matt's or the Union's.

"Go on," Matt said.

"What would the locations of four operational Hu-Max research facilities, on Union Core Worlds, do for your cause?" Roth asked, the hint of a genuine smile playing at his mouth.

Wow. That was more than Matt had expected.

"Four?" Matt asked. "On Core Worlds?"

A nod. "Core Worlds."

"But—but why Planet 5? Why was that one lab so remote, if they're doing HuMax research on Core Worlds?" Matt protested.

"Planet 5 is—was—the crown jewel. The most extreme. The most long-term. The best data. But there are still monsters in our midst."

"HuMax aren't monsters."

"To the Union, they are." Roth's voice was mild.

Matt reeled. If that was true, they could go in with

force, liberate the HuMax—and broadcast everything in real time to the entire Union. The evidence would be right there in front of them, huge and incontrovertible. They couldn't ignore it.

"And there is Arcadia," Roth said. "On Eridani."

"Arcadia?"

"The lab of labs. It may be the origin of the HuMax themselves. It is, I understand, largely inactive. But it may have evidence—evidence of Union-HuMax activity dating back to the Expansion."

Matt licked his lips. "Why not do it yourself?"

"Unlike you, I do not have the advantage of surprise. I also do not have sufficient control over my Mecha pilots, as you have demonstrated to great effect yourself a number of times."

"What do you want in return?" Matt asked.

Roth formed his lips into a smile. It was a mechanical gesture, like something programmed into an automaton. "I only wish to see the Union returned to balance, like you."

Matt shivered, despite the warmth of the room. Somehow Roth wanting nothing from him made the offer even more terrible.

I will pay the price in the future, Matt thought. *No matter what he says.*

But what could he do?

Matt made himself extend a hand.

Roth did the same.

19

LIBERATION

In the Space Between the Union's Core Worlds, Free Stars Alliance Displacement Drive ships gathered. Five in all. FSS *Helheim*, led by Matt Lowell. FSS *El Dorado*, led by Captain Horatio Gonsalves. FSS *Midgard*, another Last Rising ship, now led by Lena Stoll. FSS *Niflheim* and FSS *Utgard* rounded out the Corsair ships, commanded by Anne Raskin and Uve Next, a HuMax, respectively.

Each ship was only one jump away from its destination. All Core Worlds: Aurora, Geos, Greenland, Utopia, and Eridani.

"If Roth's bullshitting us, we're all dead," Soto said, his voice distorted by the FTLcomm transmission.

Matt nodded, but didn't respond. He was deep in the pilot's cockpit of his Demon, cradled by magnetorheological fluid and watching the world through his wraparound viewmask. It was as if he were fifteen meters high himself. Matt smiled, basking in the warm glow of Mesh. It had been a long time since he'd been in the Mecha.

I want to stay here forever, Matt thought.

Yes, this is your place, this is your time. Scratchy, like static and dust.

But that was the Mesh talking, eating deeper into his

mind. It was a risk he had to take. He would deal with the addiction if—when—he got out of this alive.

Matt surveyed his screen. Five insets showed key POVs of his Mecha commanders on board each Displacement Drive ship. Four new faces, and Soto. Soto had introduced Matt to his best Mecha pilots the night before. All four were HuMax. Soto seemed embarrassed, muttering about the lingering effects of Rayder's programming and the rushed program, but Matt wasn't surprised. HuMax and genemod made better Mecha pilots. Which made Soto's proficiency that much more startling.

Unless he was a genemod himself, and didn't know it. There were so many secrets hidden in the human universe, Matt didn't think he could be surprised anymore.

And what the top pilots were didn't matter. Genemod or HuMax or human. They were all just people. What mattered was that Soto trusted them, and Matt trusted Soto.

Soto was inside an Aesir, within *El Dorado*'s familiar spaceport dock. Waiting for the command.

Numbers spun down in front of Matt. Everything falling into place. Right vectors. Right timing.

Three.

Two.

One.

"Displace," Matt said.

In the Space Between, four of the five ships winked out of existence. Only one, *Helheim*, remained behind.

From here, Matt would watch and wait. For now.

Soto's POV was at first a jumble: a quick puff of escaping gas from the *El Dorado*'s docks; then the lush green surface of Aurora filled the screen. Every one of their drops was a deep one, to avoid the worst of the orbital weapons platforms.

Other Aesirs came to fly alongside Soto, joined quickly by squirming masses of silver Lokis as they descended deeper into the atmosphere. White contrails of flash-frozen ice crystals streamed from every razor edge of the Aesirs.

As he watched Soto descend over the fuzzy FTL-comm link, Matt's Perfect Record recalled his rationale for the mission. *If the Union can use Mecha to surgically extract diplomats with no civilian casualties, why can't we use them to extract HuMax from research facilities the same way?*

"But you know someone will die," Soto had told him.

"We don't know that," Matt had responded.

"We might not kill anyone, but the Union will," Soto had said.

Matt hadn't responded to that. Soto knew this was necessary. He knew there wasn't any choice. They had headed down this road, and they needed to drive it to its end. Soto just wanted to make sure Matt understood the consequences, and accepted it when the Union pulled out the stops.

ANTIMATTER WEAPONS TARGETING, Soto's POV screamed. Lock sensors traced lines down to the surface of Aurora—to the same nondescript installation they were heading toward, a university lab set at the edge of a broad bay.

Of course. The Union wasn't stupid.

"Break formation!" Soto yelled. "Lokis, dive deep and try to get a line on the target. Aesirs, use antimatter arms!"

"No antimatter weapons!" Matt said. "You'll wipe out the whole facility."

ANTIMATTER WEAPONS LOCK, Soto's POV shouted.

The world went white. Soto sheared off, his Mecha tumbling wildly. One of the other Aesirs beside him disintegrated with a shrill, high-pitched explosion that sounded eerily like a scream.

ANTIMATTER WEAPONS TARGETING.

"If no antimatter, looking for suggestions!" Soto yelled.

Matt ground his teeth. The facility had finally wavered into view. They were still a hundred kilometers out. A hundred kilometers of antimatter beam through atmosphere was a recipe for disaster. They could easily slice the whole lab to ribbons.

"Move in fast and loose! They won't be able to lock on you. Use the Mecha like you mean it!" Matt said.

"What?" Soto spat. "I can't move like you do in a Mecha!"

"You can if you want to! Do something unpredictable!"

ANTIMATTER WEAPONS LOCK.

Another beam split the sky, like reverse lightning. This one went wide and wavered for a moment, only grazing one of the Aesirs.

Matt grinned. A hundred kilometers of atmosphere also meant the Union's targeting would be off too.

ANTIMATTER WEAPONS TARGETING.

Soto groaned and muttered something about impossible moves. Then his flight jets screamed upward an octave, and he rammed himself into the nearest Aesir. Soto's cockpit reverberated like an immense gong, and the two Mecha fell toward the surface, their jets still screaming.

But the ANTIMATTER WEAPONS TARGETING icon flashed off.

Above Soto, two other pairs of Aesirs performed the same stunt as another brilliant lance came from the research facility. One of the Aesirs evaporated in the beam.

But now they were close. Less than ten kilometers. The research lab swelled in Soto's enhanced vision. Low-set concrete tilt-up buildings huddled on a spit of land that extended into a bay. A single, well-maintained road stretched through the grasslands and forests back into the mainland. It looked completely innocent: researchers performing routine science in the middle of nowhere.

Except, of course, for the antimatter gun installation at its near side.

"Targeting lock capability!" Soto yelled. "We can take out the gun now."

ANTIMATTER WEAPONS TARGETING. LOCK.

"Do it!" Matt yelled.

Even before his words left his lips, Soto targeted the antimatter weapon and fired his arm gun. The two beams met in midair and interacted with a deadly concussion. A sonic boom flattened the grass on the hilltops and spread concentric waves to grassland miles away. Intense heat fried the skin of Soto's Mecha, and internal temperatures screamed toward overload. Down on the surface, grass exploded into fire and concrete melted and ran red like lava as the beam impinged on the antimatter gun installation.

Two other beams joined Soto's. The lab's antimatter gun flashed briefly through all the colors of the heat spectrum: orange, yellow, white, blue—then it was nothing but an expanding gas ball at the edge of the research labs. Molten steel and stone showered down on the facility, burning craters in the reinforced concrete roofs.

"Down, all Mecha!" Soto yelled.

The wave of Lokis accelerated in front of Soto like a flying carpet. To his side, the three remaining Aesirs dove straight at the facility.

Depleted-uranium shells streaked at Soto's Aesir as they reached the edge of the facility. They *spanged* off the Aesirs and Lokis without any effect. Soto brought in his Mecha squad to land—just as two Hellions stepped out of a concrete bunker.

The Union Hellions never even got a chance to raise their weapons. The Lokis bored into them, pinning the black Hellions with their crablike pincers. And when they struck, the Hellions spasmed and fell prostrate on the ground, immobilized.

"Careful!" Matt said. "They may have countermeasures for the system disrupter, according to Roth."

"Acknowledged," Soto said.

Sure enough, the Hellions began struggling to their feet. Fireflies erupted from their chest launchers, scattering the Lokis. Compartments opened on the sides of the Hellions as they began to draw their Zap Guns.

With a roar, Soto charged the nearest Hellion. His antimatter arm vibrated and thrummed with power as he slammed it into the Hellion's visor. It vaporized in a resounding explosion, and the Hellion dropped to its knees.

"No antimatter on the ground!" Matt shouted.

"Relax, I know what I'm doing," Soto said. "You may be good at Merging, but I'm good at fighting."

Soto turned to see two more of his Aesirs taking out the other Hellion. It went down, hard, on the Aurora grass, digging long furrows behind it. Like the first, they'd only destroyed the sensor arrays, so the pilots inside were safe.

Lokis poured into the main building, shattering glass and pulverizing concrete as they went. They flowed down wide utilitarian corridors, smashed through steel-reinforced doors, and cleared the way for the Aesirs. Soto's POV showed the heat signatures of the scientists retreating in front of the Mecha horde. Guards returned fire at the Lokis. Bright muzzle flashes from within the building spoke of energy or missile weapons.

But the Lokis quickly overwhelmed the guards, drilling deeper into the complex. Merged with the local computing systems, they quickly confirmed Roth's data: two hidden sublevels to the complex, set twenty meters below the main buildings.

As Soto entered the research facility, the Lokis had just found the elevator shaft leading down to the sublevels. A blast took out three of the Lokis as they scrabbled down the shaft, but the structure held its integrity. More Lokis found the other mines and disabled them before Soto and his Aesir came down.

Soto took the lead. His POV that he shared with Matt descended into darkness. At the bottom of the elevator shaft, wan light flickered from an irregular opening.

When Soto reached the bottom, he had to crouch low to fit into the underground space. The Lokis had already blasted through the reinforced doors and scattered plastic cubicle walls like fallen buildings. Several frightened technical staff still cowered in a conference room near the back of the space, but none took any action against the Lokis.

"It's a damn office," Soto growled as he pushed through into other chambers. There was nothing there except cubicles, meeting rooms, and NPP displays.

"Still another level—" Matt said.

An explosion from the back of the space hit Soto like a hammer. His POV shook with the force of the blast, and billowing dust reduced his vision to IR outlines. Soto cursed and pushed forward toward the source of the explosion.

Soto's vision slowly cleared as he moved forward. Soon he stood at the edge of a gaping hole, twenty meters in diameter, which revealed the lower level of the complex. Shattered Lokis twitched and writhed at the edge of the hole. Others were Merged with door consoles in the space below. Some had sacrificed themselves to prevent the explosion from destroying everything below. Some were keeping the rest of the facility from self-destructing.

And, in the antiseptic level revealed by the blast, what they'd come here for: dozens of HuMax, cowering against the walls in abject fear. None of them were grotesquely transformed like the HuMax on Planet 5, but they were all recognizably HuMax. Wide violet-and-gold eyes stared up at Soto's Aesir, quivering in expectation of annihilation.

Matt closed his eyes. "Ione," he whispered.

"What?" Soto asked.

"Nothing," Matt said. "Go on."

Soto leapt down into the lower level. The HuMax scattered as a guard turned to open fire on Soto's Aesir with a handheld fusion pistol. Soto plucked the gun out of the man's hands and crushed it with his Mecha's talons. A gout of flame erupted from his hand, and the guard fled.

Behind the guard was a fallen HuMax and a large burn mark on the floor. The guard had been using his gun. In the face of discovery, they'd been slaughtering the HuMax.

Cleaning up their mess.

"Fuck me," Soto breathed.

Matt shook his head, his eyes filling. It was no different than Planet 5. No different than what they had done to Ione's father and what they had tried to do to Ione. He shouldn't be surprised. But it still hit him hard.

"Go deeper," Matt told Soto. "Save who you can."

Soto and his Aesir pressed deeper into the facility. In terms of scale, it was a tiny fraction of the size of the secure environment on Planet 5. The HuMax apartments were deserted. They were simple but comfortable, a far cry from the cells on that remote ice world. It seemed the only HuMax left were the dozen or so waiting to be gunned down.

In the grim images that streamed over the FTL-comms, one thing was clear: this was a secret lab. A prison. A concentration camp. One where the Union was working on HuMax. On a Core World.

"Are we still live?" Matt asked Lena Stoll.

"Yes. Our repeaters are being taken offline, but we're getting increasing rebroadcast throughout the Union," she told him.

Matt nodded. "Good."

On the other screens, similar imagery was coming in from Geos and Utopia. Only the Greenland mission had failed to penetrate the facility. In all cases, the labs were small and limited. But, also in all cases, they housed HuMax and UARL scientists. Geos's staff managed to kill most of the HuMax before Matt's Mecha team stopped them, but the images of the drugged superhumans lining up obediently for lethal injections was even more damning.

In all cases, most of the UARL scientists surrendered quietly. One, a staff director, took his own life with a depleted-uranium slug. Some remained sullen and taciturn; others gave halting questions about their research, their guilty eyes darting away from the cameras' glass eyes.

"Roth was right," Soto said, after the research lab had been secured.

"You don't sound very happy," Matt told him.

"When you make a deal with the devil, do you smile when he delivers?"

Matt frowned, nodding his head in silent assent. *No. You start worrying about the bill.* Just because Roth didn't want anything up front didn't mean there wasn't going to be a cost.

"I'm just sorry I wasn't able to be there with you," Matt told Soto.

Soto shook his head. "Don't be. You'll soon be taking a much bigger chance."

*　　*　　*

The tearful Auroran scientist, with his authenticated credentials and unassailable records, was what sold it.

"When I found out HuMax still existed, I took this assignment for revenge. Everyone knows those monsters almost destroyed the human race. But I discovered they were people. And what we're doing to them is more terrible than anything they ever did to us. We're the monsters now."

Shot with the HuMax survivors still cowering in the background, it was a powerful image. One the Union had never seen.

The Union mass media tried to play it off. Just another violent Corsair attack, they said, emphasizing the loss of property and speculating on loss of life. Terrible hit on the home worlds, worse than Rayder. The Corsairs planted the evidence. Everyone knew the HuMax were an evil superrace bent on universal domination.

But that one scientist, that one video—it bounced through the UniNet FTLcomm links beyond the speed of thought. In one hour, as Matt's forces were fighting their way back to their rendezvous points, it had gained ten million views. In an hour and thirty minutes, it had hit a hundred million.

From there, the walls crumbled. Fast.

More UARL research personnel stepped forward. One quietly removed all the security from the Union's HuMax historical archive. In it, the creation, usage, and management of the HuMax were recorded in painstaking detail.

Ideal tool for use on desert planetoids, one report said. Where humans struggled to survive for weeks, HuMax had an "acceptable" average life span of fourteen years.

Petition for Entry into United Planets, was another popular document. More than a hundred and fifty years ago, a provisional HuMax government had gone through proper channels and tried to join the United Planets, which was the precursor to the Union. The United Planets had responded by dropping nuclear weapons on the most populous HuMax world, Prospect. When the HuMax fought back—harder than the United Planets had expected—they took over several of the Core UP worlds. Desperate, the UP absorbed several new neutral worlds and transformed itself into the Universal Union. The promise: eliminate the HuMax menace and usher in a supposed new age of peace under enlightened leaders.

In the end, nothing had changed. The Union monsters just wore new masks.

All fabrications! the Union media shouted.

But the damage was done. What had been set in motion by Matt's awkward transmissions now overflowed the banks. Hundreds of thousands poured out of the cities to see the remains of the breached labs on Geos, Utopia, and Aurora. They sent their own video and photos onto the UniNet, confirming the "Corsair" transmissions.

Aurora was the first world to burn.

At the office of the supreme chancellor of Aurora University, students flowed in, took over the hallways, and pressed close around the building by the tens of thousands. They yelled for explanations. They demanded all the archives be opened. Sprinkled throughout the crowd were the characteristic violet eyes of genemod. A tearful interview with a pretty blond genemod woman put words to fears ricocheting throughout the UniNet:

"If they torture HuMax, what's to stop them from doing the same thing to me?"

The chancellor appeared briefly to tell the students to go back to their classes. His voice could only barely be heard above the chanting of tens of thousands of students, despite the powerful public address system.

Tell the truth! Open it up! Tell the truth! the crowds chanted.

Five minutes after the frustrated supreme chancellor left the stage, the Aurora University Security forces came out. Except they weren't dressed in their friendly gray-blue uniforms, and armed only with stun sticks. They marched in behind carbon-composite shields, dressed in formfitting black body armor. There was no negotiation, no demands. They simply sprayed aerosol incapacitator into the crowd and marched forward, pushing them away from the chancellor's office. Video of writhing students being trampled by heavily armed police joined the media on the UniNet.

It was probably a student who lit the first match. Analysis of satellite images, in some future time, might pinpoint it. But it didn't matter. Less than five minutes after the Aurora Security force waded in, the chancellor's office was burning.

Raging flames shot out of the tall, first-story windows, curling outward in streamers of destruction. Cheery banners reading AURORA UNIVERITY/UNIVERSAL OPPORTUNITY caught fire and disappeared in the blaze. More windows blew outward as the fire grew.

For a moment, students and security both paused to look at the burning building. And, at that moment, one of the last images to run across the Auroran FTLcomm link was taken: a group of bloody and bruised students, their eyes reflecting the light from the fire, their expressions a mix of uncertain triumph.

Then the Union began taking big steps.

It severed the UniNet FTLcomm links to Aurora, Utopia, and Geos. Takedowns hit hundreds of tertiary media sites screaming about the Union's deception. The primary media started running nonstop refutations and propaganda. Union loyalists came out to fight with the millions already in the streets, on all twelve Core Worlds.

But the word was out. Views on all media of the Hu-Max liberations kept climbing—to the billions, then tens of billions, then hundreds. Messages poured into the Senate on Eridani, overloading their capacity. And, as on Aurora, crowds began to gather. Their chant reflected the students:

Open it up! Tell the truth!

But they added their own spin on it too. A spin fueled by the violet-eyed among them.

Open it up! Tell the truth! Right the wrongs!

Matt smiled. Right the wrongs. People's faces burned with rage or crumpled in confusion. Until this day, they'd known the Union only as a force for good. They *knew* they were on the right side, fighting the evil Corsairs.

How was it, then, that the ones labeled "Corsairs" had exposed the Union's own terrible experiments, its own buried secrets?

Matt remembered his amazement at *El Dorado*, Captain Gonsalves's Corsair ship. Full of people. Normal people. Just doing their jobs. Some nice. Some dicks. The Union had never seen the Corsairs as people.

Just like themselves.

Outside the Senate Building on Eridani, black-armored Union Security forces appeared, trying to push the growing crowd of citizens back. In the bit-rotted FTLcomms view, it looked like a razor-thin line of black ants, trying to hold an opposing army at bay.

And this citizen army wasn't like the Aurora students. Eridani was the oldest world in the Union, fiercely proud of its customs. Many of its citizens were heavily armed.

It wasn't long before shots rang out. The security line parted, and the masses stormed the Senate.

Matt nodded, still deep in his Demon, deep in Mesh. It was time. Time to join the fight.

"Displace!" he barked.

Despite the chaos outside the Senate in the city of New-home, the hills above Eridani rose peaceful and yellow-green, carpeted in the alien spring flowering of the world. The bay was calm and glassy, deep blue under a clear sky. Local time was fifteen thirteen, and the sun was falling toward another perfect sunset. Pleasure boats still churned the canals, full of eager Union citizens out for one of the first warm days of the year.

In the hills above Newhome, a kilometer-wide, silvery planetoid snapped into existence.

The thunderclap of displaced air echoed across the valley, reducing windows in Newhome suburbs to shards. Far away, panes rattled in the mirrored high-rises of the city proper.

Dirt and rock fountained outward from the bottom of the planetoid, where it impinged on the crust of the planet. The roiling dark cloud of debris charged outward toward the city like a deck of thunderclouds. Immediately the surface of the asteroid sprang to life. Tens of thousands of Lokis scrambled down the dark armored surface, their auxiliary thrusters flaring to drive them ahead of the onrushing debris.

Matt smiled as he watched on his Demon's screens. The hundred thousand Lokis came from former Last Rising worlds, now part of the Free Stars Alliance. His whirlwind tour of the last weeks had paid off, even though some of Rayder's worlds remained loyal to his memory—and some had rebuffed his diplomatic over-tures with antimatter force.

The Mecha Dock hatch sprang open in front of Matt, revealing flattened grassland and a chaos of dust.

Through the miasma, the silver spires of Newhome were just visible. The Loki barrier was already falling to ground and swarming toward the city.

"Only overwhelming force will work," Dr. Roth had told Matt. *"Your proof may win the rest of the Union, but you won't win Eridani without Arcadia."*

Arcadia. Roth had referred to it both as the "lab of labs" and the ultimate stronghold of the Union's deepest secrets. Located directly below Newhome, it was also the most heavily guarded. An orbital approach wouldn't work. A deep atmospheric insertion might not even give them enough time before the Eridani defenses countered. Only dropping *Helheim* down right on the surface of the planet had any chance.

Matt's viewmask lit with vector outlines reaching toward Newhome—his guide toward the hidden shaft leading down below the city.

On this point, Roth had been completely clear: *"only you can win Arcadia."*

Matt leapt out of the Mecha Dock, firing his thrusters in furious pursuit of the Lokis. Above him, the first missiles from Eridani defenses were streaking in across the clear blue sky, leaving bright white contrails. They arced down toward *Helheim*.

"Displace!" Matt shouted.

Helheim disappeared in another furious thunderclap. Now the only thing behind Matt was a shallow crater and flattened grassland. Ahead of him, Lokis, suburbs, and the city. Less than five kilometers. All he had to do was maintain course, find the shaft, and descend into Arcadia. Mesh high filled him as he shot forward over the narrow streets and single houses of Newhome suburbs.

Conquer these people, he heard a voice inside the Mecha command him. *Rule them. Make them what they could be.*

Matt ignored it, knowing it was the Mesh speaking. He was here to bring justice, not more tyranny.

Firefly missiles flared at the edge of the city, impacting harmlessly on the Loki storm. Bright explosions sparked off Newhome's tallest, glass-walled skyscrapers, like gigantic camera flashes.

Sidewinders quickly followed. As they found their targets, Lokis flared in dirty orange explosions and fell out of the sky, crippled or destroyed. Other Lokis dove toward the weapons emplacements, switching seamlessly to their segmented, insectlike forms. They flowed over the broadening avenues like a carpet of angry centipedes, surrounding the Sidewinder arsenals before they had a chance to retarget. Reinforced concrete exploded upward as the emplacements fell to the Lokis' missiles, opening a path into the city.

Matt's Demon passed over into the city proper. The late afternoon sun cast his shadow ahead of him, like the form of an avenging angel.

Sidewinder fire fell away behind him. Lokis swarmed on the roads, over ground cars, past terrified pedestrians, well in advance of Matt.

On the stone facade of a building ahead, doors opened to reveal a Hellion. Down the city's main street, more doors snapped open. Hellions stepped from their hiding places and launched Sidewinders at Matt.

Matt swore and dodged, firing his own missiles at the closest Hellions. Stone and tarmac disintegrated as the Hellions took direct hits.

A splash from the city's broad canals made Matt look. Something speared up, impaled a Loki, and took it down into the water. Bubbles boiled up as dozens of dark shapes roiled just below the surface of the canal.

Eels, Matt thought, as more of them leapt out of the canals to strike at the Lokis. The small semi-Mecha were only armed with pikes and depleted-uranium slugs, but the meaning was clear: Newhome would do everything in its power to stop them.

The Lokis separated—some fighting the Eels, and some moving farther ahead of Matt. They hit the emerging Hellions and immobilized them long enough for Matt to put strategically placed Fireflies in their visors. Even if they could regenerate, it would take many minutes—and he'd be at Arcadia by then.

It looked as though they were past the defenses now. An endless carpet of Lokis surged ahead, straight down the vector pointing at Arcadia. The stronghold was now less than a half kilometer away. Matt arrowed along the glowing green line, his lips skinned back in Mesh high. Nothing could stop them! Not unless the Union wanted to fire an antimatter weapon at their own capital city. And they weren't that crazy, no matter how incensed they were.

Matt's grin grew wider as they rounded the last curve toward Arcadia. Directly ahead of him was the Capitol Complex he'd visited with Michelle, its vast parklike grounds unchanged, dotted with timeless neoclassical buildings and monuments to battles long past.

Directly ahead of him lay the Senatorial Apartments, set just below the Prime Residence. A grassy hill rose behind those buildings, dotted with native Earth oak trees. Beyond were the Plaza of Technology and the Expansion Museum. Farther off, a thin streamer of smoke rose from the Senate Building itself.

As they passed over the ring road surrounding the Capitol Complex, three Lokis suddenly shot skyward, disintegrating into shattered segments. Matt pulled back on his throttle, looking for their attacker. There'd been no Mecha, no missile flash.

Two more Lokis got shredded. Matt jagged to avoid

the debris. What the hell was happening? Where was the attacker?

But there were no gun emplacements, nothing that could possibly be a weapon. The closest thing to the destroyed Lokis was a delivery truck, abandoned in the middle of the road.

No. Wait. Behind the truck, black metallic tendrils shot from the ground. Some of them wrapped around something that looked a little like a Sidewinder missile. Some of them wrapped around the truck. As Matt watched, the truck shuddered and crumpled in on itself as the tendrils seemingly sucked the life out of it.

The Sidewinder missile fired, tearing through the tendrils and annihilating more Lokis. Another began growing as the van shivered down to nothingness.

Oh, shit.

All around Matt, metallic tendrils continued to shoot from from the ground, wrapping cars and trucks in their embrace. Where they touched, metal shriveled. Where they grew, weapons blossomed. Matt saw Sidewinders, glowing fusion ports, even something that looked suspiciously like a Zap Gun. One growing mass even seemed to be forming itself into a crouching figure, a proto-Mecha. Where Lokis passed, the tendrils tracked. Weapons flashed. Segments of Lokis cartwheeled through the air as explosions echoed hollowly through the city.

Matt fired Fireflies, but they exploded harmlessly against the tendrils. He tried Sidewinders. Bright white blossoms bloomed around him. But there were just too many. All around him, metal reshaped into biometal. Missiles launched. Fusion guns spat. And Lokis erupted in fire.

Matt's mouth went dry. This was another trap. And they were so deep in there was little chance of getting out. His only chance was to charge through to a final assault on Arcadia, deep in the Capitol Complex.

But even in that vast park, other things were happening. The tendrils wrapped war memorials and crawled over the ground and through the decorative lake. A giant mass of them convulsed, extruded insectoid limbs, and scuttled toward Matt and his Lokis.

This was Newhome's final barrier. Matt had come in expecting to sweep through the city with a hundred thousand Lokis. Now the city was transforming itself into its own implacable force, all around him. Lokis fell by the thousands as Newhome fought back.

But he knew how to deal with this. It was the same as on Jotunheim. Biometal called to metal. All he had to do was Merge with the city and take out all the opposing Mecha at one go.

Matt arrowed his Demon at a building at the edge of the Capitol Plaza, and embraced it.

Merge! Matt thought.

Strands of biometal fused deep with its steel structure, searching for the invisible control lines that ran through all of Newhome. Data surged through Matt's mind, infinite gabble on the point of insanity. All he had to do was give the command.

No, an irresistible voice spoke in Matt's mind, over the feel of static and the smell of dust. *You will not contravene here.*

An immense force struck Matt like a sledgehammer, driving him right out of the system.

His biometallic tendrils shattered to dust, and he fell helpless off the side of the building. He landed on his back on the hard concrete, whooping with the force feedback from the impact. Around him, Lokis were being sliced to bits by the newly transformed Mecha. In moments, they'd be on him.

Merge had failed.

20

ARCADIA

For what seemed like an infinite time, Matt couldn't move. With his Perfect Record accelerating, calculating every possible action he could take and instantly weighing the outcome, he searched for a path that led to success.

He could simply try to escape. Fire his thrusters and blaze for orbit. But he'd seen the plot of orbital countermeasures around Eridani. Any path he could take led to the fireball of his Demon exploding in an impenetrable maze of antimatter fire. No amount of crazy maneuvering would change that. And even if he somehow avoided being annihilated, there was no *El Dorado* waiting for him. No Free Stars ship at all. The Union would chase him down to a cold death in empty space.

Or he could try again to drive deeper into the Capitol Complex. But there, the tendrils were busy converting every piece of metal and glass into Mecha and weapons. Hundreds of them. Soon to be thousands. All well armed and aimed exclusively at him. Every course of action led to the same result: Matt's Demon impaled under the city Mecha while the segments of the shredded Lokis twitched impotently on the carefully maintained Earth grass.

He could head back into the city itself. But there,

madness reigned as well. His enhanced sensors showed every building coated in thick ropes of biometallic muscle. Some skyscrapers shuddered, as if they were coming alive. Others swiveled new-made gun turrets at him. There was only one conclusion: his Loki outgunned, his Demon overcome by Newhome itself.

Every path led to his death.

Was that what Roth wanted? To see him twisted and broken in the middle of the Union's most powerful city? Had he set this trap for him?

No. That made no sense. Roth might have a hidden agenda, but he wasn't a Union stooge. And these tendrils, this defensive system, was acting different than anything Roth had shown Matt. And if it was Roth's, why would he need Matt to get past it? This was something bigger than Roth, something to protect a great secret.

How close you are, the static-dusty voice grated, close in Matt's ear. It seemed amused by him. *In so many ways.*

The voice of the thing in the Mecha was louder and closer than he'd ever heard it. Matt bit back his response.

Because it didn't matter if the ghost in the machine was a reflection of his own mind, or some artificially intelligent thing in the Mecha. Not now. Not when he was so close to uncovering the truth behind the Union. Even if there was no way out, he'd at least finally know the truth. And maybe everyone else would too.

Outside Newhome's madness, the Union revolution continued to reel off in Matt's inset video. Government-toppling protests were flaring now on every major world.

That was what Roth really wanted, Matt analyzed. To claw his way to the top of a crippled Union. That was the perch Roth was after.

Concrete shattered around Matt, breaking his chain of thought. Matt scrambled to his feet and triggered his thrusters, quickly climbing away from the carnage on the street.

Below him, the city came to life. Shining biometallic tendrils joined together to form thick ropes, wrapping around abandoned cars and trucks, snaking up buildings and plunging deep into their steel cores, covering advertising billboards and holosign projectors. Where they touched metal and power, the biometallic ropes coiled and throbbed with life, swelling into a thousand different forms. Some changed into Mecha with spiderlike legs and sharp, origami-like edges. Some transformed the sides of buildings into flocks of dartlike kites.

Skyscrapers sprouted bulbous black gun emplacements, and Fireflies and Sidewinders began a continuous hail of brilliant destruction on Matt's carpet of silver Mecha.

Shattered segments and torn biometallic muscles fountained into the air as Lokis fell by the thousands. Matt's Demon rang with the impact of depleted-uranium slugs and the explosions of Firefly missiles.

Matt balled his fists in frustration. The coordinates of the Arcadia entrance were so damn close. If he could just get across the Capitol Plaza, no matter what he lost in the process . . . but there was no way to make it. No other Mecha to Merge with, no—

Merge with the Lokis! It was the only probability with any chance to make it to Arcadia.

He didn't hesitate. He slammed his thrusters full reverse and headed for the most concentrated mass of Lokis. Landing hard, he grabbed the closest pincers and thought, *Merge!*

Matt felt the Lokis' rudimentary computing cortexes like a chorus of simpleminded voices, chanting in unison. At first, they struggled against the Merge. *Not programmed! No rider! Unsupported configuration!*

Matt used his Perfect Record to show the Lokis their

probable outcomes. Their simple machine minds ran the numbers and, as one, made their decision.

We accept, they told him. The Lokis shimmered and melted like lead, joining with the main mass of Matt's Demon. The giant red Mecha bulked up with silver veins and bulging biometallic muscle.

Let us help, the Lokis' machine brains said. *We are faster than you.*

Matt suppressed a smile. *Let's see what you can do,* he told the Lokis.

The Merged Demon's arms suddenly swept into life, triggering rapid-repeating Fusion Handshakes as they moved. The shock waves expanded out from Matt's Demon, reducing the origami city Mecha to smoking hulks and melting still-transforming biometallic tendrils into slag.

Leaping free from their attackers, the other Lokis streamed toward Matt now. They grabbed on to Matt's Demon and became one with it, growing his size twofold, threefold. Matt's Demon took on a paler red tone, with shining silver segments outlining every part of his body. The screaming in his mind became a chorus of machine voices, calculating and scheming.

Like you, that static-dusty voice boomed over the cacaphony. Something like stale laughter echoed through Matt's mind. The voice was almost irresistibly strong now.

Matt clamped his mouth shut and refused to answer. But was the ghost in the machine a little bit right? His super–Perfect Record was like an ultimate computing machine, assimilating and assessing probabilities at unreal speed.

Matt's Demon was now as tall as some of the buildings in Newhome. He looked down on the Capitol Complex, now shrunk to the size of a model.

Newhome's origami Mecha swarmed toward him. Pinpoints of pain flared all over Matt's body as they skittered up his legs and reached his chest. Fusion weapons flashed, puncturing his hide. A dozen drilled through his biometallic skin and used their Handshakes to blow away biometallic muscle and tendon. Sharp pain tore into his gut.

More Mecha came. Like a wave, they flowed out of the city.

No choice. Matt crouched down, instantly transforming from his humanoid Mecha form into something sleek, low, and streamlined, like a racing ground car on grand scale. Jets lit on his back, shooting white-hot flames two hundred meters behind him into the city's broadest avenues. Building facades melted and windows blew out in the heat. Origami Mecha flicked out of existence with little sparkling pops.

Matt barreled forward toward the Capitol Complex, as surviving building guns pelted him with depleted-uranium and fusion explosions. More Lokis flowed in to fill the raw gashes on his back, but the pain was red-hot, like being sprayed with acid.

Matt shot out onto the ring road and into the capitol itself, right over a sentry gate entwined with transforming biometallic ropes.

Matt followed the road deeper into the complex, dodging swarms of transformed Mecha, using his Fusion Handshake to sweep them away. The vector leading to Arcadia shot straight ahead and then slammed down into the ground—right at the location of Landing Pad 100.

Matt's Perfect Record yanked him back to the day he'd first seen Landing Pad 100. Standing there with Michelle. Wanting to feel what she felt. The place where humankind first landed on Eridani. The place where the Expansion really started.

What bullshit.

Matt realized he'd never really believed all these stories about the glories of humanity and the Expansion. At least in part, he'd always been searching for what was really going on in the Union and beyond, and here he was, on the verge of finding out.

This was what he was supposed to do. He was a mongrel, and mongrels never stop fighting.

Just beyond Pad 100 was the Expansion Monument, a five-hundred-meter-tall spire celebrating the beginning of humanity's reign over other planets. The vector leading toward Arcadia pointed straight at the monument, then dove beneath the ground.

The lab of labs, the ultimate stronghold—existed under a monument in the capitol? Why would they put something like that here?

This is much more than a lab, the scratchy voice taunted. *This is a place no one is worthy to enter.*

A shadow fell across his visor. Strong hands seized Matt's Demon and plucked it from the ground. He yelled and transformed back into his humanoid shape, thrashing against his attacker. But the thing held him in a vise-like grip and shook him with a fury. It took several seconds for his visor to clear enough so Matt could see what was happening.

The Expansion Monument, the five-hundred-meter-tall black spire that marked the beginning of humanity's reign on other planets, had been transformed into a giant Mecha.

And it had him.

At the spire of the Expansion Monument, a flaming orange gash opened. The sharp-edged hands of the transformed Monument-Mecha brought Matt's Demon inexorably upward toward its fiery mouth. Shining black orbs split through the surface of the Expansion Monument, rotating quickly to fix him with pinpoint pupils.

Matt grabbed the monument's arm and triggered his Fusion Handshake. Power thundered down his Demon's arm and reverberated from the Monument-Mecha. Pieces exploded outward in all directions, showering the fresh green grass of the Capitol Plaza with obsidian-colored rubble.

But its grip didn't loosen. Beneath the stonelike exterior, massive coiled ropes of biometallic muscle gleamed, mercury-bright in the late afternoon sun.

Matt screamed, triggering Handshake after Handshake. But the giant didn't falter. Matt tried to draw his Zap Gun, but the Monument-Mecha tightened its irresistible grip.

In seconds, the damn thing would throw him down its burning maw. Every thread led to that outcome. There was no escape, none at all. A momentary shock of pure hopelessness overcame Matt.

What to do? He dared not Merge with the thing. It was part of the city. It would just overpower him, as Newhome had done.

But there was nothing to Merge with. He'd already absorbed all the surviving Lokis. But even if there were ten thousand more, he'd never match the mass of this gigantic spire.

He was at the thing's mouth. Deep inside it, a crystalline orb pulsed with pure power, ready to sear him to oblivion.

Matt stretched his Demon's hands out in front of him and triggered one last Handshake. The monument rocked back briefly. A new arm shot out of the side of the monument and grabbed Matt's arm, crushing his Fusion Handshake in a crescendo of pain. It twisted the crushed arm out of its socket, shearing cords of biometallic muscle with deep, thrumming bass twangs. Matt screamed as icons flared in his viewmask:

ARM REGENERATION: INDETERMINATE
CQFA REGENERATION: INDETERMINATE

One arm down, the rest of me to go, Matt thought hysterically. It really was over.

Boom. Blue-white brilliance flared in front of Matt, and a shock wave rattled his broken Mecha. The Monument-Mecha's mouth blew open, bricks expanding outward in a cloud. The thing screamed, an unearthly alien ululation.

Tags in Matt's viewmask told the tale: another Demon had arrived, delivering a Zap Gun blast right into the mouth of Matt's giant enemy.

Another Demon? That meant . . .

"And the teacher again saves the protégé," a voice said, across the comms. Its identifying icon flared DR. SALVATORE ROTH.

In a flash, the Monument-Mecha shot out another arm and grabbed Dr. Roth's Demon in its implacable talons. Roth's Zap Gun exploded in a flare of antimatter fire. Roth yelled over the comms and triggered Fusion Handshakes. The Monument-Mecha's talons glowed red with the fusion fire, but held fast. The backfire energy concussed Roth's Mecha with punishing heat waves.

Now the Monument-Mecha held both of them fast. Its hands rose toward its mouth, toward destruction.

"Thanks, Doc," Matt said, dripping sarcasm.

"I could not possibly estimate the power of this—of this technology—"

Matt cut him off. "I figured it wasn't yours."

Roth fumed silently, his comms icon still lit. The Monument-Mecha's mouth was very close now. Beyond it, the city of Newhome boiled under coils of biometallic muscle. The transformation continued.

It was over. Completely over. Matt would never know how or why Roth had shown up to help, or what Eridani's underground biomechanical secret was. All probabilities pointed to a single end point, in the gut of the towering Mecha.

Roth's Demon was now close. Close enough to see all the damage. The thing was a quarter gone, blown away in the Zap Gun explosion. Not that it mattered. Even whole, he was no match for the Monument-Mecha.

"Merged Demons increase power exponentially." Dr. Roth's instruction came back to Matt.

"Merge," Matt said.

Roth croaked something unintelligible. It could have been a compliment or a condemnation.

Matt reached with an arm, willing it to elongate and touch Dr. Roth's Demon. Immediately power shot across the connection to Matt. Power, and Roth's dark thoughts.

Dark not for evil, but for their obscurity. Roth was actually trying to shield his thoughts from Matt. Matt was incredulous. He didn't know you could do that. He believed that sharing minds in Merge was absolute.

Still, pieces bled through. Roth was as surprised as Matt by the biometallic ropes that had shot up out of the ground of Newhome. He'd really thought Arcadia was just a grand lab, maybe more than that, perhaps even the enigmatic Source, the one he'd found, the one the Union had found, the one he suspected Rayder of using . . .

Roth's thoughts clamped down tight on that. His voice grated over the comms: "If we are to survive, I suggest we act now."

Matt jumped. The heat of the Monument-Mecha's fusion mouth was hot on the Mecha's skin. They were moments away from being consumed.

Complete Merge, Matt thought.

Matt's and Roth's Demons flowed together like molten steel, forming biometallic cuffs around the Monument-Mecha's arms. Matt's power levels shot up as the Merge continued, peaking at 1.7x, 2.5x, 3.3x what he'd had before. His REGENERATION warnings disappeared, and new strength flooded through his body.

The Monument-Mecha beat the Demon cuffs against its mouth, unable to ingest it.

Zap Gun, Matt thought.

Gone, Dr. Roth corrected.

Not mine, Matt shot back.

The Demon cuffs extruded arms and swiftly unfolded the shining silver gun out of its biometallic body. The Monument-Mecha keened again, its tiny eyes swiveling in fear. Its arms pushed them away now, desperate to fling them away.

Too late. The Zap Gun was aimed and ready.

Fire, Matt/Roth thought.

Pure light shot down the Monument-Mecha's throat. Molten biometal erupted out of its gullet. Its scream of pain shattered the few remaining panes of glass in the Capitol Complex.

The giant thing reeled backward as its head split in half, erupting hot plasma. Slowly, the five-hundred-meter-tall Expansion Monument started to topple toward the ground.

Matt/Roth flowed out of its slack fingers and reformed in a humanoid shape: a super-Demon twenty-five meters tall. Thrusters on its back flared to hold it in midair. For long moments, the two men could do nothing but watch the show.

The Expansion Monument fell across the pristine park of the Capitol Mound. A noise like distant thunder rolled across the still-transforming city.

Matt/Roth's enhanced senses zoomed in on New-home, now little more than a tangled jungle of biometal-lic sinew.

Complete conversion, and with such speed, Roth thought. His dark mind fed Matt feelings of awe and wonder. Not a single thought for the inhabitants of the city, or what might have become of them. No sympathy at all. Roth dreamed only of what he could do with such power. But his dreams were blurry, indistinct. His ulti-mate motive was well shadowed.

What would you do with that power? Matt thought.

Roth's mental barriers clamped down tight. *You are such a simple man, for all your abilities,* Roth told Matt. *Would you be content to leave the Union in charge of our destiny?*

As opposed to you? Matt thought. Out loud, he said, "What's happening to the city?"

Roth sent deep amusement to Matt. For one moment, his barriers were down. Matt shivered in revulsion. He was here, Merged in Mecha, sharing his mind with Dr. Roth.

"Simple mind, simple answers," Roth said. On Matt's viewmask, the map to Arcadia came to the fore. The lo-cation vector pointed straight down to Platform 100. "We inspect the installation."

Matt nodded. "Let's do it."

Matt/Roth shot down to Platform 100. The vector pointed solidly at the center of the fused black granite plinth. There was no obvious entrance, not even using the Demon's enhanced sensor array.

Matt shivered. It was as if the early settlers had buried something here, something they wanted to stay hidden for all eternity.

Stop being dramatic, Roth thought. But beneath that, he was unsettled. Whatever he had expected Arcadia to be, he hadn't expected this.

"No time for subtlety," Matt said. Matt/Roth drew their Zap Gun in one smooth motion. They aimed it straight down at the platform and pulled the trigger. Antimatter power slammed down their Mecha arm. Fused stone flared red and ran like water while clouds of black smoke shot skyward.

Matt's viewmask lit with new tags. Far above Newhome, three Mecha were descending. Each was tagged DEMON.

"Yours?" Matt asked, out loud.

No, Roth thought.

Great. Even if they broke through to Arcadia, those Demons would follow them in. And that would be the end. And that could surely be their end. Two crippled Demons against three shiny new ones, in close-quarter combat. It was a simple equation to solve. Just like so many of Matt's gifts, it was a blessing and a curse to have the ability to deduct with extreme scrutiny every possible future. Matt/Roth's Zap Gun beam flickered in uncertainty.

This is too fascinating not to follow to the end, Roth thought.

Matt ground his teeth. "Even if the end is our end?"

Roth's amusement poured through the mental link. "Are you scared, prodigy?" he said, out loud.

Matt's anger flared. "Hell no!"

Suddenly their Zap Gun beam went pure white as the barrier in front of it disappeared. They were through. In front of Matt/Roth was a deep shaft. Its walls still glowed faintly red from the antimatter beam. Matt's sensors pegged the depth of the hole as over a hundred meters.

Behind them, the Demons streaked closer.

No time for subtlety, Matt thought again, and jumped.

Matt/Roth fell through the just-cut shaft, thrusters lighting the vitrified walls. They descended into a large chamber, easily three hundred meters around and fifty tall. Along the walls were fantastic frescoes carved into the naked stone. But they weren't like the work on Esplandian or *El Dorado*—or anything like Matt had ever seen before. They didn't show anything recognizable at all. The frescoes were repeated geometric patterns, so complex as to be almost fractal.

Below the frescoes, several tunnels pierced the stone, dark thresholds that revealed nothing beyond.

Matt checked his coordinates. According to the viewmask, they were inside Arcadia. Arcadia was all around them, extending in a diffuse cloud outward.

This is it? Matt thought, confused.

Deeper perhaps, Roth thought, indicating the tunnels.

But the tunnels were too small for their Merged Demon. *We'll have to deMerge,* Matt thought.

Leaving me without a Zap Gun, Roth thought.

"And me without an arm or Fusion Handshake," Matt said, out loud.

Still, waves of distrust emanated from Roth.

Matt laughed. "*You* don't trust *me*?"

Only silence from Roth. What was he calculating? Matt wondered. *How to get the Zap Gun and overcome me too?*

From the shaft above, three flickering lights appeared. Matt's viewmask tagged them all as DEMON. The new Union Mecha had caught up with them.

"No choice," Matt said. *DeMerge.*

The two Demons flowed apart. Roth's shattered Demon staggered to the side as its biometallic skin flowed to reintegrate. Matt grimaced in pain as the REGENERATION counters for his arm and CQFA reappeared in his viewmask.

"After you," Roth said, over the comms.

Matt shook his head. He didn't like the idea of Roth

being at his back. But what choice did he have? Matt picked a corridor and ran down it, propelled by his thrusters toward their goal.

Matt and Roth descended, circling a shining vector that led down into the heart of the Arcadian cloud. There was no elevator; the corridor simply corkscrewed down for ten thousand meters into the planet.

That was so *wrong*. Why wouldn't they simply sink a shaft and drop a cage down to the bottom? And where did all the other corridors lead?

The walls themselves were ancient, pure Eridani stone and dirt. They'd once been polished to a high gloss; now cracks radiated over their surfaces, and fragments of rock, some the size of boulders, lay in the middle of the floor. It was like some incredibly ancient ruin.

But how could it be more than two hundred and fifty years old? Matt thought. The walls weren't scarred from battle or use. They were eroded away, as if over a great amount of geologic time.

Plink. Clink. Stones fell from the ceiling above Matt and Roth. He looked up. Biomechanical tendrils waved down at his Mecha. Matt yelled and crouched. But the tendrils extended no farther. They seemed content to announce their presence, nothing more.

Deeper, the dusty-static voice told Matt.

Matt shivered. This was beginning to feel like a tomb. Whether the Mecha behind them sliced their Demons to shreds, or the tendrils caught them in their web of destruction, it looked as though everything ended here today, one way or another.

Come closer, the voice said.

Down they went, at fifty, a hundred, two hundred kilometers an hour. The tags of their Demon pursuers inched closer as they descended. Matt's sensors showed nothing ahead of him. Dodging the boulders became automatic, reflexive.

Suddenly a black opening appeared before Matt. Matt skidded on his heels, sliding into another vast, open chamber far too big for his Mecha lighting to illuminate. The only thing he could see was a vaguely curving roof in the distance, and glittering crystals lining pale, faraway walls. The crystals reflected outward seemingly to infinity, making the chamber seem almost endless.

No. Wait. Matt's viewmask overlaid an enhanced-sensor reconstruction of the chamber. It didn't just seem big. It was huge. The area extended beyond the sensors' resolution range, which meant it was kilometers wide. Maybe tens of kilometers.

Or more, the dusty-static voice of the ghost in the machine came, closer than ever before.

Light rose throughout the giant underground cavern, and Matt gasped. The cavern was bigger than any enclosed space he had ever seen. It was supported throughout its length by massive columns of pale, vitrified stone and earth. Nodules glowed dull green in the columns, the ceiling, and the floor. In some places, large polished black spheres were embedded in the planet's rock. Biometallic tendrils emerged, almost tentatively, from every surface, to wave at Matt like Aurora's plains grass in the wind.

And it wasn't just one endless chamber. Ahead of him, a large hole in the floor opened on deeper darkness, where more green embers glowed.

"What is this?" Roth asked. His voice was hushed, awestruck.

Matt shook his head in mute answer. This wasn't a lab. This wasn't a hidden military base. This wasn't an abandoned colony. This was something fundamentally inhuman.

This was alien.

Yes, the scratchy-dusty voice said.

But that wasn't possible. They'd never found a single alien race, even after almost three hundred years of Expansion. There were no aliens. Only humans. And HuMax. Only people.

ANTIMATTER WEAPON TARGETING, Matt's viewmask flashed. Tags showed that the three pursuing Demons had just arrived.

Matt collapsed to the floor. Above him passed a single beam of perfect brilliance, sizzling the air centimeters away from his Demon's back. Kilometers away, the chamber walls flared red and melted.

A Zap Gun. Shit!

Matt scrambled across the floor as another bolt came his way. It seared a hundred-meter-long scar in the floor, leaving behind a line of red lava. Roth fired thrusters, heading for one of the nearby stone columns. He was trying to hide.

Too late. Another Zap Gun bolt clipped Roth's Mecha. He went crashing down to the rough floor, out of sight. Matt fired his thrusters to get away, but he knew it was pointless. The Mecha with the Zap Gun would pick him off just like Roth.

Matt's comms snapped on. "Mr. Lowell, surrender now!"

A familiar voice. A familiar icon: MICHELLE KIND.

They'd sent her. Of course.

Matt fought back manic laughter as she continued. "Mr. Lowell, we are authorized to use deadly force."

Was it him, or did her voice break a little on those last words?

Matt came back to ground and faced the three Demons. They burned ember-red in his thermal imagery, against the cool dark tunnel they'd emerged from. The ridiculousness of the situation suddenly struck him: their capital city was being consumed by alien ropes, but the Union had sent three Demons to arrest him.

Matt laughed, snapping on his own comms. "You think I did this?"

"It doesn't matter!" another voice spat. Marjan's voice. One Mecha raised his Zap Gun and aimed it straight at Matt. "You're under arrest. Come with us now."

"What about Newhome? Your Union? Don't you have other things to think about?"

"We'll sort that out later!" Marjan cried, twitching the Zap Gun barrel back toward the tunnel. From his tone and posture, Matt knew Marjan would much rather fire than have him comply.

"Who else is there with you?" Matt asked. "Mikey? Norah?"

"Captain Posada," snapped another voice. Norah.

Matt frowned. Michelle, Marjan, and Norah against his half-crippled Demon. Roth seemed out of the fight. Matt had no Fusion Handshake, and there was no way he'd be able to aim and fire his Zap Gun before they blew him to pieces.

"Enough!" Michelle snapped. "Stand down, hand over your Zap Gun, and jettison all missile weapons. Now!"

But there was something in her tone, something that said, *I don't want to do this. I don't know about all of this anymore.*

One Mecha kept stealing glances beyond Matt, looking at the vast chamber beyond. Michelle. Michelle knew there was something very wrong here.

"Aren't you even a little curious?" Matt asked, nodding over his shoulder at the cavern. "Don't you want to know what's really going on here?"

"The Union . . . always has its reasons," Michelle said, her voice breaking.

"You think the Union built this?" Matt prodded. "Do you think any human did?"

"Enough of this shit!" Marjan yelled back, his Zap Gun twitching up toward Matt. "The Union wants you arrested. Major Kind, I will relieve you of command if you disobey this order."

Silence fell for long moments. Finally Michelle replied, "By whose authorization, Captain Marjan?"

More silence.

"I received no changes in our orders since going underground. Answer me, Captain! Whose authorization?" Michelle prodded.

"By the Union! By common sense!" Marjan's voice was thin and screechy. His Zap Gun wavered from Matt and swung toward Michelle's Demon. Midswing, Marjan seemed to realize what he was doing and pulled the barrel away.

This was Matt's chance.

He lit thrusters one hundred percent, going forward full speed. Michelle and Marjan hardly had a chance to react before he was on them. Matt's Demon slammed into Michelle and drove her back into Marjan. Norah sidestepped out of the way, pulling her Zap Gun out of its holster in one fluid motion.

Michelle's thoughts ricocheted in Matt's head as their Mecha made contact. Shrill, panicked thoughts: *I don't know, I don't know, I don't know what's going on.*

And other thoughts leaked out: Michelle still burned to take down Matt. For the Union. For her ideal, for her life. She had made it off Earth. She wouldn't let anyone take that away from her.

But the ideal of the Union was now warring with the reality.

Marjan's mind was spiky and raw like blades. *Hate you, hate this, hate everything, this life, everything.* Marjan had volunteered for this, and he'd vowed to kill Matt Lowell.

And now Norah was raising her weapon. He couldn't hold Michelle and Marjan down and deal with her as well.

Merge, Matt thought.

No! Michelle screamed, in his mind.

Marjan said nothing intelligible, but his brain vibrated with rage.

The three Mecha flowed together, legs and arms becoming a mass of spiky appendages as Michelle and Marjan fought against the Merge.

But Matt didn't need ultimate control. He focused all his energy on a single extrusion, extending a single Mecha claw from the mass of their three Demons. It shot out and grabbed Norah by the wrist. Her Zap Gun went clattering to the floor as her mind screamed in protest.

The three minds pulled Matt apart, as if he were being tortured on a rack. He groaned with the pain, and struggled to hold the Merge together. They were too strong; he wouldn't be able to hold it for long.

But there'd be time enough for one more thing.

Matt opened his mind and showed them everything: Jotunheim. Planet 5. Esplandian. Last Rising. Rayder's death. The shattered HuMax labs on Aurora, Utopia, and Geos.

And he asked them, *Who gives the Union the right to choose someone else's future? Is it all orchestrated from this cavern, by something else?*

For a moment, Michelle wavered. The images had reached her, stunned her. But she couldn't act.

Marjan roared and pulled away as hard as he could. Matt's grip on the Merge melted away, and Marjan's Demon slithered out of the main mass. Norah followed. Matt let them. This was all about speed now, not finesse.

In one malformed appendage, Matt held Norah's Zap Gun. In the other, he held his own.

Matt raised both weapons and fired, slicing Marjan's Demon neatly in half, and punching a giant hole in Norah's leg joint. Marjan's Mecha spouted superheated vapor from every single joint and slumped forward on the floor. Marjan went down hard and slumped into a keening ball. Their screaming over the comms confirmed he was still alive.

Matt turned the gun on Norah's Demon, but Michelle forced a deMerge, sending Matt's Zap Guns clattering harmlessly away on the floor. Even before she had completely re-formed into a humanoid Mecha, she had drawn her own Zap Gun and trained it on Matt.

"Stop!" she yelled as Matt went for his own guns. Her voice was strident, commanding.

Matt stopped. Michelle had come into a crouch. Her Demon's talon was tense on the Zap Gun's trigger. She had it pointed directly at Matt's midsection.

She's going to kill me. Simple as that. Those were her orders, and Michelle always executed her orders.

Even if she cried for him in her Demon's cockpit, she would kill him, because he would never be simple, and things needed to be simple.

But as the moments passed, Michelle didn't fire. Was it possible she was having doubts?

Say the right thing. Save the universe, Matt thought.

Matt opened his mouth and said, "You came from Earth and saw the stars. Don't you want to see if there's anything beyond humanity?"

For an instant in time, nothing changed. Michelle stood tense. Norah didn't move. It was as if the whole world were holding its breath.

Then, softly, Michelle's voice: "Yes."

Michelle's visor snapped up, and her Mecha's talon loosened on the trigger.

"Traitor!" Norah cried, shambling forward. Her Zap Gun shuddered upward to fix on Matt.

Michelle brought her Zap Gun up as Norah fired wide. Both Matt and Michelle swept her legs with scintillant beams, and she pitched forward with a biometallic clang. Michelle picked Norah's Zap Gun out of her fingers.

"I think I may lose some R-and-R days over this," Michelle told Matt over the comms, her tone trying for wry humor.

"Only if you go back to the Union," Matt said, thinking, *And only if any of us get out of here alive.*

The black biometallic tendrils all around them waved as if agitated now. *There is only one,* boomed a voice in Matt's mind. Razor talons stroked the surface of his consciousness as his nostrils filled with dust and the prickle of static.

"What was that?" Michelle yelled.

What is here. What has always been, the voice of the ghost in the machine boomed in answer. The thing in the Mecha. The thing he'd heard from his first Mesh. The thing all Mecha pilots heard.

"Did you hear that?" Matt asked.

"Yes," Michelle said, her voice hushed.

"What are you?" Matt said.

What we have always been: your masters, the voice said, swirling with hate.

21

SOURCE

As the voice in Matt's mind echoed, the green glow of the orbs and crystals in the pale walls of the endless underground chamber pulsed brighter.

"I don't have a master," Matt said, out loud.

We have controlled/crafted you since the beginning of your history, the voice said, now sending waves of an emotion like chill amusement. The green glow seemed to pulse in time with its statements.

Sudden insight unfolded, sped by Matt's Perfect Record calculations: this must be the connection between everything. This was where Mecha came from—an unimaginably vast cache of supertechnology from before the Union. Something profoundly alien.

This is where all your greatest achievements come from, the voice whispered, sending images of Dr. Roth and Rayder and HuMax scientists and Union researchers, all blurred and jumbled together.

But if this was the source of Roth's technology, why had he seemed so surpised? And if the Union knew about it—and were actively hiding it—why didn't they have their own Mecha? How had Rayder found it? And why were they all at odds?

This location is/was only one of many, the voice boomed in response. *And conflict is only the most entertaining part of the plan.*

And in that moment, Matt got a momentary image of something so huge, so unimaginable that his mind recoiled in instinctual revulsion. This giant cavern was just a tiny part of a network that spanned all of Eridani, riddling the crust and mantle of the planet like a giant ant farm. Its power conduits wrapped the molten core itself, drawing power from the near-infinite source of the planet.

And this was just one of a universe-spanning network of planet-sized nodes and conduits, all packed with biometallic tendrils, fractal fibers, and thinking nodes. Something had created a giant computing network and built it throughout the stars.

Too simple, the voice rasped. *Concepts still small/limited.*

Tendrils shot out and drilled pinprick holes in Matt and Michelle's Demon. Their ends were like red-hot embers, burning deep into his body. It happened so fast neither of them had a chance to scream.

And, in a flash, they were elsewhere.

Matt stood on an infinite plain of glowing white, under a bright pale sky. Only the thin gray line of a horizon gave any indication of distance or dimension. He couldn't see his body. He existed as pure consciousness, stretched out on a blank canvas.

As we are, the static-dusty voice boomed. In the distance, a pale shadow flickered. The voice, a thing of razor spines and slicing claws, devouring Matt.

"Who are you?" Matt asked.

We are Omphalos. Echoes chased the voice: *Nonexact. Closest concept/representation in your mind.*

Omphalos. Matt's Perfect Record brought a memory of his Ancient Mythos class in Aurora U. Omphalos was the pin on which the world turned.

Flickers of thought came from the Omphalos, shadowy representations of twisted shapes growing peacefully in the seas of a long-extinct world. No, not twisted. Just complex. Like tumbleweeds, branching and rebranching.

And they sang. They sang a dusty, lonely song, full of overtones and harmonics that carried the data of their thoughts from one plant to the next.

Like Centauri, Matt thought. The Palos. The underwater bushes that sing.

Sudden anger struck him like a blazing wind. The voice rasped. *Degenerate forms! No longer part/integrated! Disunified!*

Images flooded Matt's mind, grandiose images of swarms of these plantlike things breeding and growing in giant diamond bubbles as they made their slow way across the stars. Crashing into new watery worlds and remaking them to their needs. Then discovering ways to transform themselves into forms that could live on land, in deserts, on desolate stone wastelands.

"Aliens," Matt breathed. The reality of it all finally sank in. The Omphalos had always been there on Eridani. Here hidden throughout time. *Waiting for us. Playing with us.*

Something like ironic amusement washed over Matt. *More than you believe/imagine.*

The window into the Omphalos consciousness opened a little wider. Matt saw them swarming over inhabited worlds. Primitive furred quadrupeds looked up at the Omphalos' dark ships as they fingered their spears nervously, in an amazingly human gesture.

Do not interpret as genuine/actual, the Omphalos

voice grated. *Representational filtering, redacted to compatibility with your mental faculties.*

And more: worlds with giant floating cities and races that played gracefully in the seas, gas giants with floating jellyfish brains, another insectoid race with advanced armaments, which beat back the Omphalos for a time.

But we prevail, the Omphalos voice said.

And they did. Cities burned, civilizations fell, and entire planets flared with nuclear annihilation. Omphalos changed the remaining population to suit their needs: making them stronger, smarter—and more obedient.

At its height, the Omphalos civilization spanned a million races and spread across the entire Milky Way galaxy. Snail-slow Omphalos ships crawled their way across the voids between stars at sublight speeds as the millennia ticked away. For all their brilliance, they'd never invented the Displacement Drive.

"How could plants take over the universe?" Matt asked, incredulous

Not accurate. Not plants. The Omphalos showed him more: their nanoscale technology, building their diamond ships an atom at a time. Their minds, reaching into the more animal-like races' thoughts and turning them into their minions.

"Slaves," Matt said.

An expression of ourselves, the Omphalos said. *The most glorious expression.*

At the same time, Omphalos changed themselves to meet any environment, via their advanced bioengineering technology. Their protean biometallic Interstructure Suits became their permanent homes.

Interstructure? "Mecha?" Matt asked.

That is what you have made of it. A simple perversion of an elegant concept, the Omphalos answered. The Omphalos lived their entire lives in shining biometallic enclosures, completely dependent on their transformational capabilities. An Interstructure Suit was much more complex than any Mecha, serving as both life support and life extension for the Omphalos.

And now, Matt realized, that was what the shining nodes and crystals in the walls of the chamber were—millions of Omphalos seeded throughout the planet. They had become their technology, permanently inseparable.

In the Omphalos' mind, it was a glorious dream. But that wasn't entirely accurate. The Union had capped their realm. They hadn't yet swarmed over the whole human race. Why not?

"What happened?" Matt asked. "Why are you stuck here while humans take your stars?"

Instant, hot anger. *Humans minor/unsustainable.*

"We're doing pretty well for a minor race," Matt said.

Hot anger washed over him. *It is more entertaining/interesting to act at a distance.*

But they showed him. While the Omphalos' diamond ships never exceeded the speed of light, their FTLcomm networks became more intertwined and massive. The Omphalos, in all their varied forms on all their perfected worlds, retreated into the infinite space of the mind.

More space within than without, the Omphalos told Matt.

The Omphalos had built the sprawling Arcadia network on Eridani, as they had built millions more across the galaxy. It wasn't just Eridani. On every Union world, on every frontier world, on nearly every place in the explored universe where humanity could live, there were Omphalos networks. If humanity dug long enough, it would find the Omphalos. Just like on Keller.

But there was something else. Something hidden. The Omphalos guarded their secrets carefully.

All to plan. We led/brought you here.

"For what?"

Unification, the Omphalos said, its voice suddenly sharp-edged, hungry.

And in that moment, its grip on Matt's mind loosened, and he caught a glimpse of the grand plan: transform humanity through genemod, and then assimilate them into the Omphalos mind-space.

Of course. The HuMax.

And you/yourself, the Omphalos said.

"Me?" Matt recoiled, a chill shooting down his spine. How was that possible?

Our influence is felt/perceived evermore, the Omphalos told him. *You are one of the most pure expressions of desired genome, but also failed/incomplete.*

Most pure expression? Matt rocked back. Was that the source of his Perfect Record? His enhanced probability-calculating capabilities?

Causal interpolation, we see all/most/some eventualities.

Matt's shock drove him deeper, and for a moment he was directly connected to the Omphalos mind, seeing every point in time as a single continuum.

Early U.S. Expansion missions had found Arcadia on Eridani, just as planned. They'd eagerly taken the technical data the Omphalos had prepared for them, and they'd quickly used it to create the HuMax, as well as the first earliest FTLcomm devices.

But humanity was cagier than the Omphalos had expected; they isolated their most critical systems from the biometallic tendrils, and probed for information that lay deeper in the infinite universe of the Omphalos mind. They saw the shadows that lurked within. And they took steps.

Even before the Human-HuMax War, the proto-

Union was already putting additional safeguards in place, and working on drawing only the useful information out of the Omphalos, not the information they wanted the Union to have.

Yet time overcomes all, the Omphalos voice told Matt. *Our tendrils now infect/control much human communication. It is time for direct action. To prevail.*

Matt shivered. That voice. So alien, so implacable, so confident. And he saw the truth behind it. While UARL believed they had sealed Arcadia, the Omphalos had always been present throughout their systems, changing directives, altering reports, slowly moving them forward toward their ultimate goal. Toward assimilation.

The Union had done their best to contain the Omphalos, but their containment had crumbled over time until it was little more than a ruse. Everything was part of their plan. Roth had found his own outpost of Omphalos deep in Corsair space, and they'd been feeding him the technology to create his biomechanical Mecha. Rayder had undoubtedly done the same. Matt's own father had gone deep into Union records to give what he thought was a priceless genetic gift to Matt. All these ambitious people, each driven to use the Omphalos' technology for advancement, for power, for personal gain. But in the end, all those wonders would lead only to enslavement.

Balance/divide. Embrace/conquer. The Omphalos voice sounded almost smug. *You will be our general in the coming battle, imperfect as you are.*

General? Matt suddenly saw himself commanding the tendrils of Omphalos, spreading over the Union and converting it to the whims of these alien masters.

"What about Michelle?" Matt asked.

Not optimized, the Omphalos told him. *Her mind is only mildly interesting.*

Help, Michelle said. She was trapped on the same infinite plain as Matt, terrified and alone. Matt's anger rose, but he was powerless, bodiless, in the grip of the Omphalos.

Not powerless, a new thought came. A familiar, dark thought. Gray lightninglike bolts streaked across the infinite plain. The Omphalos keened in surprise.

Suddenly Matt was seeing the scene through his viewmask inside the Demon once again. Ahead of him, orange-hot stone flowed from the Arcadia chamber supports.

Dr. Roth's Demon had staggered to its feet and joined him. He had partially Merged with Matt and was firing Matt's Zap Gun deep into the Omphalos' chamber. The tendrils waved angrily and whipped up to reach Roth's Demon, but they were instantly vaporized by the all-powerful antimatter stream. Nearby, Michelle's Demon remained wrapped in the biometallic ropes.

"They lied to me," Roth croaked, by way of explanation.

Matt took control of his other Zap Gun and aimed it at the tendrils surrounding Michelle. They disappeared in giant blue flames, and Michelle staggered free. She scooped up Norah's Zap Gun and joined Roth in firing into the Omphalos' chamber. Matt turned his own weapon at the same target.

Where the antimatter beams struck, stone melted and flowed like water. Smoke and steam billowed out, obscuring the destruction. The Omphalos cried out in his mind. But it was more in surprise than in pain.

After what seemed like infinite moments, Matt stopped firing. Molten stone flowed throughout the chamber. But the irresistible antimatter force just splashed harmlessly off the glowing nodules and sharp-edged crystals buried in the rock. They remained unscathed.

And the Omphalos laughed.

*   *   *

"Probability disruptor," Dr. Roth croaked, over the comms. "They see all probabilities, and choose the outcome."

Matt's guts twisted in momentary awe of the Omphalos' power. They'd shifted the beam around their Interstructure Suits, dancing through quadrillions of possibilities to find the one where they were not harmed. Their most powerful weapons, their Zap Gun, couldn't touch the aliens.

The Omphalos' surprise turned to rage. *We prevail,* the voice echoed. Matt's Zap Gun fell from numb Mecha fingers. Roth's and Michelle's Demons stiffened and dropped their guns as well, fully controlled by the Omphalos. Matt's mind expanded to feel Michelle's fear and Roth's deep disappointment. They were sharing feelings, as if in a Merge.

"It is over," Roth said. "I was to be a god. Now I am nothing."

But behind his words, there was something more. Some deep calculation, something that Roth himself had held back. The biometallic devices implanted deep in his skin. It gave him an ability to control the connection with the Omphalos. Not enough for movement, but maybe enough to—

Merge, Dr. Roth thought, sending his will through the biometallic nerves of the Omphalos.

Matt's and Michelle's consciousness came with Roth. Their minds expanded into vast new dimensions. For an instant, the secrets of the universe appeared to be laid bare ahead of him. So much technology! So much capability! With this, humanity could be as gods.

But down deep, the Omphalos had buried their mysteries. Things they didn't want to examine. The very nature of causal influence. The principle behind humankind's Displacement Drive. The (meaningless sounds) direct mental connection, without physical intermediation. The Omphalos had disregarded the deepest secrets, the most baffling principles. At their core, they were a race of convoluted mental games, infinitely recursive, like two pedants arguing over the proper use of a comma. But the Omphalos took it to a universal scale. So many minds, raised in chorus of argument. No wonder they felt like static to him.

A force like a Fusion Handshake knocked Roth, Matt, and Michelle out of Merge. He came out, hard whooping air through his viewmask in the Demon. The Omphalos still held them all fast.

You will probe us no more, the Omphalos said. *You will simply submit.*

In that moment, every fragment of anger in Matt assembled into a painful, vibrating whole. The Omphalos were no better than Rayder and his mind control, no better than Union politicians and scientists and their genetic modification experiments on the HuMax. They were the ultimate expression of power, the ultimate suppression of choice.

"I won't let you win," Matt said, out loud.

Amusement from the Omphalos washed over him.

Who/what are you to refuse? they asked him.

"I'm Matt Lowell," Matt said. "Mecha Cadet. Mecha Corps. Corsair. Esplandian. Free Stars Alliance Leader."

Static laughter shuddered in Matt's infinite virtual space. *You are a broken/fractured thing.*

Broken and fractured. In the Omphalos' mind, the thought carried with it a feeling of disgust.

Matt's speeding Perfect Record assembled the pieces. The Omphalos were all about order and perfection. About control and ultimate union. Even their technology pushed toward Merge.

But what if they turned the tables? Matt thought. It

was like the Lokis' simple minds. When hitting a problem head-on didn't work, they'd invert the logic and try again.

And conventional logic said that their only way out of this was for Matt to find a giant, well-armed Mecha to Merge with. One with weapons powerful enough to launch an attack so massive the Omphalos couldn't calulate all the probabilities.

Which meant—

Understanding hit Matt like a giant hammer. Inversion. Not big. Small.

Not one path. Many.

Roth and the others heard his thoughts, through the connecton with Omphalos. Roth sent waves of doubt. *Mecha were never intended to support a sharded operational mode,* he thought. It would take an amazing mind to control each piece effectively—

Roth suddenly stopped himself. Inference to the point of precognition. Matt's Perfect Record might be able to integrate and control a sharded Mecha.

Shard, he thought, imagining his Demon shattering into a thousand pieces, ten thousand. Each not much larger than a man. Each with a tiny fusion thruster on its backside, and a tiny antimatter torch at its front.

Matt's Demon dissolved. Matt's entire body screamed. His Mecha wasn't just falling apart; it was being sectioned, piece by piece, by atomic lasers. Intense agony shot through every inch of him, until it was his entire soul.

You are not permitted, Omphalos boomed.

But Matt's Demon dissolved and flowed through the tendrils like sand in the wind. Ten thousand tiny shards darted in a constantly shifting pattern to avoid the tendrils.

Matt's shards found Michelle. "Join me," he said. One touch, and her Mecha dissolved into ten thousand more.

And Roth. His Demon also joined the ranks. The swarm of shards shot for the entrance to the cavern, seeking escape. Omphalos' tendrils shot out of the walls on all sides, weaving together into an impenetrable wall. The leading edge of Matt's shards impacted the wall and were caught and held by Omphalos. Their way out was blocked.

And now something new was happening, deep in the cavern. The Omphalos' Interstructure Suits were powering up. Glowing orange eyes and razor-sharp limbs unfolded from their mirror-smooth surfaces. Wriggling free of the walls, they fired their own fusion drives and accelerated wildly toward the intruders.

Matt grinned. A cloud of enemies. No exit. Hopelessly overmatched. Impossible odds. This was what he was meant for.

Matt turned to meet the Omphalos, shard versus Suit. He barely knew where he was within the cloud of Mecha shards, but he knew the rush of Mesh, the feeling of being able to do anything. Suddenly everything was completely clear. He knew what he had to do.

The Omphalos fired. Bright antimatter flashes brightened the walls of the awakening cavern, and Matt felt the hot pinpricks as his shards were destroyed. Matt's own antimatter weapons sought, targeted, locked. Matt grimaced in the moments before firing. If the Omphalos were able to shift probability on more than a single attack, they were done.

Fire, he thought.

Five thousand beams lanced out from Matt's shards, turning the cavern interior into day. They touched the Omphalos' Interstructure Suits—

And where they touched, orange blossoms bloomed, reverberatingly loud in the giant underground space. Rolling bass booms echoed up and down the cavern.

The Omphalos screamed, a silent wave of hate and pain.

Matt grinned. The Omphalos' probability disruptor couldn't counter his masses all at once. Some Interstructure Suits survived, but over half of them were destroyed. Michelle's and Roth's shards shot forward to meet Matt and began lancing the Omphalos with their own energy. Interstructure Suits exploded by the thousands.

"How does it feel?" Matt asked Omphalos.

You will stop! We prevail!

But the Omphalos' Interstructure Suits were no match against Matt's shards' antimatter blasts. Where they touched, Omphalos blossomed in deadly fire. Where they passed, only carbonized biometal was left in their wake. The only advantage they had was in numbers.

The cavern came crawlingly alive as Omphalos disengaged en masse from the biometallic matrix and launched their Interstructure Suits at Matt's Mecha shards.

Soon there weren't just thousands, but millions.

And the battle turned. Antimatter blasts from the Omphalos cut hot swaths in continuous waves. Matt's shards exploded as the Omphalos pressed them deeper into the cavern. Matt increased the speed of his retreat and dove down into a lower mezzanine.

"We're going the wrong way!" Michelle yelled, over the comms.

"I know!" Matt said.

"So, what's the plan?"

"Find a way out!" Matt yelled. That was the only thing they could do. Trapped down here with the Omphalos, they'd eventually be cut down by sheer numbers.

"Our opponents know this," Roth grated. "They're massing above us."

Matt's viewmask confirmed Roth's words. The space

above their shards was a virtual cloud of tags showing UNKNOWN MECHA.

"Did you get a map of this place when you were digging into their mind?" Matt asked Roth. "Any directions?"

"No," Roth said, and then fell silent. But his comms icon remained lit. Finally he continued. "I believe we may need something more than bravado."

"It's what I have," Matt said, grimacing as the Omphalos' Interstructure Suits annihilated even more of his shards. Only about half were left, and his sensors showed no upward-turning caverns ahead.

Matt shot downward again, to a cavern where a giant red-hot column, a full kilometer in diameter, thrummed with power. Around it clustered millions of the nodules and crystals of the Omphalos, all of them coming to life. Matt recognized the column as part of the Omphalos' power network that reached down to the planet's core.

"Attack the column!" Matt yelled. "Maybe we can take it down!"

Matt's, Michelle's, and Roth's shards unleashed sheets of antimatter fire at the column. Vitrified rock melted and flowed in orange rivers.

But the column was simply so massive it was like shooting a pistol at a Displacement Drive ship. Their beams had little effect. And a new swarm of Omphalos were on them.

Matt and Michelle turned to face their attackers.

But Roth didn't. His shards recoalesced into a Demon, or at least something very much like one. He'd lost a lot of mass to the Omphalos' Interstructure Suits attack. He perched on the smooth edge of the glowing power column, clinging tight with his Mecha's talons.

"What are you doing?" Matt yelled.

"Providing something more than bravado," Roth said.

Snaking biometallic tendrils caught Roth's Demon and bound it down to the column. Roth struggled against them, but couldn't escape.

A new icon flared in Matt's viewmask, one he'd never seen before. It showed a bright red Mecha, like a Demon, with a warning triangle and exclamation point within it.

ANTIMATTER POWER SYSTEM OVERLOAD, the icon read.

"I'm nothing here," Roth said, before Matt could ask. "I will carve my sphere out of the Omphalos mind."

"By blowing yourself up?" Matt yelled.

"By Merging, then eliminating any place for my mind to live afterward."

Matt rocked back, as if struck. This wasn't a sacrifice. This was Roth, trying to extend his empire inside the Omphalos' own universe-spanning network.

He'd given up on humanity.

Matt grimaced and ran his thrusters up to redline, yelling for Michelle to follow. The cloud of Mecha shards arrowed away from the radiant column, toward the masses of Omphalos in Interstructure Suits.

"If you have a plan . . ." Michelle trailed off.

"I have hope," Matt told her.

Because even if Roth's action wasn't really a sacrifice, maybe it could disrupt the Omphalos long enough for them to get out.

Maybe.

Behind Matt, the chamber lit in perfect incandescence. Yellow-white clouds of vaporized rock and biometal engulfed them in a turbulent wave. Matt's shards tumbled uncontrollably into the middle of the hordes of Omphalos.

But the Omphalos faltered too. Some sputtered and fell dead. Some went in wild corkscrews. Some fired randomly, cutting down their own comrades.

"Come on!" Matt yelled at Michelle. "Go up!"

They pushed through the last of the Omphalos and into empty caverns. Behind them, the giant column of power had been half destroyed. It flickered dull red as it struggled to provide power to the remaining Omphalos.

So not a mortal hit, Matt thought. *But a solid one. Hopefully it would be enough.*

We prevail, the Omphalos said. But the voice was weak, and pain came in waves.

Matt's and Michelle's shards flew up through the chambers. The Omphalos still came at them in their Interstructure Suits, but there were only a handful of them. Matt and Michelle picked them off with relative ease.

Their position tag slowly moved upward toward the corridor where they'd entered.

At the original cavern, the archway was no longer netted with biometallic cords. Some waved weakly at Matt and Michelle as they passed.

Up and up, they went through the corkscrew and out into the Capitol Park. At the fallen Expansion Monument, Matt and Michelle reassembled into tiny red Mecha, the only thing their Demon could create from the few shards they had left. In the distance, night was falling over the city. Union Mecha strafed the biometallic tendrils and transformed buildings.

"It's not over," Michelle said.

"It may never be over," Matt told her. They'd dealt a hard blow to the Omphalos on Eridani, but what about their other caverns buried on humanity's worlds? And how long would it take the Omphalos to recover from the damage they'd done here?

"Then why do you sound so cheerful?" Michelle asked.

Matt said nothing for a long time. Because they overcame impossible odds. Because the cloak has dropped.

Because nothing will ever be the same again. Those were all things he could say.

But he knew there was something more. And it was finally time to say it.

"Because I'm here," Matt said, eventually. "With you."

Michelle's Mecha turned to look at Matt, its visor almost questioning. "Are you serious?"

"Yes. I am."

Michelle said nothing for a long time. Finally her Mecha's hand reached out and took Matt's own talons. It felt almost warm through the force-feedback.

"It's about time," she told him.

For a while, they stood there, content. But there was still a job to do. Matt nodded at Newhome. "Should we go help them?" he asked.

"You'll be arrested," Michelle told him.

"After all this?"

"You know the Union," Michelle said.

Matt laughed. "I'll take my chances."

Two small Mechas ascended into the sky, toward Newhome.

ABOUT THE AUTHOR

Brett Patton, in the words of a friend, "was watching Evangelion while you were reading Heinlein." Actually, don't tell anybody, but he was doing both. And actually, don't tell anyone, but he's also taking liberties with the quote. He's been writing fun, action-oriented science fiction for years, and currently in Los Angeles, California.